IRA FISTELL'S
MARK TWAIN:

Three Encounters

IRA FISTELL'S
MARK TWAIN

Three Encounters

August 18, 2011

Ira Fistell

Library of Congress Control Number: 2012904021
ISBN: Hardcover   978-1-4691-7871-4
               Softcover   978-1-4691-7870-7
               Ebook   978-1-4691-7872-1

To order additional copies of this book, contact:
Xlibris Corporation
1-888-795-4274
www.Xlibris.com
Orders@Xlibris.com
104103

Contents

Acknowledgments

The author wishes to recognize the contributions of a number of people whose interest, assistance, and support helped to make this book possible.

First, I wish to thank Charles Neider, editor of Mark Twain's *Autobiography* and Susy Clemens' *Papa,* who has both inspired and encouraged me in my efforts to understand the complex man who was both Samuel Clemens and Mark Twain.

Dan Fuller of Kent State University, my longtime friend, has always been willing to give freely of his time and advice, not to mention appropriate doses of encouragement when needed.

Jack Savage, for many years my colleague on radio, turned artist and supplied the cover for this book.

Rachel Oriel Berg, Ph.D., read through the manuscript and contributed many constructive comments and ideas.

To Mrs. Anna Howland of Anaheim, California, a fellow sufferer of "delirium Clemens," go my deepest and most sincere thanks for her aid in researching this book. Without her help, I doubt that I would have ever gotten it done.

Dr. Larry Moss of Los Angeles volunteered to read the manuscript and gave me great encouragement when I needed it.

A number of libraries and their personnel have offered indispensable assistance. I wish to thank specifically Victor Fischer and Simon Hernandez at the Mark Twain Project, University of California, Berkeley; Frank Lorenz, Archivist at the Hamilton College Library in Clinton, New York; Mark Woodhouse of the Center for Mark Twain Studies at Elmira College, Elmira, New York; and the staffs at the Mark Twain Memorial and Stowe-Day Foundation, Hartford, Connecticut; the University of Virginia Library, Charlottesville, Virginia; and the Huntington Library, Pasadena, California. Without the kind and helpful assistance of these individuals and institutions, I could not have written this book.

Neither could anyone have read it without the help of my dedicated typist, Ms. Sherrie Gogerty, to whom I am hopelessly indebted.

To my two universities, the University of Chicago and the University of Wisconsin, Madison, I owe whatever analytical and literary skills I may possess. Whatever I have done right is to their credit; wherever I have erred, the responsibility is totally mine.

Ira Fistell
Los Angeles, Ca.
August 18, 2011

An autobiography can distort, facts can be realigned. But fiction never lies: it reveals the writer totally.

— V.S. Naipal

Part I

Encounters of the First Kind:
Mark and Me

Introduction

There were always books in our house, and one of my juvenile volumes contained an excerpt from *The Adventures of Huckleberry Finn*, Chapter 7, "I Fool Pap and Get Away." That was how I first encountered the works of Mark Twain.

Then, sometime around my tenth year, I somehow acquired a matched set of *Tom Sawyer* and *Huckleberry Finn*. I have no idea, now, how I got them; most likely somebody gave them to me as a gift. These books were part of the *Illustrated Junior Library* published by Grossett and Dunlap, and they contained not only Twain's writing but also marvelous pen and ink drawings by Donald McKay. Today, at least forty years later, both volumes are well-worn with what must be thirty or forty readings each. They are childhood mementos become adult treasures.

Sometime later, I acquired a copy of *A Connecticut Yankee in King Arthur's Court*, which I read in snatches (leaving out the boring parts). These three Mark Twain volumes have been with me ever since, through seven residences in three states.

As a juvenile reader, I liked the books, read and reread them, and even came to know passages and scenes by heart; but the depth of my comprehension was limited by my youth and inexperience, and I neither understood nor even suspected the subtle messages beneath the surface. As to the author of these works—well, I knew from the start that he had been a steamboat pilot named Samuel Langhorne Clemens, that he had grown up in Hannibal, Missouri, and that I liked what I knew of his writing. In those days, I gave the man no more thought than that.

Even as a graduate student in American history, with a minor in American literature, I felt no need to go deeper than the pages of such lesser-known Twain works as *Pudd'nhead Wilson, Roughing It,* and *The Mysterious Stranger.* The books made a shallow impression; the man behind them remained no more than a pen name.

I don't know exactly when, or why, my attitude began to change. It may have been when I read the *Autobiography* for the first time in my second or third year of graduate school. Whatever and whenever, I began to grow curious about the author, as much or more than about the books he wrote. Slowly, gradually, the life of Mark Twain began to fascinate and obsess me. I wanted to get to know the man, to understand the mind that produced those books—books which, as an adult, I found infinitely greater works of art than I had ever suspected.

At first, I admired his adventurous life. Samuel Clemens went everywhere, did everything, and knew everybody. The mere catalogue of his successive careers is intriguing: printer's devil, journeyman, steamboat pilot, soldier (for two weeks), prospector, reporter, humorist, travel writer, platform lecturer, correspondent, novelist, publisher, inventor, philosopher, polemicist—he was all of these. He traveled around the world, ranging freely from Hawaii to Berlin, counting friends everywhere and from every station of life. His accomplishments, his adventures, and his acquaintances made Samuel Clemens an object of envy. For some time, I thought that he was the man I would most like to have been.

The more I became aware of the darker side of his life, however, the less I wished to stand in his shoes. If he enjoyed a public life filled with triumph and adventure, he more than paid for it in a private existence damned with adversity and tragedy. A child of poverty, he suffered the additional frustration and humiliation of his father's bankruptcy. Two of his siblings died before he turned seven, and he lost his father before turning twelve. He lost a favorite brother to a steamboat explosion, an infant son to diphtheria, one daughter to meningitis, and a second to epilepsy. He buried his mother, his older brother, his sister, and his wife. Of all his immediate family, one daughter alone survived him.

Additionally, while Clemens undoubtedly earned more money from his works than any other American writer of his century, his business sense was such that he managed to spend himself into bankruptcy at the age of fifty-nine, thus repeating his father's fall from economic grace at a time in his life when he thought he had long since achieved financial security. He managed to lose $300,000 of his own and his wife's money backing the Paige typesetting machine, while rejecting the opportunity to invest in the telephone when that invention was new. Few men of Clemens' sagacity can have been so disastrously unsuccessful in business. All in all, the proverbial dog had a better personal life.

The paradox of public success and private disaster symbolizes Clemens' whole life. In many ways, he was a living incarnation of duality, a human Yin-Yang. A native of the Missouri frontier, casually at home in the Nevada mining camps and in roaring Gold Rush San Francisco, he lived half his life in Eastern domesticity and a sixth of it in European cosmopolitanism. In his own lifetime, he became a symbol of a virile, vibrant young America, while simultaneously (in private) lapsing into fatalism and cynicism, decrying the helplessness of man, and bewailing the "damned human race."

This sense of paradox applies as well to his work. *The Adventures of Huckleberry Finn,* a masterpiece of adult literature expressing the conscience of America, is frequently dismissed as a boy's adventure story. It is a glorious tribute to the dignity and equality of mankind, yet it is regularly attacked by do-gooders who want to keep it off library shelves because it contains the word "nigger."

Likewise, Twain's brilliant and devastating satire of nineteenth-century America, *A Connecticut Yankee in King Arthur's Court,* is often treated (even by literary critics) as an awkward desecration of Malory's tales of the Round Table. In fact, few Americans take Mark Twain seriously as a writer. He is often dismissed as a funny man who also wrote adventure stories, a sort of cross between Artemus Ward and Robert Louis Stevenson. His literary reputation is greater abroad than in his own country.

The theme of dualism and paradox extends to the man's own personality. He began by using "Mark Twain," the leadsman's cry meaning two fathoms (or safe water) on the Mississippi River, as his pen name. In time, however, this persona seems to have almost become a second personality. Consciously or not, Mark Twain began to diverge from Samuel Clemens to the point where it is sometimes difficult to think of these alter egos as part of the same individual.

I grew increasingly fascinated by this man. I began to feel the need to understand him, to grapple with his mind, and to feel the passion of his emotions. I needed to get a handle on him, get inside him, to know him. Mark Twain became an obsession I find impossible to explain.

I devoted several years to my quest, and sometimes I feel that I know the man as well as anyone in his own time could. There are even moments when I feel as if it were really me in his place, seeing, hearing, and feeling what he saw, heard, and felt. Yet at other times, he remains as elusive as ever, a will-o'-the-wisp, to be forever chased and never caught.

In this book, I have tried to describe three encounters I have had with the man who was both Clemens and Twain. First, I discuss some of his work—why it is so great, and how it is so overlooked. After all, it was the writer's output which attracted me to him in the first place, and it is because of his work that he is important to the world.

The second section of the book consists of a number of essays in which I try to make contact with the man by visiting the physical sites which were important to his life—his homes, the places where he worked, the places he visited, and his grave.

Finally, in the third section, I venture some speculations about Clemens' life—about the processes of his mind and about emotional energy which drove him. Here I freely admit I am on shakier ground, without much bedrock of facts to support my suggestions. Yet I think I can make the pieces of the puzzle fit to give a coherent explanation of why and how Samuel Clemens came to be the man that he was, and why and how so much of his life has been an enigma for so long.

I have relied on the voluminous sources about Clemens as well as his professional and private writings. Still, much as we know about the man, there is no telling how much more material may have been suppressed or destroyed—by Clemens himself, or after his death by Albert Bigelow Paine, his literary executor, and/or by his surviving daughter, Clara Clemens. Paine and Clara had no intention of revealing anything which would not support the portrait of Samuel Clemens, which they had painted for public consumption, and they did not hesitate to conceal anything which they felt did not fit that picture. I have tried to surmise how some of the questions unanswered by the official portrait might be resolved.

Unlike most serious writers on Mark Twain, I hold no faculty appointment and claim no special credentials as an expert in American literature. My academic degrees are in law and US history, although as a graduate student in that discipline, I minored in American lit. While I have had extensive experience in teaching, my professional career has been outside academia, as a radio and television personality. My previous books have been travel-oriented rather than literary, and I doubt that I will ever again write a biographical/critical study of any other author.

While I do not claim the credentials of a Walter Blair, a Henry Nash Smith, or a Bernard DeVoto, I am an interested and devoted amateur with (I hope) the intelligence to match the intensity of my involvement with Twain and his work. I have, in addition, background, discernment, and ideas. I have come to Mark Twain's work without the burden of preconceptions: I have tried to discover what he wrote, not what others say he wrote. My hope is that my book, which is intended as much for the general reader as for the Twain student, will throw new light on the life and works of this complex, talented, difficult, and altogether remarkable man.

I wish to stress that *Ira Fistell's Mark Twain* is in great measure the product of my thinking about the author and his work, attempting to supply (by the process of original reasoning) answers to the questions they pose.

In my discussion of *Pudd'nhead Wilson*, I have emphasized the message which Mark Twain wrote into that book—namely, that stereotypes and restrictions on the free range of thought are ultimately both misleading and disastrous. I have taken that principle as my guide in rethinking the life and work of the artist whom William Dean Howells called "The Lincoln of our Literature."

A Note on the Use of Nomenclature

When an author writes under a pen name, as Samuel L. Clemens did, it is tempting to use the real and signature names interchangeably. This may be acceptable practice in some cases, but I have tried not to do this with Clemens/Twain—first because it seems to me somewhat sloppy usage, and second because this man really was two widely divergent personalities simultaneously. Samuel Clemens, for example, built an extravagant house in Hartford and eventually went bankrupt pursuing big money through the Paige typesetting machine—while at the same time, Mark Twain was writing "Overreaching Don't Pay" and producing the most devastating attack on Victorian cupidity ever written, *A Connecticut Yankee in King Arthur's Court*.

Therefore, I have endeavored to use the names "Sam" or "Clemens" when referring to the husband, the father and the businessman, and the names "Mark" or "Twain" when writing about the artist. Sometimes the two personalities mesh closely; Samuel Clemens took to the lecture circuit to raise quick cash, but it was Mark Twain who enthralled audiences from the podium. On the other hand, there were times (especially later in his life) when the two personalities were so far apart that integrating them seems difficult if not impossible. Susy Clemens, Sam's oldest daughter, was one who perceived the split. She came to hate Mark Twain because she felt her own personality obscured by her father's literary persona. Samuel Clemens was her loving, if difficult, father, but Mark Twain was a stranger and an interloper.

My own feeling is just the reverse. As I came to greater and greater familiarity with the man, I found myself liking Mark Twain more and more, and Samuel Clemens less and less. The relationship between the two personalities is an important subject of this study.

A Basic Biography

For those unfamiliar with Samuel Clemens' life, a brief biographical sketch is appropriate here.

He was born on November 30, 1835 at the hamlet of Florida, Missouri, several miles inland from the Mississippi River. His father, John Marshall Clemens, came originally from Virginia and had the pride and dignity (if not the financial resources) of an Old Dominion aristocrat. He met and married Jane Lampton in Kentucky in 1823. She was a lively, witty, and independent woman who possessed little formal education but had a keen intelligence. Sam was her sixth child; she was later to bear one more.

He was a premature baby, born at seven months while Halley's Comet, then making one of its periodic approaches to the earth, streaked through the skies. Mrs. Clemens mentioned later that when she first laid eyes on her son, she "could see little promise in him." He was a sickly infant who nevertheless contrived to survive his childhood, something three of his older siblings failed to do.

John Marshall Clemens had come to Missouri full of great expectations, but the Panic of 1837 and his own lack of business sense made the hamlet of Florida a disappointment. He decided to move his family to the more prosperous river town of Hannibal, several miles to the northeast. The death of a daughter at around this time may also have influenced Mr. Clemens' decision to pull up stakes. In any event, father, mother, and the four surviving children settled in Hannibal in 1839, when Sam was three.

In later years, he recalled his boyhood as an idyll, though the dark side of life in a rough frontier town is reflected frequently in his books. However pleasant Sam's early years may have been, they ended abruptly with the death of John Marshall Clemens on March 24, 1847. The family was left in poverty; within a year, young Sam had to leave school and was apprenticed to a printer. Later, he worked for his older brother Orion, who tried to run a local newspaper. Orion, however, proved to be even more ineffectual in business matters than his father had been, and throughout his life, he was continually falling back on Sam for financial support. Indeed, none of the other Clemens children could be said to have done anything remarkable with their lives. They all seemed to have been rather colorless, ordinary personalities, totally lacking in the wit and crackling intellect that Sam shared only with his mother.

In 1853, when he was seventeen, Sam Clemens (by then a passably good journeyman printer) left Hannibal, returning afterward only to visit. He worked as a printer in New York, Philadelphia, St. Louis, Cincinnati, and Keokuk, Iowa, for a few years, a period of his life of which he wrote little, and of which we know comparatively few details.

We do know that he spent much of his free time reading (contrary to the popular view of Clemens as a sort of literary bumpkin, he was extremely well-read in history, philosophy, and belles lettres). He was conversant with all the major English and American novelists, particularly Dickens, Thackeray, Sir Walter Scott, and James Fenimore Cooper. For a man who never saw the inside of a school after the age of twelve, he possessed a remarkably good education, nearly all of it self-acquired.

His journeyman period lasted for about four years. Then, in 1857, Clemens embarked on a new career—he set out to become a Mississippi River steamboat pilot. With money borrowed from his brother-in-law, Sam arranged with Horace Bixby to learn the river from New Orleans to St. Louis. It took Clemens the better part of two years to become a competent pilot, but it was the fulfillment of a boyhood ambition, and he later wrote that of all the jobs he had ever held, steamboating was the one which gave him the most satisfaction.

He got his federal certificate in 1859 and worked on the boats for two years until the outbreak of the Civil War shut off traffic on the river and put him out of work. However, as with his Hannibal boyhood, Mark Twain, the writer later drew on Clemens' piloting years for literary material. Much of *Life on the Mississippi* is based on his experiences in the wheelhouse.

With river traffic abruptly cut off after Fort Sumter, Clemens was left jobless. He returned to Missouri, where he joined a disorganized band of Confederate irregulars who called themselves the "Marion Rangers." This seems to have been more the result of Clemens' feelings for his friends rather than of any proslavery conviction on his part. Indeed, Sam was popular enough to win the rank of second lieutenant by vote of the company.

However, it did not take long for Clemens to decide that soldiering was not for him. To use his own term, he "quit" the military under murky circumstances. One story is that his unit disbanded: another is that he obtained medical leave. It is possible that he simply deserted. Whatever the truth, Mark Twain drew on Clemens' two weeks as an army officer when he wrote "The History of a Campaign that Failed" many years later. Sam Clemens suffered no consequences from his self-demobilization—his quick departure for the Nevada Territory saved him from any potential unpleasantness.

The Nevada experience came about by chance. Sam's inept elder brother, Orion, had been living in St. Louis. There, he met a local attorney named Edward Bates, who was a power in Republican politics. When Abraham Lincoln was elected president of the United States in 1860, he chose Bates to be Attorney General in his new administration; through Bates' influence, Orion wangled an appointment as secretary to the new governor of the Nevada Territory, James W. Nye. He took his younger brother Sam out to the Comstock with him, as a sort of secretary to the secretary. Sam wrote later that the arrangement was less than one-sided generosity on Orion's part; it was Sam's savings out of his piloting wages which paid the stagecoach fare to Nevada for both brothers. In any event, the move was crucial; it took Sam safely away from the fighting, which was as fortunate for American letters as for Samuel Clemens himself. Instead of charging the Union cannon at Shiloh, or starving in the baking trenches before Vicksburg, Sam spent the war years prospecting and newspapering at Washoe. Neither a stray federal bullet nor a case of dysentery would kill him off before he became Mark Twain.

Once safe in Nevada, Sam left Orion to try prospecting for silver at a camp called Aurora. The idea of easy money was always a lure to Sam Clemens, and the Aurora venture was only one of many efforts he made to get rich quick. Like all of these schemes, it ended in failure. By the middle of 1862, Sam had come to realize that digging holes in the ground was hard work, and the chance of turning up a fortune was next to nil. He began to contemplate other ways of escaping poverty, and thus he began to write.

He sent a series of sketches to the *Territorial Enterprise* at Virginia City, probably the most colorful of all American newspapers. Its editor, Joe Goodman liked them, and not only printed them but offered the writer a job on the *Enterprise* staff, sight unseen. The salary was $25 a week, and Clemens was desperate. Still he hesitated to leave prospecting until August,

1862, when he finally made up his mind. It was 130 miles to Virginia City; Sam walked the whole way, eventually staggering into the *Enterprise* office on a hot, dusty day, more dead than alive but ready to take up still another career.[1]

He remained with the *Enterprise* staff for a little less than two years, writing mostly humor sketches and covering the territorial legislature in an outrageous manner well suited to its deliberations. It was while reporting from the capitol at Carson City that he used, for the first time in print, his immortal pen name—Mark Twain.

Clemens managed to make Virginia City too hot to hold him, and in May of 1864, he moved on to California, but he left his mark on the Comstock, where he appears to have been a well-known and popular character, and it left its impression on him, for his work on the *Enterprise* began his literary career.

There is a surprising paucity of information about Clemens' private life in Virginia City, however. We know that he drank a good deal, as one would expect of a vigorous young reporter in such a roistering spot as the Comstock. Yet neither in his *Autobiography* nor in his fictionalized account of his Nevada experiences (*Roughing It*, published in 1872) has he left so much as a clue to his love life. To my knowledge, no letters have turned up touching on Clemens' relations with the women of Virginia City, amateur or professional. His reticence on the subject is consistent, if frustrating for the biographer.

It's hard to believe that he was a celibate—not there, not then. Indeed, we have one hint that he was anything but. A rival journalist, sniping at Clemens' reputation, alleged that he had contracted venereal disease from a prostitute. Whether or not the story is true (it is impossible to confirm), the point is that

---

[1] Though not yet twenty-seven, Clemens had by this time already been a printer, steamboat pilot, and silver prospector.

the charge was apparently credible at the time; in other words, it had to be accepted in Virginia City that Clemens was getting around the town. That Sam was so secretive about his sex life strikes me, then, as an indication that he felt he had something to hide.

Clemens left the Comstock one jump ahead of the sheriff, and wound up becoming just as unpopular with the San Francisco police, with whom he also had run-ins. He thus retired for a time to the gold diggings at Jackass Flat, near Angel's Camp, and it was while living there that he heard and subsequently transcribed the amusing story of "The Remarkable Jumping Frog of Calaveras County." Twain intended it as his contribution to a book of humorous sketches to be edited by Artemus Ward, but that project failed and the "Jumping Frog" story first saw print in the *New York Saturday Press* in November 1865. It won Mark Twain his first general acclaim as a professional writer, and two years later, it was the title story in his first book, a collection of his humor pieces.

At this time, Clemens arranged to travel to Hawaii as correspondent for the *Sacramento Union*. His letters to that newspaper, including a journalistic scoop covering the wreck of the clipper ship *Hornet*, not only earned him a reputation as a correspondent, it also provided him with the material he used to present his first platform lecture, which he delivered to a packed house in San Francisco during October 1866. For the rest of his life, Clemens was acknowledged as one of the kings of the lecture circuit, though he professed to hate platform speaking. He could always fall back on lecturing whenever he needed some quick cash, however, and he returned to the circuit periodically over the next forty years.

It was following his lecturing debut that Clemens embarked on the pivotal adventure of his career, his voyage to Europe and the Holy Land aboard the steamer *Quaker City*. He arranged the sponsorship of the *Alta California* newspaper, which paid his fare and printed his impressions of the trip and of his fellow passengers.[2]

Not only did this voyage provide the material for Mark Twain's first travel book, *The Innocents Abroad* (published with great success in 1869) but it also resulted in Clemens' acquaintance with Charles Langdon of Elmira, New York. Young Langdon, in turn, showed his shipmate Clemens a picture of his sister, Olivia, and as Twain tells us in the *Autobiography*, it was love at first sight. The couple met for the first time in New York, after the *Quaker City's* return in December 1867. Their first date was a lecture by Charles Dickens. Sam Clemens visited Olivia and the family in Elmira in August 1868; the couple was formally engaged some six months later, and they were married in the parlor of the Langdon home in Elmira on February 2 1870.

The marriage was the central event in Samuel Clemens' life, marking his metamorphosis from steamboat pilot and rollicking journalist to newspaper owner, householder, and establishment citizen.[3] The newlyweds took up residence in Buffalo, New York, where Clemens had purchased part interest in a newspaper. The furnished house into which they moved was a wedding gift from the bride's father. His motives certainly included concern for the way her new husband might lodge his daughter; Jervis Langdon made sure that they had what he considered respectable quarters by providing the house himself.

At this point, Sam Clemens seems to have been making a genuine effort to "be good" in the Victorian sense. His letters, when they talk about religion, are obsequious enough to be

---

2. The *Alta* paid $1,250 for Clemens' passage, a huge sum for those days. Thus the value of Mark Twain's byline is clearly demonstrated.

3. At least in part, the degree to which this chameleon-like transformation affected the man who was also Mark Twain is the key question in understanding his life and work.

positively embarrassing. Also, Olivia soon became pregnant, and Sam delighted in the new experience of being both lord of the manor and an expectant father.

But the euphoria did not last; within a year, Clemens admitted to himself that running the *Buffalo Express* was tedious and boring, and his heart was not in his work. Nor was his religious orthodoxy more than a facade. Also, soon after the wedding, Jervis Langdon developed stomach cancer; he died on August 6, 1870, and his passing occasioned a nervous collapse on the part of Livy. She had a difficult pregnancy, suffering a near-miscarriage in autumn and finally delivering a boy several weeks prematurely. Born on November 7, 1870, Langdon Clemens weighed only four and a half pounds and appeared so sickly that his father did not think he would last a week.

Stymied in his attempt to write a second book (it would eventually become *Roughing It*), and sick of his life in Buffalo, Clemens made a decision. He sold out his interest in the *Express* (at a sizable loss), liquidated his holdings in the city, including the house his father-in-law had bought for him, and pulled up stakes. His goal was Hartford, Connecticut, home of his publisher Elisha Bliss, where he felt he could write, free of the burden of editorship. Livy's inheritance from her recently deceased father made the move financially possible. The Clemens family spent the summer at Quarry Farm, the home of Livy's adopted sister, Susan Langdon Crane, which stood on a hilltop overlooking Elmira. That fall, they moved to Hartford, the city which would be their home for the next twenty years.

The next two decades proved to be the happiest and most productive period of Clemens' life. Artistically, he produced a string of critical and popular successes: *Roughing It* (1872); *The Gilded Age* (with Charles Dudley Warner, 1873); *The Adventures of Tom Sawyer* (1876); *A Tramp Abroad* (1880); *The Prince and the Pauper* (1881); *Life on the Mississippi* (1883); *The Adventures of Huckleberry Finn* (1884), and *A Connecticut Yankee in King Arthur's*

Court (1889). Also, Clemens scored a publishing coup when his firm, the Charles Webster Co., brought out the memoirs of General Ulysses S. Grant in 1884.

Socially, Clemens earned more than grudging acceptance into the narrow society of patrician America, while he was lionized abroad. He may very well have been the best-known American personality of the last quarter of the nineteenth century.

Domestically, Sam and Livy became the parents of three more children, all girls: Susy (b. 1872); Clara (1874); and Jean (1880). Little Langdon, who never developed normally, died on June 2, 1872, at nineteen months. His passing (for his father, at least) was almost more relief than sorrow. Besides, the birth of Susy who, unlike her brother, was a healthy and normal baby from the beginning seemed more than compensation for his loss.

In 1874, the Clemens family moved into their own house in Hartford, a fantastic structure which symbolized Sam Clemens' success. There, the family lived regally and entertained on a lavish scale, in the process running up expenses which would have challenged even the income of a captain of industry. Mark Twain may have made more money from his writing than any other literary figure of his time, but it's a cinch that Sam Clemens spent more than any other. He had grown up in poverty; now he was wiping out its memory.

Even during these most placid years, there was a shadow on the horizon, which was to prove disastrous in the next decade. It was the Paige Automatic Typesetting Machine, and James Paige, its inventor, was blessed with an uncanny ability to mesmerize Samuel Clemens. Beginning with a $5,000 investment in 1884, Clemens eventually sunk $300,000 of his (and Livy's) money into the Paige machine. It was so complicated and impractical that it never went into production and never earned a penny for Clemens, who literally bankrupted himself in the hope of earning enormous riches from the infernal machine.

The eighties were by and large a good time for the family. All of them had their health, their home in Hartford was joyous and stimulating, and Mark Twain was doing some of the finest literary work of his career. He had long since earned commercial success; in 1888, he received further recognition when Yale University made him an honorary Master of Arts.[4]

The financial strain, stemming from the family's lavish lifestyle and the insatiable demands of the Paige machine, was not getting any easier. By 1891, the Clemens family had exhausted their resources. They could no longer keep up the Hartford house; they closed it and went to live in Europe, where they could maintain their standard of living at somewhat less expense.

In autumn, 1890, Susy enrolled at Bryn Mawr College near Philadelphia but withdrew the following spring. Her failure to finish has never been explained. Clemens wrote, "Bryn Mawr began it. It was there that her health was undermined . . . ," but in what way, he does not say.

For four years, the Clemens family lived in Europe, chiefly in Germany, Italy, and France. Clemens made several transatlantic crossings during this period in an attempt to stave off financial disaster, but the Panic of 1893 proved fatal. Livy's inheritance was affected and her income reduced, while the voracious demands of the Paige machine went on and on. Clemens took money from the publishing company to help pay for the machine, only to have the Webster firm collapse into bankruptcy in 1894 with unsecured debts of more than $125,000.

At the age of fifty-nine, Samuel Clemens, America's most successful author and lecturer, its foremost literary personality and its best-known citizen, was broke. He had repeated his

---

[4.] The same institution later went the rest of the way and conferred a Doctor of Literature degree upon him in 1901.

father's humiliating tumble into insolvency, and the situation was all the worse because he had done so long after he thought he had achieved lasting financial security.

His savior was Henry Huddleston Rogers, a rapacious capitalist who was one of John D. Rockefeller's chief associates in the Standard Oil monopoly. Rogers' business reputation was less than flattering, but to Clemens, he became the next thing to a saint. Rogers took over the management of Clemens' business affairs, and negotiated an agreement with creditors of the Webster firm, who accepted the promise of fifty cents on the dollar while allowing Livy, as preferred creditor, to keep control of the valuable Mark Twain copyrights and title to the Hartford house. To fund the agreement, Mark Twain agreed to undertake a year-long, round-the-world lecture tour to be followed by the composition of a new travel book. The tour was set to begin in July 1895 at Cleveland. It took Clemens to Japan, India, South Africa, and on to Europe by way of the Atlantic. To prepare for the trip, the family finally returned to the United States in May 1895.

Susy, as the eldest daughter, was offered the chance to accompany her parents on the journey, but she declined the opportunity. Her sister Clara went in her place. Susy remained in America, studying voice and trying to build up her stamina in the hopes of an operatic career.

The world tour was a huge artistic and financial success. It ended in London, during the summer of 1896, where Clemens took a furnished house while awaiting the arrival of Susy, Jean, and their faithful maid Kate Leary from America. Then came the news that Susy was ill. Livy and Clara boarded a steamer for New York, but while they were still at sea, Clemens received a cable message that Susy was dead. She had contracted spinal meningitis, endured a raging fever and suffered delirium, and then lapsed into a coma, which lasted until her death on August 18, 1896.

It was a blow from which Clemens/Twain never fully recovered. Little of the vast amount of writing he did after her death has the magic of his earlier work, and with the exception of *Following the Equator*, a travel book about his round-the-world lecture tour, he never again was able to complete a full-length book.

The family remained in Europe for four years after Susy's death. Clara asserted a degree of independence and went to study piano with the great teacher Leschetitzky in Vienna. Although she never had much of a musical career herself, she later married another of Leschetitzky's pupils, the distinguished Russian pianist and conductor, Osip Gabrilowitsch.

Sam and Livy spent the years 1900-1903 in and around New York, with summers at Saranac Lake and in Maine. The summer of 1903 was the last at Quarry Farm. Livy was very ill, and Sam took her to Florence for the winter, vainly hoping that her health would improve. She grew progressively worse and finally passed away on June 5, 1904, at the relatively youthful age of fifty-nine. Her death terminated a marriage which had endured for more than thirty-four years.

Clemens returned to New York, renting a house at 21 Fifth Avenue, which was his base for the next four years. He made a last trip to England in 1907 to accept a Doctorate of Letters from Oxford, and the next year moved to his final residence, a new home near Redding, Connecticut. Clara named it "Stormfield" (it was paid for in part by royalties from "Captain Stormfield's Visit to Heaven"). Designed by John Howells, the son of Clemens' friend William Dean Howells, Stormfield was the scene of Clara's wedding to Osip Gabrilowitsch in October 1909. Jean was maid of honor, and Clemens wore his Oxford gown. This occasion was his last great happiness.

Soon thereafter, on Christmas Eve 1909, the epileptic Jean suffered a seizure while taking a bath. Her heart stopped, ending her life at twenty-nine. Clemens' tribute to her, written the next day and incorporated into his *Autobiography*, was his last significant literary work.

He wintered in Bermuda, but feeling himself failing, he returned to New York on April 14. He was taken to Stormfield, where, true to his own prediction, he passed from the world as he had entered into it—with Halley's Comet streaking overhead. Clara, his only surviving child, was at his deathbed. He wrote her a note beginning, "You never told me . . ." which then becomes indecipherable. It may have referred to her pregnancy (the following November, she bore Clemens' only grandchild, Nina Clemens Gabrilowitsch). The dying man addressed his last words to Clara—"Good-bye, dear . . . if we meet again . . ."[5]

Samuel L. Clemens was buried in the Langdon/Clemens plot at Woodlawn Cemetery in Elmira, beside the ashes of his wife and the graves of the three children he had outlived. Later, at his own request, Osip Gabrilowitsch was buried at Clemens' feet, and still later, Clara was interred in the same plot. Nina Gabrilowitsch, Sam Clemens' only grandchild, died a suicide in Hollywood, California, in 1966. She never married and left no children. There are today no survivors of Samuel Clemens' immediate family.

He left behind an enormous literary legacy. Apart from his published novels, travel books, short stories, and essays, Mark Twain wrote a staggering amount of fragmentary materials, much of it now in print, and an even more amazing number of letters. Considering that he did not even begin to write seriously until he was nearly thirty, the sheer size of his output is astounding. How the man could have led a busy domestic life,

---

[5]   In so doing, he echoed the dying action of his father. John Marshall Clemens, on his deathbed, kissed and addressed his daughter Pamela alone among the members of his family. He neither held nor spoke to his wife or his three surviving sons before expiring.

lectured widely and traveled extensively, entertained lavishly, and often conducted business affairs (however unsuccessfully), and yet still found time and energy to write so many words is one mystery which will never be explained.

I have attempted to clear up some others, and to my own satisfaction, I believe I have explained much about the man and his work, which had previously been puzzling. As my approach to him was made through his work, let me begin with my first encounter with Mark Twain—the study of some of his best-known and most significant books.

Part II

Encounters of the First Kind: Reading
Mark Twain's Major Novels

The Necessity of Selection

With an author as prolific as Mark Twain it is simply impossible to study in detail all of his published work unless one is prepared to write not a book but an encyclopedia. The mass of material is so great and the range so wide that one must necessarily set some limits on the study.

Fortunately, in the case of Mark Twain, it is probably more than fair to disregard his travel books when attempting to explore his literary legacy. However good they might be—and *The Innocents Abroad* in particular is very, very good—the travel volumes are relatively superficial. I believe that it is upon Mark Twain's novels that his literary reputation must, and will, ultimately rest. Only in his longer prose fictions does the full range of Mark Twain's art appear to advantage: his concern with the problems of good and evil, conscience and consciousness, and individual and society. Likewise, it is in the novels that we see most clearly Mark Twain's technical skill as a writer in his command of construction, character development, irony, satire, and humor. It is on the novels, therefore, that I have concentrated.

In particular, I have written in detail about *The Adventures of Tom Sawyer, The Adventures of Huckleberry Finn, A Connecticut Yankee in King Arthur's Court,* and *Pudd'nhead Wilson.* In lesser detail, I have also discussed *The Prince and the Pauper, Life on the*

Mississippi, Personal Recollections of Joan of Arc, and *The Mysterious Stranger.* It is these works upon which I have fastened my critical attention, and it is from them that I have derived a theory about Mark Twain's work and its relationship to the life of Samuel Clemens.

Note on Criticism

Since this portion of *Encounters With Mark Twain* consists of commentary on a number of his works, it seems relevant to begin with a statement of my views on the function of literary criticism.

I do not believe that criticism should be limited to "I liked it" or "I hated it." That sort of commentary does nobody any good and may do the author much harm. Neither do I believe in the sort of criticism which relies on the obfuscation of jargon to conceal the lack of any serious ideas.

Criticism must, I think, seek to explore the work to elucidate the author's meaning and to raise questions which may help the reader formulate his own conception of the work in question. In the case of much of Mark Twain's work, this kind of analysis is sadly lacking. To my mind, few of the many writers on Twain's work have really explored his structures, explained his many paradoxes, or made an honest effort to achieve a cogent synthesis of his output as a whole. Too much Twain criticism goes off on tangents; too little is based on what Twain actually wrote and published as compared with common misconceptions about his books. For example, it is generally accepted that *Tom Sawyer* is a boys' adventure story, that *Huckleberry Finn* degenerates at the end, and that *A Connecticut Yankee* is a burlesque of Malory's tales of King Arthur and represents Mark Twain's favorable defense of nineteenth-century American institutions. None of these ideas can be supported on the internal evidence of the novels if they are read carefully and with intelligence. It is my hope that my comments will lead to critical reassessment of Mark Twain's novels, giving them at last the great stature that they so richly merit.

Defining Literary Terms

In the course of my discussion of Mark Twain's works, I will refer frequently to his use of irony and satire. These two literary tools, coupled with his use of humor, are at the core of his writing technique; his work simply cannot be understood without them.

It is well, then, to define specifically the meaning of these tools, which are so important in Mark Twain's writing. Unfortunately, I find that frequently they are used (even by scholars in English) too loosely or even incorrectly. Irony and satire are clearly defined terms which should be used carefully, not tossed haphazardly about as if they had no precise meanings.

Irony is the technique of making a point by saying the exact opposite of what is really meant. One of Mark Twain's most pointed ironies is found in the "Notice" at the beginning of *Huckleberry Finn* (which I will refer to at length later on). It says in part, "Persons attempting to find a plot in this book will be banished . . ." Twain's real meaning is that the reader should be aware that there *is* a plot, and that he should look out for it.[6]

---

6. In a broader sense, irony can be thought of as the reversal of expectations. Perhaps the best known practitioner of irony in American literature was

Satire should not be confused with irony. While they are frequently employed together, they are quite different. Satire is the technique of attacking or deflating a particular object through indirection. A substitute object is attacked, and the reader is left to draw the deadly parallel by inference. One of many examples of satire in Twain's work can be found in Chapter 33 of *A Connecticut Yankee* titled "Sixth Century Political Economy." The apparent object of attack is the economic situation in Arthurian England; the real object is the foes of free trade in Victorian America.

In fact, the whole of the *Yankee* is a satire; an indirect and surprisingly bitter attack on the world of Samuel Clemens, the United States in the last decades of the nineteenth century. Arthurian England is the straw man, the object of apparent attack. America, with its similar problems and equally corrupt institutions, is the real (though indirect) object.

Given these specific definitions of "irony" and "satire," the reader will be more easily able to comprehend both Mark Twain's work and my observations about it.

O. Henry (pen name of William S. Porter) whose many short stories often end with a sudden twist in which the reader's expectations, built up throughout the tale, are completely frustrated. Mark Twain did this too—consider my discussion of *Pudd'nhead Wilson* later in this book.

Early Works

Mark Twain made his debut as an author of full-length books in 1867, when publisher Charles Webb brought out a collection of twenty-seven of his humorous sketches headed by and titled for the "Jumping Frog."[7] By its very nature, this was no sustained novel but merely an olio. At that stage of his career, Twain was primarily a newspaper correspondent and platform lecturer who sometimes dabbled in comedic sketches.

His second book, the one which earned him his first great success, was also a compilation. *The Innocents Abroad,* published in 1869, grew from a series of travel letters he had written for the *Alta California,* the newspaper which financed his trip to the Holy Land aboard the *Quaker City.* Similarly, *Roughing It* (1872) is a semi-fictionalized account of his Nevada adventures during the Comstock rush. Like *Innocents,* it is a travel book in which the sequence of events provides the plot line without the necessity of constructing the story from scratch.

[7.] By one of those inexplicable, delightful ironies of circumstance, the book was printed by the New York firm of Gray and Green, where Sam Clemens had worked as a journeyman fourteen years earlier.

Even *The Gilded Age* (1873) is less than a real Mark Twain novel, in that it was a collaboration between Twain and his friend and neighbor, Charles Dudley Warner. The book grew out of a social evening during which the wives challenged their husbands to produce something, and while *Age* contains the wonderful Colonel Sellers, it lacks any sustained literary distinction. Whether this is the result of authorship by committee, or whether at this stage, neither Warner nor Twain was sufficiently adept at long fiction is a moot point. For me, at least, *The Gilded Age* is most significant for its presentation of the follies and foibles of the post-Civil War decade, introducing for the first time in Twain's fiction the theme of social criticism, which runs through all of his subsequent work and is his *raison d'être* as a novelist.

Before 1874, then, Mark Twain had never attempted a cogent, full-length novel which required him, as sole author, to construct a plot and mesh his characters together in the course of telling a story. In that sense, the four books he wrote in the first years of his career as a writer were in the nature of apprenticeship. They were learning experiences for Twain on the way to his first real novel, *The Adventures of Tom Sawyer.*

The Adventures of Tom Sawyer

In the summer of 1874, Samuel Clemens was a new father for the third time; Livy had given birth to a daughter, Clara, on June 8. At thirty-eight, he had behind him careers as journeyman printer, steamboat pilot, silver prospector, newspaper reporter, correspondent, and editor/publisher. He had won great success as a platform speaker and as a humorist. His travel books, especially *The Innocents Abroad,* had earned him both fame and fortune. He had been lionized in England and had been applauded on both sides of the Atlantic, and he had built his dream house in Hartford, the symbol of his rise from poverty and obscurity to affluence and glory. He was understandably in a mood to look backward.

Clemens' boyhood years in Hannibal had been drawing his imagination into the past for some time. In 1870, as a newlywed struggling with the demands of his position as editor and co-owner of the *Buffalo Express*, Mark Twain wrote a memory piece about his boyhood days. Known as the "Boy's Manuscript," it featured a character called "Billy Rogers," and was based on people and events the author remembered from his youth. Two years later, Twain explored the same material in an unperformed play. This time, "Billy Rogers" was given a different name, which Twain had taken from a San Francisco bartender he had known; he became "Tom Sawyer."[8] Now, just as his marriage seems to have stimulated him to write the Boy's Manuscript and the birth of Susy seems to have led to the abortive drama of 1872, the arrival of the new baby appears to have turned Mark Twain's attention once again to his own juvenile days.

Four days after the birth of Clara at the Langdon mansion in the middle of Elmira, the Samuel Clemens family moved up to Quarry Farm on East Hill, high above the town. This property had been purchased by Jervis Langdon some years before, and bequeathed at his death to his eldest child, Susan Langdon Crane, and her husband, Theodore. Born in 1836, Susan Crane was an adopted child, nine years older than Livy and a year younger than her brother-in-law, Sam. Herself childless, she was always the favorite aunt of the Clemens and Langdon children, and her farmhouse on the hill was their summer paradise.

Sue Crane was an intelligent woman who got on particularly well with her famous brother-in-law; she called him "Holy Samuel," and he retaliated by addressing her as "Saint Sue," and by making her the namesake for his eldest daughter.[9] She seems to have appreciated his intellect, perhaps more fully than Livy did; it was Susan Langdon Crane who presented Mark Twain with the gift which further stimulated him to write.

Recognizing her brother-in-law's need for a quiet place in which to do his work, she presented "Holy Samuel" with

---

[8.] Mark Twain had a predilection for calling his heroes Tom. Besides Tom Sawyer, there is Tom Canty in *The Prince and the Pauper* and Tom Driscoll in *Pudd'nhead Wilson*. One doubts that the identity of names was intended to indicate a relationship between the characters, however.

[9.] Born in Elmira on March 19, 1872, the child was baptized Olivia Susan Clemens after her grandmother, mother, and aunt. Throughout her life, however, she was always called Susy by the family. Only at Bryn Mawr College was she known by her given name, Olivia.

an octagonal study built on the side of the hill away from the house. Overlooking the valley and the town of Elmira, this little eight-sided room, reminiscent of a steamboat pilot house, offered Mark Twain the seclusion he needed to produce his best work. Between the summer of 1874 when he used it for the first time, and 1889, when he finished *A Connecticut Yankee*, much of Twain's best writing was done here. The first fruit of "Saint Sue's" gift was *Tom Sawyer*.[10]

The novel was begun in the summer of 1874 and finished the next year after eighteen months of intermittent work. It did not appear in print, however, until December 1876—too late for the Christmas book trade. Always alert to the monetary side of authorship, Twain was infuriated by the delay. Partly as a result of this mismanagement, Samuel Clemens began to interest himself in the publishing business as a way to maintain more control over Mark Twain's literary output. Six years later, the result was the founding of the Charles Webster Publishing Company, over whose imprint *The Adventures of Huckleberry Finn* was published in 1885.[11]

[10.] The octagonal study still exists. It is now located on the campus of Elmira College, where it was moved to protect it from vandals and curiosity seekers after Elmira College acquired Quarry Farm by gift of Jervis Langdon, Jr. (Susan Crane's great nephew), after the death of his father in 1952. The interior is not open to casual visitors, but one can look through the windows and see the inside, which is devoid of furniture but does have a fireplace. Mark Twain loved this little study, and from it came most of his immortal characters and best work. Had Saint Sue not given him this ideal working environment, one wonders whether he would have written so much and so well as he actually did.

[11.] While the firm bore the name of Clemens' nephew-in-law (Charles was married to the daughter of Clemens' elder sister, Pamela), the principal stake in the firm always belonged to Sam. Beginning well,

Of course, *Tom Sawyer* grew out of Clemens' boyhood in Hannibal as he recalled it years later. Some of the story is presaged in the Boy's Manuscript of 1870, including the juvenile romance of Tom and Becky Thatcher. Some of the tale is fiction based on fact; for example, there really was an "Injun Joe" in Hannibal, but he was a kindly old sot who never hurt the proverbial fly—nothing at all like the bloodthirsty murderer and thief who is the villain in the book. The buried treasure plot, however, is entirely a fabrication—nobody in Hannibal ever found $12,000 in an old, tumbledown house.

Likewise, the characters are an amalgam of memory and creative invention. Becky Thatcher was modeled on a girl named Laura Hawkins; Joe Harper, Tom's best friend, on John Briggs. The original of Huckleberry Finn was Tom Blankenship, son of the town drunkard and the undisguised envy of every boy in town because he was completely free of any restrictions whatsoever.

Hannibal landmarks, which show up in Twain's writing, include Jackson's Island (called Glasscock's Island in the real town;) Holliday's Hill, which becomes Cardiff Hill in *Tom Sawyer;* and McDowell's Cave (called McDougal's Cave in the book.) Many other characters and references can be found in Mark Twain's manuscript, "Villagers of 1840-43," now at the University of California Library.[12]

---

with *Huck* and the memoirs of General Grant, the firm later made some miscalculations, suffering when Clemens took money from it to invest in the Paige Typesetting Machine. Ultimately, the firm went bankrupt in April 1894, with losses in the neighborhood of $125,000, still another Clemens' venture gone sour.

[12.] Mark Twain Papers, DV 47. It can also be found in *Mark Twain's Hannibal, Huck, and Tom,* edited by Walter Blair (Berkeley and Los Angeles: University of California Press, 1969, pp. 23-40). "Villagers" is

Perhaps the best way to explore the novel is to attack it structurally. This technique opens the door to thematic explication and character analysis without admitting the misreadings, which so frequently arise from taking observations out of context. At the same time, it clarifies the points the author considered most important to the story.

---

a remarkable piece of writing. Clearly never meant for publication, it was written in 1897, more than fifty years after the period it describes, and forty-four years after Clemens moved away from Hannibal for good. Moreover, Clemens was in Switzerland at the time he produced these notes, so he can hardly have had much, if any, material with him to check his recollections. If nothing more, this fragment demonstrates that the memory Clemens used to become a licensed Mississippi River pilot had not deserted him at the age of sixty-one.

The manuscript identifies 168 people, most of them under their own names, though Professor Blair notes that Clemens renamed his own family as the "Carpenters," using false names beginning with the appropriate initials for each family member (thus Orion Clemens becomes Oscar Carpenter, Pamela is called Priscilla, and Sam himself becomes Simon). Professor Blair checked each of the 168 individuals described in the MS and was able to confirm the identities of no less than 120.

Among the other people named are Sam Clemens' friends John Robards, John Briggs, and their families; the Blankenships; the Widow Holliday, who served as the model for "the Widow Douglas," and many more. Among the more interesting entries is that describing Neil Moss, son of the local pork packer, who was sent to Yale and came home foppish and pretentious. He must have been in Mark Twain's mind when he created "Tom Driscoll," the villain of *Pudd'nhead Wilson*. Anyone interested in the material Mark Twain mined when creating the characters in his Mississippi Valley books must read "Villagers."

I
Plot and Structure

The Adventures of Tom Sawyer is anything but a carefully constructed, cogently plotted novel. There are no less than four principal story lines. The first is essentially a detective story—the murder of Dr. Robinson, the subsequent capture and trial of Muff Potter, the escape of Injun Joe, and his eventual death in the cave. The second is the "romance" between Tom Sawyer and Becky Thatcher, introduced in Chapter 6 and culminating with their adventures in the cave and ultimate deliverance in Chapters 30-32. The third story, Tom's pirating career, is self-contained in Chapters 13-19, occupying the physical center of the book; while the fourth and final subplot, Tom and Huck's search for and eventual discovery of the treasure, begins only with Chapter 25 and continues through the presentation of the gold in Chapter 34. In addition to these four interlocking principal narratives, there are other chapters devoted to Tom and his friends at play, to pictures of village life (including the school recitation scene in Chapter 21), to local folklore, and to descriptions of nature. Finally, there are other scenes, particularly concentrated in the first eight chapters, which center on the personality of Tom Sawyer himself and define his relationships with his environment, his peers, and the village adults, while at the same time, presenting us with his moods and motivations. Taken in all, it is a rich mixture: the question is what holds it all together?

One answer to this poser is found in the time framework of the book. All of the action takes place in the course of a single summer, commencing on a Friday afternoon in June and concluding before the reopening of school the following autumn.[13] I have found it useful to work out the whole time frame of the novel, which appears below.

The Time Frame of Tom Sawyer

Chapter number/Name	Day/Date	Time of Day
1. Tom Plays, Fights and Hides	Friday 6/14	Afternoon
2. The Glorious Whitewasher	Saturday 6/15	Morning
3. Busy at War and Love	Saturday 6/15	Afternoon
4. Showing Off at Sunday School	Sunday 6/16	7-10:30 a.m.
5. The Pinch Bug and his Prey	Sunday 6/16	10:30-noon
6. Tom Meets Becky	Monday 6/17	Morning
7. Tick-Running and Heartbreak	Monday 6/17	Morning (later)
8. A Pirate Bold to Be	Monday 6/17	Afternoon
9. Tragedy in the Graveyard	Monday 6/17-Tuesday 6/18	Midnight
10. Dire Prophecy of the Howling Dog	Tuesday 6/18	12-2 a.m.; 10 a.m.
11. Conscience Racks Tom	Tuesday 6/18—	Noon; a week afterward
12. The Cat and the Pain-Killer	Tuesday 6/25	Morning
13. The Pirate Crew Set Sail	Tuesday 6/25 Wednesday 6/26	Afternoon; night 2:00 a.m.
14. Happy Camp of the Freebooters	Wednesday 6/26	Dawn; afternoon; evening

---

[13]   We know from Chapter 23 that the murder in the graveyard took place on June 17. Working backward, it is possible to place the opening scene of the book on Friday afternoon, June 14. The year is not given but must be before 1850, when T. H. Benton lost his Senate seat. It is probably around 1844-45.

15. Tom's Stealthy Visit Home	Wednesday 6/26-Thursday 6/27	Night; early morning
16. First Pipes-"I've Lost My Knife"	Thursday 6/27-Friday 6/28 Saturday 6/29	
17. Pirates at Their Own Funeral	Saturday 6/29-Sunday 6/30	Afternoon; morning
18. Tom Reveals his Dream Secret	Monday 7/1	Morning; noon
19. The Cruelty of "I Didn't Think"	Monday 7/1	Noon
20. Tom Takes Becky's Punishment	Monday 7/1	Afternoon
21. Eloquence—And the Master's Gilded Dome	Unspecified	
22. Huck Finn Quotes Scripture	End of June-July 4; Five Weeks of Illness (This hiatus in Tom's summer carries the story into the second week of August)	
23. The Salvation of Muff Potter	Three days in August	
24. Splendid Days and Fearsome Nights	Unspecified (following the trial)	
25. Seeking the Buried Treasure	A Wednesday and Thursday in August	
26. Real Robbers Seize the Box of Gold	The next afternoon; (Friday) Saturday	Afternoon
27. Trembling on the Trail	Saturday night	Sunday Morning
28. In the Lair of Injun Joe	Sunday through Thursday	Night 11:00 p.m.
29. Huck Saves the Widow	Friday Saturday	Morning All day and Saturday night
30. Tom and Becky in the Cave	Sunday	Morning-afternoon
31. Found and Lost Again	Saturday through Tuesday (In the Cave)	

32. Turn Out! They're Found!	Tuesday through Sunday,
	then two weeks later
	(taking the story to the
	last week in August)
33. The Fate of Injun Joe	Unspecified
34. Floods of Gold	Unspecified
35. Respectable Huck Joins the Gang	Unspecified

The reader will note that while the time schedule for the first twenty chapters is very specific, it becomes much less definite later in the novel. The consistency with which the book is laid out is remarkable; I can find only one inconsequential error, in Chapter 28, when the watch on Temperance Tavern #2 skips from a Sunday night to a Tuesday, omitting any mention of Monday. Other than this one slip, all of the many references to passing days check out perfectly.

The time scheme chart indicates that *The Adventures of Tom Sawyer* is constructed in two major parts. The first comprises Chapters 1-20 and, with the exception of the chapters dealing with the murder in the graveyard (9-11), it is concerned with Tom's more juvenile adventures and with the Becky Thatcher romance. The second part, Chapters 25-35, centers on the buried treasure story and includes the resolution of the murder mystery and the culmination of Tom and Becky's romance and their salvation from the cave. In this portion of the book, Tom generally acts older, if no less self-centered. Connecting these two major sections of the novel is a "bridge" of four chapters (21-24), including the self-contained stories of the school exercises, Tom's illness, the trial, and Tom's subsequent terror.

The sections are connected by the continuing thread of the murder story, which appears in all three parts. The killing occurs halfway through Section I, the trial and acquittal of Muff Potter is found in the bridge, and the story is concluded with the discovery of Injun Joe's dead body two chapters before the end of the book. This is the only one of the four main narratives which appears in all three sections of the novel.

If unity of time is the first structural device which holds *Tom Sawyer* together, unity of place is the second. The entire novel takes place in and around St. Petersburg, which is a thinly disguised portrait of Clemens' own Hannibal. The characters hardly ever get further from the center of town than Cardiff Hill and the Haunted House in one direction, or the cave in the other. Those who do—Injun Joe after his escape from the courtroom and Becky Thatcher when she goes to Constantinople for the summer—drop out of the story when they leave the village and reenter it only when they return. The novel is confined to the same narrow world as Tom Sawyer himself.[14]

The surprising thing is the degree to which Mark Twain's description of this world is ambiguous. The casual reader almost certainly retains the image of St. Petersburg as "the white town drowsing in the sun," a kind of Eden nestled between the great river and the green hills, a boy's paradise and the prototypical American town.

Yet the novel also gives us another view of St. Petersburg—a dull, dreary, mud-spattered backwater in which little happens to break the monotony of existence and in which the atmosphere is stifling. Its citizens have pretensions to commerce, culture, and class, but they are all too often ignorant, foolish, short-sighted, prejudiced, superstitious, and poor. The town belongs as

---

[14]   The constant presence of Tom would have made it possible for Twain to have presented the novel as through his eyes, and we know he considered that device before deciding to tell the story in the third person. In *Huckleberry Finn,* he did use first-person narration, with implications and results which I shall discuss later.

much to Muff Potter as to the Widow Douglas; Injun Joe is as characteristic a citizen as Judge Thatcher.

A catalogue of the unpleasantries we encounter in the novel is surprisingly inclusive of the sins of the world. St. Petersburg is filled with drunkenness, duplicity, habitual theft (sometimes excused as mere "hooking," and thus not forbidden by Scripture), obscene cruelty (foiled in the attempt), and burglary, not to mention grave-robbing and murder; and always and everywhere is the pervasive wrong of slavery, which escapes notice by its very familiarity.

Not only is St. Petersburg a cruel and violent place but the level of ignorance in the town is appalling. The children believe that US Senator Thomas Hart Benton stands twenty-five feet tall, and are disappointed to find out that he does not.[15] Religion is mostly a combination of tedious sham and memorized platitudes in which most of the congregation is hardly more interested than Tom himself. Recall the difficulty the minister experiences in trying to collect his salary, or how the church sounds on the unique occasion when the congregation puts its heart into "Old Hundred" upon the return of the pirates.[16] Nor is education more meaningful, consisting as it does in rote memorization enforced with cruelty. In short, when one looks at St. Petersburg more closely, the "white town" is no Eden at all but something much closer to what Huck Finn would call "t' other place."

This microcosm of the world is the stage upon which *The Adventures of Tom Sawyer* plays. That the entire book is focused so narrowly is one of the important means by which Twain holds his material together.

The third (and probably most important) factor unifying the novel is the character of Tom Sawyer himself. He dominates

---

[15.]   See Chapter 22.

[16.]   See Chapter 17.

the book from first page to last, and he is at the center of nearly every incident in it. The only exception is the salvation of the Widow Douglas from Injun Joe's revenge, which is Huck's work, not Tom's. Everything else in the book is brought about by, or is defined by its effect on, Tom Sawyer himself. Therefore, it becomes vital to a complete understanding of the novel to focus on Tom's character and to define his position relative to his juvenile peers and the community as a whole. The proper study of *Tom Sawyer*, to paraphrase Pope, is Tom Sawyer.

To put this another way, we can say that structural analysis of the novel indicates that it is fundamentally not a narrative but a character study, and that therefore full understanding of the book demands that we explore the personality of the central character in detail.

II
Tom

Tom Sawyer belongs to one of the most respectable families in St. Petersburg, though the precise intrafamilial relationships in the Sawyer clan are left somewhat obscure. We know from Aunt Polly herself that Tom is her own dead sister's son.[17] We also know that Sid is his half-brother and that Mary is his cousin. No mention is ever made of Tom's father, or for that matter of whether Mary is Aunt Polly's daughter by an unremarked (and presumably dead) husband or the daughter of still another sister, also presumably deceased. We learn in *Huckleberry Finn* that Aunt Polly and Aunt Sally Phelps are sisters and also that Sid's family name is indeed Sawyer, and from this, we can infer that Tom and Sid are sons of the same father but different mothers.

[17.] See Chapter 1.

In any event, the Sawyer family pedigree is full of confusion and impossible to sort out.

Tom's age presents another problem. It is never given, and more than one commentator has pointed out that through the course of the book, his actions are not consistently appropriate to any single age. For example, in the "I dare you!" confrontation with Alfred Temple in Chapter 1, Tom acts no more than seven or eight, while in the buried treasure sequence, he seems to be thirteen or more. His showing off to Becky Thatcher is the attention-getting of a little boy, but his taking her punishment in school is the act of an adolescent. Again, there can be no real resolution of these inconsistencies; the best we can do is infer that Tom is perhaps twelve or so, Mary about fifteen, and Sid about ten.

Nor is it enough to simply identify Tom in the novel with the young Samuel Clemens. Indeed, while there is a lot of Sam in Tom, and some of the adventures of which we read really did happen to the author when he was a boy (the tale of the cat and the painkiller, for one), there is at least as much fiction in Tom as Clemens. Mark Twain wrote, in the preface of the novel, that Tom Sawyer was created out of a combination of characteristics belonging to three boys; with however many grains of salt one takes that remark, one still cannot simply identity Tom with the young Sam Clemens.

The only way to really understand the character of Tom Sawyer is by close analysis of what he does in the book and why he does it. Only when we have done this will we be able to say with confidence that we know who Tom Sawyer is and what this novel is about.

We begin with the first chapter. Tom's very first action in the book is theft of the jam, which he has been eating in the closet while Aunt Polly looks for him. When she catches him red-handed, so to speak, he escapes her switch by the old April Fool's trick of shouting, "Look behind you, Aunt!" and scrambling over the fence when she does so.

Aunt Polly's subsequent soliloquy tells us of Tom's cleverness—"He 'pears to know just how long he can torment me before I get my dander up, and he knows if he can make out to put me off for a minute or make me laugh, it's all down again and I can't hit him a lick." She also clues us in to one of Tom's most important characteristics—"He hates work more than he hates anything else." A page or two later, he is stealing sugar at the dinner table, and through Sid's observation of the thread on his collar, his hooky playing comes to light. Next he gets into a fight with the new boy in town (later we learn his name, which is Alfred Temple), a fight which obviously stems from Tom's jealousy of the new boy's clothes, shoes (and it was only Friday!), and bearing.

In short, after just one chapter, we know Tom to be both cunning and selfish, with an inferiority complex that drives him to actions which will inflate his ego and make him more satisfied with himself.

Chapter 2, "The Glorious Whitewasher," is probably the best-known part of the book, and Tom's ruse to get the other boys of the village to pay him for the privilege of doing his work is the best-known thing he does.[18] In the popular mind, this trick is much admired, as proving Tom to be smarter than the other village lads and somehow more worthy of our appreciation. I venture to say that if a survey of all the readers of *Tom Sawyer* could be made, the vast majority would admit that their impression of Tom's trick is favorable and that they admire him for pulling it off.

[18.] The curators of the Mark Twain Home and Museum in Hannibal have reconstructed the famous fence. They could hardly afford not have done so—the fence is probably the biggest attraction at the site, so far as the public is concerned.

It is well to remember, therefore, that Tom's ruse is designed for two purposes. The first is to escape the work of doing the fence, and the second is to profit by the deception. In the pantheon of American virtues neither of these purposes is enshrined; Tom acts more like a young crook than an all-American hero. His motives are self-aggrandizing, and he succeeds simply because he *does* possess a cleverness beyond the dull wits of his friends. However, his behavior can hardly be called admirable if one overlooks the humorous aspect of his accomplishment.

So it goes throughout the novel. Everything Tom does is for the purpose of furthering himself, gathering more glory, amusing himself, or accumulating some kind of wealth. He is totally heedless of the feelings of others and blissfully insensitive to the consequences of his actions.

In Chapter 3, we see another facet of Tom's character. Caught in the act of stealing sugar again, Tom is delighted when brother Sid, attempting a similar theft, breaks the sugar bowl.[19] Tom expects Sid to get a rap from his aunt's palm and is stunned when she belts him instead—more or less on general principles. He retaliates by sulking to make Aunt Polly feel guilty; presently, he begins to feel sorry for himself in earnest and sits brooding on a raft, thinking about how pleasureful it would be to inflict sorrows on those others in the village (to wit, his aunt and the new girl he has just met) who don't appreciate him enough, by suffering a painless martyrdom. The scene ends comically, when the Thatcher's housemaid dumps the chamber pot out the window upon him, but another part of Tom's makeup has

---

[19.]   Sid is worthy of a character study of his own. While generally depicted as the "good boy," in contrast to Tom, he is actually far more complicated than that. As Tom points out in Chapter 34, he has a mean streak in him, which is the most unattractive, and he is plainly jealous of his elder half-brother.

been revealed; he longs to manipulate the feelings of others into giving him the love and respect which he feels he does not get.

In Chapter 4, Tom goes to Sunday school and, again by using his superior wits, contrives to collect the right number of tickets to earn a Bible. He hardly wants the Bible for its own sake, though—his motivation is to earn himself a place close to Judge Thatcher at least equal to that enjoyed by his friend Jeff as one of the Thatcher family, to win some longed-for glory before the congregation (all of whom, from the superintendent down, are equally desirous of showing off), and especially to earn the attention of "the new girl" (Becky) whom he hasn't even met yet. In short, Tom's motives are the already familiar ones of self-aggrandizement, ego-boosting, and attention-getting. In the course of his performance, he does indeed earn feminine attention—from Amy Lawrence. But he pays no attention to her, and presently "breaks her heart" (not for the last time either). Tom is forever trifling with the feelings of his two love objects, Amy and Becky, although in all fairness, it cannot be denied that they do the same thing to him, and all three of them survive uninjured.

As he was deflated at the end of Chapter 3, so Tom gets his just desserts again at the end of Chapter 4, when he is forced to identify the first two disciples and can come up with no better answer than "David and Goliath!" But these temporary setbacks never turn him from his goal of glory-seeking; he will try again.

He only dreams of glory in the next chapter, while the minister sermonizes on the picture of the lion and the lamb lying down together, and the little child leading them. Tom thinks only of how much attention that child would be getting, and how he would like to be that child (if it were a tame lion). Before the real action of the novel begins, then, we have a complete picture of its hero drawn with some detail. It is not a very pretty portrait if taken at face value, yet somehow Tom has escaped serious censure from over a century of affectionate readers, who tend to recognize him as a rascal, but refuse to take him too seriously as a villain.[20]

Tom's next big adventure—his pirating experience—is first conceived of in Chapter 8, after Becky rejects his brass andiron knob. He muses on how she would feel if he died, like Jimmy Hodges, and then he thinks about dying temporarily. He rejects in turn the ideas of becoming a clown, a soldier, and a savage, finally hitting on piracy as a way to awe the town. He is confirmed in his decision to run away when his aunt berates him for "breaking her heart so," when Becky returns his andiron to his desk at school, and finally and completely when she snubs him after he shows off for her upon her return to school after an illness. In other words, his real motivation for running away is to manipulate the feelings of others, to punish them for not loving him enough, and ultimately to return gloriously to an awe-stricken village.[21]

---

20. In *Love and Death in the American Novel,* the perceptive Leslie Fiedler calls Tom the archetype of the "good bad boy," and points out that this is precisely America's image of itself—a bit of a rapscallion, not so good as to be sissified or goody-goody but with a heart of gold. Fiedler also recognizes (correctly, I think) that Tom, despite his many "bad" actions, never really breaks the social norms; he may pull at the leash, but in the end, he is a tame puppy. More on this point later; in my opinion, it is crucial to understanding not only *Tom Sawyer* but *Huckleberry Finn* as well.

21. Just to show how subtle and how well-read Mark Twain really was, consider Aunt Polly's line after she hears from Sid (in Chapter 10) that Tom has been out all night. Instead of flogging him, she makes him feel guilty by saying that he will "make her bring her gray hairs with sorrow to the

The pirating sequence, which occupies the center of the novel, is telling in several ways. First, it indicates that Tom (and the other boys as well) are so thoughtless of the future that they do not even think about making any preparations in the event of bad weather; Twain comments that in their heedlessness, they were no more than representative of their generation. Second, the pirates' adventures on Jackson's Island are interrupted by Tom's visit home, which is motivated by certain stirrings of conscience but ends instead in an even more blatant decision in favor of a triumphant return (at the funeral) at the cost of the feelings of others. To put it another way, even when Tom does show some consideration, he is willing to put aside such concerns in favor of anticipated triumph and glory for himself. Then he makes matters even worse by lying about his visit home, presenting it in the form of a dream and making Aunt Polly an object of ridicule as well as a sacrifice to his ego gratification.

The pirating story culminates in the most important chapter of the novel; Chapter 19, "The Cruelty of I Didn't Think!" Here,

---

grave . . ." To me, this seemed just typical speech for Aunt Polly (though, in fact, we hear it only second-hand, through the narrator).

However, my young daughter, who studies the Bible assiduously, recognized these words immediately. They come from Genesis XIV, V.29, where Jacob uses them to his sons. They in turn repeat the old man's speech to Joseph when he demands that they leave Benjamin in Egypt; the ultimate effect of this touching line is to make Joseph reveal himself to his brothers.

The point is that Twain clearly knew the verse and incorporated it into Aunt Polly's speech. Whether the author expected his readers to recognize the reference, or whether he just used the words for their power and beauty, we cannot know. The fact that the biblical source can be traced, however, proves beyond question the range of knowledge and the subtlety of the author.

for the only time in the book, Tom is confronted by one of his victims. He hangs his head and says he is sorry but excuses himself by saying he didn't mean to be mean—he just didn't think.

"Oh, child, you never think. You never think of anything but your own selfishness," replies Aunt Polly, thus summing up Tom's character in a single line.

Even Tom's supreme gesture in the novel—his assuming the punishment Becky deserves for tearing the master's anatomy book in Chapter 20—is done not out of altruism or of desire to spare her pain and embarrassment. It is the product of his lightening realization that it will impress her and win her favor, a calculated acceptance of pain in return for the expectation of ego-gratifying pleasure.

Moreover, Tom does not change during the course of the book. Toward the end, he leaves Huck alone when he goes to investigate the Temperance Tavern in Chapter 27, because "He did not care to have Huck's company in public places" (that would be socially demeaning). Likewise, he abandons Huck, who is on watch for the robbers, while he goes off to enjoy Becky's picnic. Again, in Chapter 34, he quite rightly criticizes Sid for spoiling the Welshman's secret and upstaging him at the Widow's party—and then immediately does the same thing himself when he brings in the bags of gold (Like Hank Morgan in *A Connecticut Yankee*, whose spiritual ancestor he is, Tom can never resist "getting up an effect" for the glory of it.[22]) Finally, in the last chapter of the novel, he insists that Huck return to the Widow's house and endure the torments of "sivilization",

---

[22.] Robert Keith Miller has pointed out the similarities between Tom Sawyer and The Boss; he calls Tom "a pint-sized Hank Morgan" in that both are addicted to power, profit, and prestige. See *Mark Twain* (New York: Fr. Ungar Publishing Co., 1983), p. 68.

not because he sees any benefit in it for Huck but because Tom Sawyer's Gang (that is, Tom Sawyer) would lose social status if it accepted such a déclassé outcast as Huck in his unreconstructed state.

In short, every one of Tom's actions in the novel is the product of his never-ending search for self-aggrandizement, ego massage, or the desire to manipulate the emotions of others to make them feel pain for not appreciating him enough. Never does he demonstrate any serious consideration for the feelings of others; on the one occasion when his conscience stirs him to take some action in that direction—his midnight visit home from Jackson's Island—the overwhelming attraction of a glorious return to his own funeral diverts him. In brief, Tom Sawyer is as selfish and unfeeling a character as American literature has produced.[23]

Yet it is abundantly clear that Tom's deeply flawed character is overlooked or ignored as much by the other villagers of St. Petersburg as it has been by more than 125 years of delighted readers. As an example, look to Aunt Polly. She is quite aware of his insensitivity and selfishness since she suffers from it more than anyone else. Still, she is all too willing to forgive him everything, even when she is perfectly cognizant that she ought not to. Other people, like Judge Thatcher and the Widow, see only a great future for Tom; his image as a not-too-good boy blinds them to his real inadequacies. They see him *as they want him to be,* not necessarily as he is, and generations of readers,

---

[23]. One is reminded of the lyrics to "As Time Goes By," which might have been written to describe the life of Tom Sawyer, "It's still the same old story, A search for love and glory, A case of do or die . . ."

seduced perhaps by the attitude of St. Petersburg's residents, have done the same thing.[24]

It is easy to see how this misreading of Tom's character comes about. Both the people of the novel and the readers as well see so much of Tom in so many varied situations (including the charming Robin Hood scenes) that we lack perspective to recognize him for what he really is. Then, too, there is a cheeky quality about everything Tom does which is never quite saucy enough to make us see him as a brat but is quite attractive in comparison with the dullards in town. Finally, as Fiedler again has pointed out, the ultimate source of Tom's charm is that he is bad without being truly outside the pale. He plays at evil, and it is no accident that Tom's games of being a robber and a pirate are contrasted with the reality of crime as carried out by Injun Joe and his partner. Tom, whatever he is, will never be an Injun Joe—he is part of the town, not hostile to it.

The personality of Tom, then, as contrasted with the other drab youngsters in town on the one hand, and with the reality of what he only plays at being on the other, is a principal factor in holding the novel together.

[24.] In a previous footnote, I remarked on Mark Twain's predilection for naming his characters "Tom." Insofar as Tom Sawyer is a "bad good boy," he combines elements of Tom Canty (a "good boy") from *The Prince and the Pauper* and Tom Driscoll (a very bad person indeed) from *Pudd'nhead Wilson*. The name also evokes ideas of an independent and self-serving male cat. Whether any of this was conscious or intentional on Twain's part, I cannot say.

III
Huck

While Tom is certainly the central character in the novel, a sensitive reader cannot but feel the growing presence of Huckleberry Finn in the latter part of the book.

Huck makes his first appearance midway through Chapter 6, when, in the immortal phrase of Bernard DeVoto, he "marches into history, swinging a dead cat." Based on a boy named Tom Blankenship, who was the son of the town drunk, Huck is truly outside the accepted society of St. Petersburg. He has the freedom from rules and conventions Tom supposes that he wants, and so Tom associates with Huck whenever he gets the chance; but in reality, Tom would never choose to change places with his friend. For all Huck's freedom, he is truly an outcast, eating with the slaves and toting water for Ben Rogers' father's Uncle Jake in return for a place to sleep. Huck has his place in Tom's life, but it is a limited place.

It is by contrast with Huck that Tom's real position in St. Petersburg becomes clearer. He is indeed selfish and unfeeling, but at the same time, he is part of the town society. When Tom sees himself as a desperate outlaw, it is mere romanticizing; actually, he is a pillar of the younger set in town.

In short, the introduction of Huck Finn is a key device in the novel, for it is by comparison with Huck that Tom's social position is fixed. Similarly, Tom's character is defined by comparison with the real villain, Injun Joe. We can only conclude, then, that Tom Sawyer, whatever his character, is part of the St. Petersburg establishment; he stands with the town, not against it. He is of it, not hostile to it, and I submit that it is crucial to understanding the book to recognize this point.

We can summarize, then, by saying that structurally *The Adventures of Tom Sawyer* is not a complicated novel. The four principal story lines and its other independent scenes are held together by the unities of time and place and by the presence of Tom Sawyer himself in nearly every scene. It is, then, primarily a novel of character rather than plot, and its central character, Tom, is clearly presented as a selfish, unfeeling, manipulative, grasping boy who is at the same time closely identified with the community in which he lives.

IV
Other Points

While character is central to *Tom Sawyer*, the book has other dimensions which help to make it the ripsnorting good read which it always has been. Among these are its language, its description of nature, and its catalogue of superstitions.

The language of *Tom Sawyer* is hybrid. Its dialogue is the vernacular speech of the Missouri frontier, while its narration is the diction of the educated sophisticate. One would expect the two styles to clash, but Twain somehow makes them blend together so artfully that the seams rarely show. Admirable as the caulking is, however, the lack of a consistent narrative style does, I think, have a negative impact on the book. One of Mark Twain's greatest assets as a writer was his unexcelled ear for vernacular speech, and his ability to reproduce it in such a convincing matter that his characters come fully alive. To the extent that we hear them speak, we cannot fail to believe in them completely.[25] In *Tom Sawyer*, we do indeed get to hear the characters speak, but the constant intrusion of the impersonal and sometimes biting narrator has the effect of distancing us

---

[25] Ironically, Twain's uncanny skill with everyday speech was one of the reasons why his books were so roughly attacked for their alleged "coarseness" by the effete elite. Without intending to do so, his attackers were actually paying the author a supreme compliment.

from them and, I submit, of weakening the potential impact of their conversations. Even though *Tom Sawyer* may well have been the finest and most sustained presentation of colloquial frontier American speech ever put on paper at the time of its publication, its author was destined to eclipse it completely in *The Adventures of Huckleberry Finn,* where there is no narrator to temper and blunt the effects of the dialogue.

While surely *Tom Sawyer* is above all else a novel of character, it is also, to a surprising degree, a novel of nature. St. Petersburg is very much on the borderline between civilization and the untamed natural world, and in this novel, Twain, for the first time in his literary career, presents nature as an elemental force of great power and endurance, yet impersonal and disdainful of human conduct.

First and always foremost aspect of the natural world is the Mississippi itself, lapping eternally at the forefront of the town as it takes its patient, never-ending course down to the sea. The river gives economic life to the town; indeed, it can be said to have created it. Moreover, it is more than a fluid highway. The people of St. Petersburg live with, on and in the river; it is their fishing hole, their swimming pool, and their cleansing agent all in one. For Tom Sawyer and the other boys in town, it is all of these things, even more clearly than for the adults, and it is also their friend.[26]

Nature also pervades the novel in other forms. In Chapter 2, its beauty contrasts with Tom's drab task of whitewashing the fence; in Chapter 14, we encounter the first of Mark Twain's

---

[26] Injun Joe's nameless partner, the "ragged man," is found drowned near the ferry landing. The ferryboat serves the town as vehicle for searching for the missing boys, who are presumed drowned as well; it is also the means by which the picnickers go to the cave. At various times, we see Tom go swimming in the river, go fishing in it, hunt turtle eggs on a sandbar, and use it as a highway to the cave to retrieve the gold. In truth, no one and nothing in St. Petersburg is ever very far from the river.

several pictures of dawn on the Mississippi; in Chapter 16, we witness the awesome power of an electrical storm on the island; and in Chapter 33, the indifferent, eternal enormity of nature is symbolized by the drop of water which falls from the stalactite overhead once every three minutes, day after day, year after year, century after century, millennium after millennium.[27]

Tom Sawyer is also pervaded with various superstitions, whose effects govern the lives of its characters to an amazing degree. Twain seems to have delighted in cataloging the weird and wonderful beliefs of his boyhood town. Whether it is curing warts with a bean or a dead cat, finding marbles with the proper incantations, crossing a stream to keep from being pursued, or identifying a person soon to die by the howling of a stray dog, *Tom Sawyer* contains a fascinating collection of superstitious beliefs.

Yet, as clearly as Twain sees them for what they are, the author never completely discredits superstitions. For example, Tom and Huck are saved by their recognition that Friday is a bad day to go hunting buried treasure. Is Twain, then, giving some respect to folk wisdom, or are we meant to take its occasional rightness in the spirit of the blind hen who sometimes scratches up a worm? Twain leaves this question unanswered.[28]

[27.] If I am not mistaken, this passage is Twain's first reference in fiction to an idea which was to pervade his thinking in the last years of his life—the insignificance of man and the meaninglessness of human existence. The author refers to Injun Joe here as a "flitting human insect" in comparison with the endless dripping of water in McDougal's cave.

[28.] A similar treatment of superstitions will be found in *Huckleberry Finn*. Jim's folk beliefs are the object of ridicule on more than one occasion, yet more often than not he turns out to be ironically right. He predicts that the snakeskin has not yet done its evil job and that he will someday be rich again. It has not—the travelers miss Cairo in the fog—and he does become rich, obtaining the priceless gift of freedom at the end. Also,

Language, nature, and superstition are thus three facets of
Tom Sawyer, which lend color to the novel and help it to become
the wonderful adventure in reading which it really is.

V
Interpretations

The Adventures of Tom Sawyer has been wildly popular ever
since it first appeared in December 1876. Even today, it remains
Mark Twain's best-selling book, and it will probably remain in
print forever.

It is not hard to explain this fabulous popularity. *Tom Sawyer*
has everything: a blood-and-guts murder plot, complete with a
frightful villain; an appealing devil-may-care hero (as long as one
does not look at him too closely); a childhood romance; Gothic
horror; a tale of buried treasure; and lots of comedy as well. Put all
these elements together, and they add up to a publisher's dream.

Yet *Tom* is such a ripsnorting good story that it is tempting to
overlook a good deal of serious material, not at first apparent,
but clearly seen by a careful and perceptive reader. The book is
full of themes and ideas, some of them not worked out, which
when recognized not only help to clarify this novel but to put it
firmly in its proper context among the author's other works.

In common with most readers, I used to dismiss *Tom
Sawyer* as great juvenile adventure unworthy of serious critical
consideration. I can no longer subscribe to that proposition,
and I shall try to demonstrate why I now see *Tom Sawyer* as more
like than unlike its great successor, *Huckleberry Finn,* and why I

---

note *Connecticut Yankee* in this regard; despite all The Boss accomplishes
with the magic of science, it is Merlin and the magic of folderol who
triumphs in the last chapters.

now see the book less as sui generis and more as a part of Mark Twain's steadily developing and interrelated body of work.

Of course, the book is a remarkable example of juvenile adventure—certainly among the finest novels of this type ever written. Very few other examples of this genre can match its blend of action and terror, comedy and romance. Only Robert Louis Stevenson comes immediately to mind as Mark Twain's peer in writing this kind of fiction.[29] *The Hardy Boys* and their many imitators and competitors are a bad joke by comparison. The danger is that the reader may get so wrapped up in the adventure story that he misses the other aspects of the book.

One of these, as I have already mentioned, is that *Tom Sawyer* is a character study. It is not, however, a classic "Bildungsroman" (the German term for a story of education). Tom does not grow or change in the book; neither his formal schooling nor his experiences teach him anything or make any perceptible mark on his character. Tom behaves at the end of the book just as he behaved in the beginning, and just as he will continue to behave in *Huckleberry Finn*. One can hardly speak of a novel of education when the central character learns nothing and remains static throughout the book.

Tom Sawyer, then, is not more or less than a romance, in the classic definition—a narrative written in the vernacular which tells a story for its own sake. Yet even if the book makes no pretense at being a novel of manners and morals (as its successors in Twain's catalogue do), on close examination, *Tom*

---

[29] I had thought that Stevenson must have influenced Twain until I checked the dates and found that *Tom Sawyer* antedates *Treasure Island* by several years and *Kidnapped* by a decade. One wonders instead to what degree Stevenson was influenced by *Tom Sawyer*, which he must have encountered during his visit to the United States in 1879-80. According to the *Autobiography* (Chapter 59), the two writers met at least once—for an hour on a Washington Square park bench.

Sawyer may be seen to contain many of the same elements which we find in the later, more "serious" works.

First, in common with practically everything Twain wrote, *Tom Sawyer* incorporates a sizeable chunk of social criticism. One hardly thinks of the book in this connection—yet what is the entire chapter on the school graduation exercises, if not a biting attack on the kind of education they represent, on the pedagogue who inculcates it (by vigorous application of his rod), and on the society which accepts such trash as real education?[30] Likewise, religion as it exists in St. Petersburg's little church is so dull, so boring, and so irrelevant that Tom is far from the only congregant who tunes the minister's sermon out.

Nor is this all. Among the specific targets of Twain's criticism are the townspeople who first want to lynch Injun Joe but don't dare to do so, and afterward circulate a petition to the governor for his pardon. Then, of course, there is slavery; one of the most bitter criticisms in the book is the one contained in that little footnote about the howling dog, whom the boys take for "Bull" Harbison.[31] Mr. Harbison's dog is called Bull Harbison; if he had owned a slave named Bull, he would have been known as "Harbison's Bull," slaves not being entitled to a family name. Huck reinforces the absurdity of this fact in Chapter 25, by pointing out that kings have only one name too.

But *Tom Sawyer* is a novel of social criticism on a different level, too. The people of St. Petersburg never see through Tom himself—his posturing, glory-seeking, and manipulation of the others go ignored, and he is hailed by the leading citizens, Judge Thatcher, and the Widow as a young man with a great

---

[30.] See *Tom Sawyer,* Chapter 21.

[31.] See Chapter 10.

future. The apparent object of attack here is Tom, but on second thought, one can see the whole story as a satire in which the real object of attack is not the boy himself but the society of which he is a part and for which he stands. That is why it is so important to distinguish between Tom, the "bad good boy," Huck, and Injun Joe, who really do stand outside of and against the community. An attack on Tom's character is by implication an attack on St. Petersburg as a community; and the trouble is that this whole society is as heedless, thoughtless, self-deceiving, and manipulative as Tom himself. No wonder nobody in the village recognizes Tom for the flawed character that he is—they are all too much like him.

When we recognize that social criticism is an integral part of *Tom Sawyer*, always present if lying just below the surface, the ambiguous picture of St. Petersburg comes into focus. The townspeople see their community as an idyllic new Eden, ignoring or deliberately refusing to recognize the abundant evidence that it is something much less. They are as blind to the reality of their condition as they are to the character of Tom Sawyer, the boy who personifies them and everything they stand for. In the gap between their self-delusions and reality lies the opportunity for the reader to appreciate the unstressed but clearly present criticism of St. Petersburg society; but all too often, the reader, swept along by the excitement of the adventure stories, misled by the novel's overwhelming energy, and without the assistance of careful plot construction or extended thematic development to aid him, winds up at the end of the book no more aware of its deeper significance than the self-deluding townspeople.

That such social criticism should indeed be found in *Tom Sawyer* should come as no surprise to anyone familiar with Mark Twain's earlier writing. From Clemens' first use of the pen name, while covering the antics of the venal and crooked politicians in the Nevada territorial legislature back in 1863, it is

always associated with the most outspoken and biting attacks on
pomposity, stupidity, and social injustice.[32]

His earlier books are all laced with characteristic Twainian
attacks. *The Innocents Abroad* is as much a demolition of the smug
and stupid travelers as it is a description of the countries they
visit. *Roughing It* continues Twain's wry observations on society,

---

[32.] Clemens had used many other pen names in his earlier years, among
them W. Epaminondus Blab and Thomas Jefferson Snodgrass. When he
began writing for the *Enterprise,* his pieces were signed "Josh." But when
he decided to adopt a new, permanent pen name, he chose the sonorous
Mississippi River called "Mark Twain," the leadsman's term for twelve
feet of water under the bow—safe depth for a steamboat to navigate.
Later in life, Clemens claimed to have taken the name from a Mississippi
River Captain named Sellers (whose last name he appropriated for the
hero of *The Gilded Age*) who used to write long, pretentious letters to the
New Orleans newspaper over the Mark Twain signature. Captain Sellers
having passed on, Clemens took over the name.

Another possibility is that he picked it up in a saloon, where drinks
on credit were written up on a slate. "Mark Twain" would then have
meant, "Write down two drinks on credit." However, he came to it, we
know Clemens first used the Mark Twain name in the *Enterprise,* and it
was associated with political and social criticism from the beginning.

His editor on the *Territorial Enterprise,* Joe Goodman assigned his new
writer, Sam Clemens to the legislative beat in full knowledge that he knew
little or nothing about legislative procedures, parliamentary debate, or
government in general. Goodman saw this as an advantage; he knew that
in the absence of technical knowledge, Clemens would inevitably focus his
reports on the failings and foibles of the legislators, which is exactly what he
did. The result was precisely the kind of colorful invective Editor Goodman
knew his readers wanted. From the very first, then, the pen name "Mark
Twain" was associated with deflation of the pompous, exposure of the phony,
and criticism of the unjust.

and *The Gilded Age*, of course, is about little else. It would have been surprising had Mark Twain *not* continued his critical analysis of society in *Tom Sawyer.*

Moreover, one can draw some telling parallels between events in *Tom* and episodes of *Huckleberry Finn*, which point up just how present that critical attitude is the earlier novel. For example, the school exercises in Chapter 21 of *Tom* are echoed in the poetry and art (?) of Emmeline Grangerford in *Huck*. The irrelevancy of religion as practiced in St. Petersburg is highlighted by comparison with two parallel sequences in *Huck;* the Grangerfords and the Shepherdsons come to church to hear a sermon on brotherly love—and keep their rifles within easy reach during the preaching, while the folks at the Pikesville camp meeting are so affected by the king's phony testimony that they are moved to rapture and shower the old fraud with money (whereupon he runs off with the collection).[33]

The unsuccessful attempt to lynch Colonel Sherburn in Chapter 23 of *Huck* is presaged by the mutterings of St. Petersburg against Injun Joe in Chapter 11 and then against Muff Potter in Chapter 23 of *Tom*. Tom and Huck discuss kingship in Chapter 25 of the earlier novel, just as Huck and Jim will do in Chapter 14 of the later. The point, I think, is adequately made—to ignore the social criticism apparent just beneath the surface of *Tom Sawyer* is to violently misread the book.

The Adventures of Tom Sawyer, then, belongs squarely in the mainstream of Mark Twain's work, which is characterized by deflation of the pompous, compassion for the oppressed, and criticism of the unjust from his earliest writings onward.

---

[33]. There is another interesting parallel with *Tom Sawyer* here. In the earlier book, Tom plays at being a pirate; in *Huck*, the King does the same thing; and in both instances, the mummer winds up aggrandizing himself as a result.

Carrying that analysis one step further, we find that *Tom Sawyer* introduces, if only in passing, most if not all of the themes which preoccupied Mark Twain in his later works. For example, Tom struggles with his conscience over the question of whether to tell what he saw in the graveyard, and eventually, despite his most solemn oaths sealed in blood, testifies at Muff Potter's trial and saves his life.[34] On a lesser level, he confronts his conscience again when, on his midnight visit to the village, he almost leaves Aunt Polly a message telling her that he is not dead but only off pirating.[35] Though the treatment is different (Tom's conscience clearly motivates him to do the right thing), these events bring to mind the central issue of *Huckleberry Finn*—Huck's titanic struggle with his superego over whether to tell on Jim.

Likewise, careful reading discloses a little passage embedded in Chapter 27, which in itself is innocuous, but in the light of the author's later career takes on much greater significance. It occurs at the beginning of the chapter, just after Tom and Huck have watched Injun Joe and his nameless companion dig up the great Murrel treasure from beneath the floor of the Haunted House. It is now the next morning, and Tom feels as if the events of the day before happened long ago and far away. So powerful is this sensation, in fact, that he begins to wonder if it happened at all or whether the whole scene was actually a dream. He is not certain that it wasn't until he finds Huck and gets independent corroboration that the treasure is indeed real.

What makes this little passage so interesting, of course, is Mark Twain's later idea that in fact all life is a dream and

---

[34]   See Chapters 11, 23, and 24.

[35]   Chapter 15; in this instance, Tom overcomes his conscience and leaves no message; the thought of the grand glory, which will be his when the pirates attend their own funeral and then march into the church very much alive, is too powerful for him to resist.

that there is no reality in existence; that whatever man does is ultimately futile, insignificant, and inutile; and that consequently no individual man can be held guilty for whatever misdeeds he may have committed. This "dream philosophy," if I may so call it, will be seen again in *A Connecticut Yankee* and is at the core of *The Mysterious Stranger.* It is generally seen as the aging Sam Clemens' attempt to deal philosophically with his own overwhelming feelings of guilt, as it surely was. Yet here we find the germ of the idea introduced in the author's very first full-length novel, written at a time when he was not yet forty, basking in the sunshine of young marriage and recent fatherhood, and many years away from the financial distress and domestic tragedies of his later years. Obviously, the relationship between dream and reality was at the back of Mark Twain's mind many years before it developed into his final philosophy, for here it is, in outline at best but unmistakably present, in a book written in 1874-75.[36]

I have already noted how *Tom Sawyer* introduces the characteristic Twain themes of kingship, nobility, and character, although in this novel they are only raised not worked out. Also present in the book, although not elaborated upon, are other typical and recurrent Twain themes; over-romanticism and its crippling effects; the motif of escape; the overwhelming attraction of "getting up a dramatic effect," the torpedoing of pomposity and sentimentality; the cowardice of mobs; the duality of human nature and its capability to reach the highest level of conduct or the lowest; and the one theme which is explored most completely in *Tom*—the consequences of thoughtlessness. Every one of these ideas reappears and is treated in greater depth in Twain's later writing, especially in the twin masterpieces of

---

[36]   The theme also appears in another guise in *Tom Sawyer;* Tom telling the story of his visit home as if it were a dream. The circumstances are different, but the theme—relationship of dream to reality—is the same.

his maturity, *The Adventures of Huckleberry Finn* and *A Connecticut Yankee in King Arthur's Court.*

Because they are eclipsed by the electrifying adventure stories, which dominate the novel, and because they are so often merely introduced rather than explored, the presence of these themes in *Tom Sawyer* is easily overlooked. Yet the careful student of Mark Twain's writing must inevitably conclude that nearly everything of importance in the author's later work is present to some degree, however slight in his "juvenile" first novel.

This fact in turn raises another question: what was Mark Twain trying to do when he wrote *Tom Sawyer,* and for whom did he intend it?

In the Preface to the book, written just before publication and more than a year after completing the manuscript, Mark Twain explains, "Although my book is intended mainly for the entertainment of boys and girls, I hope it will not be shunned by men and women on that account, for part of my plan has been to try to pleasantly remind adults of what they once were themselves, and of how they thought and felt and talked, and what queer enterprises they sometimes engaged in."

This is pure moonshine. In a letter to Howells dated July 5, 1875 (just after completion of the manuscript), Twain wrote "It is *not* [his emphasis] a boy's book at all. It will only be read by adults. It is only written for adults."[37] By November, Howells and Livy had managed to convince him " . . . the book should issue as a book for boys, pure and simple . . ."[38] The Preface seems to split the difference.

Actually, one doubts that Twain had any plan at all when he wrote *Tom Sawyer,* and, if he did, he surely did not intend to recall anybody's childhood but his own. Few readers of *Tom*

[37.] Quoted by Kaplan, p. 205.
[38.] Ibid., p. 206.

were likely to have had graveyard murders and buried treasure discoveries in their younger days.

Give Howells (and Livy Clemens) credit for recognizing that the sales potential of *Tom* as a juvenile classic was enormous. Yet it is more than likely that Mark Twain wrote the book out of his own recollections and basically for his own delectation. There is more than ample internal evidence that the novel was never written with a juvenile audience in mind; the language of the book alone is enough to disprove that proposition, as Robert Keith Miller has sagely pointed out.[39]

The hypothesis that Mark Twain wrote *Tom Sawyer* primarily for his own enjoyment is supported by its origin in the Boy's Manuscript of 1870, which was never intended for publication at all but was intended as a "memory piece" by means of which the author reexplored his youth. Likewise, we have Twain's own testimony that the book "has no plot in it" and that as little as two weeks before he ended the story, he still had no idea of where it was going.[40] Notes on the first page of the MS indicate that an early idea was to carry the story of Tom well into adulthood.

If indeed I am correct in proposing this idea, it would explain not only the clear lack of focus which makes *The Adventures of Tom Sawyer* such a salmagundi of a novel, but also the casual throwaway treatment of so many themes which are introduced in this book but worked out only in Mark Twain's later fiction. It is as if these ideas were introduced semi-consciously, coming to the surface from the deep well of the author's subconscious under the stimulus of putting the story down on paper. To put it another way, the adventure stories dominate the deeper themes which surface in *Tom Sawyer* partly because the author himself never consciously intended those other aspects to come to the fore.

---

39. See his *Mark Twain*, a perceptive and thoughtful critical study.
40. Letter to Howells dated June 21, 1875. Quoted by Kaplan, p. 205.

In this reading, *Tom Sawyer* becomes more than a story of Samuel Clemens' boyhood. It is also his own first exploration of his subconscious concerns. One can argue that Mark Twain's greatness as a novelist derives in part from his willingness to recognize the significance of what he had dredged up while writing *Tom*, and to consciously explore its implications in his later books.

Likewise, if Twain wrote *Tom Sawyer* for himself, another quality of the novel is explained. I refer to its peculiar exuberance, a quality which I find nowhere else in Twain's fiction and which helps to explain the book's overwhelming and continuing popularity. The sheer youthfulness and energy of *Tom* overwhelms the reader and carries him along so forcefully that he tends to ignore any of the more subtle contents in the book. Never before—in *The Innocents Abroad,* in *Roughing It,* or in *The Gilded Age*—nor ever again, even in *Huckleberry Finn,* did Twain recapture this quality of youthful enthusiasm, which is so apparent in *Tom Sawyer.* I suggest that in the earlier books, he had not yet tapped the wellspring of his youth, which is widely accepted as the source of his best fiction, while in the later books, he probed and explored the themes and concerns which had first presented themselves to his consciousness in the course of writing *Tom.* He became a deeper, more philosophical thinker and writer as a result, but the sheer joy of writing about his boyhood was spent.[41]

For those who would discount this theory on the ground that the creative process must be conscious in all respects, I can

---

[41.] Mark Twain was aware, I think, of the process which was going on in his mind. I shall point out the reason why I believe this to be true when I reach my discussion of *Life on the Mississippi,* the relevant part of which was written in the winter months of 1875, before the completion and publication of *Tom Sawyer.*

reply from personal experience that "it ain't necessarily so." One of my close friends is a well-known American novelist who has written several popular books. I met him after he had produced his first book, and our friendship deepened to the point that I was invited to read the manuscript of his third. In the course of so doing, I was struck by what appeared to be a significant growth of my friend as a symbolist. When I congratulated him on the way he had used a particular symbol to clarify and unify his novel, he looked at me with genuine surprise and said, "Did I actually do that? I was not aware of it at all." His subconscious mind had taken over during the creative process, and it was not until I as a critic read his book that he realized just what he had put into it. I suspect that much the same thing happened to Twain during the composition of *Tom Sawyer*—the process of writing the book evoked from within him ideas which he had never consciously planned to employ.

But if Twain was not consciously aware of the deeper, more complex implications of his "paean to boyhood," at least not at the beginning, I think there can be no doubt that he at least began to realize them as the book developed. Once again, there is both internal proof of this proposition from within the novel itself, and external support of it in the form of letters to Howells, Clemens' close friend and literary conscience.

The internal evidence can be seen in the way *Huckleberry Finn* gradually takes over the last third of the novel.[42] Twain must

---

[42]. A close look at Huck's career in the book is instructive. He makes his famous first appearance in Chapter 6, where he discusses curing warts and trades his tick for Tom's tooth, then is absent from the next two chapters to reappear as Tom's companion on the midnight excursion to the graveyard. After witnessing the murder of Dr. Robinson, Huck joins Tom in flight to the old tannery, where the two boys swear never to tell about what they have seen. Huck is merely present the next morning

have realized that he had run into a dead end with Tom; he could not grow or develop as a character without changing his relationship to the village and the society around him, yet his identity with that world was and is the essence of his existence. Huck, on the other hand, offered more possibilities. As an outcast to begin with, he was the more flexible character, who could be used to explore the social problems with which Twain was becoming concerned.

The external evidence that Twain realized that Huck would have to be the center of any further novels exists in a letter from Twain to Howells, in which the author recognized that he could not take Tom past boyhood, without making him "just like all the other one-horse men in literature." He still planned to carry the story of "a boy of twelve and run him through life, but not

---

at the discovery of the crime (Chapter 11) and does not reappear in Chapter 12. He is more or less along for the ride during the pirating sequence (Chapters 13-17), where his presence is really superfluous, except for his experience in handling his tobacco, and when the boys return to town, he disappears completely from the next four chapters. In Chapter 22, he is present only as a shadow, reflecting the town's religious revival by greeting Tom with a scriptural quotation and later reflecting the communal relapse by sharing a stolen watermelon with Joe Harper. Huck comes alive again in Chapter 23, when he and Tom renew their vow of silence, which Tom promptly breaks. From here on to the end of the novel, Huck appears in every chapter except 31 (the story of Tom and Becky in the cave), and he takes an increasingly active part, culminating with his saving the Widow from Injun Joe's vengeance and ending with him agreeing to be "sivilized" for the sake of joining Tom Sawyer's gang. In short, he starts out as a minor character and winds up as central to the last part of the story. Clearly, Mark Twain realized that Huck, not Tom, offered the best potential for future adventures.

Tom Sawyer—he would not be a good character for it."[43] The subsequent book, which Twain was already considering before *Tom Sawyer* was finished, ultimately became *The Adventures of Huckleberry Finn*.

Not only did Mark Twain fail to realize the implications of his material when he began to write *Tom Sawyer*, he also lacked at the time the technical skill as a novelist which he was to acquire increasingly during the writing of the book and to further refine and sharpen later on. Proof of this proposition can be found in the major mistake he made at the very beginning; he used the device of third-person narration.

The advantages of the omniscient, impersonal narrator are considerable. He allows the author to portray all the action without having to rely on the presence of any one character in every scene, and he allows the author to act as a Greek chorus in commenting upon and clarifying the action. But these advantages are offset by drawbacks; the impersonal narrator stands between the characters and the reader. He also makes it impossible for the reader to understand the thoughts of the central character from within. The creator of any work of fiction must weigh the characteristic strengths and weaknesses of each technique against the demands of his material and against the intention of his work and choose the device most suited to his purpose.

In writing *Tom Sawyer*, Twain made an inappropriate choice in setting the narration in the third person. One reason why the novel lacks the focus and concentration of its sequel is that the intervention of the nameless, faceless, impersonal narrator distances us from the people in the book. We never understand

---

43. *Mark Twain—Howells Letters*, Edited by Henry Nash Smith and William M. Gibson, 2 Vols., Cambridge, Massachusetts: Harvard University Press, 1960. Quoted by Kaplan, p. 205.

Tom Sawyer from within; we see him only from the outside. We feel less about the world of St. Petersburg because we are kept at arm's length from by the intervention of the narrator, and I have already commented on the clash between the language of the people in the novel and that of the narrator. The impact of *Tom Sawyer* as anything but an adventure story is much weakened as a result of the mistaken choice of technique.

Moreover, Mark Twain was perfectly aware of the problem, at least by the time the book was completed if not before. "I wonder if I did not make a mistake writing *Tom* in the third person," he wrote to Howells. Clearly the question was rhetorical; he knew his error and corrected it. *Huckleberry Finn* is in the first person from the very first line, with Huck as the narrator and Tom reduced to his proper status as a contrasting but secondary personality.

In another technical area, Twain's growth as a writer contributes mightily to the superiority of *Huck Finn* over its predecessor. I refer to the vastly superior plot structure and organization. *Huck* has been attacked as a loose, episodic novel, but that criticism is much more appropriate to *Tom Sawyer.* In 1874, writing his first long piece of fiction, Twain simply had not acquired the facility to create a strong, unifying plot. The internal evidence of *Huck* demonstrates that sometime during the next few years he did.

In summary, I suggest that the raw material in the two books is quite similar, but *Tom* evokes it from the author's subconscious rather than attempts to explore it; also that the principal differences between the two novels is less thematic than structural and technical. The result is that *Tom Sawyer* ultimately succeeds as a string of adventures largely unified by the none-too-admirable character of its central figure, while *Huck Finn* emerges as a provocative novel of ideas and social criticism glorified by the wonders of Huck's vernacular narrative.

In the process of writing *Tom Sawyer,* probably for his own enjoyment and amusement, Mark Twain found in himself themes and ideas which he recognized as the stuff of literature, and he began to hone the technical skills which would later enable him to explore those problems in future books. He must also have recognized at some point that once these demons had been let loose, he would never again be the same writer, let alone the same personality; yet he had resolved, by the time he finished his "paean to boyhood" to follow the dictates of his literary conscience and to explore the problematic, even terrifying questions, *Tom* had evoked from his subconscious. If Tom Sawyer learns nothing and remains untouched by his experiences in Mark Twain's first novel, his creator by contrast learned much and was never the same heedless young man afterward. The greatness and torment of Twain alike date from the composition of *The Adventures of Tom Sawyer.*

Between Tom and Huck

T he span of nine years which passed between the completion of the manuscript of *Tom Sawyer* (mid-1875) and the first publication of *Huckleberry Finn* (late 1884) was Mark Twain's most productive period, and in some ways, the happiest time of his life. In that decade, he produced four major books, wrote three plays (one of which became a major hit), traveled and lectured extensively on two continents, involved himself in a number of nonliterary pursuits, and fathered his fourth and last child.

In January 1876, Twain delivered a speech to the Monday Evening Club in Hartford. It was called "The Facts Concerning the Recent Carnival of Crime in Connecticut," and it recounts the meeting between Mark Twain and his dwarf-sized, moldy conscience. In the end, Mark murders his tormenting superego and goes on to murder thirty-eight people in two weeks, burn down a house that interferes with his view, swindle a widow and some orphans out of their last cow, and generally go on to commit scores of other crimes in the most lighthearted and untroubled imaginable manner.

The importance of "Carnival" (which saw publication in the *Atlantic* for June 1876) is, of course, its relationship to the theme of conscience. In *Tom Sawyer,* which Twain had finished only five months or so before writing "Carnival," Tom's conscience torments him into testifying at Muff Potter's trial, nearly leads him to spare Aunt Polly's feelings by leaving her a note to tell her that he is not dead, but only off pirating, and generally serves as a reliable guide to "good" behavior. In *Huckleberry Finn,* begun about the time "Carnival" saw print, Twain takes the analysis a step further to deal with the question of whether conscience, which is, after all, a product of the process of socialization, is really a reliable guide to behavior. The assumption we make in this direction is comfortable and appealing, but Mark Twain must have been obsessed with the fact that in his youth, Samuel Clemens never realized the enormity of the wrong that slavery represented, for there was no one to challenge its universal acceptance by Hannibal society. Sam's conscience bothered him about many little acts—handing matches to a tramp who later used them to burn down the jail and accidentally incinerate himself was one—but never about the gross evil all around him which he never recognized or questioned. "Carnival of Crime" demonstrates that, having raised the theme of conscience in *Tom Sawyer,* where it is treated in the conventional manner, Twain was still thinking about it while the manuscript was on the way to the printer. Six months later, he began to write *Huckleberry Finn.*

He did about seventeen chapters in the summer of 1876, and on August 9, he wrote to Howells that he liked what he had done " . . . only tolerably well, as far as I have got, and may possibly pigeonhole or burn the MS when it is done."[44] He did indeed put it aside at the end of the summer, and it was three years before he picked it up again.

In the meantime, Twain collaborated with his old California friend Bret Harte on a play called *Ah Sin,* based on Harte's *The Heathen Chinee.* The object of this effort was simply money;

---

[44]   Twain-Howells letters, 144. Quoted by Kaplan, p. 226.

Harte was broke and Clemens, burdened by the expense of his
dream house, was forever cash short. They hoped to cash in on
the big money that a theatrical success promised, and to that
end worked together through the last three months of 1876.
Ah Sin reached the stage in Washington, DC, in May and played
in New York for five weeks in the summer before closing at a
loss to the producers. Meanwhile, travel rather than literature
preoccupied Twain and his family. In May, he visited Bermuda
with Joe Twitchell, and the following April Sam, Livy, Susy (then
six), Clara (age four), and an entourage sailed for Europe on a
trip that would last seventeen months. Twitchell came over in
August 1878, joining Clemens in Germany and accompanying
him on a walking tour which contributed material for Mark
Twain's next book, *A Tramp Abroad.* It was during this grand tour
that Twain set down the first notes for *The Prince and the Pauper*
and produced the speech on the Science of Onanism, which has
somehow come down to us in print—a fact which would have
undoubtedly shocked its author had he only known about it.

The family finally returned to Hartford in September 1879,
and Twain worked on *A Tramp Abroad* through the fall, delivering
the manuscript to his publisher, Elisha Bliss, in January.[45]

Also, around this time, Livy became pregnant for the fourth
and last time, and in July 1880 gave birth to the couple's third
daughter. Baptized Jane Lampton Clemens, after her paternal
grandmother, she was called "Jean" by the family, perhaps to
avoid confusion. During 1880 and 1881, Mark Twain composed
his next book, the tale of *The Prince and the Pauper.*

According to Albert B. Paine, the original idea for the
story had taken three years to germinate, and its background

[45.] When published two months later, *A Tramp* was immensely popular, sixty
thousand copies were sold in a year, Twain's best figure since *The Innocents
Abroad.*

may go back further than that.[46] Mark Twain had first visited England in 1872 when he became, at least for a while, a total Anglophile, and his temporary interest in all things English may have contributed to his decision to write a book set outside the United States for the first time in his career.

The Prince and the Pauper, unlike the problematical *Tom Sawyer,* was frankly and from the beginning conceived of as a children's book. Set in the sixteenth century, it is a fantasy in which the young Prince of Wales (later King Edward VI) and a London beggar boy called Tom Canty meet, exchange clothes, and then are accidentally separated. The real prince is exiled from the palace, while the pauper is taken for the (temporarily deranged) son of King Henry VIII.

From the point of view of historical authenticity, the book is total nonsense. The boys are supposed to be fourteen when they switch places, and Edward is still Prince of Wales (his father, King Henry, dies in the course of the story). Actually, Edward was born in 1537 to Jane Seymour, Henry's third wife. He ascended to the throne upon his father's death in 1547, when he was not quite ten years old. His reign lasted a mere six years, however, as he died of complications from multiple diseases in 1553, at the tender age of fifteen. In his brief time on the throne, he did find time to execute both of his uncles, Thomas the Lord Admiral and Edward, Duke of Somerset. When he died, he left only his two half-sisters, Mary Tudor and Elizabeth, both of whom would occupy the throne. Edward had been persuaded, however, to will the crown to his first cousin, Lady Jane Grey,

---

46. Since his teenaged days, Clemens had been familiar with Dickens, an author who always had a special attraction to him (It was to a Dickens reading that he took Olivia on their first date.) The melodrama in both *The Prince* and the later *Connecticut Yankee* is markedly reminiscent of the English author.

then sixteen years old. Her father-in-law, John Dudley, Duke of Northumberland, was behind the scheme. Lady Jane knew she was not entitled to be queen and did not want the crown, but she was bullied into acceptance of the scheme. Mary Tudor ended her "reign" at a mere nine days and had her executed together with her young husband and relatives. "Bloody Mary" then began a tumultuous, violent reign of four years, during which she burned two hundred "heretics," married Philip II of Spain and experienced two false pregnancies, imprisoned her half-sister Elizabeth in the Tower of London for a time, and then died in 1558 when only forty-two. Elizabeth, the last living child of King Henry, then took the throne to begin a dazzling reign of forty-five years during which England emerged as a great, powerful, and productive nation.

Of all Mark Twain's books, none was more highly praised by his own family than the *Prince*, and none is so easily dismissed as trivial and insignificant today. In fact, there were those who saw it as a waste of his talent even at the time. While even Howells (normally a perceptive critic of Twain's work) liked the book, Joe Goodman, Clemens' old boss on the *Territorial Enterprise*, was disappointed in the remoteness of the subject matter and the milksoppiness of the story and told his old writer how he felt. He also said he hoped Twain would come to his senses and get back to writing what he ought to be writing.[47] Fortunately, Twain did; within months of publishing the *Prince*, he was back at work on *Huckleberry Finn*.

Yet for all its artificiality and vacuousness, the *Prince* is not, it seems to me, without significance in Twain's growth as a writer. Just as *Tom Sawyer* raises a number of characteristic Mark Twain themes, which are worked out in later books, so *The Prince and the Pauper* exhibits ideas which we will find in the author's later work.

---

[47]   See Kaplan, p. 278.

First, the *Prince* sees Twain's first use of the device of switching identities. We find this hoary idea reappearing in a different form in *Huckleberry Finn,* where Huck masquerades as Tom and Tom as Sid; and it is central to the story of *Pudd'nhead Wilson.* It is possible that Twain was stimulated to use this device by its appearance in Gilbert and Sullivan's *H.M.S. Pinafore,* which was first produced in 1878 and was running in London the following summer while the Clemens family was staying there.[48]

Second, the *Prince* presages Twain's later satiric masterpiece, *A Connecticut Yankee in King Arthur's Court*—not only in its use of an historical English setting but in its use of antique British speech. He uses it quite well, but he never seems truly at home with it, and it lacks the ring of utter authenticity which is so evident in the dialogue of the Mississippi River novels. Mark Twain never heard anybody speak like Edward VI or Tom Canty; he was only copying what he read. Thus, his matchless ear for vernacular dialogue was wasted in this book, although in the *Yankee,* he could at least apply it to the speech of Hank Morgan, if not to the Knights of the Round Table.

Third, the *Prince* can be seen as an elaborate illustration of the maxim "Clothes make the man." The idea that social standing is the product of nothing more than education and raiment is,

---

[48]   G&S were satirists themselves; *Pinafore* is partly a jab at Verdi's *Il Trovatore,* whose plot also turns on the deliberate switching of babies in their cradles. Musically, the satiric point is made by having Little Buttercup sing her confession of baby trading in the same key used by Azucena in the opera.

That Twain employed the same device, even after G&S got through pillorying it, implies either that he thought he could get away with it in a children's story, or that he used it realizing that he was lending an aura of artificiality to his book—something he certainly did later in *Pudd'nhead Wilson.*

of course, the ultimate expression of the egalitarianism which underlies American democracy, and in 1881, Mark Twain was still a believer in that principle, however much his faith may have already been shaken. A few years later, in the much more complex *Yankee*, Hank Morgan professes the same credo, only to discover that it may not be true.

In the *Prince* Tom Canty (the beggar boy) is thrust practically unprepared into the role of monarch, where he performs as well as any king born to the purple could have done—and in the obvious opinion of his creator, better than most actually did. Tom quickly earns the love and appreciation of his "subjects," whom he treats with wisdom and compassion; he solidifies his popularity by relaxing the most vexing laws which oppress the common people. Yet he not only lacks any royal lineage, he is almost completely untutored, his only preparation for the role of ruler being a little Latin and his experience of life in Offal Court. The conclusion to be drawn from this is either that no special background or training is necessary for a wise leader—or that nobility of character is to be found in whom it is found, regardless of the accident of birth.[49]

Fourth, *The Prince and the Pauper* returns to a theme Twain raised in *Tom Sawyer* and had clearly been mulling over ever since—the theme of conscience, its formation, and its reliability as a guide to behavior. In the *Prince,* it is nothing more or less than Tom's conscience which leads him to turn the throne over to the real Edward. Stirred by a chance encounter with his mother,

---

[49]. Even in this first presentation of the theme of nobility, Twain dispels any notion that he is thinking in terms of an elevated "herrenvolk" as superior to the corrupt noblemen. Tom's family, and his father in particular, has no touch of the character he himself displays: they are the "human muck" Hank Morgan decries in the later book. Character is a personal not a class characteristic.

whom he at first denies, Tom must overcome the courtiers' conviction that he is the true king. Indeed, out of his guilt at denying his mother, he himself devises the test which ultimately validates Edward's claim and leads to his own removal from the throne. What is more, he does so at a real cost to himself. Clearly, Tom likes being king and is easily accustomed to the privileges of the position, of which he takes full advantage (recall that one of the first things Tom does is to triple the number of his servants!). Once awakened, however, his conscience will not permit him to continue the deception, even though he could easily remain king for life by merely keeping his mouth shut. In short, as it was in *Tom Sawyer*, conscience is still a reliable guide to good conduct.

Finally, we find in the *Prince* Mark Twain's first use of the structural device which underlies both *Huckleberry Finn* and *A Connecticut Yankee*, a character is thrust into a foreign and sometimes hostile environment, where he both observes and experiences a world much different than his own. In the *Prince*, the device is doubled—both Tom Canty at court and Prince Edward in the slums are strangers to the world in which they find themselves.

Twain may have stumbled upon this technique unawares, for it was the natural and inevitable consequence of a story based on switching identities. The fact remains, however, that he clearly saw the potential of the idea of setting a character in conflict with a society different from the one of which he is a part or from which he has come. Coupled with the use of first-person narration, this is the formula Twain employed to produce his two greatest novels.[50]

[50.] Note that the *Prince* is written in the third person, like *Tom Sawyer* before it. Twain had yet to put all the structural pieces together; he was still learning his craft, experimenting and growing as a creative artist.

For all its triviality and artificiality, then, *The Prince and the Pauper* should not be overlooked. It is one more step, thematically and structurally, toward *Huckleberry Finn*.

The book is also significant in a nonliterary way. Clemens was more than a little disturbed by the way Elisha Bliss had mishandled the manuscript of *Tom Sawyer*. The book was finished by July 1875 and was in the publisher's hands that same autumn; what is more, Twain had it copied on a typewriter for easy reading by the editors and printers, giving him claim to having been the first author to present a typewritten MS for publication. Expecting the imminent appearance of the book, Clemens sent a set of proofs to Howells for review, and Howells dutifully produced a rave in the *Atlantic* for May 1876. At this point, the horrified author discovered that Bliss had taken on too many projects and was unable to get *Tom Sawyer* printed and sold before December.[51] Always sensitive to the monetary side of writing, Clemens began thinking about a new publisher, and although he did publish *A Tramp Abroad* through Bliss, it was to be their last association. Clemens could hardly have been upset at Bliss' handling of *Tramp,* which sold better than any of his previous books (excepting *The Innocents Abroad*), but Bliss by 1880 was in failing health and he died later that year.

To publish the *Prince,* Clemens arranged a deal with James Osgood of Boston, which reversed the usual arrangements between author and publisher. Instead of assuming the risks and production costs and paying a royalty to the author, Osgood merely acted as sales agent for the book, with Clemens paying all the production costs himself; it was Osgood, who got the royalty of seven and one-half percent. Nominally Clemens' publisher,

---

[51.] See Kaplan, pp. 229-230. Ironically, it was Clemens himself, as an investor in Bliss's American Book Company, who brought in some of the authors whose work delayed the publication of his own book.

Osgood, was, in fact, no more than a salesman.[52] From this arrangement, it was no great leap to the creation of Clemens' own publishing house, handling not only his own works but also books by other authors. In effect, Clemens entered the publishing business with the *Prince,* and if he had known in 1881 what was to come of that venture, he would probably have remained a mere author.

The great burst of creativity which produced *The Adventures of Tom Sawyer* in 1874-75 also bore other fruit.[53] For the *Atlantic Monthly,* Mark Twain wrote a series of seven articles based on Clemens' experiences as a cub pilot, which appeared between January and June 1875 under the collective title, "Old Times on the Mississippi." Written mainly at the new Hartford house during the winter of 1875, these pieces were done during the composition of *Tom Sawyer,* which Twain had laid aside in September of the preceding year and upon which he resumed work only after returning to Quarry Farm in the summer of 1875. The river and his boyhood memories remained in the forefront of his consciousness through the summer of 1876, when Twain wrote the first part of *Huckleberry Finn;* but (except for some work done on *Huck* in 1879 and 1880) travel, *A Tramp Abroad,* the birth of Jean, the expansion and decoration of the Hartford house, and *The Prince and the Pauper* preoccupied him from the autumn of 1876 through the winter of 1882.

It was then that Clemens began to feel a nostalgic impulse to see the great river again. Except for a quick visit to Hannibal

---

[52.] See Kaplan, p. 276.

[53.] The birth of Clara Clemens on June 8, 1874, seems in some way to have turned her father's mind back to his boyhood. The birth of Susy in March 1872 appears to have had the same effect—it was followed a few months later by the writing of the earliest version of *Tom Sawyer,* the abortive drama of 1872.

in 1867, he had not seen it since his piloting career ended
with the outbreak of the Civil War back in April 1861, and he
was undoubtedly feeling his age—he was approaching fifty. So
accompanied by his "publisher" Osgood and a stenographer
named Roswell Phelps (whose job was to take down anything
Twain said about the trip in order to include it in the new travel
book he planned to write about it), Clemens left for St. Louis
in April 1882. His trip took him down the river to New Orleans,
then back upstream on the "City of Baton Rouge," (Horace
Bixby, master—the same man who taught young Sam Clemens
the river back in 1858) all the way to the head of navigation at
St. Paul, Minnesota. The trip took five weeks in all and resulted
in the creation and/or completion of two significant books, the
first being that giant grab bag of river lore entitled *Life on the
Mississippi.*

From the critical point of view, it is simply impossible to write
about *Life* as if it were a cohesive whole; in fact, Twain made
no effort at all to produce an organized volume with a plot or
story line. *Life on the Mississippi* is better treated as a notebook,
a collection of material about the river, the people who lived
on or near it, the steamboats which navigated it, and just about
anything else Twain happened to be thinking about at the
time.[54]

---

[54] Chapter 1 describes what might be called the dimensions and character
of the Mississippi. Chapter 2 is devoted to an account of early exploration
by DeSoto, Marquette, and LaSalle. Chapter 3 contains the so-called
"raftsman" episode, which was cut out of *Huckleberry Finn* in order to
shorten that book and is reincarnated here. In Chapter 30, we find
another of Twain's word pictures of dawn on the great river; In Chapter
38, his description of his uncle, John Quarles' home extolled as "The
House Beautiful;" In Chapter 46, his indictment of Sir Walter Scott on

Yet within this disconnected olio, there is a cohesive story with considerable importance in Mark Twain's creative career. I am speaking of the "Old Times" articles, which form Chapters 4-20 of the larger book.

The central character in this tale (which is actually a novella) is the Cub pilot who narrates the story. While his adventures are based on Samuel Clemens' real-life experiences, and while his chief, Horace Bixby, was Clemens' own tutor and master, the nameless Cub is not necessarily Clemens himself. We can be reasonably certain that the real man was nowhere near as credulous and as unaware as the Cub, who is a supremely naïve character. Nor was Clemens so lacking in memory, as his own literary career demonstrates. No, the nameless Cub is first cousin to the Mark Twain who narrates *The Innocents Abroad* and *Roughing It*—a figure of credulity who is the object of humorous deflation as well as the protagonist of the story. He might have been called "Mark Twain," except that the author did not begin using that pen name until after he left piloting.

There is another way in which we can infer that the Cub is not necessarily Samuel Clemens. If the "Old Times" section had been nothing more than a personal memoir, it should logically have carried the story through Sam's earning his pilot's certificate, if not through the end of his river career when the Guns of '61 began to shoot. The tale of the Cub, however, reaches neither point; it ends with the death of Henry Clemens in the explosion of the steamboat "Pennsylvania," on which he was working. I contend that this abrupt ending should put us as readers on notice that "Old Times" is something other than a purely historical narrative. Why, we must ask, does Mark Twain end the Cub's story not with his own accomplishment, but with

---

the charge of instigating the Civil War. *Life* is a very rich book, but a cohesive whole it is not, and was never meant to be.

his brother's death? In the answer to this question, I suggest we will find a clue as to what the Cub's story is really about.

The story begins with the Cub as a boy, experiencing the awakening of his sleepy town with the arrival of a steamboat and harboring the permanent ambition to be a boatman someday. In pursuit of his dreams, he tells us, he ran away from home.[55] But he does not get a job on the river at first; he merely becomes a passenger on the old "Paul Jones," en route from Cincinnati to New Orleans with a vague plan of exploring Brazil in mind. Merely being a traveler on a steamboat puts him in a "glorified condition." He keeps his hat off and stays out in the wind and sun to get the bronzed look of a seasoned trekker. He virtually swells up like a toad at the thought of being accepted by unknowing landsmen as part of the "Paul Jones'" company. He is immediately deflated by the mate, and this sequence, coming at the beginning of Chapter 5, sets the pattern for the rest of "Old Times." It is a story of alternate peaks and valleys; each time the Cub learns something and thinks he is really getting somewhere, he is immediately brought back to earth by some subsequent happening or realization. The gravity of the incidents deepens in the course of the manuscript; at the beginning, as we have seen, the Cub is inflated by the trivial and immediately deflated by the humorous. Later, his achieving knowledge of the river is offset by his notorious scare at Island 66 (Chapter 13). At the end, the Cub's greatest triumph—his victory over the bully Brown in defense of his brother Henry—is followed by the terrible tragedy of Henry's death.

---

[55]. Here is another case where the Cub's story deviates from Clemens' true history. He did not run away from home, and he did not leave with the idea of going on the river—he was then a journeyman printer, and he left Hannibal intending to go east and to see New York. This was in 1853, when he was seventeen.

The whole story is a dialectic, a tale of gains and losses. With each step of the Cub's growth into a competent river pilot, something is lost to him. Another example of this technique is to be found in the famous passage at the end of Chapter 9, in which the experienced boatman compares the effect of a spectacular sunset on the uninitiated passenger with its meaning to the professional steamboat pilot. The boatman has a much deeper understanding of the natural signs, but he has acquired it only at the cost of his capacity to appreciate the sunset as poetry, grace, and beauty. It is not that the boatman regrets his tremendous accomplishment at learning to read the river, but he realizes that his knowledge has not come to him without a serious cost. This is the theme of "Old Times," and it is clearly the philosophy of a man who feels the passing of his youth with nostalgia, if not regret.

In short, buried beneath the semi-comic adventures of the silly young Cub pilot is a finer, deeper story; the story of how a young man learns, one step at a time, to achieve and to cope; to develop his knowledge and skill, while at the same time learning understanding and self-control. He loses his youthful innocence but gains adult self-knowledge and compassion.

In a very real sense, then, "Old Times on the Mississippi" is the book *Tom Sawyer* is not—Mark Twain's Bildungsroman. Where Tom learns nothing and changes not at all, the Cub learns much and grows from youth to adulthood. The pinnacle of his development is his confrontation with death, when he helps to carry his brother to the "death room." The Cub emerges from the experience a man at last. The death of Henry Clemens is also the birth of Mark Twain.

He practically says as much in the three paragraphs which make up Chapter 21, the bridge between "Old Times" and the rest of *Life on the Mississippi*. In these less than two hundred words, one finds a tone of subdued nostalgia, of warmth without exuberance, of an adult looking backward at his youth with fond memories but without the desire to be wet behind the ears again. It is important to recall that for all he made of his boyhood, Samuel Clemens the Hartford Squire had no desire to live in Hannibal again, or in San Francisco or Virginia City either. His youth was a mother lode of material for Mark Twain to mine, but he did not care to return to it outside literature. It does not seem unreasonable to conclude that if *Tom Sawyer* was Twain's "paean to boyhood," then "Old Times on the Mississippi" was his valedictory to youth.

From the technical point of view, "Old Times" may be seen as the counterpoint of *The Prince and the Pauper*. In the *Atlantic* articles, Mark Twain for the first time coupled his memories of the Mississippi with the device of first-person narration. He had used that technique in both *The Innocents Abroad* and *Roughing It* but in neither of those earlier books is his narration as effective nor his subject so attuned to his style. In the *Prince,* as I have already noted, he stumbled across the formula which would permit his narrator to be an effective social critic as well as a figure of fun. Combine the significant qualities of *The Gilded Age, Tom Sawyer,* and *The Prince and the Pauper* and you have the ingredients of *Huckleberry Finn*.

Completion of Mark Twain's greatest novel was the other significant product of Clemens' return to the river in the spring of 1882. He had put the manuscript away again in 1879 and 1880; now, as he was struggling to turn his travel notes into the last forty chapters of *Life on the Mississippi*, he took up *Huck* again as well.[56] The two books were written symbiotically, with work

---

[56.] There is an interesting (if probably insignificant) parallel between Mark Twain's on-again, off-again composition of *Huck* and Richard Wagner's work on *Der Ring des Nibelungen*. It took Twain eight years to finish his masterpiece. Wagner, likewise, put aside the Ring cycle and his hero Siegfried for ten years, writing *Tristan und Isolde* and *Der Meistersinger*

on one leading the author to work on the other. This went on through the summer of 1882. *Life* was finished and in print by July, 1883, and the manuscript of *Huck* was basically completed later that same summer, though Twain spent much of the next year tightening and polishing it. Neither book came easily. Twain wrote of *Life*, "I never had such a fight over a book in my life before," and *Huck*, of course, took eight years of sporadic labor to complete.[57] Whatever the difficulties, the author surmounted them at last. In *Life of the Mississippi*, he painted a wonderful portrait of a bygone era. In *Huckleberry Finn*, he did even more; he created in triumph his greatest, most cohesive, most sophisticated, best-executed book. Even more than that, he produced what is in all probability the greatest American novel.

---

von Nuremburg before taking up Siegfried again and going on to write the music for *Gotterdammerung*. The result in both cases was the same; a talented artist left off the composition of his work—and a mature master picked it up again.

[57.] See Kaplan, p. 289.

The Adventures of Huckleberry Finn

All modern American literature comes from one book by Mark Twain called *Huckleberry Finn.* If you read it you must stop where the nigger Jim is stolen from the boys [*sic*]. That is the real end. The rest is just cheating. But it's the best book we've had. All American writing comes from that. There was nothing before. There has been nothing as good since.

> —Ernest Hemingway
> *Green Hills of Africa*
> Chapter 1
> (New York: Charles
> Scribner's Sons, 1935)

There may occasionally be dissenting opinions, but the mainstream of American literary criticism agrees with Hemingway in calling *The Adventures of Huckleberry Finn* a great book, if not our greatest American novel. So does the reading public, which has been buying it steadily ever since it first appeared well over a century ago. It is probably fair to assume that *Huck* would appear on nearly any list of the best books written in the United States.

Not that the novel has been beyond criticism or controversy. Most commentators agree again with Hemingway in considering it a masterpiece, but a flawed masterpiece. They generally consider the last dozen chapters (at the Phelps plantation) "just cheating"; a burlesque letdown unworthy of the rest of the book. Nor has *Huck* escaped the attention of would-be book banners and burners. Within a month of its publication, the Library Committee of Concord, Massachusetts ordered the book removed from its shelves—with the predictable results that sales soared, and Mark Twain expressed his gratitude to the protectors of the public's morals whose actions poured dollars into his bank account. The general complaint in the genteel 1880s was that *Huck* was uncouth, indecorous, crude, and an unfit model for American youth. In our own day, presumably well-meaning people have sought to ban the book because of alleged racism.[58]

Not to worry. *The Adventures of Huckleberry Finn* has long outlasted its Victorian critics, and it will never stop selling as long as English is read or the United States continues to exist. While perhaps not as popular a book as its companion volume, *Tom Sawyer, Huck* has long since become a classic. Indeed, I think it deserves to be called "The Great American Novel."

As a matter of fact, while most critics concede that *Huckleberry Finn* is a masterpiece, few, if any, of them seem to have realized how great the book really is. Far from being flawed, *Huck Finn* is in my view as nearly perfect as a novel is ever likely to be.

---

[58]   To be sure, the word "nigger" appears in the book 219 times, but it is hard to believe that anyone who has read *Huckleberry Finn* could miss the larger message—that the brotherhood of man transcends skin color and that nobility of character knows no bounds of poverty or race. Have the book's contemporary critics really read it?

Take the question of plot, for example. It is a truism among literary critics that Mark Twain could not write tight, well-integrated plots; *Huck Finn* is seen as an episodic, loosely-strung-together book on the order of its predecessor, *Tom Sawyer.* On the contrary, it appears to me that *Huck* is in fact a tightly constructed, thoughtfully planned whole, by far Mark Twain's best-planned and best-executed book. I believe I can demonstrate this proposition through reference to the novel itself.

Likewise, I am unwilling to concede that the ending of the book is (as Hemingway put it) "just cheating." I shall attempt to show that in fact the final section of the novel is a brilliant resolution of the story, entirely consistent with the earlier chapters, which in fact could not have been improved upon as a way to bring this difficult, deeply thought novel to a conclusion. In fact, I shall go even further; I shall attempt to show that these last twelve chapters give us our clearest clue to Mark Twain's real intentions in writing this brilliant, cruel, hilarious, and totally fascinating book.

I shall also try to point out some of the other factors which make *Huckleberry Finn* such a masterful work, among them use of satire, irony, language, and skill in characterization. Also, I shall try to put the novel in its proper perspective as the culmination of all of Mark Twain's previous writing, and to demonstrate its thematic links with both his earlier works and with the books he was to write in subsequent years. In short, I shall try to show why *The Adventures of Huckleberry Finn* deserves the appellation I have already bestowed upon it—"The Great American Novel."

Nor do I use that phrase carelessly. *Huckleberry Finn* really is a novel in the strict sense of the word—a long prose fiction exploring the manners and morals of a particular society, as illuminated by conflict with an outsider to that world. By contrast, *The Adventures of Tom Sawyer,* despite clearly novelistic elements, is really a romance. That was the term given to a simple story of adventure or amour, though the term has nothing to do with falling in love; the English word "romance" derives from the French "roman," meaning a long prose fiction.

Moreover, *Huck* is beyond question an American novel. Its setting, its concern with the defining American question of race relationships, and its marvelous capture of vernacular border state and Southern American English leave no room for further discussion. The book could not possibly have been written by an Englishman, an Australian or a New Zealander, and to conceive of its being the product of a Canadian is no more than barely possible.

Not just any American author could have produced *Huck* either. It could never have come from the pen of one of the genteel New Englanders, who recoiled in shock at the book's "coarseness" and "irreverence."[59] Only a product of the frontier West could have written such a naturalistic, sardonic, and supremely funny book as this.

Shall we now take a look at this remarkable novel and try to understand why it has stimulated such praise, such criticism, and such controversy?

Let us begin, as Twain must have begun, with the central problem for a novelist who set out to write social criticism in America during the Victorian period. The readers of books at that time and in that place were disproportionately female and genteel. Men were supposed to engage in the rough-and-tumble of the marketplace; their wives and daughters were charged with the task of taming and civilizing them with culture.

Thus, to keep up his sales, an author had to write books that this sentimental, socially upper-class, and basically establishment

---

[59.] See Justin Kaplan, *Mr. Clemens and Mark Twain* (New York Simon and Schuster, 1966), p. 314, for some of the negative reactions printed in New England journals after the book appeared in February 1885.

constituency would buy and read. That, in turn, meant "morally uplifting" tales to which these ladies could not object. To sell such readers on a work of social criticism was no mean task.

Mark Twain found a way to do so. He masked his savage attacks on Americans and their institutions in a triple cloak of irony, satire, and humor so that the perceptive and thoughtful reader could recognize the attacks easily enough while the rest would buy and enjoy the book without ever realizing just what they were reading.[60]

He enjoyed a perfect foil within his own family. Olivia Langdon Clemens was very near typical of the "sophisticated" ladies to whom Mark was selling his books. It has long been known that he submitted his manuscripts to her for approval and that she crossed out anything she felt to be indecorous or improper. It has generally been accepted that Twain did this because he did not trust his own judgment, being by birth and upbringing a Western wild man and that he needed her approval and acceptance. I beg to disagree.

Far from needing Livy's advice and approval, I believe Mark used her as a barometer of what his readers would accept. If he could get a scene or a passage past her, he could be pretty sure that his genteel lady readers would not object to it. If, on the contrary, she blue-penciled something, he knew that his subterfuge had failed in that instance and that the passage would have to be rewritten.

It is well-known (in fact, Mark Twain wrote it himself) that he often played tricks on his connubial editor by putting in things he knew she would excise. It is also no secret that on occasion, he simply restored things she cut out. He was no slave to her judgment, even when he was supposedly submitting his work to it.

[60.]   I have defined satire and irony in specific terms earlier in this manuscript.
    See page 12.

It makes sense, then, to conceive of him playing other tricks with her editorial instincts. I think he employed her for his own purposes, while letting the world think that he was actually submitting to her. It seems unlikely that she ever fully comprehended her husband's intelligence, and he, in turn, made certain that she never did by assuming a pose before her and his public as well.[61]

The danger in perpetrating a subterfuge on the audience is, of course, that the reader may not realize that there is more to the manuscript than appears on the surface. Mark Twain, having written a social criticism in which the ultimate purpose was masked by irony, satire, and humor, had to confront that possibility. He did so by use of a brilliant, unique device at the very beginning of the book.

Before the narrative of *Huckleberry Finn* begins, the reader encounters the following:

Notice

[61.] It is appropriate here to discuss Livy Clemens. Her biographer, Resa Willis (*Mark and Livy*: New York, Atheneum, 1992) asserts that she was a well-read woman. Yet there is nothing in her letters that indicates that she (or for that matter, anyone else in the family) saw anything exceptional about *Huckleberry Finn*. To Livy and her daughters, *The Prince and the Pauper* was Mark Twain's best book. That in itself is a telling remark, indicating that Livy remained unaware that her husband had written a masterpiece which operates on a level light years beyond that of the relatively simplistic *Prince*. One wonders how well she understood her husband; I suspect that he never entirely revealed himself to her in all their thirty-four years of marriage. Ms. Willis, by the way, notes that whatever Livy did with his manuscripts, he did not change a word unless he wanted to and that he himself was on occasion a tougher editor than she (p. 155).

Persons attempting to find a motive in this narrative will
be prosecuted; persons attempting to find a moral in it will be
banished; persons attempting to find a plot in it will be shot, by
order of the Author, per G. G., Chief of Ordnance.[62]

This splendid little advice of forty-four words can have but
one possible function. It is an irony itself; it says exactly the
opposite of what it means. It alerts the reader to look for a
motive, a moral, and a plot in *Huckleberry Finn*. It is the author's
red flag to the reader—his wake-up call to the drowsing peruser.
It tells the reader to watch out for this novel; this is not another
Tom Sawyer or *Prince and the Pauper*. As Dr. Seuss wrote in another
such notice at the beginning of one of his books, "This book is
dangerous."[63]

On the assumption, then, that the "Notice" is there for a
reason, we should look for a plot, a moral, and a motive in
Huckleberry Finn, and indeed, I think, it is quite evident from a
structural and textual analysis of the book that it has all three.[64]

---

[62] It is an enormous temptation to attach a real identity to "G.G." I have
never been able to do so, and perhaps it cannot be done. One of my
students suggested that perhaps "G.G." might stand for "Great Guns." I
suspect that Mark did not really have anyone or anything in mind here;
but if anybody has any suggestions on the point, I would be delighted to
hear them.

[63] Dr. Seuss: *Fox in Socks*. New York: Beginner Books, 1965.

[64] Since the discovery of the missing manuscript of the first part of
Huckleberry Finn in 1991, we now know that the "Notice" was written after
the three-year hiatus in the composition of the novel—that is, not earlier
than 1882. This suggests that part of the reason for the long gap may
have been less a plot problem than the author's attempt to focus his
material before proceeding further.

I
Plot

A good deal has been written about how *The Adventures of Huckleberry Finn* is put together, and most critics seem to agree that the novel is a loosely structured, episodic book modeled on Cervantes's classic, *Don Quixote.*

I do not dispute for a moment Twain's debt to Cervantes, whose masterpiece is reflected in *Huck Finn* in several ways. Both books are satiric attacks on foolishness, pomposity, hypocrisy, and over-sentimental, over-romantic literature. Both are basically optimistic, and both feature unforgettable and (in their own way) admirable heroes.

Nor can it be denied that *Huckleberry Finn* is an episodic novel; it consists of a series of individual incidents, strung together on the thread of Huck's journey from the Widow Douglas' to the edge of the territory.

Episodic though it is, however, *Huck* is *not* loosely structured. The two are not synonymous, and I think a close reading will demonstrate that, far from being a tossed-together hash like *Tom Sawyer,* this novel was constructed with great skill and care. In fact, it enjoys the most cohesive, most well-planned, and well-executed plot Mark Twain ever created. This, I submit, is one reason why *The Adventures of Huckleberry Finn* is clearly the best piece of full-length fiction Twain ever produced.

Even a cursory reading of the book can hardly fail to disclose that *Huckleberry Finn* consists of three large sections, each of which may be delineated geographically. Chapters 1-11 are set in and around St. Petersburg; Chapters 12-31 describe Huck and Jim's raft voyage and their adventures on and around the mighty Mississippi; Chapters 32-43 take place at the Phelps plantation. The opening and closing sections are approximately equal in length and parallel in theme, in that both involve the motif of separation from or escape from society. The long central section is, in essence, a traditional novel of manners and morals, exposing the flawed society with which Huck comes into contact.

It should be immediately apparent that this tripartite structure corresponds to the dramatic structure of a three-act play. Section I (or Act I) is devoted to the exposition of the plot problem and the presentation of the major characters; Section II (Act II) contains the complications of the plot; Section III (Act III) is devoted to the ultimate resolution. I submit that on a structural level, *The Adventures of Huckleberry Finn* operates in just this way. The first eleven chapters set forth Huck's problem and Jim's and are devoted to their withdrawal and eventual escape from St. Petersburg. In the central twenty chapters, Huck is thrown into contrast with the corrupt world around the river and with its emissaries, the king and the duke. In the final section, the book is resolved with Jim's freedom and Huck's liberation from Pap's shadow and his ultimate flight from "sivilization." Exposition, development, resolution—the structure is as clear as can be.

Moreover, Twain has carefully constructed his novel so that it contains landmarks at structurally significant places. Chapter 15, "Fooling Poor Old Jim," marks roughly the one-third point of the manuscript and contains Huck's apology to Jim—a vital step in their increasingly close bond. At the two-thirds mark of the book, we find Chapter 31, "You Can't Pray a Lie," in which Huck takes the decisive and monumental step of tearing up his letter to Miss Watson and undertaking to steal Jim out of slavery, even if it costs him an eternity in hell. Not only this, but the center of the book, Chapter 23, "The Orneriness of Kings," is occupied by the dramatic contrast between the discussion of the amorality and general uselessness of kings (fraudulent and otherwise), and the touching scene of Jim grieving for his family and berating himself for the mistreatment of his little girl. In short, the heart of *Huck Finn* depicts the humanity of the runaway slave. It is the most heartrending scene in the novel.

We can go much further into the structural analysis of *Huckleberry Finn* to demonstrate even more completely the effectiveness and cohesiveness of its plot.

Each of the three large sections consists of smaller component parts. Section I, for example, can be conveniently broken down into three subsections. Chapters 1-3 provide a "bridge" from *Tom Sawyer,* involving readers of the earlier book in the world of the later one. These three chapters also introduce nearly all the major characters in the novel; Huck himself, the Widow Douglas and her sister, Miss Watson, Tom Sawyer, Jim, and Pap.[65] Finally, they express Huck's sense of malaise at the Widow's (the highest level of St. Petersburg society), his practical, unromantic mindset as compared with Tom's characteristically unrealistic fantasy world, and his fear of his father.

There are two interesting points relating to the exposition of characters in this first section. Huck is nearly blackballed by Tom Sawyer's Gang because he doesn't have a proper family to hold as hostages. He gets around the difficulty by offering the boys Miss Watson. The irony of this little scene is that to be a member of Tom's fantasy band of robbers and murderers, one must have the correct social standing. In the real world, social position is hardly a prerequisite for a career in crime. But Tom

---

[65].   One of the interesting points about the novel involves the name "Huckleberry." Apparently nineteenth-century frontier slang used the term "huckleberries" as we would use "shucks," to indicate something insignificant or of no great importance. Twain's choice of this name for his greatest hero may have been descriptive as originally used in *Tom Sawyer,* but it is supremely ironic in the later novel, where "Huckleberry" is anything but insignificant or of no importance.

Incidentally, the word is used again in this context in Chapter 26 of *A Connecticut Yankee,* where Sir Palamides the Saracen is described as "no huckleberry himself."

Sawyer would never be a *real* robber or murderer, anymore than he would be a real pirate in *The Adventures of Tom Sawyer* or a real nigger stealer at the Phelps plantation. Tom only plays at such deliciously outrageous careers. In reality, he is a completely integrated part of his society—he is "sivilized."

The other character introduced in a significant manner in this opening section is Jim. When we first meet him, he is the very stereotype of the ignorant, superstitious darkie St. Petersburg wants and expects him to be, and Tom gets a rise out of him by taking his hat off as he sleeps and hanging it on a tree limb over his head.

We may think of this incident another way; we see Jim here as Tom and the town see him. Only later, through Huck's developing closeness with him and through Huck's unprejudiced judgment, do we see him as a man.

The second subsection of Section 1 is made up of Chapters 4 through 7 and is dominated by Pap. The action of the novel really begins in Chapter 4, when Huck sees tracks in the snow and realizes from the cross on the boot heel that his father has come back. His immediate response is to go to Judge Thatcher and divest himself of the reward he acquired at the end of *Tom Sawyer*, when he and Tom found the treasure in the cave. Of course, one can question the legality of a transaction in which an adult schooled in the law buys a $6,000 fortune from an underage juvenile for a $1 consideration but that's hardly the point. What is important about Huck's action is that by ridding himself of his money (at least apparently), he has taken the first major step in disengaging from "sivilization" as it exists in St. Petersburg. No longer having property, he no longer has a stake in society. Possession of wealth is a mark of success, and standing in a materialistic world; in one quick stroke, Huck has renounced both.

Pap appears in the flesh in the last line of Chapter 4, and he is undoubtedly one of the most striking, most memorable characters in all American literature. His active life in the book occupies no more than two and one-half chapters—less than twenty printed pages—yet his shadow falls upon the entire novel, and no reader who has encountered him can ever forget him. Pap Finn is the most vividly drawn character portrait Mark Twain ever created; an archetype of the drunken, insecure father who is jealous of his son, angry not at himself but at the world in general for his low estate; manipulative and hypocritical, illiterate, grasping, ignorant, prejudiced, and small-minded.

To create this tremendous character, Twain uses precisely one paragraph of descriptive prose. All the rest of Pap Finn is brought out through his conversations with others and his long monologues; he talks himself into literary immortality. Twain's feel for the language of the frontier lowly was never more sure, and he never used his tremendous ear with more telling effect. If the manuscript of *Huckleberry Finn* had been left unfinished at the end of Chapter 7, this fragment alone would assure the book a lofty place in the American literary pantheon.

Pap makes Huck quit school, makes a fool of the bleeding-heart new judge who tries to reform him (one of Mark Twain's favorite targets was the well-meaning but naïve reformer who refused to see true evil where it was all too evident), takes Huck away from the Widow Douglas' house and keeps him in a cabin across the river on the Illinois side, gets drunk, and attempts to kill Huck in his delirium. Huck determines to run away, and in Chapter 7 he stages a masterpiece of evasion, thoughtfully planned and perfectly executed. The end of this subsection finds Huck alone on Jackson's Island, uninhabited (thus symbolically outside civilization) but within easy canoeing distance of the town.

Chapters 8-11, the third and final subsection of Part I, describe Huck's finding Jim on the island and agreeing not to betray the runaway; their encounter with the House of Death; Huck's visit to Mrs. Loftus and the flight of the two fugitives on their raft.

The St. Petersburg section of the novel is thus concerned with Huck's step-by-step disengagement from the society into which he has been adopted, a process to which he himself contributes but which is furthered by Pap. Note the steps involved; first Huck renounces his fortune, then Pap takes him out of school and shortly thereafter physically removes him not only from the Widow's house but from the town itself, and from the state of Missouri (which was slave territory) to Illinois (a free state). Huck then uses his own ingenuity to escape from Pap and get away to the wilderness of Jackson's Island. So effective is his staged kidnapping and murder that the St. Petersburg folks search unsuccessfully for his body; as far as the town is concerned, he is dead. Finally, he meets Jim on the island, and fearing discovery and recapture by the town, the two flee the area altogether. By the end of Chapter 11, Huck has been economically, socially, and physically separated from St. Petersburg society, and is even more a complete outsider than he was before the Widow adopted and "sivilized" him.

The gradual process of disengagement from society, which begins in Chapter 4 and is complete at the end of Chapter 11, is interrupted by Huck and Jim's first adventure together—the House of Death incident which occupies Chapter 9. This sequence seems to me to be quite important both to the technical functioning of the plot and to the larger meaning of the novel.

The House of Death is a two-story frame building which comes floating downstream, one paragraph after Huck and Jim catch their soon-to-be famous raft. While Twain never explicitly says so, his description of the house and its contents make it clear that it was a bordello and thieves' den; and it contains a corpse. Huck does not want to look at the face—Jim tells him not to and covers it with rags. But Jim immediately identifies the body; it is that of Pap, shot in the back.

From the technical standpoint of plot work, the House of Death furnishes Huck with the girls' clothes he uses to visit the town in disguise (Chapters 10 and 11). It is also important technically that Huck not know the identity of the corpse; if he had learned in Chapter 9 that his father was dead, he would have had no further motive to flee St. Petersburg and the plot of the novel would have been aborted.

But it is not enough to look only at the technical points. One must ask *why* Jim did not tell Huck that the body in the House of Death was that of his father.

Putting oneself in Jim's position, it becomes clear that to disclose the corpse's identity might cause Huck to abandon their flight, leaving Jim alone; even worse, it might lead Huck to betray the runaway to the town. In short, the unspoken reason behind Jim's silence is that he does not yet trust Huck completely. Therefore, Jim keeps him in the dark about his father's death because that is the best course for Jim to take to further his own best interests.

What is more, there is proof that Jim was right in not completely trusting Huck at this stage. In Chapter 15, some forty pages further on in the novel, Huck plays a Tom Sawyerish trick on Jim when he lies about his being away in the fog. Jim is hurt and says so; he even has the guts to call Huck, a white boy, "trash." "Trash is what people is dat puts dirt on the head er dey fren's an makes 'em ashamed."

Huck, in turn, has the guts to own up to what he has done. "It was fifteen minutes before I could work myself up to go and humble myself to a nigger; but I done it, and I waren't every sorry for it afterwards, neither." At the time of the House of Death incident, the process of bonding across racial lines had not yet reached the stage where the two could trust each other to this degree. Huck did not then understand that Jim was a human being with deep feelings and even deep pride, despite his status as a slave, and Jim clearly knew it.

It may also be instructive to look at the House of Death from a symbolic point of view. This den of iniquity, scene of whoring, robbery, and murder, may be seen to stand for the corruption and violence of the riverside community from which it came. Throughout the novel, the river itself is treated as a pristine Eden, while the life along its banks is full of evil. That the river ultimately claims the House of Death and is continually eating at the rotten foundations of the shoreline homes may be seen as indicative of the ultimate cleansing of man's sins by nature. Passive, silent, patient, yet ultimately all-powerful, the Mississippi itself becomes a character in the novel. It eventually destroys man's puny works of evil and cleanses the scenes of human crimes.[66]

This view of the river as a cleansing avenger recalls Richard Wagner's similar use of the Rhine in *Gotterdammerung*, the final part of his massive tetralogy *Der Ring des Niebelungen*. *Gotterdammerung* (usually translated in English as "The Twilight of the Gods") received its first performance at Bayreuth, Germany, in 1876. Whether Twain was aware of what Wagner had done, and whether he was influenced at all by the German author/composer, I cannot say. It is true, however, that Samuel Clemens knew German and spent some time in that country in 1878, between the debut of the Ring cycle and the completion of *Huckleberry Finn*. He was alert to new developments in science and the arts (case in point; his use of fingerprints in *Pudd'nhead Wilson*), and it is just possible that Wagner's work may have influenced Mark Twain's portrayal of the Mississippi in *Huck*. This might make an interesting topic for some future study.

The last chapter in the first section of *Huckleberry Finn* is noteworthy because it contains the depiction of Mrs. Judith Loftus, another in that galaxy of wonderful character portraits

---

[66.] The river not only claims the House of Death in Chapter 9, but it is destined to get the wreck of the steamboat "Walter Scott" in Chapter 13 and will someday carry off the houses of Bricksville (Chapter 21).

with which this novel bulges. She is delineated with the same extreme economy of means that Twain employed in defining Pap, carried even further. Aside from Huck's remark that she is about forty years of age, we have absolutely no physical description of her whatsoever. Even so, she is vividly and eternally alive through her talk; she is garrulous, exposing a sharp intelligence and a thorough knowledge of masculine and feminine behavioral traits. Through her, Huck learns that the town is after Jim, largely because of the $300 reward on his head. From the technical point of view, she provides the motivation for Huck and Jim to leave St. Petersburg altogether.

It is easy to forget that while Jim is running from the very tangible threat of recapture and future slavery, Huck is also running from something almost as fearsome—his father (whom Mrs. Loftus reports as being seen around town with a couple of hard-looking strangers) and from "sivilization" in general. In other words, both black man and white boy are fleeing from authority sanctioned by society, Huck as much so as Jim.[67]

Before leaving this first section of *Huckleberry Finn,* there are some additional comments I should like to make.

First, when Huck returns to the island after his visit to Mrs. Loftus, he says "Git up and hump yourself, Jim! There ain't a minute to lose. They're after us!"

Now this is a remarkable speech. Remember, while Huck still fears his father, as far as St. Petersburg is concerned, Huck is dead. The townspeople aren't after him—they are only after Jim, the runaway slave. Huck could have said, "They're after you!",

[67] When the Widow tried to get guardianship over Huck, the new Judge in town said that courts must not interfere and separate families and refused to take Huck from Pap. Thus, Pap's position of power over Huck is as directly sanctioned by the law of society as Ms. Watson's hold over Jim, her slave.

but he uses the plural pronoun "us" instead. He has thrown his lot in with Jim to the point where he himself does not even think about the fact that nobody is really after him at all. The relationship between the two outcasts has grown closer.

The reason is clear—Huck's foolish prank in leaving the dead rattlesnake on Jim's blanket, causing Jim to be bitten by the snake's mate (Chapter 10).

This prank is another of the mindless sort of tricks Tom Sawyer is always playing on people for his own amusement, never thinking of how the victim may be emotionally or even physically hurt as a result. Huck sees Jim's suffering due to the snakebite and feels guilty about having caused such pain to his fellow fugitive. He has already gone further, then, than Tom Sawyer in developing sensitivity toward others; but he has not yet reached the point where he can apologize to Jim for what he did. He says, "I warn't going to let Jim find out it was all my fault, not if I could help it." Nor does Huck learn fully the lesson that mindless pranks can cause pain to others. He resolves not to handle snakes again, now that he has seen the results, but he does not forswear playing pranks on Jim, and he plays another heartless one in Chapter 15, as I have already observed. Huck is gaining in sensitivity but is not yet at the point of seeing Jim as a man with feelings and emotions identical to those of whites.

I have already noted that *Tom Sawyer* often serves as a reference point in explaining some of the events in *Huckleberry Finn*, for the two novels are closely related. An example of this is found in Chapter 7. When Huck and Jim flee to Jackson's Island, their action parallels Tom, Joe Harper, and Huck leaving town for the same location in the earlier novel. In both cases, the island serves as a temporary refuge for the fugitives.

However, the two incidents, while parallel, are completely different. Tom's disappearance was planned to punish those he felt did not love him enough, while Joe and Huck were simply along for the ride. Tom evolves the plan to stay solely for the effect which he can generate by returning to town at the moment of his own funeral. His motive in going to the island is not escape from St. Petersburg, but inflation of his own ego and causing pain to others. He never really wants to escape St. Petersburg life—on the contrary, he wants more recognition from it.

By contrast, when Huck and Jim go to the island (separately) in the latter book, they do so out of real fear of the town and with the intention of escaping its threat to their freedom. While Twain uses a similar device in each novel, the difference between Tom Sawyer's character and Huck's could not be more graphically depicted than it is by their different attitudes toward Jackson's Island.

A final comment on Section I of *Huckleberry Finn*: notice how Huck's escape from Pap's cabin is analogous with the escape from the Phelps farm in Section III. Huck's own escape is a masterpiece of plotting and execution, a deadly comparison with Tom's phony, trumped-up and ultimately unnecessary "stealing" of Jim. Indeed, Huck's escape is the stuff of the novels Tom is so fond of aping. These parallel incidents, I submit, are not accidental; they are structural devices which illustrate again the difference between the foolish, playacting Tom, and the realistic and practical Huck.

Having examined Section I with care, we may now go on to Section II of *The Adventures of Huckleberry Finn*. This long central section is the core of the novel, describing the raft trip down the Mississippi from Missouri to Louisiana and the interaction between its passengers and the world on shore. It consists of twenty chapters (Chapters 12 through 31) and may be divided into five separate episodes: the story of the wrecked steamboat "Walter Scott" (Chapters 12-13), the Grangerford-Shepherdson feud (Chapters 17-18), the rape of Parkville and its camp meeting (Chapter 20), the doings in Bricksville, including the murder of

Boggs, the failed lynching of Colonel Sherburn and the Royal
Nonesuch (Chapters 21-23), and the tale of the heirs of Peter
Wilks and its aftermath (Chapters 24-31). Interwoven with these
episodes are the scenes on the raft and in the woods involving
Huck and Jim, and developing their deeper relationship.

The action of this section may be thought of in dialectic
terms. On the one hand, we have the growing trust, dependency,
respect, and finally love between Huck and Jim. On the other,
the sharply contrasting scenes ashore in which an ignorant,
prejudiced, self-deceiving, violent, and vicious society displays
its failings and foibles. The raft is a miniature Eden; the shore a
vast Sodom. In time, the emissaries of this corrupt world—those
two unforgettable scoundrels, the king and the duke—invade
the paradise of the raft, despoil it, and finally destroy it. The
section concludes with the fraudulent sale of Jim by the king and
Huck's momentous resolve to free him whatever the temporal
or spiritual cost.

The first subsection, the "Walter Scott" story, begins with
Huck's idyllic description of life on the raft in the first days of
the journey. It may not seem possible, but Twain creates his Eden
on planks in exactly eight paragraphs of descriptive prose. This
remarkable economy of means, which I have noted in the cases
of Pap and Judith Loftus, is a characteristic of *Huckleberry Finn*.
It is all the more significant in this novel because Mark Twain is
generally regarded as a discursive writer, not especially adept at
the economical use of words. His tendency toward length may,
however, have had more to do with the fact that his books were
sold by subscription rather than any lack of facility on his part.
We shall see his talent for brevity displayed again when we come
to *Pudd'nhead Wilson*.

The first of the five episodes which make up the central
section of *Huck Finn* is the story of the "Walter Scott." Huck
and Jim see this wrecked steamboat as their raft floats by, and
(motivated by the spirit of Tom Sawyer) Huck wants to land on

her. He expects a good haul—maybe seegars from the Captain's cabin, worth five cents apiece. Jim dislikes the idea of boarding the wreck; his comment is, "we better let blame well alone . . . ," but when Huck insists, he gives in.

The runaways guide their raft alongside the wreck and tie it up, but when they board the "Scott," they find a trio of desperadoes aboard, two of whom are about to murder the third. The raft breaks loose, stranding Huck and Jim on the wreck with the criminals, but through a fluke, they find the only boat first and leave the crooks stranded on the decomposing steamboat.

At this point, we are introduced to a new and significant facet of Huck's character. Up until now, nearly everything he has done is for his own benefit, in the manner of Tom Sawyer (the only exception being his flight together with Jim, which is at least partly for Jim's benefit).

Now, though, Huck begins to worry about the men on the wreck. "I begun to think how dreadful it was, even for murderers, to be in such a fix." In short, he puts himself in another's place and asks how he would like it. As a result, he goes out of his way to land on the ferryboat and gets its captain to run up to the wreck and take the men off. In the process, he uses for the first time his marvelous command of the psychology of lying, picking up from the ferryman his admiration for the monied Jim Hornback, and using it to motivate him to rescue Hornback's nonexistent niece from the "Walter Scott."

Huck acts selflessly, out of pure compassion for other human beings, even though he knows these men are robbers and killers. This incident prepares us for Huck's acceptance of Jim's humanity, which comes at the end of Chapter 15. In addition, it sets up the basic conflict which dominates the rest of the book, the conflict between Huck's socially created conscience, which tells him what the world says he ought to do, and his instinct toward noble behavior which tells him what he must do. This conflict expresses itself each time Jim is threatened, and is finally resolved in Chapter 31.

The "Walter Scott" episode can also be seen as having symbolic significance. Mark Twain is not known as a symbolic writer, and indeed, he is not one to toss unexplained symbolic images around in the manner of James Joyce. But despite his clear naturalistic bent, Twain was not beyond using symbols in his work, and I think there can be little doubt that the wrecked steamboat "Walter Scott" has symbolic significance.

First, as to the name of the wreck. Mark Twain contended (only half in jest) that Sir Walter Scott should be held responsible for the American Civil War. His romantic novels (*Waverly, Ivanhoe, Rob Roy,* and the rest) were favorite reading of the Southern people, and Twain felt that Southerners became so stewed in his work that they became unable or unwilling to see themselves and their society as they really were. Southerners saw themselves as cultured heroes and heroines and their world as a neo-Scotian paradise; in reality, the South was not far removed from frontier primitivism, and its underlying institution, chattel slavery, was an anomaly not only in the United States but in all the Western world. Less romanticism and a more realistic view of itself, Twain felt, would have led the South to a more accurate assessment of its place in the world and of its "peculiar institution," rather than to a bloody armed conflict in defense of an indefensible social convention and an unreal way of life which never actually existed.

Nor was Mark Twain alone in his feeling about the deleterious effects of too much romantic literature on the antebellum South. A number of historians have agreed with him on this point, among them Fletcher Pratt, who wrote that except in South Carolina, most Southerners never seriously thought that secession would bring war. To them, it was a typical dramatic gesture, designed to bring some concessions from the North to the effect that no more anti-slavery presidents would be permitted. It was a shock to many in the South when the Northern states took up arms to maintain the Union.[68]

By giving Sir Walter Scott's name to the wrecked steamboat, dead on a rock, isolated, destined in a short time to break apart and be washed away by the inexorable current, Twain invites the reader to see the wreck as a symbol of the old South. By extension, it can be seen as standing for any society so befuddled by a romantic, unrealistic view of itself that it is doomed to destruction for lack of a clear understanding of itself.[69]

The "Walter Scott" episode is followed by a trio of chapters which center on the relationship between Huck and Jim. In Chapter 14, "Was Solomon Wise?" we get some comic relief, while at the same time, Twain introduces once again the theme of royalty and nobility. This chapter harks back to Huck's own noble conduct as regards the three desperadoes stranded on the wreck in Chapter 13 and looks forward to the coming of the king and the duke in Chapter 19. Chapter 15 marks Huck's last Tom Sawyerish prank on Jim, Jim's heartfelt reaction, and Huck's subsequent apology and resolve not to do any more mean tricks on the man who is now, for the first time, his equal in Huck's own mind. This chapter marks a new stage in Huck's growth; now, away from St. Petersburg and its social standards, away from all riverbank society, Huck can at last accept Jim as a man, with the feelings and sensibilities of a man. His apology to Jim is profoundly significant, for it

---

[68]. Fletcher Pratt, *Ordeal by Fire (A Short History of the Civil War)*, New York: Perennial Library, 1966.

[69]. For one statement of Twain's case against Sir Walter, see Chapter 46, "Enchantments and Enchanters," in *Life on the Mississippi*. This part of the book was written simultaneously with the later part of *Huck Finn* and expresses Twain's feelings as of 1882 or 1883.

breaks down the barrier of race between the outcast boy and the runaway slave.

The new relationship between the two gets an immediate test in Chapter 16. Hearing Jim talk about Cairo, freedom, and his plans to buy or steal his wife and children out of slavery gets Huck's conscience going, telling him that aiding Jim in reaching freedom is wrong. He resolves to turn the runaway in, and actually paddles off in the canoe to do so; but Jim's last call to him across the water—"Jim won't ever fergit you, Huck. You's de bes' fren' Jim ever had; en you's de only fren' ole Jim's got now . . ." chills him. "Dah you goes, de ole true Huck; de on'y white genlman dat ever kep' his promise to ole Jim." It is too much for Huck's conscience. Immediately he meets two men in a skiff, looking for runaways. They ask him if his man on the raft is black or white, and Huck, after a moment's hesitation, answers, "He's white." When they say that they will go and see for themselves, Huck exhibits his marvelous command of psychology for the second time. Where in Chapter 13, he got the ferryman to head for the wreck by appealing to his greed, now he keeps the hunters from the raft by making it seem that he wants them to come—and playing on their fear of smallpox to not only to turn them aside but to collect $40 in gold.

Immediately after this ultimate testing of the bond between them, Huck and Jim are separated when the raft is run over by an upstream steamboat. Huck swims ashore and reaches the Grangerford house.

The feud episode occupies Chapters 17 and 18, and like the "Walter Scott" incident, it attacks the self-deluding romanticism of the old South. While the region's self-image was of elegant gentlemen and graceful ladies living a cultured life beneath the columns of their Greek revival mansions, the reality of the backwoods South was of a difficult life in a brutal, raw world not far removed from savagery. The pretensions of old Sol

Grangerford and his family are all the more out of joint with the time and place in which they live.[70]

Nothing could be more ridiculous in a harsh frontier environment than a blood feud, yet the Grangerfords and the Shepherdsons go on exterminating each other out of a misplaced conception of honor, even though nobody seems to know the cause of the fighting in the first place. This is Tom Sawyer play acting all grown up; the principals go on shooting each other because "the books" say that this is what honor demands. No one thinks rationally about their behavior, least of all young Buck, who can't wait to kill a Shepherdson for breakfast.

The feud episode contains more than the horror of organized and sanctioned murder. By contrast, we also meet Emmeline Grangerford, poetess and artist extraordinaire. I defy anyone to read Huck's description of her drawings aloud and not laugh the same way. This little segment, deflating the cultural pretensions of the frontier first families, is a parallel to the school graduation ceremonies in *Tom Sawyer*, except that Emmeline's work is even funnier.

There is also a marvelous throwaway line in this section; the Grangerfords and Shepherdsons attend the same little backwoods church, bringing their guns along and keeping them "between their knees or handy against the wall." This image alone is devastating, but the next line, delivered in Huck's ingenuous style, is the topper. "It was pretty ornery preaching—all about brotherly love and suchlike tiresomeness . . ."

These people all say what a good sermon it was and spend the Lord's Day in contemplation of faith and good works—while

---

[70.] It is interesting to note that Colonel Grangerford wears a white linen suit, so white "it hurts your eyes to look at it." As an old man, Samuel Clemens adopted the white linen suit himself; it became his trademark outfit in his final years.

they bring their firearms into the church and spend their lives attempting to kill off their neighbors. They all listen to the preacher, but no one is hearing the message.

Just as one can take the symbolic significance of the wrecked "Walter Scott" as applying to societies other than the old South, so one can read this passage as a satire as well. Twain's apparent object is the fighting and feuding families, but the deeper target is all those folks in any place and at any time who metaphorically take their guns to church and pay as little attention to the message of religion as the Grangerfords and Shepherdsons do.

One can read the feud episode in at least three ways: first, as a story of romance and tragedy, similar to "Romeo and Juliet" (though in this instance with a presumably happier ending for the lovers, if not for their kinsmen). Secondly, as an attack on the absurdity of such behavior at a time and a place so inappropriate to it. Thirdly, one can see the segment as a satire, in which the real targets are not the Grangerfords and the Shepherdsons, but all those people anywhere and everywhere and at any time whatsoever who act so foolishly and without understanding of themselves and their circumstances.

Chapter 18 ends with Buck and the other male Grangerfords dead and Huck sickened from the violence which he has been forced to witness and which he unwittingly precipitated by delivering Ms. Sophia's note. He returns to the raft, which Jim in the meantime has preserved and refitted, and in the last paragraph of the chapter, the runaways are back on the river on their wood plank Eden of a raft.

Chapter 19 begins with one of Twain's many descriptive set pieces—a depiction of dawn on the river. I have already mentioned the importance of nature in this book and indeed in all of Mark Twain's Mississippi River works. This particular scene is twinned by a similar passage in Chapter 30 of *Life on the Mississippi*, also describing a summer dawning. Both passages depict such sylvan loveliness as to evoke images of Eden, and in the *Huck Finn* case, this can hardly be accidental, given what immediately follows it.

That is the appearance of those two immortal con men, the king and the duke. Huck, who has come to feel for anyone in trouble, from murderers on up, does them a kindness and brings them aboard the raft. This is akin to opening the gates of Eden and asking the serpent to slither in; and it isn't long before Huck has cause to regret his invitation.

Of course, Huck sees through the king and duke nonsense almost immediately and recognizes the pair for the frauds they are, but he says nothing and plays along just to keep things peaceful on the raft.

Royalty dominates the last three episodes of Section II. Their first port of call is Parkville, where the duke takes over the printing shop while the king works the camp meeting.[71] This

---

[71.] The name of the town is "Pokeville," according to the king, who gives it that way while working the camp meeting in Chapter 20. But according to the chapter titles, it is "Parkville," and this is how it appears in both of my editions of *Huckleberry Finn*—the Washington Square Press paperback, published by Simon and Schuster, and the Junior Classics hardcover edition from Grossett and Dunlap.

My friend Dan Fuller, who not only teaches books but collects them as well, was confused at first by my mention of chapter titles in *Huck*. His first edition does not have them nor do a couple of other editions in his possession. He does find the chapter titles in the Bernard DeVoto edition of 1946. The fact that some versions of Huck include chapter titles, and others, including the original, do not raise the question of who wrote the chapter titles and when. I am betting on Mark Twain—they have the perfect Twain "feel"—but I am at a loss to explain why, if he wrote them, they did not appear in the first edition.

In any event, the discrepancy between "Parkville" in the chapter titles and "Pokeville" in the text remains unexplained. Twain may have meant

scene is another in that album of prose photographs which *Huck Finn* contains. The people are well-meaning and good-hearted, but so trusting as to be ripe for plucking by the king.

In Chapter 21, ("An Arkansas Difficulty") the con men mangle Shakespeare, then land in Bricksville, where we encounter another type of riverside people. The cruel, greedy loafers chewing tobacco on the tumbledown business street are the flip side of the good folks at the camp meeting. They have no apparent redeeming qualities whatsoever.

Chapter 21 is mainly concerned with the murder of Boggs, the drunken old countryman, by Colonel Sherburn. This incident is based on one of Sam Clemens' boyhood experiences in Hannibal—the shooting of Sam Smarr by a local merchant. It leads to the mob setting out to lynch Sherburn, who foils the attack in Chapter 22.

Colonel Sherburn's soliloquy, together with Jim's heartrending speech of regret in the next chapter, is literally and figuratively at the very center of the novel. These scenes portray opposite facets of the nature of man, just as the descriptive passages in the last two chapters do. The good people of the

---

us to think that the king was mishandling the name—he is, after all, no great intellect, and he is used to mispronouncing names (consider "Bilgewater" for Bridgewater and "Elexander" for Alexander, just to name a couple). If this was indeed the author's intention, there is a sly irony involved here, for there isn't much park like about Parkville; it is a lot more pokey than parky, so the king's misspeech actually gives a more honest description of the town than does its real name.

More or less arbitrarily, and because "Pokeville" appears just once, I have called the town Parkville, as it appears in the chapter titles and at the top of each page of Chapter 20. I do like to think Mark Twain meant to have the king misspeak for the reasons I have given—but I can't prove it.

Parkville camp meeting are counterbalanced by the vile loafers of Bricksville, and Colonel Sherburn's assertion that "the average man's a coward" is set off against Jim's deep feelings of guilt and humility when he recalls his thoughtless treatment of his little deaf daughter.

The placement of these portraits of the paradox of Humankind at the very center of the novel can leave no doubt about Mark Twain's real subject in *The Adventures of Huckleberry Finn*. The book is ultimately about the only animal that blushes (or needs to)—man, who is capable of the greatest good and the basest evil. The eternal problem with which Adam's children must grapple is how to discern what is right and good, and how to accomplish it.

The final episode of Section II is the Wilks sequence, which, including its treacherous aftermath—the betrayal of Jim—is played out over eight chapters (24-31). From the point of view of plot and structure, the episode is significant mostly for Huck's actions in Chapter 26. Moved by the thought of the Wilks sisters being defrauded by the king and the duke, Huck determines to steal the money on their behalf. At serious risk to himself, he pilfers the bag of gold from the king's room.

Up to this point, Huck has been primarily an observer of riverbank society rather than a participant in it.[72] Now, he deliberately involves himself to protect others, putting himself in some danger with no expectation of personal gain or reward from what he does. None of his previous acts, even his efforts on behalf of Jim, entailed any risk to him personally. For the first time, then, Huck in Chapter 26 undertakes a selfless act on behalf of others despite the possibility of harm to himself. Tom

---

[72.] True, he did carry Harney's note to Ms. Sophia in the Grangerford episode, precipitating the outbreak of feudal violence, but he was unconscious of the import of his action on that occasion.

Sawyer never does anything like this in either novel; in fact, with the single exception of Jim, none of the other characters ever do. Huck has progressed to another level in his development as a man. He is now primed to make the momentous commitment he undertakes in Chapter 31.

Huck's crisis here is the climax of the novel. He must choose between writing to Ms. Watson and telling her where Jim is, or standing by Jim and trying to steal him out of slavery. His societal norms, his religion, and his conscience all demand that he disclose Jim's whereabouts; on the other side, there is nothing but the closeness they shared on the raft journey. When Huck tears up his letter to Ms. Watson, he does so conscious not only that he is breaking the conventions of his society but also fully expecting damnation as a result. No greater love can a man have for his fellow than to lay down not only his life but his eternal soul as well. This time, when Huck acts to save Jim, he is willing to pay the ultimate cost—not only social ostracism but eternal hellfire as well. He at no time thinks he is doing good by resolving to steal Jim to freedom. On the contrary, he is convinced that this is a wicked act and that he is simply giving himself up to the evil with which he was raised.

This whole central section of *Huckleberry Finn*, depicting life along the banks of the Mississippi River, is virtually a catalogue of human misbehavior. Through Huck's eyes, we witness murder, attempted murder, mob violence, robbery, cruelty, deceit, sloth, ignorance, greed, the worst aspects of slavery, and heaven knows how many other sins. Yet these evils are so camouflaged with hilarious comedy that the reader tends to gloss over the horrors. In the phrase made famous by Sherlock Holmes, one sees but does not observe. This was precisely what Samuel Clemens himself did as a boy growing up in Missouri; it is what the people of the Old South did; it is what people do today; and it is probably what they will always do. In *Huckleberry Finn*, Mark Twain did not simply tell his readers of the human tendency to regard the world with blinders on—he made them experience it in the course of reading the novel.

Critics have often cited the end of Chapter 16, when the raft is run over by a steamboat after the runaways have missed Cairo in the fog, as the location of Twain's great plot crisis in writing the book. It was at this point that he laid the manuscript aside for several years before finally returning to it.

My view, on the contrary, is that the author's true crisis came at the end of Chapter 31. At this point, he was faced with a difficult problem—how to finish the novel?

He had faced a similar difficulty in writing *Tom Sawyer*—remember that letter to Howells in which Twain admitted that until two weeks before he completed the manuscript he did not know how the book was going to end—and indeed he writes at the end of *Tom* that when one writes of adults, he knows where to stop (that is, with a marriage) but when his subject is juveniles, he must stop where best he can. In *Tom Sawyer* that turned out to be with the discovery of the treasure and Huck's adoption by the Widow Douglas and subsequent acceptance into Tom Sawyer's Gang. That is to say, *Tom Sawyer* ends with Huck's "sivilization."

Mark Twain must have realized when he began the new book that *Huckleberry Finn* had to end differently. Huck had to escape the forces of convention to which he submits at the end of *Tom* if the social criticism in the second novel were to have its full effect. There were two ways in which that could have been done—either Huck would have to die at the end of the novel, or somehow he would have to evade the forces of "sivilization"—that is, escape.[73] To kill him off would make the tone of the book too depressing,

---

[73.] Twain faced the same dilemma at the end of *A Connecticut Yankee*, which is in many ways a mirror image of *Huck* (as I will point out later). In that book, however, his ending was not comic but tragic and mystical. In my

and yet the only way his escape could be carried out without offending the reader was to make it humorous. Therefore, the end of the novel had to be comic. However, Huck had been too well developed and become too deep a personality to be employed as a buffoon. Some other character had to be the butt of the joke. Twain hit upon an inspired solution; he brought Tom Sawyer to the Phelps plantation.

In so doing, the author both employs and attacks the overused device of deus ex machina. Tom does take over the action, but instead of solving the hero's problem, he complicates the situation with his harebrained, book-inspired plot to steal a free man out of slavery. He artificially prolongs and confuses what would have been a simple solution. Thus, Twain parodies the "God of the machine" device in the course of employing it.

From the Aristotelian point of view, bringing Tom back was a risk. Aristotle, of course, is known for his dictum that the plausible impossibility is preferable to the implausible possibility, and Tom's turning out to be Aunt Sally's nephew is certainly implausible. If *The Adventures of Huckleberry Finn* has a plot weakness, it is that no preparation was made earlier in the novel to lay the groundwork for Tom's reappearance.

Once the reader gets over the difficulty of accepting Tom at the Phelps plantation, however, he finds the ending of the novel to be both original and subtle. Tom acts in keeping with his own character and his own code of conduct; knowing all along that, Jim was already free by the terms of Ms. Watson's will, and that therefore he was not really nigger stealing but merely playacting, Tom then orchestrates a romantic and ridiculous "escape." He himself suffers nothing from it but sore hands, while he puts Jim through a mini-hell. He runs no real risk,

---

opinion, it was far less satisfying that the much-maligned final section of its predecessor.

because if he is caught, he need only disclose the fact that Jim is already free.[74] Meanwhile, he enjoys the sensation of power and the glamour of drawing a crowd to the final scene. It is Tom Sawyer's greatest performance, and it bears the hallmark of everything else he does—selfishness, ego gratification, lack of empathy for others, and blatant disregard for reality while living in a world of fantasy.

By contrast, Huck, having experienced what amounts to a religious conversion in Chapter 31, is now firmly dedicated to freeing Jim from slavery at whatever cost. He has gone beyond separation from society, and beyond observing it from the outside. In Section III of the novel, he has become an active subversive agent, working against one of his world's fundamental institutions and against many of its standards, customs, and laws. Likewise, he has moved from being an entity reacting to the actions of others to a new status, initiating action against the society which not long before had tried to "sivilize" him. His position in Section III relative to Mississippi Valley society, therefore, is directly opposite from what it was at the beginning of Section I.

This change of position on Huck's part is underlined by the many deliberate similarities between the Phelps plantation and St. Petersburg. As described in the beginning of Chapter 21, the Phelps place could as well be in Missouri as in Louisiana (in fact, we know that Twain's inspiration for it was his uncle John Quarles's farm in the back country behind Hannibal). The similarity is made closer by having the Phelps family turn out to be blood relatives of the Sawyers; Sally and Aunt Polly are sisters. Tom's presence simply brings St. Petersburg (with which he is identified) physically to the Phelps plantation. As I have

---

74. At the end, Tom does take a bullet in the calf, more or less by accident. He certainly was not intending to run any serious risk in his "evasion," however. Characteristically, he never considers the possibility.

previously mentioned, the thematic underpinning of the two sections is also parallel; both deal with the idea of escape, both physically and metaphorically, from the power and influence of the surrounding society. What has changed is Huck's character and his relationship to that world around him. What has not changed is the character and attitude of Tom Sawyer, who orchestrates the parody of escape literature known in the novel as a "mixed up and splendid rescue."

By surrounding and contrasting this hilarious but patently ridiculous performance with Huck's courageous commitment in Chapter 31 and Jim's selfless sacrifice in Chapters 50 and 52, Twain achieves the greatest of all his satiric triumphs. Tom is the butt of the joke, and because Tom is completely identified with the society from which he springs, the indirect object of attack is that society itself. In short, the last twelve chapters of *Huckleberry Finn* are not apart from the rest of the novel, as is often alleged. They are closely integrated with it, not only by characters but by structure, theme and satiric object. They constitute the funniest (yet most savage) attack on the ignorance, cruelty, and self-deceit in American society that Mark Twain levels in this novel. These chapters sum up, codify, and restate the whole central argument of the book.

It is no accident that this attack is made through the medium of Tom Sawyer either. Structurally, the plot of *Huckleberry Finn* consists of one satiric attack after another on the darker side of American society; but the objects used to bring out these attacks get progressively more uncomfortable for the reader.

In Section I of the book, the objects are Tom and his friends and their juvenile playacting, but these are easy to dismiss as immature children. The other objects are the new soft-hearted judge (whom we never really know) and Pap, who can be discounted as belonging to a lower order of society.

In Section II, the objects are the feuding families, who are socially respectable, all right, but removed from the reader by distance and lack of previous identification; the good but foolish people of the Parkville camp meeting and at the Wilks'; the vile would-be lynchers and loafers of Bricksville and, above all, the king and the duke. Like Pap, however, they can be dismissed as "not one of us" by upper-class readers.

But in the last section, the object of the attack is indeed "one of us"; Tom Sawyer himself—the all-American Boy of literature. The reader cannot dismiss attacks on him so readily. Twain turns the lance of his satire at the character in the book who most clearly stands for the society from which he comes—America itself.

Nor is this the only way in which Twain integrates these last twelve chapters into the larger plot structure. He also uses, with deadly effect, the device of parallel structure.

Huck's classic escape from Pap in Chapter 7 is a direct analogue with Tom's silly, comic-opera plan in Chapters 34-40. The attempt to "sivilize" Huck with which the book begins is echoed by his plan to escape Aunt Sally's clutches in the last chapter. Tom patronizes Jim with money in Chapter 2 and does the same thing again in Chapter 43—only the amount is different. Of course, Tom's playacting at robbery and murder in Chapter 2 is contrasted with the real thing in the body of the book and repeated in his plan to steal Jim out of the Phelps cabin. His reshaping the real world to conform with his romantic fantasies as derived from heroic literature is no different from the Grangerford-Shepherdson feud, and just as unrealistic. In many ways, then, Tom's presence in the last section underlines the point of the novel and ties its numerous attacks into a cohesive whole.

Yet it's not hard to miss the message if one does not think about the plot structure because those last chapters include some of the most gut-wrenching hilarity Mark Twain ever put on paper. The scene in Aunt Sally's kitchen, when the boys confuse her count of the spoons while one by one come accounts of shirts, sheets, and candlesticks disappearing is a virtual text of how to write comedy.[75] Likewise, the concocting and delivery of the various "witch things" is enough to make a cow laugh, and yet what underlies these scenes is anything but funny. Issues of life, death, and freedom, of man's inhumanity to other men and of nobility and baseness of character are all hidden under the cloak of laughter. Far from being a lapse on Twain's part, these eleven chapters are among the best writing Mark Twain ever did.

I hope that this detailed outline of the plot structure of *The Adventures of Huckleberry Finn* will convince the skeptics that this is no loosely-mounted, casually-thrown-together novel, but a carefully planned and tightly structured social satire in which the last and most devastating attack is aimed at the character nearest and dearest to the reader.

I believe it is important to stress that the plot of *Huck Finn* works on several levels. It can be read as a juvenile adventure story, which is probably the way most of us encounter it for the first time; it can be read as a masterpiece of comedy, which it surely is; it can be seen more deeply as a magnificent and powerful novel of social satire and criticism having no peer in American literature in that field, and it can also be understood as a form of Bildungsroman, in which Huck's sensitivity and character grow as he becomes increasingly divorced from the society into which he was born. This aspect of the novel has been little remarked, yet I think it is undeniable that Huck Finn grows in the course of this book to finally attain a nobility which Tom Sawyer, the king, the duke, and all the rest will never achieve. The careful reader will no doubt spot other plot points

---

[75.] Compare, for example, the stateroom scene in the Marks Brothers' film, *A Night at the Opera*. The technique—piling one thing on top of another until the whole thing collapses under its own weight—is precisely the same.

which I have not discussed but will validate the premise which I set out to prove—that *The Adventures of Huckleberry Finn* is no slung-together series of unrelated incidents but a well-planned, tightly plotted novel. No other fiction by Mark Twain enjoys such a strongly integrated structure.

II
Moral

Huck Finn has a plot, then. It also has a moral, which can be discerned from careful reading of the novel. I suggest the moral is that man is equally capable of the greatest good and the basest evil, that he is sometimes unable to distinguish between the two because his faculties are blinded by his preconceived ideas, and that his guides to proper behavior are frequently inadequate or grossly wrong.[76] Thus, a man might be judged "good" by his fellows when he is actually doing evil, and he may be judged wicked when he is actually doing good. Even the actor himself may not accurately assess the quality of his behavior since his internal standard setter, his conscience, may reflect corrupt values from without.

It is important to point out at the very beginning that Twain presents this ambiguity in a book written in the early 1880s, long before his own fall into bankruptcy. Those who believe that Twain's fiction reflects his personal life must recognize that just as he was a social critic from the onset of his literary career, so he dealt (in fiction) with moral vagueness long before his personal life began to fall apart.

[76.] The cost of failure to see reality because of the blinders formed by preconceived ideas is a theme to which Mark Twain returned in *A Connecticut Yankee* and *Pudd'nhead Wilson*. It is central to both these books: see my discussion later in this book.

Huckleberry Finn takes up religion, social position, and conscience as guides to behavior, and dismisses each as unsatisfactory.

Religion is surely not a reliable guide. In the course of the novel, Huck comes in contact with Christianity in several forms and in several ways. His first encounter with prayer takes place in Chapter 1—in fact, on the second page of the novel—when the Widow Douglas takes out her Bible and tries to teach Huck about Moses and the "Bulrushers." Huck's reaction is curiosity, until he learns that Moses has been long dead; then he doesn't care about him since he "don't take no stock in dead people."

In a nutshell, this little paragraph summarizes the state of religion in the world of the novel—it is dead, as dead as Moses. As Huck says, Moses is of "no use to anybody, being gone, you see . . ."[77]

Practically on the heels of this comes Miss Watson's dissertation on heaven and hell, and Huck's unspoken thought that if she were going to be in heaven, he'd rather not go there. This is a classic example of Twainiana. On the surface, it's a throwaway comic line, but on a deeper level, the reader cannot help but recognize that a Miss Watson—a spinster slave owner with mildly sadistic tendencies—makes a less than satisfactory angel. If heaven is to be the reward for people like her, then St. Peter is a very lenient gatekeeper indeed.

Huck's next religious experience is his attempt at prayer in Chapter 3, in the course of which he realizes that praying for material goods is not very effective, and praying for "spiritual gifts" is not very advantageous to the petitioner. Of course, the true object of this satire is not Huck, but those well-meaning

---

[77.] It is interesting that Twain chose to use Moses in this paragraph. He may have recognized that a reference to Jesus instead would have been too explosive for his readers.

and righteous people who debase prayer by using it as a request line or a hair shirt.

The Grangerfords and the Shepherdsons go to church in Chapter 18, but the only implication of their visit is that their attendance is perfunctory. In the midst of the feud, the preacher talks about brotherly love and "suchlike tiresomeness," while the two families keep their guns across their knees or handy against the wall. If ever there has been a more graphic description of religion as irrelevance, I have not yet seen it. They all say what a good sermon it was—but did they pay any attention to the meaning?

Then there are the folks at the Parkville camp meeting, all decent, well-meaning people who take up a collection for the king out of their fervor. To them, religion is a kind of entertainment—a combination community sing and picnic. What it does not do is alert them to the enormous wrong of slavery with which they live every day. Their Christianity has been adapted to their social milieu; instead of defining a standard of conduct, it accepts the status quo.

In Chapter 24, we encounter religion in still another way—religion as fraud. The king impersonates Harvey Wilks, the Church of England pastor, and most of the townspeople are completely taken in. Even Mary Jane Wilks, one of the most attractive characters in the book, fails to see through the fraud, despite its being pointed out to her. Is this Mark Twain's comment on the credulity of the public and the out-and-out scam of religious belief?

The crux of the novel, Huck's great struggle in Chapter 31, is set in a religious context. Harking back to Chapter 3 (in another example of the use of parallel structure which Twain employs so successfully in this book), Huck tries to pray "to see if I couldn't try to quit being the kind of boy I was and be better"; but he finds that he cannot pray. He knows it is because he doesn't really mean to give up sin—that is, he doesn't intend to betray

Jim. So he writes the famous letter to Ms. Watson for the express purpose of cleansing his soul so that he can pray. When it is written he says, "I felt good and all washed clean of sin . . . and I knowed I could pray now." But instead of praying, he gets to thinking; the result is that he tears up the letter and resolves to accept eternal damnation rather than send Jim back to slavery.

The stated conflict here, quite clearly put forward, is between praying and thinking. Praying is a selfish act, the purpose of which is to save Huck himself from hellfire. Thinking is a selfless act, which leads to saving Jim from slavery. No more graphic illustration of the failure of religion as a guide could ever be imagined.

This is where the parallel with Huck's attempts at prayer in Chapter 3 becomes so deadly. In that context, his petition for fishing lines and hooks is comic; but when it is compared with his abortive attempt to pray for salvation, it only highlights the essentially selfish nature of the latter. Fish hooks or salvation, the principle is the same, and it is obviously selfish in that the prayer is for the petitioner's own benefit or satisfaction.

Nor is Twain yet finished with religion. Uncle Silas Phelps is a lay preacher who built his own little log church and charges nothing for his preaching (which, as Huck adds, is worth the price). Silas is indeed a good and gentle old man, but he is completely ineffectual in every way. The usefulness of his preaching can be gauged by the behavior of his friends and neighbors—first toward the king and duke, after they try to stage the Royal Nonesuch in town, and later toward Jim after his recapture in Chapter 42. It goes without saying that Silas Phelps' Christianity is no more outraged by slavery than that of the Parkville camp meeting—or anywhere else in the South.

Twain immediately highlights the shortcomings of religion as practiced at and around the Phelps plantation by noting that Huck hurries to town to try to warn the king and the duke that the locals are after them—even *after* he knows what scoundrels they are and after they have betrayed Jim. In fact, he feels sorry for them when he sees them tarred and feathered and ridden out of town on a rail. Human cruelty bothers Huck; it does not have that effect on the good people of the South.

As depicted in *The Adventures of Huckleberry Finn,* religion is at best irrelevant and ignored. At worst, it is accommodating, blind and morally bankrupt, as much a fraud as the king's impersonations. As a guide to moral conduct, it is worse than useless—it is itself corrupting and only Huck's rejection of its teachings, at the risk of burning in hell, allows him to go ahead with his effort to rescue Jim.

Nor is social position or status of birth any better guide. The "well born" people in the book include the Widow Douglas, Ms. Watson, the Grangerfords and their rivals, Colonel Sherburn and the Phelps/Sawyer family. All of them share the common lack of vision toward the injustice of slavery and racial prejudice, and the Grangerfords, the Shepherdsons, and Colonel Sherburn all commit homicide during the course of the book. Likewise, Huck's comic discussions of the "orneriness of kings" point out the worthlessness and moral destitution of crowned heads. As Huck remarks, there is no sense trying to tell Jim that the king and duke aboard the raft aren't real nobility—the genuine article acts no better.

This theme of nobility at birth compared and contrasted with nobility of conduct intrigued Mark Twain through much of his literary career. It is a principal concern in *Huck,* and it is central to the *Yankee* and *The Prince and the Pauper.* Moreover, it is not treated simplistically. Twain does not say (as many Americans seem to believe) that royalty and nobility are corrupt while the freeborn democratic people of America are inherently better; on the contrary, American democracy produces such paragons as Pap Finn, the king and the duke, not to mention the loafers of Bricksville and well-meaning fools of the Parkville camp meeting. The only conclusion one can draw from *Huck Finn* is that nobility of character, as expressed in conduct, is a rare quality likely to be found in the most unlikely places—in this case, in the outcast boy and the runaway slave.

Having dismissed religion and social position/birth as guides to conduct, Twain takes on conscience. Huck struggles with his conscience on several occasions in the course of the novel, and in each case, Huck disobeys what his conscience tells him is right. Ironically, in each case, he acts nobly as a result of disregarding his conscience.

His first conflict with his superego occurs in Chapter 16, when he feels guilt for helping Jim toward freedom. His second struggle is the famous episode in Chapter 31, already discussed, and he wrestles with his conscience a third time in Chapter 33. On this occasion, he utters his famous "yaller dog" remark: "If I had a yaller dog that didn't know no more than a person's conscience does I would pisen him. It takes up more room than all the rest of a person's insides, and yet ain't no good no how." After these three stories of conscience at work, no reader can possibly think that conscience which, after all, is the product of "sivilization" could possibly be a reliable guide to conduct.

Twain thus disposes of three major sources of behavioral strictures. What he does not make clear is what guidelines, if any, are in fact reliable. This question raises a philosophical debate which goes to the heart of interpretation of *Huck Finn*, and which I shall discuss in due course.

III
Motive

Given that the book has a plot and a moral, it is no surprise to find that it also has a motive. I think it is clear that Twain intended his novel to lead the reader to open his eyes and recognize the irony of life in America: that in a nation dedicated to the proposition that all men are created equal and that they are endowed by their Creator with inalienable rights to life, liberty, and the pursuit of happiness, daily life should be marred by ignorance, prejudice, cruelty, stupidity, and violence. Our nation is committed to the highest values, but *Huckleberry Finn* alerts us to the degree by which we fall short of achieving them.

In this light, we can see clearly that *Huck* is not a literary clone of abolitionist Harriet Beecher Stowe's *Uncle Tom's Cabin*, in that it is not a diatribe against slavery. That institution had been destroyed a generation before the book made its appearance. In *Huck Finn*, slavery becomes a satiric object; a stand-in for the race prejudice, ignorance, and cruelty which were as much a part of life in 1885 as they had been before the Civil War and, indeed, as they are even today. The book does not attack slavery per se: it attacks the mental state and lack of vision which allows "good" people to tolerate such injustice.[78]

To put it another way, while satire is one of the techniques Twain employed in writing *Huck*, one can also regard the entire novel as a satire. Its apparent object of attack is slavery and the corrupt institutions associated with it in the Mississippi Valley of 1840. Its real object is the malfunction of American society at the time the book was published. To the extent that these shortcomings continue to exist, the book is just as topical today as it was in 1885. This continuing relevancy, even into our own times, is a factor which makes *Huckleberry Finn* such an enduring masterpiece.

I think we can safely conclude that when Mark Twain set out to write a book set in the period twenty years or more before the Civil War, he did not aim to expose the evils of slavery to his contemporary audience. People in the last quarter of the nineteenth century were no longer living with that institution

---

[78.] This is also true, I think, of *Pudd'nhead Wilson*. See p. 116

and had not been for a generation. *Huckleberry Finn* makes sense only insofar as Twain was writing with the objective of awakening his more sophisticated readers to the failings of their own times and indeed, the evils which Huck observes in the book had not disappeared by 1885. They have not disappeared today—they are simply invisible to people who do not care to look at them. The motive of *Huck* is to make the reader open his eyes.

Samuel Clemens' own background may well have persuaded him of the importance of writing such a book. He remarked in print that as a boy and as a young man growing up in Missouri, he never questioned slavery; he simply accepted it because there was no one to even hint to him that there might be something wrong with the institution. Like his characters, such as Tom Sawyer and the Widow, he was so surrounded by evil, and it was so completely accepted by the community in which he lived, that he simply did not see it or think about it. I suggest that it is no accident that Tom Sawyer and his generation are attacked (in *Tom*) most clearly for their thoughtlessness and that in *Huck*, prayer is presented as an opposite to thinking. A recurrent theme in Twain's works is the terrible consequences of failing to think about the implications of one's behavior.

In *Huckleberry Finn*, Mark Twain not only tells this motive to the reader, but by cloaking it in the triple disguises of satire, irony, and humor, he literally dramatizes it. I would dare to say that comparatively few of the millions who have read the novel over the last century have thought enough about it to see through to the underlying plot, moral, and motive to which the famous "Notice" alerts them. That is one of the supreme ironies about this frequently ironic novel.

Was Mark Twain's ruse in cloaking this message so effectively a success? One envisions Mr. Clemens chuckling to himself as he counts the royalties earned from sales to a legion of readers who bought and read but never understood the book. From this point of view, *Huckleberry Finn* is a triumph.

At the same time, one imagines Mark Twain's frustration in knowing that his masterwork will have little effect in opening people's eyes or changing their minds. America's faults will not go away, and "the damned human race" will continue to be damned. If the ultimate motive of *Huckleberry Finn* was to awaken the slumbering, self-deceiving people of nineteenth century America, then the book can only be called an artistic success but a didactic failure.

IV
Other Factors

Great as the conception of *Huckleberry Finn* surely is, and as finely wrought as its plot may be, the novel's greatness is enhanced by other factors as well. I have already mentioned Twain's brilliant use of satire and irony, but still other elements—humor, language, and descriptive writing—deserve consideration.

As for humor, it takes no great intelligence to recognize that *Huck Finn* is, in places, among the funniest books any American author ever produced. There are an almost infinite number of comic moments in the novel, of which I will mention merely a few.

For all his hard-headed realism and soul-disturbing struggles with his conscience, Huckleberry Finn himself is often a figure of fun. He gets bamboozled by the circus in Chapter 22, where he thinks the ringmaster was fooled by the bareback rider and never tumbles to the fact that he himself has been duped.

Huck's dialogues with Jim, particularly in Chapter 14, "Was Solomon Wise?", and in Chapter 32, "The Orneriness of Kings," are laughers, although they also have a deadly serious purpose in illustrating the "nobility" theme of the book, and in likening the crowned heads of Europe to the fraudulent ole rip of a "king" on the raft.

Huck's outrageous lies are frequently gut-busters as well. One example is his (less than totally successful) attempt to masquerade as Sara (or was it Mary?) Williams in Chapter 11. Another such moment comes in Huck's discussion with the Wilks sisters in Chapter 28. Huck is beyond comparison the most resourceful and funniest liar in American fiction, not to mention the most successful.[79]

The king and the duke may be con men, thieves, rapscallions of what have you, but they are also hilarious. Their mangling of Shakespeare in Chapter 21 is the kind of thing Mark Twain wrote better than any other author ever. Their internecine wrangling, which tends to be overlooked since they appear and function as a pair, can also be very funny. They are in fact a literary Royal Nonesuch, as fraudulent but funny between the covers of the book as the king is on the stage.

But the funniest part of the book by any measure is those much-maligned last twelve chapters, in which Twain really takes off against his favorite target, romantic literature with its "tears and flapdoodle," and the people who immerse themselves in it to the point of self-deception. The Grangerford chapters provide a foretaste of this bubble-bursting hilarity, with their unforgettable descriptions of the art and poetry of Emmeline Grangerford, but those scenes are really just a warm-up for what comes later.

In a famous essay, Twain demolished James Fenimore Cooper and his Leatherstocking novels.[80] Now in *Huckleberry Finn,* he

---

[79] One of Twain's great ironic passages in the novel is Lawyer Bell's remark to Huck in Chapter 29. "I reckon you ain't used to lying—it don't seem to come handy; what you want is to practice. You do it pretty awkward." A wonderful comment when addressed to the most accomplished juvenile liar in the history of literature!

[80] See "James Fenimore Cooper's Literary Offenses," one of Twain's funniest pieces and all the more devastating because its criticisms are so completely and thoroughly valid.

goes after Walter Scott, Dumas Pere, and all the others of that ilk. Add the juvenile shenanigans which Tom and Huck pull on poor Aunt Sally and Uncle Silas, and you have a sustained comedic scene extending through eight chapters and sixty-five pages of print—one of the funniest extended passages ever put on paper by anybody. Here, Mark Twain surpasses himself; he never wrote anything funnier, and with the possible exception of William Faulkner, it is difficult to identify any other American writer of significance who could possibly have created such a comic classic in the course of a serious novel.[81]

In fact, Twain may have made these pages too funny because the reader is laughing so hard that he tends to ignore the satiric and ironic depths of these chapters and their close connection with the first two parts of the book. I suspect that this is how Hemingway and so many literary critics have missed the significance of these last twelve chapters—they were too busy laughing to pay attention to the point.

That the butt of the joke is Tom Sawyer and the society of which he is a part and for which he stands is surely evident to intelligent readers (between guffaws). That a society simmered in romantic literature to the point of self-deception is therefore unable to see its own failings is a point made on several occasions early in the novel (see the "Walter Scott" episode, the feud chapters, and the Tom Sawyer scenes in Section I) and simply reiterated here. That these closing chapters are completely integrated thematically, by structure and character with the rest of the novel simply gets overlooked in the sheer hilarity; but the magnificent message, the scathing social criticism, and the underlying plot are there all the time, if only the reader dries his tears of laughter long enough to look for them.

[81.] Two other English-language writers come to mind immediately: Jane Austen and James Joyce. There may be others, of course.

At any rate, there is no denying that *The Adventures of Huckleberry Finn* belongs on any list of great comedic novels or that it is Mark Twain's most sustained and funniest book.

Another element which makes *Huck* the truly great novel which it is can be found in the language of the book. Once again, the author puts us on notice before the novel begins that language is important in this work. In his "Explanatory," he explains that seven different speech dialects are employed in the book. Being no philologist, I can't say whether he exaggerates in this assertion, but there is no doubt that all the characters do not speak alike, nor that their speech is possibly the best literary rendering of American vernacular ever put on paper.

Mark Twain had a fabulous ear for the rhythms, cadences, and nuances of common speech. It may have been his greatest gift as a writer, and his best works are those which take the fullest advantage of this talent. This is one reason why his Mississippi Valley trilogy—*Tom Sawyer, Life on the Mississippi,* and *Huckleberry Finn*—is so much more vivid and alive than *The Prince and the Pauper* or the dreadfully dreary *Joan of Arc*.

In none of his works, however, did Twain surpass his use of dialogue in *Huck Finn*. When the characters in this novel speak, we hear them across a century and a half as perfectly as if we were standing next to them.

I have already mentioned the remarkable skill and economy of means with which Mark Twain created the unforgettable Pap Finn, perhaps his supreme accomplishment with vernacular speech. Consider Pap's disquisition on government in Chapter 6, for example. It is only two paragraphs and about two printed pages long, yet it not only etches Pap's personality and character completely but does so in such convincing terms that the whole scene might have been a transcription of the old drunk rambling on and on.

Another brilliant example of Twain's ear for vernacular speech is found in Chapter 41—the scene around the dining table when the local folks are discussing the escape. Old Mrs. Hotchkiss and her tongue-wagging tablemates Sister Damrell, Brer Penrod, Sister Dunlap, Brer Hightower, Sister Ridgeway, Sister Utterback, and Brother Marples are never seen or described, and we meet them only in this one short scene. Yet they are so vividly presented through their conversation that we seem to be at the table with them. They are immortalized by their speech, and they will be as real to readers hundreds of years in the future as they were to Mark Twain's readers in 1885 or as they are to us today.

These are the salt-of-the-earth Americans who tolerate all the cruelties and injustices of which the novel speaks (and yes, perpetrate some as well). Yet they are not "bad people": on the contrary, they are well-meaning and religious folks unlike the deliberately crooked king and duke or the venal loafers of Bricksville. Yet they are also irrational, foolish, ignorant, and cruel without being ill-intentioned. They are, in fact, much like the readers Twain was writing for, if perhaps more crude and less educated.[82]

This passage works in different ways. It is clearly comic relief after the intensity of the escape, and in this sense, it is in the tradition of the Porter's scene in *MacBeth*; but it is also the exact reverse—a sobering, bitter, pointed portrait of unconscious evil, placed in stark contrast to Huck's truly noble (and Tom's falsely noble) rescue of Jim which precedes it, and Jim's truly noble self-sacrifice, as related by the doctor, which follows. After the

---

[82.] The conflict between the hatred and suspicion which these people express and their religious form of addressing one another as "Brother" and "Sister," is another of Twain's great ironies. His genteel readers probably would never see themselves mirrored in the farmers and their wives sitting around Sally Phelps's dinner table, but the difference between characters and readers is not so great as they might like to believe.

high hilarity of the evasion and the pages leading up to it, this passage provides a grim comedown.

There are many, many other examples of Twain's marvelous use of dialogue in the novel. In addition, there is at least one other passage I should like to point out as further tribute to the author's unerring ear for vernacular speech, where not a word of dialogue is actually printed, yet the conversation is made eerily real and presented with telling effect.

I am thinking of that little passage in Chapter 7, where Huck, floating silently down the starlit Mississippi in the bottom of his canoe, drifts past the boat landing and hears across the dark water the voices of three or four men talking. This trivial little scene is so vividly presented that the reader not only hears but feels the mood at 3:00 a.m. on a summer night at the ferryboat landing of a small Mississippi River town 150 years ago. This masterful little sketch is presented in a single paragraph of twenty lines or so, but it is so well-handled that it is simply unforgettable and utterly, completely true to life. Little gems like this are embedded throughout *Huckleberry Finn,* and they are a major factor in the book's greatness.

This little conversation, reported by Huck but not actually heard by the reader, brings us to another aspect of the novel—Twain's uncanny ability to describe objects and events in telling but remarkably economical prose. There are many such descriptive passages in the book.

In the very first chapter, after Huck has been sweating out a learning session with Old Miss Watson, he goes upstairs to his room and sits beside the open window. What follows is an eerie description of unquiet night—just a page or less of prose, but it shares with the landing conversation the greatest quality writing can have—it makes the reader *feel* with the character in the book.

To cite some other splendid descriptive passages: the vision of St. Louis seen from the raft, all lit up in the middle of the night but silent as a graveyard with everyone asleep; the Grangerford house, inside and out; the camp meeting; the muddy streets and ramshackle houses of Bricksville and the Phelps plantation as Huck first sees it. Every one of these passages is a miniature masterpiece in itself—clear, concise, and so vivid that not even a moving picture could present the material with more memorable effect.

Twain's descriptions of natural phenomena are equally effective and important to the book. I might cite his account of the storm on Jackson's Island in Chapter 9; anyone who has experienced a ripsnorting Midwestern summer electrical storm will feel this one. Of course, there are the many passages describing the majestic river itself, which have inspired more than one reader to raft his way downstream in Huck's wake.

Nature permeates all three parts of the Mississippi Valley trilogy. *Life on the Mississippi,* for example, contains pictures of the great river similar to those in *Huck,* written at the same time (Twain worked on the two books simultaneously in 1882 and early 1883). There is a storm scene in *Tom Sawyer,* which is quite similar to the one in *Huck.* But in none of Twain's other books is nature as pervasive and central as it is in *Huckleberry Finn.* As I have already pointed out, the river itself may be considered a character in this novel; in no other Twain book is the contrast between raw, crude, powerful, beautiful, and eternal nature and the sometimes impressive but often flawed works of man so clearly presented. The subtle but important place of nature in this novel is still another reason why it is Mark Twain's finest production, standing tall, proud, and alone above his other works.[83]

[83.] Descriptions of nature play an important role in *Tom Sawyer* as well, but in that book, they are simply incidents lending color to the story. They are never integrated into the plot as the river is in *Huck.* It is interesting

V
Themes

The Adventures of Huckleberry Finn exhibits a number of themes common to other works by Twain. I have already discussed the "nobility" theme, which is prominent and central in this book. Likewise, I have pointed out the nature theme, which is also important in *Huck*. But these are by no means the only recurring ideas which Twain used in this novel as well as elsewhere in his works.

Confusion of personalities—what might be called the "mistaken identity" theme—was first employed in *The Prince and the Pauper* and reappears in *Huck*, albeit in a different way. In the *Prince*, the switching of roles which makes Tom Canty become royalty while Prince Edward roams the country is accidental. In *Huck*, circumstances force the hero to assume the identity of Tom Sawyer, while Tom pretends to be his brother Sid. In addition, there are several other cases of assumed or mistaken identity in the book: Huck dresses up as "Sara (or is it Mary?) Williams" for his visit to Mrs. Loftus and Huck, Tom and Jim all appear in drag as part of Tom's ridiculous "evasion." Likewise, the "king" and the "duke" assume their titles, to which they have no real claim, and then they go on to masquerade as the heirs of Peter Wilks. *Huck Finn* is full of characters switching identities and pretending to be somebody else, though the "mistaken identity" theme is not central to the action as it was in the *Prince* and will be again in *Pudd'nhead Wilson*.

This "mistaken identities" theme is related to another frequent Mark Twain concern, the question of whether clothes (or education) make the man. In the *Prince*, they certainly do; in

---

to note the relative absence of nature as an important component in Twain's lesser works.

Huckleberry Finn they seem to. Twain's attitude, however, becomes more ambiguous in *A Connecticut Yankee,* as we shall see.

Twain's concern with this question is central to his feelings about American democracy. If education and vestments are the only things which distinguish prince from pauper, then indeed American egalitarianism is superior to European social class structure and American democracy is preferable to European monarchy; but if character is independent from education and social position, then the American claim to be the light of the world is less clear.

On the surface, *Huck Finn* appears to echo the unequivocal position in favor of nature over nurture which the author presented in the *Prince.* The king and the duke are satiric portraits of rapacious, unprincipled monarchs, and aristocrats (as Huck remarks, you can't tell the frauds from the real thing—they all act about the same). The red-blooded, all-American characters (Tom Sawyer, Aunt Sally and Uncle Silas, the Grangerfords, Mary Jane Wilks and her sisters) are salt of the earth "good" people.

But when the analysis is carried further, the author's position is less clear. Huckleberry Finn himself is by nature the ill-clad, uneducated social outcast, yet his inherent nobility of character does not spring from his adoption by the Widow and subsequent reformation, but in fact depends on his rejection of education in the ways of society and his symbolic throwing off the clothes which it prescribes (on the raft, Huck and Jim go naked much of the time). Meanwhile, the "good" characters all suffer from spiritual blindness and self-delusion about their supposedly superior society, which is founded on a horrible wrong—slavery and its related evil, the arbitrary categorization of individuals by skin color or social status. The author returns to this theme again and again in his later works; in *Huck,* his doubts about the ideas that "training is everything" and "clothes make the man" are already evident.

Another recurrent Twain theme which is central to *Huckleberry Finn* is the question of conscience and the degree to which the superego is a reliable guide to behavior; again the author's attitude can be seen to change as his career develops. In *The Adventures of Tom Sawyer*, really the author's first attempt at a full-length piece of fiction, Tom's conscience clearly motivates his best actions—his decision to testify against Injun Joe and save Muff Potter's life. Likewise, in *The Prince and the Pauper* it is Tom Canty's conscience, stimulated by sighting his mother, which leads him to renounce the throne. He could very well have been king for life (even his own courtiers refuse to believe him when he says he is not the real monarch); instead, Tom himself devises the test that proves Edward's true identity.

In *Huck Finn*, however, conscience is Huck's nemesis, a false guide which cannot be relied upon to lead him aright. Huck makes his famous remark about conscience being like a yellow dog that ought to be poisoned; clearly Twain's attitude about conscience was changing.

One wonders to what degree his literary questioning of conscience reflected Samuel Clemens' personal experience with his own superego. It is not implausible to suppose that were he struggling with his own conscience that experience would show up in his work. I shall return to this question later.

Another persistent Twain theme which is manifested in *Huckleberry Finn* is the terrible cost of thoughtlessness and the sad consequences of self-delusion. This theme appears in Twain's work as far back as his very first short story, *The Jumping Frog*. It is seen in *The Innocents Abroad,* and it is clearly remarked in *The Gilded Age.* Later, it is central to the Cub's education in *Life on the Mississippi* and it is at the very heart of *Tom Sawyer.* As I read *Huck Finn*, this concern seems to me to be the crux of this novel as well—the source of its moral and motive. So pervasive is this theme in Mark Twain's writing that it may be said to be one of his foremost concerns.

Moreover, the theme of self-deception turned inward appears in different form in the *Yankee* and still later in *The Mysterious Stranger,* where the author finally concludes that life itself is a delusion. From first to last, Mark Twain's writing reveals a preoccupation with the question of perceptions of reality and the cost of failing to honestly face the reality of existence.

Coupled with the tragedy of self-delusion is the even more heinous crime of thoughtlessness, yet another of Mark Twain's continuing concerns. Tom Sawyer and all his generation—which was, of course, the author's as well—is characterized as heedless, headstrong, and lacking concern for the consequences of its actions. In *Huck Finn,* thoughtlessness lies behind the whole idiocy of the Grangerford/Shepherdson feud, and it is the basis of Tom's callous treatment of Jim, whom he uses like a plaything. In the larger sense, thoughtlessness and its partner, self-deception, are the pillars of slavery and Southern romanticism alike; similarly, they are the twin banes of Victorian America, leading directly to its shortsighted cruelties and preoccupation with commerce at the expense of community.

All these themes are prominent in *Huckleberry Finn* as well as in the author's other books. Through them, it becomes evident that Mark Twain's work over more than thirty years in fact forms a continuum, for while his treatment of his underlying concerns may change, they are generally present in one form or another throughout his fiction. *The Adventures of Huckleberry Finn* may indeed stand out from the author's other books by virtue of its sustained plot structure, its masterful treatment of character and speech, and its great imagination and superior craftsmanship; but it is thematically related to all or most of its creator's other works.

VI
Interpretations

There are many ways of looking at a novel as rich as *Huckleberry Finn.* One of these is to perceive it as a novel of escape.

In Sam Blufarb's book, *The Escape Motif in the American Novel,* he calls *Huck* " . . . the first American novel in which the theme of escape is dominant . . ." and he sees the novel as the progenitor of a significant stream of later works by such writers as Dos Passos, Hemingway, Steinbeck, Carson McCullars, and Richard Wright in which the theme of flight or escape figures prominently.[84] Furthermore, Mr. Blufarb writes that *Huck* is an optimistic book, in that the hero's "light out to the Territory" promises real freedom for him, in contrast with the inward flight of Wright's Biggar Thomas which cannot hope to give him any real escape at all.[85]

Mr. Blufarb's analysis is, I think, right on. Having recognized the evils of "sivilization" (which of course go far beyond such trivia as smoking in the house, not appearing on time for meals and sitting up straight), Huck knows he must escape Aunt Sally's well-meant but menacing threat to adopt him and "sivilize" him; that he can still do so by running West ends the novel on an optimistic note. Indeed, as long as there is freedom for Huck beckoning in the territory, the implication is that all of us yet may escape the deadly mesh of contemporary civilization.

There is another facet to Huck's final flight in the novel which has been little noted by critics but which seems to me to be significant; it bears an uncanny resemblance to what Samuel Clemens himself did during the first year of the American Civil War.

While he later became a strong foe and uncompromising critic of slavery, Clemens actually spent two or three weeks as an officer of the Marion Rangers, a group of Confederate irregulars operating in his home state of Missouri in the spring of 1861. He enlisted more because his friends were doing so than out of any conviction for the Rebel cause, but however lightly Clemens has portrayed the event in his own writing, the stakes were deadly

---

84. Sam Blufarb, *The Escape Motif in the American Novel* (Columbus: Ohio University Press, 1972).

85. Ibid., p. 162.

serious.[86] Missouri at this time was split, Union sympathizers controlling the area around St. Louis, while the Confederate sympathizers, led by Governor Claiborne Jackson, dominated the further reaches of the state. Not until the battle of Wilson's Creek in August was Federal authority in most of the state assured.[87]

Sam Clemens, however, quickly decided that soldiering was not for him, and the opportune appointment of his brother Orion as secretary to the new Territorial Governor of Nevada gave him the chance to flee the war zone and sit out the conflict in Virginia City. He literally "lit out for the territory" and escaped the cataclysm which gripped the rest of the nation. It was as neat an evasion as Huck Finn's escape from Pap, and far tidier than Tom Sawyer's plot could hope to be.

It seems to me that Clemens' own escape from the war deserves more attention than it has received. He has long been viewed as a "wild man" whose subsequent taming blighted his literary career, yet here we have a clear instance of Clemens' ability to disengage himself from society, not only intellectually but physically as well.

The decision not to participate in the war could have been made by millions of young men, north and south alike. In fact, it was made by a relative handful. The vast majority chose to fight for whichever side they considered right, and these men

---

[86.] See "The History of a Campaign that Failed." How much of this tale is true and how much exaggeration I cannot say, but Clemens certainly did join the Rangers, only to quit within a very short time. Call it resignation, retirement, or desertion—the important thing is that he chose not to fight in the war.

[87.] The Missouri campaign was strategically crucial; it established the basis for Grant's moves on Belmont and Forts Henry and Donelson the following spring.

willingly accepted the risks and hardships of campaigning in the bloodiest armed conflict in American history. Clemens was one of the few who opted out; it follows that if he was not above escaping the war, he could similarly choose to avoid other less pressing constraints whenever he elected to do so.

Indeed, there is plenty of evidence to indicate that he did precisely that, although usually in private ways. Clemens was known for the quality and quantity of his profane vocabulary; his religious views were hardly orthodox (he eventually wooed his wife away from her conventional faith); and in his Mark Twain persona, he was the author of *1601, The Science of Onanism* and the supremely subversive (to use Charles Neider's term) *Connecticut Yankee*. Far from being an artist suppressed by social convention, Mark Twain, the author and his alter ego, Samuel Clemens, were capable of repeated escapes from social constraints and mores.

Seen in this light, *Huckleberry Finn* is even more reflective of its creator's mental state. I have already pointed out that in this book, Clemens attacks the kind of thoughtless blindness which he himself exhibited as a young man in Missouri. To the extent that Tom Sawyer can be identified with the boy Sam Clemens once was, Mark Twain attacks his own other self. In Huck's escape from society, the author mirrors Clemens' own wartime evasion.

If there were shackles on Mark Twain's art, they were imposed by the tyranny of his genteel readers and by his alter ego's desire for big sales. If there were constraints on Samuel Clemens' conduct, they arose mostly out of the need to do what he wished, but to do it in such a way that nobody would find out about it. To see Clemens as the victim of a Puritan/Presbyterian conscience, a view suggested long ago by a Freudian critic of great renown, now seems absurd. Not for nothing was John Marshall Clemens a freethinker, and his famous son next of kin to an agnostic. Not by chance does Huck Finn say that if he had a yaller dog that didn't know any more than a person's conscience, he'd pisen him. Not by happenstance is *Huck Finn* at bottom about the problem of distinguishing good from evil and about how noble behavior can be achieved.

In short, both Clemens and Twain, the two sides of this fascinating double personality, were escape artists. Clemens escaped the social constraints of religion and war; Twain escaped the narrow standards of the New England literary establishment and the strictures of his genteel readers.

The *Adventures of Huckleberry Finn* may also be read, as I have said before, as a kind of Bildungsroman or novel of education. In this view, Huck's own personal development is put center stage; there is little doubt that he does grow and change from a kind of Holden Caulfield-like malaise to a clear recognition that civilization is the enemy which he must challenge or escape. Along the way, Huck first evades his biological father and then finds in Jim a substitute father who has aspects of both father and lover.

Yet it seems to me that the critical question in interpreting *Huckleberry Finn* is not how the book should be read, it is what the book means; and at the center of the book is an enigma—the question of what motivates Huck's tremendous commitment to do good, when he sincerely believes he is doing evil?

The first possibility is that Huck is Mark Twain's depiction of Jean Jacques Rousseau's "natural man." Rousseau believed that man was good by nature but was corrupted by society. In this view, when Huck disregards the dictates of his socially created conscience, he is simply acting out his innate, internal human goodness.

But there is an alternative view. It is also possible that Huck should be taken at face value when he says he will go to hell for Jim—that he has no innate goodness but rather intends to do evil out of purely selfish motives and accomplishes good entirely by accident. This is a terribly disturbing idea—that while our standards of behavior are unreliable, there is nevertheless no quality inherent in the species which can offer us any better guidance. In such a moral vacuum self-interest and expediency are man's only motivations, so that while on this occasion Huck's selfish desire to rescue the man who has become his father substitute and only true companion produces a result that we all recognize as good, it is only a chance result. What if Huck had been Tom Sawyer? *His* selfish actions lead not to good but to hardship and suffering for others!

Certainly, we would prefer to see the novel in the first, Rousseau-like perspective. It is far more comforting to think that the universe has a moral center, that there is goodness in the innate human character and that only social reform is necessary to bring it out. However difficult and costly such reforms may be—whether they entail an American Revolution or a French Reign of Terror—there is always the hope, belief, and expectation that the right institutions, once attained, will produce a just, honest, peaceful, and happy society.

However, the alternative cannot be discarded. If Huck, in violating the clearly evil norms of his world, acts purely from selfish motives and without any innate goodness, then the triumph of good his actions ultimately attain is the product of mere serendipity. This view implies a universe governed solely by chance, a monstrous vision in which all ideas of choice between good and evil are vitiated. Tom, attempting to act in accordance with what his conscience tells him is "good," does evil; Huck, defying his conscience and intending to do evil, accomplishes good only by accident.

If, in fact, this moral vacuum is at the center of the book, then *Huckleberry Finn* takes its place not only as one of the most bitterly ironic novels in American literature but also as one of the most depressing. In this view, the book penetrates into the heart of human character and finds there a darkness beyond anything Conrad could have imagined.[88]

---

[88] In discovering a "heart of darkness" at the center of the universe, Mark Twain anticipated Conrad's famous short novel by several years. *Huck*

Arguments can be made for each of the two positions. In favor of the optimistic, Rousseau-like view is the clear import of Twain's previous works—*Tom Sawyer* and *The Prince and the Pauper*—which are grounded on an unambiguous moral universe where right is right, wrong is wrong, and there is no confusion of the two. Also, *Huckleberry Finn* dates from 1884 at the latest, a time when Clemens' life was still uncomplicated by financial disasters, and it is commonly thought that he was still, on the whole, optimistic and cheerful.

On the other hand, the dark and morally ambiguous view is consistent with Twain's later thinking, and the idea that choice between good and evil is illusory leads directly to his final philosophy that life is a dream and that man is neither culpable nor accountable for his life's course. In fact, the book which immediately follows *Huck Finn, A Connecticut Yankee in King Arthur's Court*, exhibits precisely the same terrifying view of good and evil, as we shall see. It is important to remember that this novel too was also written before Clemens' financial collapse and self-exile.

On the whole, I think it more likely than not that the black hole at the center of *Huckleberry Finn* is the first manifestation in Twain's fiction of the overwhelming pessimism and guilt which dominate his later works. He may not have worked out all the implications of his moral vacuum at this time—as we have seen, Twain had a way of introducing ideas almost unconsciously, only to explore them more fully in later writing. At the very least, I think it is safe to say that by the time he finished *Huckleberry Finn*, Twain's conception of the

---

Finn was first published in England at the end of 1884, and *A Connecticut Yankee* (in which the theme is ever more clearly delineated) five years later. Conrad's *Heart of Darkness* did not appear until 1902.

morality of the universe was no longer simple, straightforward, or unambiguous.

The obvious question is whether something occurred in Samuel Clemens' life between the publication of the *Prince* in 1881 and the completion of *Huck* in 1884 which might have caused his alter ego to amend his world view, or whether Mark Twain's changing attitude toward conscience and the problem of moral choice was simply the result of probing deeper and deeper into his own thoughts and feelings.

Without attempting to answer the question at this time, I think it enough to point out that if one reads *Huckleberry Finn* as a morally ambiguous novel, then the entire critical view of Twain as an "optimistic" writer who turned sour only after his own financial crisis of 1891-92 is exploded. I have heard intelligent Twain readers and critics tell me that the *Yankee* must be optimistic because it was written before Clemens' embarrassment. On the contrary, I suggest that the internal evidence, not only of the *Yankee* but (in this interpretation) of *Huck Finn* as well indicates that Twain's change in worldview occurred earlier than has been commonly believed, and that therefore it was occasioned by factors other than his alter ego's problems with the Paige typesetter and the Charles Webster publishing house.

Indeed, even if the more optimistic view of Huck as Rousseau's natural man is accepted, one cannot dismiss so easily the dark tale of the *Connecticut Yankee.* Surely (as we shall see) that book, written prior to 1889 when Clemens was still flush, exhibits a worldview markedly more pessimistic and ambiguous than the *Prince, Tom Sawyer,* or *Huck Finn.*

In short, I am suggesting that the evidence of Mark Twain's writing suggests that his turn away from the simplistic view of good, evil, and moral choice began a good deal earlier than has been generally thought. What this may imply about the author and his personal life, I leave for discussion in a later chapter.

VII
Summary

In this long and detailed discussion of Mark Twain's greatest novel, I have endeavored to show how and why it differs from and surpasses his other works in construction, technical facility, characterization, and use of language, and how it meshes thematically with the author's other works. I have also attempted to show how *Huckleberry Finn* is a multifaceted work which may be read as comedy, social criticism, Bildungsroman, novel of escape, and finally as a novel of moral ambiguity. My point has been throughout that *Huckleberry Finn* is, even more than is generally accepted, a truly great American novel, indeed The Great American Novel, and that its creator was a far greater literary craftsman and far more complicated personality than is commonly supposed. These characteristics are equally in evidence in Twain's next work *A Connecticut Yankee in King Arthur's Court*, which is surely his most misunderstood, most difficult and most disturbing novel.

A Connecticut Yankee in King Arthur's Court

n the autumn of 1884, Samuel Clemens found himself in need of cash once again. *Huckleberry Finn* had not yet been published and sales of *Life on the Mississippi* were below expectations, yet the bills kept coming in, and Clemens needed money. He did what he usually did in such circumstances—he resorted to the lecture circuit. This time he teamed with George Washington Cable on a seventy-city, ten thousand-mile tour, which lasted four months. From the point of view of literature, however, the most important moment of this odyssey occurred one night in Rochester, New York, when Cable introduced his partner to the tales of King Arthur and his Table Round, as told by Sir Thomas Malory. Twain read and fell in love with the stories and characters in the *Morte d'Arthur*, and his infatuation with them was the beginning of the powerful novel we know as *A Connecticut Yankee in King Arthur's Court.*[89]

His first notes for the book, written late in 1884 just after that memorable December day in Rochester, are comic: "Dream of

---

[89.] See Kaplan, p. 310.

being a knight errant in armor in the middle ages. Have the notions and habits of thought of the present day mixed with the necessities of that. No pockets in the armor. No way to manage certain requirements of nature. Can't scratch. Cold in the head—can't blow—can't get at handkerchief, can't use iron sleeve. Iron gets red hot in the sun—leaks in the rain, gets white from frost and freezes me solid in winter. Suffer from lice and fleas. Make disagreeable clatter when I enter church. Can't dress or undress myself. Always getting struck by lightening. Fall down, can't get up."[90]

Actually, Twain's conception of a knight in metal armor at King Arthur's Court is a complete anachronism. Arthur (if there really was a historical Arthur) lived in the sixth century, while iron armor dates from about the eleventh—a good five hundred years later. If Arthur actually existed, he was probably a good deal more like a primitive tribal chieftain than the noble national monarch of legend. Mark Twain never let such historical complications interfere with his stories, even if he was aware of them, and it's unlikely any of his readers cared, anyway. Talk of Arthur and his Knights of the Round Table to the man on the street today, and he will think of shining armor—with no help from Mark Twain either.

Not that the original armor jokes play more than a minor part in the novel as it eventually developed. As was common with Twain, the original comic conception of the book became transmogrified into something much deeper, darker, and more complex as the novel emerged. According to Justin Kaplan, the grimmer dimensions were present as early as January 1886, when the first three chapters of the *Yankee* were written.[91]

At almost the same time Mark Twain was beginning to set the story of Hank Morgan's adventures in Camelot down on

90. *Mark Twain's Notebook,* p. 171. Quoted by Kaplan, pp. 344-345.
91. Kaplan, p. 345. Also, see p. 329.

paper, his alter ego Samuel Clemens was involving himself in the disastrous business venture which was eventually to bankrupt him and to stain his life. At the beginning of February 1886, Clemens assumed half ownership of the Paige typesetting machine in return for his commitment to finance construction of a prototype and to pay for manufacture and promotion of the invention.

Clemens' involvement with the Paige machine was the biggest and the most expensive of all his attempts to make big money, and it was the most costly of his many failures in that direction. By the time he made his major commitment to the machine early in 1886, he had already invested $13,000 in it. By December 1887, his stake had grown to $50,000, and by the time the invention was finally written off as an impractical failure, it had consumed $300,000 of Sam's and Livy's money. The draining expense was the result of Clemens' greed, coupled with his self-deception about the Paige device (its rival, Mergenthaler's linotype machine, was already in existence at the time Clemens put his money behind the fantastically complicated Paige device). In *Huckleberry Finn*, Mark Twain had written, "Overreaching Don't Pay"; the cost of thoughtlessness and self-deception were familiar Twain themes. Yet simultaneously Samuel Clemens was doing exactly what Mark Twain was warning about.

The fascinating breach between Twain's writing and Clemens' actions grows increasingly pointed at the time of the *Yankee,* which was written between January 1886 and May 1889 and published in December of that year. During that period, Clemens' financial position was growing progressively more precarious, largely as a result of his continuing to pour money into the Paige project in search of the quick riches which had escaped him as a miner, inventor, publisher, and promoter. His deteriorating position is reflected in Mark Twain's increasingly bitter diatribes in the *Yankee;* unfortunately, Clemens seems to have been unable to live by his alter ego's acute and ruthlessly honest perceptions.

It has now been well over a century since *A Connecticut Yankee* first appeared in print, yet contemporary critics seem as bewildered by the book as those in Clemens' time seem to have been. Most of them see it as an attack on the ignorance and superstitions of Old England, on monarchy and the established Roman Catholic Church, and even on the institution of chivalry itself.[92]

I contend, on the contrary, that analysis of the *Connecticut Yankee* will reveal it to be simply one step further along the path of *Huckleberry Finn*—it is another ironic, comic, and satiric novel in which the ultimate object of the author's attack is the society in which he lived; that is, late Victorian America. That the *Yankee* may be less successful as a work of art than its predecessor does not take away from its own merits, particularly as the outstanding example of satire in American literature. By studying the elements of the book's plot, characterization, themes and devices, and by creative interpretation, I shall demonstrate that the *Yankee* has been too often misread and more often shunned, and that it deserves instead recognition as the most biting, most damning, and most imaginative attack ever leveled at the unchecked abuses of capitalism and the mindless avarice of late Victorian America. I shall also show how the book reflected the growing dichotomy between Samuel Clemens and Mark Twain, who were well on the way to becoming two personalities in the same body.

[92.] Even so well known a scholar and critic as Henry Seidel Canby has written that the *Connecticut Yankee* is "a burlesque which dirties the idea of chivalry" (see *Turn West. Turn East*). Professor Canby should have known better.

I
Plot

The basic plot device of the *Yankee* is that of the old formal novel of manners and morals; a character from the outside is set down in a world not his own, whose characteristics he proceeds to explore and bring out. In this case, the process goes one step further—not only does the central character discuss the world into which he has been thrust, he attacks and attempts to destroy it in order to replace it with the commercial culture from which he has come.

It will be seen immediately that this is a return to the basic device of *The Prince and the Pauper,* save that the distance between the two worlds is created by time rather than social class. It is also the underlying technique of *Huckleberry Finn,* though carried in a different direction—while Huck attacks the basic institution of his world by attempting to steal Jim out of slavery, he never thinks of actually destroying it, and his eventual way of dealing with "sivilization" is flight rather than conflict. In fact, *A Connecticut Yankee* has more than a little in common with its great predecessor, a fact which has been too often ignored.

Structurally, the two books are remarkably similar. Like *Huck Finn,* the *Yankee* may be conveniently divided into three parts, defined as much by geography as by dramatic function and corresponding to the traditional three acts of a stage drama. Section I (or Act I, if you will) describes the Yankee's arrival in and conquest of King Arthur's court and is unified by its setting in the town of Camelot. Just as the first three chapters of *Huck Finn* serve as a bridge from *Tom Sawyer,* the first four chapters of the Yankee's manuscript form a link to Mark Twain's late night interview with the stranger at the inn. Mark has been reading (between pegs of Scotch) Malory's account of how Sir Kay, with the aid of Sir Launcelot, captured three knights. Here, Chapter 1 of the Yankee's manuscript begins: he is a prisoner of Sir Kay, who brings him to Camelot, which is described in this first chapter. In Chapter 2, he meets the page, whom he calls (for no apparent reason) Clarence, and from him learns the date—June 19th, 528. For a moment, the Yankee is puzzled: how can he tell if he is really in the sixth century or only in an insane asylum? But then he remembers that the only solar eclipse in the first half of the sixth century took place at 12:03 p.m. on June 21, 528, and that there was no eclipse of the sun in the current year (1879). In forty-eight hours, he will know the truth.

How likely is it that anyone would know to a certainty the date and time (let alone the place!) of a sixth-century solar eclipse in England? When one considers this staggering bit of knowledge, one is entitled to question the veracity of the whole story. Coupled to the coincidence (?) of the Yankee's arriving at Camelot as a prisoner of that same Sir Kay about whom Mark Twain was reading that late, windy, rainy, boozy night at the Warwick Inn, we are entitled to wonder if this whole tale is not Mark Twain's own dream. More on this idea later.

It had always bothered me that the Yankee seems to pick "Clarence," his name for Amyas le Poulet, the young page, out of thin air. At last, while in the final stages of preparing this book for publication, I made a special trip to the library and found an excellent book on the meaning of names. It is called *From Aaron to Zoe* by David Avram Richman, published by Little, Brown and Co. in 1995, and from it I learned that the name Clarence comes from early English and means "Bright," "shining," or "clear." Amyas is any and all of these things in the novel, in which he is perhaps the most appealing character. In short, his name perfectly describes him: the Yankee may have pulled it out of thin air, but his creator, Mark Twain, surely did not.

Intrigued, I went on to look up the Yankee's own name, Hank. I found that it is diminutive of Henry, a name which means "powerful," "commanding," "leader," "lord," or "ruler." Don't try to tell me that Twain called his character "Hank" by accident, because I simply won't believe it.

Chapter 2 concludes with a vivid description of the great Table Round, with its carousing knights and unruly dogs. This scene continues into Chapter 3, which contains a portrait of Queen Guenever and her unseemly passion for Sir Launcelot. Here, too, we meet Merlin and hear his drowsing tale, which puts the whole court to sleep.

The Yankee hits bottom in Chapter 4, when he learns that he is to be burned at the stake the next day and is thrust naked into a dungeon cell in the meantime.

The real career of the Yankee begins in Chapter 5, when he has his great inspiration: knowing in advance of the eclipse, he has Clarence tell the court that he is a powerful magician, so potent that he can and will blot out the sun if he is harmed. In Chapters 5 and 6, he uses the eclipse to gain not only his safety but also fame and power. He soon discovers, however, that he needs to produce a second miracle to convince the people that he really is the great wizard that Merlin has been disparaging before the public. This he produces (with help from Clarence and a convenient thunderstorm) by blowing up Merlin's tower in Chapter 7.

With his position now solidified, the Yankee muses in Chapter 8. *What a jump I had made*, he thinks.[93] "My power was colossal." But he is prescient enough to see that as strong as he was—more potent

---

[93.] This thought might well have been in the mind of Samuel Clemens in the years following his marriage and sudden rise to wealth, fame, and social status.

than the king himself—there is still a force in the country more powerful than he and the king together. That is the Church.

In time, he earns the one thing he has lacked—a title. He becomes known England-wide as "The Boss."

In Chapter 9, the Yankee tells of his first creation—a patent office—and later, he attends a tournament and utters a fateful line about Sir Dinadan the humorist: "I hope to gracious he's killed!" Sir Sagramor overhears this, and thinking it meant for him, he challenges the Yankee to a bout. This contretemps is not to be resolved until the last section of the novel.

Chapter 10 contains the Yankee's account of his creating the foundations of a nineteenth century society out of sight but under the noses of the people of the sixth. It concludes with King Arthur hinting to his minister that it was high time that he went out in search of adventures, so as to build a reputation that would make him a worthy opponent of Sir Sagramor when the time came for them to fight. This is the device which leads the story into the long central section of the book—the Yankee's adventures in the kingdom.

This second section (or second act) of the *Connecticut Yankee* encompasses twenty-eight chapters and 202 pages of text in my Signet Classic edition of the book. It is similar to the middle twenty chapters in *Huck Finn*, which describe the river journey and the people and adventures Huck and Jim encounter along the way. The parallel can be carried even further: in the early novel, the central section can be broken down into two subsections, the first of which comprises the "Walter Scott" and feud episodes (which involve only Huck and Jim) and the second, including the rape of Parkville, the Bricksville scenes, and the Wilks family saga (which also feature the king and the duke). In the *Yankee* too, the central section is divided: first come the Boss' travels with Sandy, culminating in Chapter 26, and then his incognito ramblings through the country in company with King Arthur himself.

The tone of the first sixteen chapters in the second section is basically comic, although darkened by the Morgan Le Fay sequence (Chapters 16-18) and the encounters with the freemen (Chapter 13) and the troop of slaves (Chapter 21). Sandy appears prominently in Chapters 11-15, again in 19-20, and 22. Then she drops out of the narrative, and except for a quick mention in Chapter 24, we do not meet her again until the last four chapters of the novel.

The last three chapters of the second section (24-26) each describe triumphs won by the Yankee on his crusade to replace the sixth century with the nineteenth. The last of the three, "The First Newspaper," comes shortly after the center of the novel and is described in glorious terms: it is the Yankee's greatest moment. "Yes, this was heaven. I was tasting it once, if I might never taste it more."

Indeed, the tone of the last twelve chapters in Section 2 is much darker. Here we find the tragedy of the smallpox hut, in which Arthur shows how truly noble he is when he risks his life to carry the dying girl downstairs to her mother. This is followed by the terrible story of the manor house, interrupted by three deadly chapters propounding free trade over protectionism—a hot political topic in late nineteenth-century America but far less interesting to contemporary readers. Then the Yankee and the king are hunted down, sold as slaves, and saved from execution only at the last possible moment by Sir Launcelot and five hundred knights arriving on bicycles. This comic moment marks the end of a nightmarish part of the book.

It will be immediately apparent to any reader who compares the two books closely that while *Huck Finn* and the *Connecticut Yankee* are structurally similar, their central sections are violently different. In the *Yankee,* Section 2 is far too long—more than half the length of the whole novel. Moreover, it both horrifies and bores the reader, and it lacks completely the close identification between characters in the book and the reading public that is one key to the tremendous power of the earlier book. We like Huck and feel with him: we are not emotionally close to the Yankee and lack empathy with him.

The third section—the resolution of the *Connecticut Yankee*—is set back in Camelot. But if the second section is too long, this last part is too short—only six chapters covering just forty-eight pages in the Signet Classic edition. It seems curiously foreshortened and rushed, especially in contrast with the long central section. Whereas *Huckleberry Finn* is perfectly balanced, with the first and third sections together just the same length as the center, the *Yankee* is strikingly lopsided. The resolution leaves the reader feeling as though he has been mugged by too many events following each other too quickly. This glaring lack of balance between its three major parts is one of the book's most obvious and most irksome flaws.[94]

---

[94] Twain was fully aware that the *Yankee* was somewhat less than perfect. In a famous letter to Howells, dated September 22, 1889, he wrote, "Well, my book is written—let it go. But if it were to be written over again there wouldn't be so many things left out. They burn in me, and they keep multiplying, but now they can't ever be said. And besides, they would require a library—and a pen warmed up in hell." (Quoted by Kaplan, p. 354.)

There is yet another structural similarity between the *Yankee* and its predecessor. I refer to the preface, which Twain places at the very beginning of the *Yankee*. Here, he writes, "The ungentle laws and customs touched upon in this tale are historical, and the episodes which are used to illustrate them are also historical. *It is not pretended that these laws and customs existed in England in the sixth century: no, it is only pretended that inasmuch as they existed in the English and other civilizations of far later times, it is safe to consider that it is no libel upon the sixth century to suppose them to have been in practice in that day also* [emphasis mine]."

This preface, it seems to me, is the exact counterpart of the famous Notice at the beginning of *Huckleberry Finn*. The Notice warns the reader, in ironic terms, that the book he is about to begin has indeed a motive, a moral, and a plot. This preface warns the reader that the *Yankee* is not an examination of the laws and customs of Arthurian England but those of "[an]other civilization of far later date . . . ," i.e., late Victorian America. The preface is Mark Twain's announcement to the public that *A Connecticut Yankee* is a classic satire.

Of course, Twain was a master of the satiric technique, which he used with telling effect in his earlier books, especially in *Tom Sawyer* and *Huckleberry Finn*. Indeed, the *Connecticut Yankee* itself contains many individual satiric attacks; one classic is to be found in Chapter 40, where The Boss sends the knights through the country as traveling salesmen. "They went clothed in steel and equipped with sword and lance and battle-ax, and if they couldn't persuade a person to try a sewing machine on the installment plan or a melodeon or a barbed wire fence or a prohibition journal or any of the other thousand and one things they canvassed for, they removed him and passed on."

Now it is quite apparent (once you get beyond the incongruity of armored knights bludgeoning customers into buying) that the real object of attack here is not the Arthurians of the Round Table but the American drummer of the Clemens' period, who lacked the weaponry for "removing" uncooperative potential customers but otherwise was known for high-pressure sales tactics hardly less effective than those of the armed knights.[95] There are countless such miniature satiric attacks embedded throughout *A Connecticut Yankee,* most of them aimed at the American vices of moneygrubbing and thoughtlessness.

Yet the *Yankee* employs satire on a level beyond these multiple petty attacks. The entire novel is one great satire from beginning to end. Far from being a simple-minded comparison between "bad" sixth-century England and "good" Victorian America, the book is a devastating attack on the avarice, boorishness, and self-deception of The Boss and the society for which he stands. Victorian America had itself all the evils Hank Morgan attacks in Arthurian England, though sometimes in different forms (monarchy is gone, its place taken by plutocracy; for servility to the established church, Morgan's America has substituted worship of money). Tally the evils of Arthur's realm, as The Boss sees them—ignorance, cruelty, slavery, avarice, and superstition—and you will realize that all of them have counterparts in Hank Morgan's America, and in our own.[96]

The novel's very title may have satiric significance. At the time Mark Twain began to plan his book, the president of the United States was Chester A. Arthur, honest and goodhearted, if something less than lightning-quick mentally. Twain's description of the Monarch is a near-perfect picture of the president, a

---

[95.] It is interesting to remember that Mark Twain's books were sold door to door by agents who solicited orders prior to publication. It is hardly likely that this little satiric attack was written without regard to that fact.

[96.] That the *Connecticut Yankee* was published in 1889, the centennial of the ratification of the Constitution may have been accidental, but the coincidence only reinforces the ironic message of this bitterly critical satiric masterpiece.

resemblance which was not coincidental. Moreover, before becoming president Arthur had been manager of the New York Customs House, and while he himself was honest, the institution which he headed had such an unsavory reputation for graft that Arthur's political opponents called him "king of the spoilsman." Thus the United States in the mid-eighties could literally be called "King Arthur's Court." The felicitous coincidence of names would have been far easier for alert readers of the period to appreciate than it is today, when few Americans have even heard of President Arthur. It may, in fact, already have been in Twain's mind when he began turning his early comic notes into a full-fledged satiric novel. At any rate, the title *A Connecticut Yankee in King Arthur's Court* may have been intended (at least in part) to point to the satiric purpose of the book. The apparent object of attack was Britain in King Arthur's time; the actual object was America in Chester Arthur's.

There are subtle indications of the novel's satiric intent right at the beginning in the "Word of Explanation," which precedes the first chapter. For instance, consider this: when Hank Morgan wakes up in the sixth century to find himself a prisoner of Sir Kay, he is marched along through the strange but pleasant countryside until he sees "a faraway town sleeping in a valley by a winding river; and beyond it on a hill, a vast grey fortress, with towers and turrets . . ." Morgan points to it and says, "Bridgeport?" "Camelot," replies his captor.

This short, seemingly innocent conversation is full of significance; first, it suggests—almost as much as says—that it is indeed Bridgeport, and all the other Bridgeports which make up Victorian America, at which the book is aimed. Second, the deliberate juxtaposition of the two names suggests that while we may think of our Bridgeports as Camelots—that is, as enchanted places where nothing ever goes wrong—they are in fact no better than Camelot really was: not the stuff of legend but cramped, mean, dirty, and foul. One cannot help recalling the dual nature of St. Petersburg in *Tom Sawyer*—a fantasy playground of youth and, at the same time, a dreary, mud-spattered, dull, violent little town. I think it is not without significance that Twain has the Stranger's narrative end with this pointed little scene, thus adding even more emphasis to it.

Next, we learn that the Yankee has written his manuscript on old parchment bearing "fragments of old monkish legends" beneath his own words. Why is his story a palimpsest if not to suggest that it is a legend as well, to be taken with as many grains of salt as all those tales about princesses being held captive by giants and ogres?

Finally, the beginning of the Yankee's manuscript is illustrated in the first edition by a Dan Beard drawing of Morgan tweaking the British Lion's nose, above the words, "The Tale of the Lost Land." This is a peculiar way to describe Arthur's England, which may never have existed but certainly has never been lost, thanks to Malory. In no sense can Arthurian England reasonably be described as a "lost land"; but if we think of the Yankee's England, the industrial society he built there on the ruins of chivalry, then and only then does the idea of a "lost land" make sense.

"Lost" in this connotation may mean lost in the sense of "forgotten" or lost in the sense of "defeated" or lost in the sense of "without direction" or "without knowledge of one's true position." All three meanings apply to the Yankee's attempt to build the society of the American nineteenth century in the England of the sixth.

Besides, the "lost land" appellation, in its third meaning, applies not only to the Yankee's reproduction of Victorian America but to the real thing, the society which existed as Mark Twain wrote the book. Here is another double entendre, another indication, another warning that we are dealing with a master satirist disguising his violent criticism of the Yankee and all that he stands for and is associated with behind the cloak of attacks on a world which never existed.

For after all, what would have been the point of attacking the institutions of Arthurian England, except to highlight how superior those of Victorian America were? But if this was the intended meaning of the book, it could not end as it does or be written as it is. On the contrary, a reasonably perceptive reading of *A Connecticut Yankee in King Arthur's Court* leaves not the slightest doubt that this is the supreme example of satiric attack in all the canon of American literature.[97]

There is also another indication that *A Connecticut Yankee* is intended as a satire; the original edition is illustrated with more than two hundred drawings executed by artist Dan Beard and a number of them make apparent reference to Americans of the nineteenth century. The most famous and most obvious of these satiric drawings is that of the slave driver with the face of Jay Gould. Gould was widely regarded as the most rapacious and unethical of all the robber barons of the period; he made a practice of cheating his own partners as well as everybody else, and his appearance in the book clearly underscores the point that what Twain was writing about King Arthur's England was really directed at President Arthur's America.[98]

[97.] Writing about the book in *Harper's Magazine* in 1890, William Dean Howells, while perhaps not comprehending all of the satire, was perceptive enough to remark that "the noble of Arthur's time, who fattened on the blood and sweat of his bondsmen, is one in essence with the capitalist of [1889] who grows rich on the labor of his underpaid wagemen . . ." Quoted in Howells, *My Mark Twain: Reminiscences and Criticisms,* Edited by Marilyn Austin Baldwin (Baton Rouge: Louisiana State University Press, 1967), p. 124.

[98.] For a brief sketch of the kind of shenanigans, Jay Gould pulled off with (and against) his own associates, see Charles Francis Adams, Jr. and Henry Adams, *Chapters of Erie* (New York: Henry Holt, 1886). It's great reading and would be extremely humorous if only it was not so tragic.

Nor can one dismiss Beard's work as his own conception unrelated to Mark Twain's. It was Twain himself who chose Beard to illustrate the book, and it was Twain's publishing house, Charles Webster and Co., which published his drawings. Under the circumstances, one can hardly imagine that the artist's work was not at least approved by the author and publisher. In fact, Beard was clarifying through his sketches what Twain was saying in words.[99]

Between the evidence of the preface and that of the Beard illustrations, then, there cannot be much doubt that Twain intended the *Yankee* to be something other than a desecration of Malory's tales of the Table Round. When the ending of the book is considered—in his hour of apparent triumph, the Yankee and his nineteenth-century civilization meet total, humiliating rejection—the thing becomes certain.

Nor are we yet finished with discussing the structural framework of the novel and its bearing on the proper interpretation of the book. *A Connecticut Yankee in King Arthur's Court* contains an additional element unique in Mark Twain's work; it is a story within a story, a picture inside a frame. I suggest

---

Beard used a number of other public figures as models, either drawing them from life or from their photographs, among them were Queen Victoria, Sarah Bernhardt, the Kaiser of Germany, and the Prince of Wales. As his prototype for Hank Morgan himself, Beard used a Connecticut native who happened to be working in the next studio. See Milton Metzler, *Mark Twain Himself* (New York: Bonanza Books, 1960), p. 210.

99. "I am not going to tell you what to draw," Twain said to Beard. Clearly, he didn't have to (or perhaps he explained the nature of the novel in general and then let Beard have free rein). In any event, the Beard illustrations leave no doubt about the true object of the vitriolic attacks in the book. See Metzler, ibid.

that the use of this entirely new device has enormous bearing in understanding the novel.

Like *Huckleberry Finn*, *A Connecticut Yankee* employs the device of first-person narration. Unlike *Huck*, however, and unlike any other book Mark Twain wrote, the *Yankee* begins with Mark Twain, the author, telling how he met the Stranger (Hank Morgan), who first tells part of his story and then submits his manuscript of the rest of it. In other words, Mark Twain narrates only the first and last pages, "framing" the rest of the story, which is told by the Yankee himself. It will be useful to explore this framing technique in more detail.

Mark Twain writes that during his visit to the castle, this "curious stranger" accompanied him at the tail end of the touring group. The guide indicates a suit of armor said to have belonged to Sir Sagramor and points out the bullet hole over the heart. "Can't be explained, supposed to have been done by Cromwell's soldiers," drones the guide. But the stranger smiles and mutters, in the language of the sixth century, "Wit ye well, I saw it done . . . I did it myself." With this remark, he disappears.

Late that night, while the rain beats on the windows and the wind roars around the eaves and corners, Mark Twain sits in his room at the Warwick Arms, reading Malory. He has just finished the story of how Sir Launcelot first rescues Sir Kay the Seneschal from three attacking knights and then demands that they yield not to him as their conqueror but to Sir Kay. It is past midnight. There is a knock at the door and the stranger enters; four whiskeys later, he begins his narrative. After a time, he is close to sleep; he takes Mark to his room and hands over to him a long palimpsest written on parchment. Twain takes it back to his room and reads through the night.

Having finished the manuscript at dawn, Twain takes it back to the Stranger's room. The man takes Mark for Sandy, his sixth century wife in the MS. Believing himself to have returned to the time of King Arthur, he implores "Sandy" not to let him go out of his mind again, and soon after dies.

One must ask why Twain employed this framing device, something new to his work. I submit there can be only one logical purpose in its use—to make it clear that the narrator is Hank Morgan, the Yankee, The Boss; and that Hank Morgan is *not* Mark Twain. In short, we are meant to understand that the narrator of the story is not the author of the book. This is, I submit, a vital point; for once it is established, we realize that the opinions of Hank Morgan on the total superiority of nineteenth-century America are not necessarily those of Mark Twain. In other words, the framing device puts us on notice that Hank Morgan belongs to that most fascinating of all literary populations—the unreliable narrators.

If Mark Twain did not intend his readers to question anything Hank Morgan says, the whole framing device would be gratuitous and unnecessary. We must assume, on the contrary, that Twain used it consciously and for an important reason, and the only reason that makes sense is that Twain wants us to recognize that Morgan's narrative voice is not his own.

What is more, the Yankee may be unreliable as a narrator for the good and sufficient reason given in the book—he is insane, in the sense that he cannot distinguish the nineteenth century from the sixth. According to his own account, he woke up at Camelot after taking a severe blow on the noggin from a crowbar, and at the end, he thinks the sixth century to be his real world and the nineteenth only a dream.[100] One can hardly accept his account without cavil.

---

[100] See the "Final P.S. by M.T." Twain's evocation of the Dream Philosophy here, written early in 1889 before his financial collapse, European exile, and the death of Susy, is among the most unequivocal proofs that it was something else entirely which caused Clemens to think of seeking

Moreover, the framing device raises still another question; did the stranger whom Mark Twain encountered at the castle really knock on his door that midnight, or is the entire story the author's own dream? Recall—it was a dark and stormy night; Twain had been dipping into Malory between pegs of hot Scotch; he was alone, it was late, and he tells us that he was "steeped in a dream of the olden time".

That the stranger existed, we can accept readily enough; he was a lunatic wandering around Warwick Castle. That he mysteriously reappeared at Twain's hotel room after midnight, had himself a room at the same inn, produced first the tale, then the manuscript, and then died in a fit of delirium the next morning we are entitled to doubt. It may all have been a dream of Mark Twain's—and we have a further piece of evidence to support this proposition. The last thing Twain read before laying down his Malory was the tale of Sir Lancelot, Sir Kay, and the three knights who became his prisoners; the Yankee's tale begins when he is taken prisoner by that same Sir Kay. We may, then, have not only the unreliable and insane narrator but also the unreliable author who presents his story to us. When one recalls how Samuel Clemens later in his life escaped into a dream state, it begins to look as if in the *Yankee* he wrote the script which he himself was to act out some years later.

We therefore have at least three layers of personality in this remarkable novel. Hank Morgan narrates the story through Mark Twain, who himself is and yet is not Samuel L. Clemens. Thus, the structure of the novel, the preface and the use of the framing device make it clear that this is not a simple novel to be

---

escaping from the environment in which he lived to a dream world. What that something else may have been I shall discuss in the last section of this book.

raced through carelessly, but a powerful satire which demands the reader's total engagement for its full understanding.

II
The Narrator

I have just inferred from the structure of the *Yankee* that its central character, Hank Morgan, is not to be taken at his word. We must take a closer look at who Hank Morgan is, if we are to understand this complicated story of which he is the principal narrator.

By his own description, Hank is "an American; a Yankee of the Yankees—and practical; yea, and nearly barren of sentiment, I suppose—or poetry, in other words."[101] His antecedents are prosaic: his father was a blacksmith, his uncle a horse doctor, and he was both at first. His real trade, however, is making things; anything a body wanted.[102]

As the story progresses, we learn that Morgan is not above sharp dealings: note how he saves money by handing out new but less valuable coins at the king's evil in Chapter 26. He is keenly aware of his own finances; in his dealings with Arthur, he demands to be made first minister of the land in perpetuity, and to be paid one percent of the state's increase in revenues under his administration. He starts a patent office to

---

101. This is what he tells Mark Twain in "A Word of Explanation," which precedes the first chapter. Hank's close self-identification as an American first and a "Yankee of Yankees" is not without significance. He clearly stands for the society from which he comes.

102. One could say this about the United States as a nation. As Calvin Coolidge put it some years later, "The business of the United States is business." Again note the close identification between the character of Hank Morgan and the ethos of his country.

encourage new inventions, and while it is not discussed further, who do you suppose would have held the patents on all those nineteenth-century mechanical and technological improvements Morgan introduced? His grasping nature is perhaps most clearly demonstrated at the Valley of Holiness, where he harnesses the praying hermit to a sewing machine and by working him seven days a week for five years is able to sell eighteen thousand shirts at a dollar and a half each. Then when the hermit shows signs of aging, the Yankee sells the business to Sir Bors de Ganis and reaps another fortune, leaving Sir Bors and his investors holding the bag when the hermit dies a year later.[103]

Not only is the Yankee a self-serving money-grubber, he is also power hungry. Not satisfied with being The Boss, he harbors secret ambitions to declare a Republic and become its first president himself.[104] His supposed commitment to democracy does not prevent him from musing that "unlimited power *is* the ideal thing when it is in the right hands" (i.e., his own).[105]

Hank Morgan also possesses other character traits which are somewhat less characteristic of stereotypical Connecticut Yankees. He is, for one thing, an incorrigible show-off; he cannot resist a dramatic moment. As he says himself, "I never care to do a thing in a quiet way. It's got to be theatrical or I don't take any

---

[103] See Chapter 22. I defy any honest and intelligent reader to make sense of this passage except as a satiric attack on American industrial practices of the Victorian era. For those who do not believe *A Connecticut Yankee* to be a satire, this passage must be difficult to explain away.

[104] See Chapter 40. Morgan's actual words are, "I was beginning to have a base hankering to be its first president myself." Given the meaning of his given name and the powerful position he was starting to covet, this pun on "Hank" is a remarkably apt word to use here!

[105] See Chapter 10.

interest in it."[106] His best moments are when he is working up one of his "effects," whether it is manipulating a solar eclipse, blowing up Merlin's tower, or unclogging the well at the Valley of Holiness to the accompaniment of fireworks. Hank Morgan glories in the attention he gets on these occasions; he is just a grown-up Tom Sawyer.[107]

This aspect of Hank Morgan's character recalls not only Tom but also another Connecticut Yankee of Mark Twain's own time. Showmanship (then and now) is synonymous with the name "Barnum."; Phineas T. Barnum was born in Bethel, Connecticut, and spent most of his life in and around Bridgeport.[108] At the time *A Connecticut Yankee* was written, he was not only still alive but was at the height of his fame.

Barnum was not only a showman—like Clemens, he was also a journalist, lecturer, and businessman who made fortunes and went bankrupt before ultimately dying a wealthy man. There is a lot of Barnum in Hank Morgan—and a lot of Samuel Clemens as well.[109]

[106.] See Chapter 31. Note that Hank's un-Yankee-like characteristics are Clemens' characteristics.

[107.] The affinity of the youthful Tom with the adult Hank has already been pointed out. See p.43, footnote # 22.

[108.] The Yankee takes Camelot for Bridgeport in the "Word of Explanation," with implications which I have already discussed on p. 84. Since Bridgeport and Barnum were synonymous, the mention of this city may have been a hint on Twain's part that "The Prince Of Humbugs" is present (if only in spirit) in *A Connecticut Yankee.*

[109.] We know what the young Samuel Clemens thought of Barnum's Museum when he saw it on his first visit to New York; he called it "a vast peanut stand" and asked "Why does not some philanthropist burn it down again?" (See Metzler, *Mark Twain Himself,* p. 85) Yet in later years,

Another of Hank Morgan's un-Yankee-like character traits is profligacy. He declares himself "one of the worst spendthrifts that ever was born."[110] The dinner that he throws for Marco, Dowley, and their friends is pure swank; Morgan enjoys showing off by spending money as much as by working miracles.

In fact, he enjoys conspicuous consumption to the point of deliberately humiliating Dowley, the well-to-do blacksmith, by his spending—as mean-spirited, a thing as a man could do. What is more, not only does Morgan enjoy distressing the blacksmith but he also demonstrates a sickening lack of empathy. "I don't know when I ever put a situation together better or got happier effects out of the materials available," he says. "I wouldn't have felt what [the blacksmith] was feeling, for anything in the world." Morgan shows not the slightest guilt for having made the poor blacksmith feel that way—he merely glories in his clever handling of the situation. Such thoughtlessness and callous disregard for the feelings of others is familiar to readers of *Tom Sawyer*.

By this time, it should be evident that Hank Morgan, the Connecticut Yankee, is something less than a paragon. In fact, he is depicted as a decidedly unattractive personality, but Twain presents this portrait with such subtlety that it is easy, as it was in the case of Tom Sawyer, for the reader to overlook the many character faults the Yankee exhibits. To do this is to invite serious misunderstanding of the novel, I suggest that failure to

---

Clemens not only became a Connecticut Yankee himself, but began to emulate Barnum's activities; of this, more later.

[110.] He might have been speaking with the voice of his creator. Samuel Clemens was born in poverty, and when he had some money, he spent it with reckless abandon. One year, he managed to put out $100,000 for dinners and entertainment, a sizeable sum today and a staggering figure for his times. The Yankee's blowout in Chapter 32 has nothing on the affairs his creator used to stage.

see through the character of Hank Morgan may be one of the reasons why *A Connecticut Yankee* has so often been misunderstood or dismissed without the consideration it deserves.

The Yankee also oozes overweening pride and is disgustingly condescending to those he believes to be his inferiors—that is, everybody in Arthurian England from the king on down. In Chapter 5, for example, he refers to himself as "a superior man." In Chapter 8, he calls himself "a giant among pygmies." He calls the Arthurians "white Indians," "children," "animals," and "rabbits."[111]He compares himself to Robinson Crusoe on his island, and to Columbus confounding the natives by taking advantage of an eclipse (which of course is precisely what he does himself in Chapter 6).[112]

Then there is Hank Morgan's love life. He admits to forty years of age, but his passion is for a fifteen-year-old telephone operator referred to in the book as "Puss Flanagan."[113]

Finally, the Yankee harps on the force of inherited ideas, and while he recognizes that he, too, is largely a product of his inculcated baggage, he fails to see that his ideas are not necessarily any better or more appropriate than those of the Arthurians. When he fails in his effort to remake sixth-century England in the image of nineteenth-century America, he is reduced to

---

[111.] See the many references in Chapters 2-8.

[112.] It is interesting to point out that for all his technical skills, the Yankee is of course no more a real magician than Merlin—and maybe less. Merlin does have one great power—he can put people to sleep, as he does in Chapter 3 as well as at the end of the book.

[113.] The great disparity in ages is a kind of red flag, calling attention to Hank Morgan's character. I think there is an explanation for it, which I shall present later in this manuscript.

calling the people whose thinking he failed to change "sheep" and "human muck" and himself a donkey.[114]

These character traits add up to a single, inevitable conclusion—that despite his superficial amiability and chatty style of speech, Hank Morgan is not a very nice person. Completely self-centered, obsessed by wealth and power, he is utterly incapable of seeing his own flaws even when he recognizes them in others. Add to this his fatal lack of appreciation for beauty or poetry, and his declared passion as a man of forty for the fifteen-year-old Puss Flanagan, and you have a man whose character is completely in keeping with his untrustworthiness as inferred from the structure of the novel.[115]

There is also another aspect of the Yankee to be considered—the name which Mark Twain bestowed upon him. "Hank Morgan" sounds innocuous enough—just a good old-fashioned American name. Yet on close examination, it reveals some deeper implications.

Was it accidental that Twain has Morgan share his name with Arthur's vile sister, Morgan LeFay, whose outstanding characteristic is her utterly callous and shameless use of others for her own amusement? It is easy to overlook, but Hank is guilty of precisely the same behavior. Compare Morgan LeFay's hanging the composer in Chapter 17 (an episode in which Hank participates) to Hank Morgan's hanging Sir Dinadan the Humorist in Chapter 40. Similarly, while LeFay finds imaginative ways to amuse herself with the prisoners in her dungeons, Hank

---

[114.] See Chapter 43. From rabbits to sheep is not a great distance; the real change is in Hank Morgan's recognizing his own folly in supposing he could change others. This is why he now sees himself as a "donkey"—which is a synonym for an ass.

[115.] As I have already noted, Hank Morgan is very much the adult Tom Sawyer might have grown up to be. See the footnote on p. 43.

does the same by degrading the knights errant; for example, his turning Sir Ozana le Cure Hardy into a plug-hat salesman in Chapter 21. He is not a whit less insensitive than she, and Twain seems to have been underscoring their similar characters by having them share the same name.[116]

The Yankee's name also has other implications. It must have been difficult for any American in the 1880s to encounter the name of Morgan without thinking of the famous financial family. The first banking Morgan, Junius S., was at that time still alive, and his son, the famous J. P. Morgan, headed the investment firm of Drexel, Morgan and Co. They made the name of Morgan analogous with business, money, and power. Bestowing it on the Yankee heightens the identification with late Victorian America and sharpens the focus of Mark Twain's satire.

Moreover, just as he demonstrates aspects of P. T. Barnum, Hank Morgan also shares an interest in money with his famous namesake. Nearly everything he engineers in Arthur's England stands to benefit him financially, and he is not bashful about taking his percentage.[117]

There is also another small but striking point, which emphasizes the identification between Hank Morgan and the peerless J. P. It is a little-known fact—I didn't realize it myself until I looked it up—that Junius Pierpont Morgan was a Connecticut

---

[116.] In the course of reading and rereading the *Connecticut Yankee*, I was amazed to discover that the central character's full name—"Hank Morgan"—appears only once in the entire novel. Moreover, while we have known his first name since Chapter 15, his full name does not appear until Chapter 39, when it is used in the newspaper story about his coming fight with Sir Sagramor. Also see my discussion of the Yankee's given name—Hank—on p. 148.

[117.] I have already discussed Hank Morgan's moneygrubbing on p. 163.

Yankee himself, born in Hartford in 1837.[118] Just how widely that would have been known in Mark Twain's time, I cannot say. But it is difficult to believe that the implications of the name "Hank Morgan" were unintended. I have not such a capacity for believing in coincidences.

Digesting all this material, we can reach some conclusions about Hank Morgan, the narrator of *A Connecticut Yankee*. From the use of the framing device, which has the effect of distancing Morgan's comments from Mark Twain; from the portrayal of the Yankee's character, which is keyed by his love of money, glory, and power, and marred by his insensitivity; and through the associations evoked by his name, we are forced to regard Hank Morgan as a less than sympathetic personality. We are prepared not to like him too much or to identify too closely with him. We find it difficult to believe in him because Mark Twain does not intend us to.

In short, Twain has depicted Hank Morgan in such a way that we are warned against accepting anything he says without deeper consideration. We have been prepared to take him as an unreliable narrator, and if we swallow everything he says uncritically, we will have done so only after disregarding the red flags Twain has put out for us.

The relevance of our attitude toward Hank Morgan is that it bears on our interpretation of the novel. Were Hank another Huck Finn, a character we instinctively like and trust, we would

---

[118.] Junius S. Morgan, the senior financier, who founded the family business, came originally from Massachusetts, where he was born in 1813. Eventually, he took over a London banking house, which he headed from the Civil War era until his death in 1890, the year after Twain published *A Connecticut Yankee*. His son, Junius Pierpont Morgan, entered the banking profession as American agent for his father; in 1871, when he was thirty-four, he founded his own firm. From that date until his death in 1913, J. P. Morgan was the foremost financier in the United States.

take his speeches praising his own Victorian America at the expense of Arthur's England as truth. Twain tries to warn us not to do so, by endowing his "hero" with very large feet of very soft clay. Hank Morgan and the society he stands for are the butt of the joke; if we fail to understand, it is because we have failed to heed the author's warning.

III
Recurring Themes

I have already pointed out how certain themes recur in Mark Twain's fiction, from *The Adventures of Tom Sawyer* onward. *A Connecticut Yankee in King Arthur's Court* presents a number of them.

One of these themes is conscience. In *Tom Sawyer* and *The Prince and the Pauper,* the hero's conscience urges him to do right, although not always successfully. In *Huckleberry Finn,* however, the dictates of conscience are "right" only in the context of the society which has inculcated them, and Huck does right only by going against what his conscience tells him to do. In the *Yankee,* Hank Morgan, too, encounters the dictates of his conscience, which makes him ask to see the prisoners in Morgan LeFay's dungeon.[119] He remarks at this point that if he had the remaking of man, "He wouldn't have any conscience. It is one of the most disagreeable things connected with a person, and although it certainly does a great deal of good, it cannot be said to pay, in the long run; it would be better to have less good and more comfort . . . I have noticed my conscience for years, and I know it is more trouble to me than anything else I started with."[120] After

---

[119.]   See Chapter 18.

[120.]   This is a particularly interesting remark, for with his "man-factories" and his attacks on chivalry, the Yankee is attempting this very thing—the

Huck Finn and the "Carnival of Crime" article, this is a relatively mild statement, but it illustrates that Mark Twain had not lost his concern with the question of whether one's conscience is worthwhile as a guide to positive behavior or whether it is simply a useless burden imposed by social conditioning.

In connection with the question of conscience and its worth, one should not be surprised to encounter (in Chapter 21) the attitude of the pilgrims toward the whipping of a girl slave; they all comment on the expert way in which the lash was handled. "They were too much hardened by lifelong every-day familiarity with slavery to notice that there was anything else in the exhibition that invited comment. That was what slavery could do, in the way of ossifying what one may call the superior lobe of human feeling; for these pilgrims were kind-hearted people, and they would not have allowed that man to treat a horse like that."

This passage demonstrates once again Twain's own feelings of shame about growing up in a slaveholding Hannibal without ever realizing that there was anything wrong with the "peculiar institution." One can also infer that not only chattel slavery (which was destroyed by the Civil War) but also wage slavery (which was very much a current concern in the 1880s) is implied in this passage; all the way back in Chapter 8, Hank equates bond slaves with "freemen," whom he describes as "slaves in fact, but without the name . . ." This is as true in Victorian America as in Arthurian England—and maybe more so.

A Connecticut Yankee also develops the theme of how action may be governed by the thoughtless acceptance of inappropriate

---

remaking of man. Mao Tse-Tung tried it, too, so did a number of perfectionist social experiments in the United States in the nineteenth century. None of these attempts seem to have succeeded any more than did the Yankee in the novel.

ideas. We saw this concept elaborated in *Huckleberry Finn* in the "Walter Scott" episode, in the feud, and in the general attitude of the frontier toward slavery. Now Twain reworks this theme under the heading of "inherited ideas," and it is a central idea in the novel.[121] Hank Morgan is forever complaining of the inability of the Arthurians to conceive of a reordering of society because of their inherited ideas about monarchy, nobility, and the Church. He never recognizes the extent to which he himself is controlled and limited by his own inherited ideas.

Take, for example, his first experience with armor, which appears in Chapter 12. Hank Morgan has ridden off with Sandy in search of the castle with the forty-five princesses imprisoned in it—though his first reaction to the idea of traveling together with an unchaperoned young lady is "it's scandalous."[122]

On the way, he finds his armor heating up in the sun to the point of extreme discomfort. Then comes darkness and the need to camp, but Hank can't take off his armor by himself and can't bring himself to have Sandy help him, even though he has clothes on underneath, "because it would have seemed like undressing before folk." So he suffers the pains of his iron straitjacket because his mental straitjacket will not permit him to do the rational thing.

Another familiar theme which surfaces in the *Yankee* is the cowardice of mobs. In Chapter 30, the Yankee and the king encounter the charcoal burner who has helped to hang his

---

[121.] It is also central to *Pudd'nhead Wilson;* see my discussion pp. 95-96.

[122.] Hank Morgan never does get over his Victorian morality—in Chapter 41, he tells us that he finally married Sandy for no other reason than his New England sense of propriety, which considers that she would be "compromised" sooner or later by traveling around with him. "She couldn't see how . . . ," but then, she hadn't inherited nineteenth-century ideas.

innocent neighbors after the murder of the local baron; Morgan gets him to admit that he did so out of fear for his own life and those of his associates as well. This incident is not quite a parallel to the failed lynching of Colonel Sherburn in *Huck,* but the similarities are sufficient to make the point—man as part of a mob will do that which he alone would not attempt, but the mob at bottom is made up of cowards.

Identity switching makes another appearance in the *Yankee* as well. Arthur assumes the role of a farmer when he goes with The Boss to investigate the country, and Hank Morgan avails himself of disguises on several occasions. Merlin assumes the aspect of an old woman at the end of the story.

This "disguise" theme is, of course, closely related to the question of whether indeed clothes make the man or whether there is some inborn distinction between people apart from that conferred by their social position. In the *Yankee,* Hank Morgan keeps asserting that "training is everything" that "we have no nature, we have no thoughts of our own, no opinions of our own: they are transmitted to us, trained into us [Chapter 18]." Yet he recognizes the true nobility of King Arthur when he risks infection in the smallpox hut and that of Sir Launcelot when he helps nurse the sick Hello Central. Just as the question of how nobility of character is created is left unanswered in *Huck Finn,* it is similarly unresolved here. One thing can be said; while he never defines it in so many words, nobility of character for Twain means the willingness to put others first without expectation of any reward, even when it costs something to do so. Arthur risks his life in the smallpox hut; Launcelot gives up the chance to make a killing on the stock market to nurse The Boss's child.[123]

[123.] This takes place in Chapter 40. Later, Clarence describes how Sir Launcelot, a bear in the market, did engineer a stock coup that skinned many a knight and incited two of his victims, Mordred and Agravaine,

This true nobility of character is lacking in the Yankee himself; he always acts with an eye toward what he can get out of the venture. Nor is it to be found in the other knights, among the freemen of the realm, or even among the slaves. It is not the product of religious fealty—Hank remarks that whatever else they may have been, the nobility of Arthur's England were deeply and enthusiastically religious—or of conscience. It is a quality independent of all apparent origins, and it is found in those in whom it is found. The great unanswered question in *A Connecticut Yankee* as in *Huckleberry Finn* is "what is the source of good conduct?"

In my analysis of *Huck,* I raised the two possible answers to this vital question.[124]One can take a Rousseauian view and assert that man is naturally good and that his evils are the product of bad societies corrupting or twisting his basic inclinations. In this view, Huck's escape from the slaveholding society of which he was at least tangentially a part allows his natural goodness to come forward and demonstrate itself in his decision not to betray Jim but to help steal him out of bondage.

But I also pointed out that there is an alternative explanation—that Huck really believes that his action is evil that he will go to hell for it and that the fact that what he does turns out to be "right" or "good" is simply an accident. In this

---

to get revenge on Launcelot by informing the guileless King Arthur of the continuing affair between the peerless knight and Queen Guenever. This action results in civil war, disaster, and eventually the Interdict and the Yankee's destruction (Chapter 42). Incidentally, it is in connection with the Launcelot/Guenever romance that Hank Morgan gets off one of the worst puns in American literature. He says, in Chapter 26, "I never meddled in these matters [illicit couplings], they weren't my affair . . ." That one should produce no less than a chorus of groans.

124. See p. 138.

view, man has no basic nature, there is no moral center in the universe, and there is no way to define any objective good or to teach it to others. Morgan LeFay is no better or worse than Hank Morgan—they merely reflect the accepted values of different epochs.[125]

The more optimistic, Rousseauian view is possible in *Huckleberry Finn* because Huck is outside any social structure, partly by circumstance and partly by choice. It is more difficult to justify in *A Connecticut Yankee,* however, because Hank Morgan is so closely identified with the society of the United States in the Industrial Age. He does not represent, cannot represent "natural man" as Huck does. Moreover, he is an adult, not an untutored boy; his socialization is complete. Unless the world to which he belongs can be said to represent the inherent natural goodness of man (which it surely does not), we are barred from finding the origin of good actions in Hank's inherent nature.

Indeed, we have a clear example to the contrary. Perhaps the best thing Hank Morgan does in the novel is to marry Sandy and become the parent of Hello Central. His marriage, insofar as we see it, is no less than idyllic, and his love for the child clearly manifest. Yet he admits that he married Alisande La Carteloise more or less by accident; she insisted on traveling everywhere with him, since she conceived of herself as his property by custom of chivalry; and Hank, with his New England morality and rigid ideas of propriety, married her only when he saw that

---

[125.] Writing to Mary Fairbanks in November 1886, Mark Twain called the *Yankee* a "contrast" of life in Arthur's time and in his own. This somewhat puzzling description of the book may make more sense in the context of the present discussion.

he could not get rid of her. That the marriage worked out so perfectly was nothing more than pure chance.[126]

It appears, then, that *A Connecticut Yankee* is philosophically one step beyond *Huckleberry Finn.* In the earlier book, it is still possible to believe that in the absence of guidance from social standards, religion or conscience, man can still rely on innate natural goodness as a guide to conduct. In the *Yankee* that escape hatch is closed, and we are forced to confront the terrifying idea that the world is amoral, and that "good" or "right" conduct occurs only by accident.[127] The discovery that a moral vacuum is at the center of the universe is the underlying idea of *A Connecticut Yankee.*

So bleak and so horrifying is this concept that it should be no surprise when the theme of "dream versus reality" also takes center stage in this novel. One way of escaping from a vision of terror is to dismiss it as merely a dream, and *A Connecticut Yankee* abounds in dreams which may or may not be real.

Just after arriving in Camelot and getting his first view of the Table Round, Hank Morgan falls asleep in his dungeon cell. He wakes with the thought that he has been dreaming the whole adventure, and is disabused of this notion only when Clarence informs him that he is to be burned at the stake the next day.[128] Furthermore, just as the Yankee's narrative begins with a confusion between dream state and reality, so does it close; in the "Final P.S. by M.T.," Hank takes Mark's voice for Sandy's and,

---

[126.] See Chapter 41. That Twain's comments might also refer to Clemens' own marriage, which was a signal success although his original motivation in choosing a mate may be questioned, I merely point out.

[127.] Thus, Huck Finn does good while believing himself to be doing evil, and Hank Morgan works ultimate evil while convinced that he is doing good.

[128.] See Chapter 5.

believing himself to be back in the sixth century, raves about his horrible dream of being in the nineteenth. For him, the dream has become reality, and reality the dream. Unable to distinguish between the two, he has reached the state Tom Sawyer pondered after visiting the Haunted House, and the state Mark Twain contemplated in his last work, *The Mysterious Stranger.*[129]

Nor is the theme of dream vs. reality confined to Hank Morgan. It also applies to Mark Twain himself.

One can see the entire tale of the Yankee and his manuscript as Twain's own dream, induced by his meeting the lunatic at Warwick Castle that afternoon, by a dark and stormy night, by his "dipping into Malory's enchanting book" and by a handy bottle of Scotch. We may be dealing with a dream within a dream—a completely unique literary device, as far as I am aware. I shall take up the question of why Mark Twain may have employed such a remarkable device in due course.

Perceptive readers will have no trouble recognizing other characteristic Mark Twain motifs in the *Yankee.* One, for example, is the idea of escape, so prominent in *Huckleberry Finn.* It is perhaps not without significance that where Huck successfully evades not only his father, all the sentinels searching for Jim and eventually "sivilization" itself, the Yankee's escape from slavery is

---

[129.] Hank Morgan also has other dreams in which the two centuries become confused. In Chapter 41, for example, while living in the sixth century, he dreams of his lost love Puss Flanagan, the telephone girl in the nineteenth. So often does he mutter "Hello Central" in his dreams that Sandy, taking the phrase to be the name ". . . of some lost darling of mine," confers it on their daughter. Incidentally, he refers to the child as "the center of the universe"; given the moral vacuum which the book discovers there, this is a fair description of the Yankee's attitude—and probably of his creator's as well.

foiled and he survives only as the object of a dramatic and comic rescue.[130]

Another familiar theme is that of superstition, which (as in *Tom Sawyer* and *Huckleberry Finn*) is treated with disdain, yet to a degree turns out to be triumphant after all. It is Merlin, the Yankee's chief object of ridicule, who makes those curious passes in the air over The Boss's head at the end of the manuscript.[131]

Other familiar themes will also be apparent. Whatever else one can say about *A Connecticut Yankee,* one fact about the book is beyond dispute—nobody but Mark Twain could have written it.

IV
Language

I have remarked that the brilliance of *Huckleberry Finn* is due in no small degree to the marvelous rendering of American vernacular speech with which that novel abounds.

By setting the *Yankee* in old England, Mark Twain immediately forfeited this particular asset—perhaps his greatest literary talent. Yet when it comes to language, *A Connecticut Yankee* is not without merit.

We may discount, I think, Twain's presentation of Arthurian speech. However effectively he uses "an" for "if", and "marry" and "mayhap" and all the other linguistic antiquities, they are not reported speech; these words are simply Malory transposed from one printed page to another.

[130.] See Chapters 36-38.

[131.] I have already discussed Merlin's notoriously unsuccessful career as a magician and noted his only true power—the ability to put people to sleep. See footnote 112 on p. 166.

But Twain does have some field for use of his great gift in the language of Hank Morgan himself.

Hank, to begin with, does not sound at all like Huck. He speaks an American vernacular, to be sure, but it is the vernacular of a lower-middle-class artisan with pretensions to business success who comes from New England. His speech is therefore completely different from Huck Finn's, yet it is recognizably American. Hank's conversational style is chatty but somewhat edged with irony. He is fond of puns (something completely foreign to Huck or Tom Sawyer, by the way), and his vocabulary is reasonably large. He has an authoritative tone appropriate for a foreman with a couple of thousand "rough men" under him. In short, he is another of Twain's linguistic triumphs—a character whom we get to know and understand in part through his own speech. If he does not emerge as colorfully as Huck, it may be because his segment of American society did not speak with the same fascinating vernacular as the Southwestern frontier.

Two of Morgan's speech characteristics are worth noting; his favorite expression of surprise, shock, or horror is "Great Scott!" which would be innocent enough if we did not know Mark Twain's feelings about the work of Sir Walter. When we are aware of Twain's attitude about Scott's overromanticism, the Yankee's using his name (even accidentally) can only be seen as ironic.[132]

Hank Morgan also uses the term "Sheol" frequently. For those unfamiliar with this word, it is a euphemism for hell,

---

[132.] Twain gets in a jab at Sir Walter in Chapter 4, where he mentions the earthiness of Arthurian speech as compared with Sir Walter's idealized (and sanitized) dialogue: "The soft Lady Rowena would embarrass a tramp in our day." For the author of "1601," this is perhaps a valid criticism—but then, Twain was careful to idealize and sanitize the dialogue in the *Yankee* too.

deriving from the Hebrew. Hank's common resort to it indicates that such usage was current in the Hartford of the 1880s[133]

Perhaps Hank's most important verbal characteristic, however, is what might be called his unconscious ironies. Time and time again, he makes critical statements about others, without ever realizing that the same comments could also refer to himself. For example, he asserts that "a magician who believes in his own magic" is "an old numbskull" who can never thrive while handicapped by such a superstition. He is speaking of Merlin, but at the end of the novel, we realize that the same comment applies to the Yankee as well.[134]

This verbal technique is, of course, part of the author's subtle presentation of the *Connecticut Yankee* as a satiric work, the butt of which is the Yankee and his society. Hank's utterances prepare the way for the reader to see the true object of attack.

There is also one other small point involving Hank Morgan and his language. In Chapter 13, while discussing the exploited state of "freemen" in Arthur's England, he says, "What [they] needed was a new deal." There are a number of ideas about where Franklin D. Roosevelt got the term he used for his anti-Depression measures, but one thing is certain—it appeared in this novel, which was published in 1889, forty-four years before FDR came to power. He certainly could have picked up the term from the *Yankee,* although I cannot show that he did.

It should be enough to conclude that if *A Connecticut Yankee* lacks the linguistic virtuosity of *Huckleberry Finn,* still it demonstrates Mark Twain's great talent for creating a character

---

[133.] There are other echoes of the Hebrew Scriptures in the book; the Yankee compares himself to Joseph's rise in Egypt, and the unwillingness of the people to believe in Hank, even when miracle follows miracle, is reminiscent of the Israelites in the Wilderness.

[134.] See Chapter 22.

out of words, and for using speech to underscore his irony and satire.

V
Comparing Huckleberry Finn and the Connecticut Yankee

I have pointed out the structural similarity between *The Adventures of Huckleberry Finn* and *A Connecticut Yankee in King Arthur's Court*. The two novels are of parallel form, both using a tripartite, three-act plan conforming to the traditional "exposition, development, resolution" pattern. The difference is that while in *Huck Finn* the parts are perfectly balanced, in the *Yankee*, the central section is too long and the resolution too short so that the book is noticeably lopsided.

But this is far from the only similarity between the two books. In fact, they are so similar in both intent and design that they may be said to be brothers, if not precisely twins.

After the success of *Huckleberry Finn*, Twain returned again to the novel of manners and morals when he wrote the *Yankee*. He employed the same device—the first-person narration—with the same purpose, to expose the enormous flaws in the smug, self-confident, often thoughtless, and sometimes cruel America he knew. His tools were the same; humor, irony, and satire. His problem was the same; to write a critical novel which aimed at large sales in an environment where the principal purchasers of books were genteel ladies of the established class who were unlikely to buy such a work. His solution was the same; to obfuscate the social criticism behind the mask of humor and to make his attack indirect by means of satire and irony.

The result, however, was not the same. *Huckleberry Finn*, despite all the violence and tragedy in it, remains on the whole a joyous book, a pleasure to read. The *Yankee*, despite its many marvelous comic moments, is a bitter, disquieting book, anything but summer beach reading. In this, and in many lesser ways, *Huckleberry Finn* and *A Connecticut Yankee* appear as mirror images, alike but opposite.

Take the narrative device. As I have said, Twain repeated the first-person technique in the *Yankee,* but the differences in character between Huck and Hank leads us to trust the boy but distrust the man. We like Huck, who is frank, open, and (apart from his petty thievery and adept lying) basically honest. We are meant to believe in him, and we do. But we dislike the Yankee, who is self-serving, pretentious, and altogether too fond of himself. We are meant to suspect him, for his account of the tale is unreliable. To put it in other words, while Huck and Hank are similar, our responses to what they say are intentionally colored by the differences in their characters. Just as the structural similarity of the two novels is altered by the *Yankee*'s lack of balance, so the narrative device is modified by the differences between the narrators.

The novels are also mirror images in another way. In *Huck,* Twain took a character loosely integrated into his village society in the first place, then disengaged him completely from his home and used him to explore and expose its corruption, its cruelty and its thoughtlessness. At the end, Huck becomes an active opponent of this society's basic social institution, and ultimately finds his own resolution by escaping from "sivilization." In the *Yankee,* the central character, far from being a social outsider, is firmly and intimately representative of his world. He is sent to explore and contrast another society temporally as well as physically removed from his own, and while he does indeed expose its considerable failings, he never realizes the extent to which his own society shares them. At the end, he attacks the basic social institution of Arthurian England—knighthood—with far more success than Huck attacks slavery, and in fact, he destroys it; but the result is the destruction of his own parallel civilization as well, and for Hank, there is no escape to the territory. He dies insane. The technique and the social criticisms are similar, but the results are opposite.

The most glaring example of this mirror imagery, I suggest, can be seen in the endings of the two novels. In each instance, Mark Twain was faced with the problem of finding a satisfactory conclusion for a story which had no natural stopping place. In *Huckleberry Finn*, he found his ending by employing comic satire. In the *Yankee*, he resorted to tragic mysticism, and the result is far less satisfactory.

The last twelve chapters of *Huck* have been roundly criticized for generations, but in my view, they are the most brilliant thing in the book. The proper target of criticism is the last six chapters of the *Yankee*, which are telescoped, confused, and which leave the reader vaguely unsatisfied and wondering what the point of the novel really is.

This last section of the *Yankee* demands a closer look. After the climax reached by the rescue of King Arthur and The Boss at the end of Chapter 38, the last section of the book begins with a note of relaxation created by the words, "Home again, at Camelot." Quickly, however, a new conflict is developed, as the Yankee prepares to meet Sir Sagramor Le Desirous to resolve the challenge first made in Chapter 9. The duel is tragicomic, for its participants are a mailed knight on horseback against a cowboy with a lasso. As Hank unhorses Sir Sag, and after him seven more knights (ending with Sir Launcelot himself), the scene is the stuff of laughter—the grand and the pompous deflated by the insignificant. But when Merlin, the Yankee's arch-enemy, steals the lasso and Sir Sagramor comes at Hank with sword in hand and murder in his smile, the scene turns ugly. The Yankee is forced to use his pistol, killing first Sir Sag and afterward several other knights before the rest are put to flight. The Yankee crows in triumph, "Knight-errantry was a doomed institution. The march of civilization was begun."

The irony here is that the Yankee's "civilization" starts with killing by firearms—that is, by technology applied to the production of corpses (it is destined to end the same way). There is plenty of killing in Arthur's England, but the means are primitive and the capacity for wholesale slaughter lacking. The Yankee's introduction of nineteenth-century technology remedies this condition: where Arthur's throne rested on the murder and violent subjugation of a relative few, the Yankee's world is based on the ability to kill by the thousands.

That world is revealed in Chapter 40, and for three years, the Yankee rides high, exulting in his domination of the land and planning a future in which a Republic should replace the monarchy (with Hank Morgan as president). At this point, we find a strange interpolation in the text. Sandy rushes in to report that Hello Central is ill, and the parents nurse her with the aid of Sir Launcelot. Eventually, the doctors prescribe a sea voyage, so the Yankee, Sandy, and the child go off to France.

What makes this tale so peculiar is that at this point we do not even know that The Boss has married Sandy, let alone that they have a child. The story is out of place, injected out of context and completely unprepared. The situation is explained in the next chapter, but a mistake of this magnitude is quite uncharacteristic of Twain, and it seems inexplicable. Perhaps the fact that these final chapters were written under financial pressure and with the distractions of the Hartford social season may account for the lapse.[135]

In Chapter 41, the Yankee's new England falls apart. He returns to England to find the country in the grip of the Interdict. He makes his way to Camelot in disguise.[136]

---

[135] See Kaplan, p. 350.

[136] I am struck by the satiric implications of the phrase "new England." After all, the Yankee comes from Connecticut, which is in New England, and it

Chapter 42 includes Clarence's narration of the events which led to the Interdict, and his preparations for defense at Merlin's Cave.[137] With everything prepared for a stand, the Yankee takes the offensive by proclaiming his Republic.

It enjoys widespread support—for about a day. Then all England, led by the remaining thirty thousand knights, comes marching against Hank Morgan and his crew barricaded in Merlin's Cave. Here is one of Twain's most devastating ironies—what kind of democratic republic must protect itself from its citizens behind a mine field, a moat and a set of electric fences overshot by Gatling guns?[138]

What follows is an orgy of destruction and homicide unprecedented in American literature. First, the Yankee blows up his modern industrial society. Next the land mines, the electric fences, the water-filled moat, and the Gatling guns kill twenty-five thousand knights.[139] The Yankee and his fifty-three followers win a victory more one-sided than Agincourt. Yet the victory turns out to be Pyrrhic, for the rotting corpses will kill the victors. The Yankee lacks the guts to write the end of his story; it

---

is the world of 1885 New England, which he tries to introduce to Arthur's realm. Does the failure of the Yankee's "new England" not imply the failure of his own New England as well?

[137] Note how Clarence takes over the end of the *Yankee,* even more completely than Huck takes over the end of *Tom Sawyer.*

[138] Note that the Yankee sets up his citadel of the new Republic at Merlin's Cave, symbol of the same superstition and witchcraft he has attempted to exorcise. Whatever comes out of Merlin's Cave is not to be trusted.

[139] Twain's vision of mass murder by technology is an uncanny foretaste of the war on the Western Front between 1914 and 1918—a full twenty-five years after the publication of the *Yankee.* The author would not live to see his grim vision brought to life, but it would not have surprised him if he had.

is left for Clarence to pen the ending in Chapter 44, where all die but Morgan himself, who is put to sleep by Merlin and destined to awake only after thirteen centuries. Finally, comes the "P.S. by M.T.," which describes the stranger's confusion of dreams with reality and his ultimate death. The Yankee's experiment in bringing the nineteenth century to Arthur's England ends in mass murder and insanity.

All these events follow so quickly upon one another that the reader can easily become confused, and the glaring error in Chapter 40 does not make it any easier to follow the plot. The sure command of the story line, which Twain demonstrated in *Huckleberry Finn,* is absent in *A Connecticut Yankee.* The careful building and relaxing of tension which marks the last part of *Huck* is lacking too; the Yankee's apparent victory comes too soon, and the terrible result follows it so quickly that the full impact of the irony is lost. The Yankee's Gotterdammerung—his twilight as a god—occupies a mere three pages of the text.

In addition, the lighthearted tone of *Huck Finn,* which not only masks the satiric attack but also makes the book such a delightful read, is absent in the last section of the *Yankee.* Instead, the reader is left disquieted and depressed. It would not be exaggerating to say that *The Adventures of Huckleberry Finn* is a comic book with tragic underpinnings; its mirror image, *A Connecticut Yankee in King Arthur's Court,* is a tragic novel spiced with comedic passages. The true nature of each work is revealed in its concluding section.

I have already mentioned that the *Yankee* is seriously unbalanced—a major structural flaw. Consider this: the last section of *Huck* (Chapters 32-43) is almost exactly 25 percent of the entire novel. The resolution of *A Connecticut Yankee,* by comparison, occupies less than 15 percent of the text. All signs point to the probability that Clemens was growing increasingly pessimistic as his financial problems mounted and increasingly obsessed with finishing the novel as Paige finished the typesetting machine.[140] Finally, Twain seems to have thrown up his hands and written this strangely powerful, yet desperately vicious, pessimistic conclusion and sent the book off to the printers, even though he knew better than anyone that its ending was less than satisfactory—hence that famous letter to Howells.[141]

In fact, it might have been possible for Twain to find a better ending for the book. The Yankee might have been made to suffer another blow on the head (perhaps from Sir Sagramor's lance) and returned to the nineteenth century, subsequently recognizing its deadly correlation with the worst facets of the sixth. This is essentially the device Swift used in *Gulliver's Travels,* where the satiric point is made perfectly clear by its employ. Alternatively, perhaps, Twain could have repeated the technique used in *Huckleberry Finn* and written a comic conclusion masking the pointed satire beneath an outbreak of laughter. Because he did not, *A Connecticut Yankee* is not only Twain's most powerful satire and his bitterest irony but also his most haunting, most unsettling novel.

If *Huckleberry Finn* and *A Connecticut Yankee* share significant similarities, they also show clear differences. One of these is technical—the question of length.

I have already remarked that one of the most striking aspects of *Huckleberry Finn* is its remarkable economy of means. There is hardly a wasted word in the book, and while Mark Twain's works sometimes suffer from excessive discursiveness (i.e., *Life on the Mississippi*) there is none of this in *Huck.*

By contrast, *A Connecticut Yankee* is not only notably longer than its predecessor but it is also much less taut. Parts of the book ramble on and on; the discussion of free trade vs. protectionism occupies three chapters of blatant preaching,

---

[140.] See Kaplan, p. 343.

[141.] Quoted in a footnote on p. 82.

and if Twain had omitted Chapter 15, "Sandy's Tale," altogether, I for one would not have missed it a bit. The sure control of his material, which Twain displayed in *Huck Finn,* is too often missing in the *Yankee.* Perhaps 10 percent of the manuscript could have been cut, removing several thousand words of pure lard and leaving a tighter, better-written book. Clearly, the lack of economy in the *Yankee* is one reason why it is inferior to the earlier masterpiece.

Another is characterization. The galaxy of colorful, carefully drawn, and marvelously vivid personalities inhabiting *Huckleberry Finn* finds no comparison in the later book. Neither Hank Morgan himself nor any of the other characters in the *Yankee* step off the pages the way Huck, Jim, and so many other characters in *Huckleberry Finn* do. King Arthur, Merlin, Sandy, even Sir Launcelot are merely characters in a book—none of them truly come alive. Indeed, the only person in the book who almost does is Clarence, the page who becomes The Boss's right-hand man. This may be partly because other than Hank Morgan and Sandy, Clarence is the only significant character in the novel created by Twain himself; the others are all delineated in Malory. But even Clarence is no Pap Finn, and Alisande Le Carteloise is no Aunt Sally or Judith Loftus.[142] The people in *Huck Finn* come to life; the characters in the *Yankee* remain in the pages.

There are doubtless many other comparisons to be made between Mark Twain's two great novels of the eighties, but at the risk of neglecting something of importance, I will now go on to

---

[142.] She may, however, be in large measure Livy Clemens. She is described as a "flawless wife and mother," words which Samuel Clemens used in reference to his own consort on more than one occasion. She also exhibits a blind love for Hank Morgan, whose complexities she never understands or even sees.

discuss some implications of the *Connecticut Yankee* which appear to me to have significance.

VI
Interpreting the Yankee

What, then, can we make of *A Connecticut Yankee in King Arthur's Court*?

That the novel is a satire can no longer be in doubt. But we can and should go one step further with analysis: why did Twain describe the book as "a contrast" between the two worlds the Yankee inhabits?

I suggest that this question would be easier if the author had used the near synonym "a comparison." All the evils and virtues Hank Morgan discovers in King Arthur's sixth century England have their counterparts in President Arthur's nineteenth century America. Comparing the two societies, we must conclude that neither is either superior nor inferior to the other. The thirteenth centuries which lie between Morgan LeFay and Hank Morgan may have produced prodigies of technology, but they have made no change in the basic nature of humankind. Adam's children remain what they have always been—a conflicted species capable of the greatest good and equally of the greatest evil, sometimes simultaneously. The Victorians in both England and America at the time Twain was writing sincerely believed that their technologically exploding world had all the answers, and that the perfect society was sure to arrive in a relatively short time. In the *Connecticut Yankee* Mark Twain challenges this naïve belief: his vision of the future in which the flawed human race achieves enormous power through technology but still lacks a moral compass to check its misuse is necessarily dark, and the end of the novel appallingly grim.

Charles Neider applied the term "subversive" to this novel, and to the smug self-satisfaction of the Victorian period that is precisely what it is. No wonder Mark Twain adopted the framing device in addition to his other tools of literary sleight of hand: Samuel Clemens, apparently an avatar of Victorian standards, wanted no responsibility or criticism for this devastating attack on the world in which he moved while yet recognizing its shortcomings. In brief, the ultimate subject of *The Connecticut Yankee in King Arthur's Court* is the same as that of *Huckleberry Finn*—the damned human race.

Certainly, this is Mark Twain's most difficult, most complicated, and most frustrating book. It is no accident that so many lovers of *Tom Sawyer* and *Huckleberry Finn* have never read it, or that so many people who have read it come away with a vague feeling that they have not understood it very well.

The *Yankee* is also Twain's most uneven novel. Parts of it are brilliant and powerful, other sections drag dully. The book lacks the linguistic perfection of *Huckleberry Finn*, and its structural plan is twisted out of shape. It suffers from inferior character depiction and even more from excessive length and overhaste.

Yet with all that, the *Yankee* remains a novel of splendid imagination and rare power, both completely original and totally unique. It is a deeper, more heartfelt book than *Tom Sawyer*, and infinitely more thoughtful than *The Prince and the Pauper*, Twain's previous attempt to set a story in an old English context. If it fails to achieve the artistic perfection of its mirror image and predecessor, *The Adventures of Huckleberry Finn*, it is only fair to remark that no other American novel does so either.

The *Yankee* was completed in May 1889 and published that December. This was at least a year and a half before Clemens' growing financial distress, the product of his family's extravagant lifestyle coupled with the unceasing and ever-increasing burden of financing the Paige typesetting machine, drove the author, his wife and their daughters from their beloved Hartford home and into self-exile in Europe. It was almost five years before the effects of the Panic of 1893 and the failure of the Charles Webster

Publishing House drove Samuel Clemens into bankruptcy; and it was a full seven years before the most crushing blow of all, the death of Susy in 1896. If Clemens' world was tottering in 1889, still it had not fallen down; yet the novel clearly reflects a significant darkening of the author's vision. Indeed, of all his works, only the posthumous *Mysterious Stranger* is so bleakly pessimistic.

It can hardly be claimed, then, that Mark Twain was a bright, effervescent, and optimistic personality until his business failure and personal tragedies turned him into the haunted, bitter man he ultimately became. The uncomplicated, sunny humorist never really existed. There was always in Twain's psychological makeup a darker side, which expressed itself in his work as bitter social criticism and barbed attacks on the pompous, the presumptuous, and the cruel. We have already seen how even in so early a work as *Tom Sawyer*, the cloudy side of his personality presents itself quite clearly (if perhaps more subtly) than in his later books. In the *Yankee*, to follow up on the metaphor, there are more storm clouds than there is sunshine; yet those clouds gathered thickly even while to all appearances Samuel Clemens' life remained largely undistressed.

The operative words here are "to all appearances," for it seems likely that something must have occurred in Clemens' own life which caused Mark Twain to adopt an increasingly pessimistic and more acutely critical attitude toward the world in which he lived.

One obvious problem was the author's business mistake in accepting sole responsibility for the financial backing of the Paige typesetting machine. His motive in doing so was the oldest in human experience—the pursuit of great wealth. He saw the typesetter as a golden path to almost uncountable riches and either did not see or chose to ignore the increasingly clear signals that it would never reach the market, let alone corner it. But Clemens was always ready to chase the will-o'-the-wisp of easy money, particularly big money. He sought it as a silver miner in Nevada, as a would-be playwright, as an inventor, and finally as an investor. He seems never to have followed the advice his alter ego wrote into *Huckleberry Finn*—"overreaching don't pay."

I am not convinced, however, that Clemens' disastrous surrender to the Paige fantasy entirely accounts for his distressed mental state in the late eighties. After all, he kept pouring money into the machine because he anticipated enormous profits from it, and as late as 1894, he still had reason to believe in its success. Financing the machine was a terrible burden, to be sure, but his optimism about it remained undimmed while he was writing the *Connecticut Yankee*. According to Kaplan, he actually saw what appeared to be a successful demonstration of the Paige typesetter in action in January 1889, five months before completing his manuscript.[143] It seems to me, then, that we must look for some other factor which weighed on Mark Twain's mind at the time he wrote the book, and I think there are some clues in the text which suggest the direction in which we must turn our attention.

First, there is the use of the framing device, distinguishing Hank Morgan from Mark Twain, and its associated concept, the presentation of the narrative as a dream within a dream. Why, we must ask, did the author employ so much misdirection, creating another layer between Samuel Clemens and Hank Morgan, setting up a persona beyond his Mark Twain persona, distancing himself even further from the story he was telling?

One answer may be the old problem of selling a biting novel of social criticism to the pillars of the order under attack. This was the problem Mark Twain faced in much of his work, and he solved it satisfactorily by use of satire, irony, and humor. The excellent sales figures for *Huckleberry Finn* were ample proof that

---

[143.] See Kaplan, p. 343.

the tactic worked; why then, in the *Yankee,* did the author go beyond it?

I believe that the use of the obfuscating device of the frame and the dreams were employed to assure that the personality behind the masks of Mark Twain and Hank Morgan—the personality of Samuel Clemens—should remain hidden. His own feelings were kept carefully out of sight; whatever heresies the novel contained could be attributed to his persona or his character, and no one could hold him responsible for what they expressed. The guilt for expressing the inexpressible should never be his.

I have already observed that what Samuel Clemens did was frequently the opposite of what Mark Twain wrote, and in fact was often the very target which Twain was attacking. It was Clemens who overlooked the evil of slavery all around him during his Missouri youth, and it was Twain who wrote of the cost of thoughtlessness; it was Clemens who was obsessed with getting rich quick, and it was Twain who counseled, "Overreaching Don't Pay"; it was Clemens who played the respectable gentlemen of means, with his fantastic house and his expensive entertaining; it was Twain who created and then punctured the Connecticut Yankee and all his pretensions.

I am not the first to suggest that the author's two personalities seemed to grow further and further apart in his middle years. As Clemens' life became increasingly troubled, he found he could escape by assuming his alter ego and becoming Mark Twain. It is almost as if there were two distinct and opposing personalities occupying the same body.

Indeed, the *Yankee* hints at a disintegration of personality which appears to have begun in Samuel Clemens/Mark Twain much earlier than has usually been thought—as early as 1886 or 1887. There is a clue to this in the opening pages of the book, when Mark Twain is approached by the stranger while touring Warwick Castle. The first words the stranger speaks are, "You know about transmigration of souls; do you know about the transposition of epochs—and bodies?"[144] A psychiatrist might find this comment pregnant with meaning in the light of the Clemens/Twain personality divergence.

The pertinent question, then, is what was driving the two sides of the author further apart? The apparent engine was guilt.

It is well known that Samuel Clemens felt deep guilt from early childhood, which only intensified in his later life. We find little to indicate that guilt interfered with his life prior to his marriage and move to the East; but it became an increasingly important and debilitating force afterward. By the time the *Yankee* was written (1886-1889), the two sides of the author's personality had grown so far apart that Mark Twain was criticizing the conduct of Samuel Clemens. That may be another way of saying that Samuel Clemens was feeling uncomfortably guilty about the way he was living his life and was able to cope with his feelings only by assuming his Mark Twain mask and turning his scorn on his other self.

I shall leave aside for the moment the reasons why I believe that Clemens' lifelong guilt intensified after age thirty-five; that discussion properly belongs in a later chapter. For the time being, I shall point out that the *Yankee* criticizes by means of satire, the standards and morals of late Victorian America, and, more specifically, the conduct of certain of its leading citizens—Barnum, Morgan, and another Connecticut resident named Clemens. If there is a lot of young Sam Clemens in Tom Sawyer, a character who is demolished by Mark Twain in his earlier books, there is just as much of the adult Samuel Clemens in Hank Morgan. It seems apparent to me, at least, that one of Mark Twain's principal targets in the book is his own alter ego.

[144.] See "A Word of Explanation," which precedes the narrative.

Samuel Clemens chased money all during his life—big money, as quickly come by as possible; Hank Morgan's lust for wealth is pilloried in the novel.

Samuel Clemens was ruining himself and his family financially through his uncritical acceptance of the Paige typesetting machine and its promise of countless riches; Hank Morgan is ruined because he will not see that his idea of a nation is not appropriate for Arthur's time and rushes ahead with his plans out of desire for power and money.

Samuel Clemens spent money wildly, perhaps because he had so little of it as a boy. Hank Morgan describes himself as "one of the worst spendthrifts that ever was born."

Samuel Clemens loved public attention and adulation. So does Hank Morgan (and so does Tom Sawyer too).

Samuel Clemens was beset by attacks of conscience. So is Hank Morgan (and so is Huckleberry Finn).

In all these instances, Mark Twain takes advantage of the close parallels between those two Connecticut Yankees, Morgan, and Clemens. His attacks on the first are patent attacks on the second.[145]

[145.] In the comparisons between Hank Morgan and Samuel Clemens, consider what might have happened had Clemens not had the support and financial backing of Henry H. Rogers. It was Rogers who engineered Clemens' bankruptcy, saving the precious Mark Twain copyrights and the Hartford house for the family by getting Livy named as a preferred creditor. It was Rogers, who finally got Clemens to accept the fact that the Paige machine was a total failure and had to be written off. It was Rogers, who not only got Clemens' creditors to accept fifty cents on the dollar for what they were owed, but then arranged the round-the-world lecture tour and subsequent travel book, from which the profits allowed Clemens to pay off all the creditors in full. That restored the author's credibility with the public and at least a measure of his own self-esteem. Had Rogers

In conclusion, I suggest that in *A Connecticut Yankee*, the divergent Clemens and Twain personalities take on a new significance far beyond a literary pen name. I believe that Clemens was unable to live the life he was leading without excessive guilt and that he resolved his feelings by assuming his Mark Twain mask and criticizing in his writing the very things he was doing in his daily life.

I am not a medical man, and my knowledge of schizophrenia is nil. I do not mean to assert that Clemens became unable to cope with reality at this period of his life, or that he was the victim of this most common of mental disorders; that is for someone trained in the field to consider. But I do suggest that a careful reading of *A Connecticut Yankee* inevitably demonstrates that the book is a satire attacking Clemens' own time and place; that Hank Morgan is the butt of the joke and that Clemens himself is closely associated with the character of Morgan and is himself a target for the attacks of Mark Twain. Later I shall discuss the reasons why I believe that Clemens came to hate himself so much that he was forced to attack himself in this complicated, terrifying, powerful, and completely unique work of literary art.

---

not been there at the crucial time, Clemens might well have ended up like Hank Morgan in the *Connecticut Yankee*—defeated, discouraged, and perhaps even insane. Think how close Mark Twain came to predicting the end of his alter ego, just as he predicted the amoral brutality which plagued the Western world in the first half of the twentieth century.

The Tragedy of Pudd'nhead Wilson

Mark Twain had intended *A Connecticut Yankee* to be his last book. Expecting huge returns from his investment in the Paige typesetting machine (for which he assumed complete financial responsibility in December 1889), he contemplated a life without the necessity of labor, intellectual, or otherwise.[146] But only a year and a half later, his dreams of wealth unfulfilled, the family was effectively at the end of its resources. The expense of running the Hartford house could no longer be borne, and the Clemens family fled to Europe, where the cost of living was lower. Susy, who had entered Bryn Mawr College in the autumn of 1890, came home the following May without completing her freshman year, and on June 6, the entire family left for Europe.

They were now dependent on what Mark could earn by writing and lecturing, and after a year in Germany, the Clemens family settled at the Villa Vivani outside Florence, Italy. There, Twain began to write seriously once more. He worked on *Tom*

---

146. See Kaplan, p. 361.

Sawyer Abroad, an adventure story which was never finished; on his *Personal Recollections of Joan of Arc;* and on the short novel we know today as *The Tragedy of Pudd'nhead Wilson.*

Of *Tom Sawyer Abroad,* there is little to say. The book attempts to exploit the characters of Tom, Huck, and Jim in a ballooning adventure which seems inspired by Jules Verne's *The Mysterious Island.* It has some comic moments but never really comes to life and ends suddenly after thirteen uneven chapters.

Joan of Arc had been on Twain's mind ever since that day in Hannibal when, as a boy of about thirteen, he picked up a book from the street and read about Joan in prison. His own *Joan of Arc* was written largely for his own satisfaction (he said he wrote it out of love and not for money) and without thought of publication.[147] Susy thought it was his best book. It was not; it is a melodramatic, lifeless piece of writing most significant for its portrait of Joan herself, which was based not on the historical character but on Susy Clemens.[148]

It was the third of the three books on which Mark Twain was at work in the early nineties, which was to emerge as a minor masterpiece. *The Tragedy of Pudd'nhead Wilson* is both the shortest and the least known of Twain's major works, but these characteristics hardly reduce its worth.

Like the *Yankee, Pudd'nhead* grew out of a trivial, comic idea, The *Yankee* began with Twain's observations on the humorous aspects of life in a suit of armor, *Pudd'nhead* derived from the author's contemplation of Siamese twins. The comic possibilities of a story about two individuals of opposite character joined inseparably had been at the back of his mind as far back as the sixties and stemmed from his fascination with the original Siamese twins, Chang and Eng Bunker.

[147.] See Kaplan, p. 371.

[148.] Ibid.

Actually of mixed Chinese and Malay origin, Chang and Eng were born in Siam in 1811. There were xiphopagus twins joined at the chest by a ligature of great strength and flexibility and possibly sharing internal organs. Brought to the United States at age eighteen, they became naturalized citizens and settled in North Carolina, where they married a pair of sisters and between them sired twenty-one children. They were in all respects healthy, normal individuals, and they lived to age sixty-two, when Chang contracted pneumonia. He and Eng died on the same day.[149]

As early as 1868, while he was living in San Francisco, Mark Twain wrote a burlesque sketch on the Twins; this uninspired piece of low humor eventually led to the serious novel of a quarter of a century later.

Another early Twain sketch may also be an important antecedent of *Pudd'nhead Wilson*. This is the piece called "A True Story," which tells the story of Aunt Rachel, a slave woman sold away from her family, who years later is reunited with her son under somewhat remarkable circumstances. Aunt Rachel is certainly not Roxy of the novel, but her career may have inspired Twain in the creation of his most interesting heroine.[150]

Having started with a comic vision, Twain added the more serious aspects of the story. "It changed itself from a farce to a tragedy," he said of the book.[151] Eventually, realizing that his two stories were incompatible, he severed them; the original comic piece became the story "Those Extraordinary Twins," while *Pudd'nhead* at last emerged, after much painful rewriting, as

---

149. For a full-length biography of Chang and Eng, see *The Two*, by Irving and Amy Wallace (New York: Simon and Schuster, 1978).

150. "A True Story" first appeared in the *Atlantic Monthly* in 1875 and was also collected in *Sketches Old and New* that same year.

151. See Kaplan, p. 369.

the novel we know today.[152] It was first published in serial form, appearing in the *Century Magazine* in 1893 and went between hard covers the following year. Luigi and Angelo Capello, a pair of Siamese twins, do appear in *Pudd'nhead,* but no mention is made that they are conjoined, and it takes a careful reading to identify this pair of twins as "extraordinary."[153]

Even with the Siamese Twin theme largely subordinated, *Pudd'nhead Wilson* still somehow manages to combine a remarkable range of seemingly unrelated elements. It is simultaneously a detective story, a farce, an attack on the stupidity and injustice of racism, a character study, and a satire. It is a strikingly modern novel in several ways, belonging more to the twentieth century than the nineteenth in style and conceptions; were, say, Joseph

---

[152.] The Wallaces observe that this operation was akin to separating a pair of Siamese twins—an interesting analogy!

[153] According to *The Two,* Mark Twain had an additional model for the Capello twins. Giovanni and Giacomo Tocci, born in Turin in 1875, were Siamese twins of a different type than Chang and Eng. The Bunkers were perfectly formed individuals joined by a single ligature; the Toccis, on the other hand, were separate above the waist but shared a single pair of legs. Each twin controlled one leg, and because they could not coordinate their movements, they were never able to walk. Twain's Capello twins ("capello," in Italian, means "head") were of this type—two torsos on a single pair of legs. In the story, however, he had them able to move about, although only if one surrendered complete control of his leg to the other. In real life, the Bunkers, though they did not have to make such an agreement in order to walk, really did have to make similar accommodations to facilitate the problem of living with two people in the same body. Twain also had his twins differ in appearance as well as in personality, which is of course a physical impossibility. Chang and Eng, however, did have distinct and somewhat different personalities; Chang was somewhat morose, while Eng was more animated and good-natured.

Heller's name signed to it, one would not be surprised. Above all, *Pudd'nhead Wilson* is an ironic novel. If *A Connecticut Yankee in King Arthur's Court* is his masterpiece of satire, and *Huck Finn* his greatest comic triumph, *Pudd'nhead Wilson* is Mark Twain's finest achievement in sustained use of irony.

In several ways, then, this little book deserves our close attention.

I
Plot and Tone

By its formal structure, *The Tragedy of Pudd'nhead Wilson* is a detective novel. In this alone, it is a remarkable book, for it is among the earliest examples of this form in English.

Charles Dickens was probably the first writer in the language to produce something like a detective novel—*Bleak House,* which appeared in 1853, a mere dozen years after Edgar Allan Poe created the detective form in his short story, "The Murders in the Rue Morgue."[154] Dickens' second venture in the form, *The Mystery of Edwin Drood* was left unfinished at his death in 1870.

Wilkie Collins produced the first great detective novel, *The Moonstone,* in 1868. Incidentally, it was published first in serial form by a magazine called *All the Year Round,* whose editor was Charles Dickens. Anna Katherine Green produced *The Leavenworth Case* in 1878—the first notable detective novel written by an American as well as the first by a woman. And finally, *Pudd'nhead* was anticipated by Arthur Conan Doyle's first two Sherlock Holmes books, *A Study in Scarlet* (1887) and *The Sign of Four* (1890). Other than these six efforts, *Pudd'nhead Wilson* is first among significant detective novels.

[154.] For the history of the detective novel, I have relied on the classic *Murder for Pleasure* by Howard Haycroft (New York: D. Appleton-Century, 1941.)

Moreover, the central device in the story is criminal identification through fingerprints—a completely new idea in 1894. The first English-language treatise on the subject did not appear until 1880, and Twain actually published *Pudd'nhead* before the International Association of Police Chiefs created its fingerprinting bureau.[155] So topical was Twain's use of the fingerprinting device that it could almost be called a case of life imitating art.

In brief, the action of *Pudd'nhead Wilson* recounts the increasingly abominable criminal career of "Tom Driscoll," in reality the slave Valet du Chambre ("Chambers" for short). He goes from gambling to thievery and finally to murder. He believes himself safe from discovery but by means of his fingerprinting records, the lawyer David Wilson, known to the people of Dawson's Landing as "Pudd'nhead," discovers a switch of babies and identifies the false Tom as the killer. He is sentenced to death, but as this would cheat the creditors of the estate out of a valuable slave, his sentence is commuted by the governor, and he is promptly sold down the river.

There are also two principal subplots. One involves the visit to Dawson's Landing of the twins, Angelo and Luigi, and their relationship to the local residents. The other is the story of Roxy, Chambers' loving and trusting mother, and her dealings with her selfish and unfeeling son. It is Roxy, who initiates the action when, to prevent her child's ever being sold down the river, she switches him with the Driscoll baby. All through the novel, she tries everything she can to support and reform him, even agreeing to have herself sold into slavery on his behalf, but at

---

[155.] An article by Sir Francis Galton popularized identification through fingerprints in 1892, and the chiefs established their bureau in 1896. *Pudd'nhead* began appearing in the *Century* in 1893, anticipating the police by more than two years.

the end, all her efforts and sacrifices are for naught—Chambers is sold down the river after all.

The first peculiarity of *Pudd'nhead Wilson* as a detective story is that neither the criminal, Tom (really Chambers), nor the detective, Wilson himself, is at the center of the story. Indeed, while Wilson is present in the book from Chapter 1 on, his presence is always slight until the last three chapters. Tom is more centrally placed, but he is overshadowed by Roxy, the most appealing and sympathetic character in the story.

Pudd'nhead Wilson has been called a novel without a hero, and in the narrow sense, this is perfectly true; but it is not a novel without a heroine. Together with *Joan of Arc,* on which Twain was at work during the same period, it is one of only two Mark Twain novels in which the central character is female.

There are also other ways in which *Pudd'nhead Wilson* is something more than a conventional detective novel. One of these is the clearly intentional, studied lack of realism.

By its very nature, the detective novel is basically rational and realistic. It is an illustration of the premise that the world is a rational place and that any criminal act presents a puzzle which may be solved by the detective by the application of his faculties and knowledge. The premise of the form is that what one man may create, however baffling, can be unraveled by another if only he applies his reasoning powers sufficiently.

As a general rule, then, the more firmly the detective story is anchored to the real world, in a specific time and place, the more believable and more convincing it becomes. The application of reason has no place in a world of fantasy; thus the detective novel is generally realistic.[156]

---

156. Many if not most successful detective novels are deeply rooted in place and time. It is enough to point out how important the background of Victorian London is to the Holmes stories, or that of Los Angeles to

Pudd'nhead Wilson, on the contrary, is not only part farce, it is also deliberately unrealistic. The farcical element is introduced when Roxy switches the babies in their cradles, a plot idea so hoary that it cannot be taken seriously unless the reader is willing to make a total suspension of disbelief. This central plot element is a device so artificial that it makes acceptance of the novel as a depiction of real life practically impossible.[157]

The dry, unadorned prose of *Pudd'nhead Wilson* supports the aura of unreality created by the basic plot. So does Twain's return to the use of the impersonal third-person narrator, a device he discarded in *Huckleberry Finn* and in the *Connecticut Yankee.* In those novels, the author employed the first-person narration to bring the reader more completely into the story. In *Pudd'nhead,* he uses third-person narration to deliberately distance the

---

Raymond Chandler's work. Likewise, countless mystery writers have used the rich background of New York City to lend credibility and authenticity to their stories.

157. The moss-covered device of switching babies in their cradles was parodied by Gilbert and Sullivan in their delightful operetta *H.M.S. Pinafore,* first produced in London in 1878. Mark Twain was visiting Britain at this time, and it is possible that *Pinafore* may have suggested the device in his mind. As I have already remarked (see p. 18), he used a variation of this idea in *The Prince and the Pauper,* which was begun at about this time. He returned to the device in *Pudd'nhead,* this time employing it in its classic form, with Roxy standing in for Little Buttercup. There is one difference: in *Pinafore,* the nursemaid Buttercup switches the babies by accident, but in *Pudd'nhead,* Roxy's actions are deliberate and rationally motivated.

Both the Gilbert and Sullivan operetta and the Twain novel employ the baby-switching device, absurd as it is, to expose and attack the even greater absurdity of arbitrary class or racial distinctions in society. The striking similarity of conception in these two works seems to me to deserve at least a passing comment.

reader from the action, helping to create the atmosphere of studied detachment which he sought for this book.

To see how clearly Twain wished to distance his readers from involvement and to make the book a fable rather than a realistic depiction, compare the tone of the third-person narration in *Pudd'nhead* with that of *Tom Sawyer*. In the earlier book, the nameless narrator is garrulous, chatty, and a little patronizing toward his characters. In *Pudd'nhead*, his voice is both more reserved and less personal; this is a narration as it might be done by a computer-generated voice.

To put it another way, in his previous books set in the Mississippi Valley Mark Twain set out to depict as realistically as possible the world of his boyhood. In *Pudd'nhead Wilson*, his subject was that same society, but this time, he treats it in a detached and totally unrealistic manner. Unlike the earlier books, *Pudd'nhead* is purposely uninvolved, stylized, and artificial. It creates an atmosphere completely different from that in any other Mark Twain book. No better demonstration of the author's literary art could be presented; having created in *Huckleberry Finn* a supreme masterpiece of realistic and involving writing, he now takes the same general subject matter but treats it in an entirely different manner.

II
Other Elements

If the plot of *Pudd'nhead Wilson* successfully meshes the detective story with its essential rationalism and realism with both farce and fable, the book also manages to integrate other seemingly disparate elements. One of these is Mark Twain's pointed attack on the absurdity of racism.

Roxy, we are told, has a completely Caucasian appearance. Her eyes are brown, her complexion fair, her cheeks rosy, and her hair soft and fine. Yet having had one identifiably black great-grandparent, she is defined by her society as a Negress and a slave. The case of her son, Valet du Chambre, is even more absurd—he is exactly 1/32 black by ancestry, but by the arbitrary rules of Southern antebellum society, that is sufficient taint to condemn him to permanent social inferiority. These rules are both unreasonable and downright silly, yet they are not only strictly enforced by both law and custom but also accepted without criticism by blacks as well as whites. Roxy is perfectly aware that nobody can tell her "black" son from the "white" Driscoll baby; indeed, this knowledge leads her to switch the children in their cradles. Yet she accepts the proposition that the two are somehow inherently different. She says, in her uncharacteristically black dialect, that her Chambers "ain't only a nigger. Mighty prime little nigger, I al'ays says, but dat's ca'ase it's mine, o'course."[158]

Chambers' birth and eventual fate—he is sold down the river despite everything—raises another issue in the novel, determinism. Twain appears to be saying that there is such a thing as inescapable destiny against which no human action can triumph.

On first thought, it might seem that Chambers is marked for a bad end because he is black. Indeed, his own mother says as much in Chapter 14. When she learns that Chambers (the supposed Tom) has refused to fight a duel with Count Luigi

---

[158.] I don't know if anybody has ever transformed *Pudd'nhead Wilson* into a movie, but of all Twain's works, it seems to me to offer the most interesting cinematic possibilities. Imagine how striking would be the contrast between Roxy's appearance and her speech—far more powerfully presented on film than it can ever be on the printed page. Imagine also the depiction of the Siamese twins, Tom's disguises, the semi-comic fire brigade, and the dramatic courtroom scene. *Puddn'head* is a great movie waiting to be made.

after the Italian kicked him downstairs, she says, "It's de nigger in you, dat's what it is. Thirty-one parts of you is white, an on'y one part nigger, en dat po' little one part is yo' soul."

But on reflection, it is apparent that Chambers' destiny is unrelated to his ancestry; after all, he is hardly black at all. If he has an evil destiny, it arises not from color—he really has none to speak of—but from his character. He is doomed because he is spoiled, selfish, and thoughtless.

This theme of determinism is elaborated in *Pudd'nhead* for the first time in any of Mark Twain's works, but in fact, it simply carries Hank Morgan's frustration in *A Connecticut Yankee* one step further. Morgan tries to create a new civilization, only to find that the people on whom he was relying for support ultimately reject him; in the end, all his efforts are for naught. *Pudd'nhead* follows up this idea by suggesting that man is a helpless pawn before the power of fate. Chambers is far more clearly a creature of destiny than Hank Morgan; Roxy switches the babies specifically to spare her son from any possibility of being sold down the river, and yet that fate overtakes him in the end. In other words, the author prepares us for this particular ending. No parallel preparation exists in the *Yankee*, which is why I aver that the theme of determinism is more clearly etched in *Pudd'nhead*.

That Twain elaborated this theme more cogently in the later novel, which was published about four years after the *Yankee*, may reflect his increasingly unsatisfactory life. Between May 1889 and late 1893, Samuel Clemens lost both his mother (in October 1890) and his mother-in-law (a month later). Susy, his eldest and favorite daughter, with whom he was especially close, left home to attend Bryn Mawr College outside Philadelphia in the fall of 1890. The following spring, Charles Webster, his grandnephew whom Clemens had put in charge of the publishing company and with whom he had later had a violent falling-out, died at the age of forty. The Paige machine was consuming Clemens' money at the rate of $4,000 a month and the financial drain forced the family to close the Hartford house and leave for European exile two months later (June 1891). Then the Panic of 1893 resulted in the loss of Livy's income from her inheritance; the financial screws, already pressing, were being tightened. At the time *Pudd'nhead Wilson* was written, Samuel Clemens was a pressured, nearly desperate man. His load of guilt, which I have spoken of before, was weighing more heavily than ever; the philosophy of determinism, which he expressed in this novel, offered an escape.

For if man's fate is predetermined, and nothing he or anyone else can do will change it, then it follows that he is not responsible for his actions, and therefore need not feel guilt. If he had in fact no choices, then nothing he chose to do could be called wrong. Without responsibility, there is no guilt.

In other words, I am suggesting that *Pudd'nhead Wilson*'s elaboration of the determinism theme, never before so clearly stated in Twain's writing, reflects a deterioration of Samuel Clemens' self-esteem and an increase in his burden of guilt. Just as something seems to have happened in the author's personal life which accounts for the difference in world view between *Huckleberry Finn* and *A Connecticut Yankee,* so some further developments seem to have pushed him to suggest that man's fate is predetermined in *Pudd'nhead Wilson.*

Other more familiar Mark Twain themes are repeated in the novel. The courtroom scene immediately recalls *The Adventures of Tom Sawyer* and would soon be echoed in *Tom Sawyer. Detective* (published in 1895). The disguise theme appears again—the false Tom masquerades as a girl, more successfully than Huck did in *Huckleberry Finn.* The theme of nobility of character, so prevalent in everything Twain wrote from *Tom Sawyer* onward, appears again in *Pudd'nhead;* Roxy is among the most clearly noble of all Twain's characters, for from the beginning of the book to the end, she always stands ready to sacrifice herself for the good of others. That everything she does, at enormous cost to herself, ultimately fails does not make her conduct or her character any less noble.

Moreover, in Chambers, Twain presents us with perhaps his most complete picture of a completely ignoble character—a selfish, unfeeling scoundrel who has all the character flaws of Tom Sawyer and Hank Morgan but none of their redeeming graces or attractiveness. "Tom Driscoll" shares his name with Tom Sawyer, as well as some unpleasant character traits, but after all, Tom Sawyer never committed murder.

Of course, the ever-present theme of the evils of slavery is found in *Pudd'nhead Wilson* too. As a matter of fact, the poet Langston Hughes, in his introduction to the 1959 Bantam Classic edition of the book, sees slavery as the "basic theme" of the novel. "Had Twain been a contemporary of Harriet Beecher Stowe," writes Mr. Hughes, "and this novel been published before the War between the States, it might have been a minor *Uncle Tom's Cabin*."[159]

The trouble with this theory is precisely that Twain was *not* writing before the War, but a good thirty years after slavery no longer existed. It would have made no sense for him to write a book on the central theme of slavery when that institution had been destroyed forever a generation earlier. Certainly, *Pudd'nhead Wilson* does discuss the effects of slavery on both master and servant, but the subject is *not* the "basic theme" of the novel.

Certainly, the theme of the cost of thoughtlessness is present again. Some of Chambers' (the false Tom's) actions are not intended to hurt but are merely selfish deeds carried out without regard for the rights or feelings of others. Most notable of all his

---

[159.] See Introduction by Langston Hughes in *Pudd'nhead Wilson* (New York: Bantam Books, 1959).

actions in this manner is his treacherous sale of Roxy "down the river" rather than to some local farmer, as she had previously agreed.[160] He does this not out of malice but simply because a convenient Arkansas planter comes along at the appropriate moment and saves him the necessity of finding a purchaser. That he is sending his own mother to the slaves' equivalent of hell on earth does not enter his mind before he makes the deal, and his feelings of guilt afterward last no more than a week or so before he is able to dismiss them.

Another aspect of *Pudd'nhead* is the picture it presents of Roxy, the white/black heroine who dominates most of the novel. Though his older women (Aunt Polly, Aunt Sally, and Judith Loftus) and one or two of his young girls (Becky Thatcher, Mary Jane Wilks) are vivid portraits, Mark Twain avoided the portrayal of sexual, romantic female characters. In all his books, there are only two in which the central character is an adult woman of childbearing years, and one of these characters is Joan of Arc, who is presented in a completely nonsexual manner. Only Roxy, of all Twain's female characters, is presented as anything like a whole and normally sexual adult woman. One suspects that he was willing and able to present her so only because she is (by fiction and in manner of speech) black, and thus not threatening. However he came to create her, Twain created in Roxy his most complete study of woman.

Roxy is intelligent if uneducated, determined, and above all full of love for her wayward son. She is willing to sacrifice anything, even her precious freedom, for his sake; while she upbraids him for his senseless behavior, cowardice, and cruelty, she can never find it within herself to abandon him. Everything she does in the novel, she does for the sake of Chambers—and everything she does on his behalf ultimately fails. Yet Roxy

---

[160.] See Chapter 16.

never loses courage or hope. In one sense, *Pudd'nhead Wilson* may be seen primarily as a character study of this admirable but unhappy woman.

Not surprisingly, *Pudd'nhead* also has satiric content. The villagers of Dawson's Landing, who stand for the ignorant, foolish, and prejudiced people of Mark Twain's own world, are often the targets of the author's indirect attack. Right from the beginning, when David Wilson remarks that if he owned half a disagreeable dog, he would kill his half, and the townspeople are too dense to see the joke, they are branded with the Mark of Twain—the mark of ignorance. No less than St. Petersburg, Dawson's Landing is a microcosm of America, and its citizens are no more or less foolish and ignorant than the Boobus Americanus which Twain saw all around him.

Also characteristic of Twain is the use of comedy in what is essentially a serious, even grim, story. Aunt Patsy Cooper and Rowena, her man-hungry daughter, are figures of fun as well as occasional scorn.[161] So indeed are the people of Dawson's Landing as a group. While there is nothing in *Pudd'nhead* comparable to the sustained antics of *Huckleberry Finn,* still the humorous touch of Twain is not completely absent.

The Tragedy of Pudd'nhead Wilson, then, is remarkable first for the way in which so many diverse elements and themes are woven into this tight little book. Detective story, farce, polemic, character study, satire, and humor are somehow all made to function in concert. This is no mean accomplishment; and if there were no more to *Pudd'nhead* than this remarkable bit of interweaving, the book would be notable enough.

[161.] Twain's use of the name Rowena for this decidedly unheroic girl is another jab at his favorite target, the romantic novels of Sir Walter Scott and their effects on the Southerners who wallowed in them.

But there *is* a great deal more to the novel in addition to Twain's skill with the literary loom. The book includes at least one completely new and effective device, offers a use of irony unmatched in American fiction, and presents some particularly intriguing challenges in interpretation.

The unique characteristic of the novel is, of course, the acid comments from Pudd'nhead Wilson's Calendar which are found at the head of each chapter. There are thirty-eight of them, and it is likely that the reader who encounters the book for the first time is more likely to remember them (or at least some of them) than anything else in *Pudd'nhead.*

Many of these lines are cynical; some are serious; others (such as the one in praise of the watermelon) comic. Together they express a dark but not depressing view of life.

Moreover, Puddn'head's bon mots are not simple additions to the story, they are woven into it. In Chapter 5, we learn that Judge Driscoll was not only David Wilson's friend and fellow freethinker but also that he admired Pudd'nhead's Calendar and carried some of its quips around with him. He made the mistake, however, of reading these ironic words to the townspeople in proof of his assertion that Wilson was no pudd'nhead. The ironic result was that the dense dullards of Dawson's Landing, unable to appreciate irony, were more convinced than ever that the lawyer was a pudd'nhead, indeed.

This passage may be seen, I submit, as a parallel to the famous "Notice" at the beginning of *Huckleberry Finn* and the preface to *A Connecticut Yankee in King Arthur's Court.* Like these other passages, it puts the reader on notice that he should be on the lookout for something: in *Huck,* for plot, moral, and motive; and in the *Yankee,* for the satiric nature of the novel. In *Pudd'nhead* we are alerted to look out for irony everywhere. To read this novel as the people of Dawson's Landing read Pudd'nhead's Calendar is to run the risk of being a puddn'head yourself.

The little epigrams of Pudd'nhead's Calendar also have another function for the reader; in the manner of the Greek chorus, they comment upon and clarify the action of the novel. In some cases, the epigram appears to bear directly on the chapter to which it is attached, as is the case with Pudd'nhead's comment on circumstantial evidence. "Even the clearest and most perfect circumstantial evidence is likely to be at fault, after all, and therefore ought to be received with great caution . . ." This remark stands at the head of Chapter 20, in which the State presents its case against the twins, a case based on circumstantial evidence which is cohesive, convincing, and completely wrong. In other instances, I am unable to see a clear connection between epigram and chapter content, but there is no doubt that the quotations from the calendar do play on the story as a whole.

Additionally, the calendar allows the further depersonalization of the narrator who, unlike the third-person voice in Tom Sawyer, does not intrude upon the story at all. In *Tom*, we can practically see the figure of Mark Twain standing behind his characters; he has a palpable presence in the novel. In *Pudd'nhead*, the narrator is refined out of existence, like James Joyce's ideal literary artist. Yet, thanks to the calendar, we still have the author's (if not the narrator's) thoughts on life and death.

So far as I am aware, the use of this device was entirely original in American fiction. No one had done anything like this before; at fifty-nine, Mark Twain was still experimenting, still growing as a writer, and still trying new techniques.

Another special characteristic of *Pudd'nhead Wilson* is its compression. The whole story runs to a mere 143 pages in the paperback edition, and its very lack of length makes it remarkable among the author's works. Whatever Mark Twain was, he was often profligate with words; the *Connecticut Yankee*, for example, is three times the length of *Pudd'nhead*. Part of Twain's loquacity was due to his practice of publishing by subscription;

people bought a book sight unseen, and expected to get their money's worth in bulk, if not in quality. This accounts for the obvious padding of *Life on the Mississippi,* for example, but even without the demands of his subscribers to satisfy, Mark Twain was sometimes prone to excessive length.

All the more, then, does *Pudd'nhead Wilson* stand out among his other books. Despite its complicated amalgam of disparate and sometimes warring elements, the brevity and intensity are exceptional. In this way, too, *Pudd'nhead* is more like a twentieth-century novel than a Victorian one. It recalls another masterpiece of compression, Scott Fitzgerald's *The Great Gatsby,* which followed it by thirty years.

In language, too, *Pudd'nhead* differs from much of Twain's earlier prose and resembles twentieth-century styles more than those of his own period. One of Wilson's epigrams is, "As to the adjective: when in doubt, strike it out." In this novel, Twain follows that practice. In contrast to his earlier books, we find no passages of lyrical descriptive prose here, like the pictures of morning on the river or of storm on the island. The language of *Pudd'nhead* is colorless, stripped-down prose foreshadowing the style of Hemingway. In this, too, the book belongs to the present century, not to its own.

III
Irony

As I have pointed out, *Pudd'nhead Wilson,* despite its brevity, is a multifaceted novel, astonishingly rich and complex. Yet there is a single quality which pervades the entire book; above all, *Pudd'nhead Wilson* is a novel of irony.

Irony is, as I have already said, the technique of expressing an idea by stating the opposite. By extension, a circumstance may be described as ironic if it results in the opposite of what was expected. The essence of irony is reversal.

We are introduced to the ironic nature of the novel in the very first chapter, when David Wilson gets the nickname "Pudd'nhead" because the townspeople are themselves too puddingheaded to understand his joke about the dog. Wilson, of course, is the smartest man in Dawson's Landing—but only Roxy recognizes this.

In fact, the novel is full of little ironies—recall the fire brigade, for example, which does far more damage than the fires it is supposed to put out; or the outcome of the novel, which has the real Tom Driscoll unable to function in the society of whites, while Chambers is sold down the river—a slave with a Yale education. Indeed, on the larger level, the entire book is one great irony. The story rests on Roxy's fear that her son might someday be sold down the river and her consequent switching of the babies in their cradles; yet at the end, Chambers does indeed wind up being sold down the river despite all Roxy's efforts to the contrary. Her attempts to save him only led to his getting in more and more serious trouble which leads to his eventual destiny.

There are many other ironies in the novel. The false Tom is trapped by his own fingerprints, which he thought to be inconsequential, just at the moment when he thought himself beyond suspicion. Judge Driscoll's estate is ultimately inherited by the real Tom, who has been raised as a slave and has never had anything to do with his true uncle; while the false Tom, upon whom the old man doted, not only loses the fortune but his liberty as well. The ironic fact that the law holds a slave's value to his master's creditors more important than punishing murder results in the false Tom finding his singularly appropriate fate.[162] David Wilson, who has been shunned and ignored by

---

[162.] The law as a whole gets a pretty good working over in this book. As the concrete expression of a society whose very core is corrupt, the law itself

the townspeople of Dawson's Landing for twenty-three years, winds up the toast of the town. Having robbed the town, the false Tom is himself relieved of all his plunder by another thief aboard a steamboat and so forth. I think it is fair to say that no American novel before *Pudd'nhead,* and not many written since, has been so totally ironic in nature. In this book, no one's plans turn out as expected, and each circumstance leads to the opposite of its purpose. Mark Twain had already established himself as America's supreme satirist and one of its greatest humorists in his previous books; now Mark Twain demonstrates in *Pudd'nhead Wilson* that he is among its greatest masters of irony as well.

IV
Interpretation

As in the *Connecticut Yankee,* a central problem in interpreting *Pudd'nhead Wilson* is discovering what exactly the author means to tell us on the vital question of whether (as Pudd'nhead's Calendar tells us) "training is everything" or whether nobility or baseness of character destines a man for his particular end beyond the possibility of altering his fate. Both messages are found in the novel, and they are irreconcilable. The question also has larger implications, for it bears centrally on the question of whether Mark Twain was the quintessential American democrat, for whom

---

is foolish and unjust—a ready target for Twain's scornful attacks. Perhaps there is some intended significance in the fact that Wilson, while a lawyer by profession, is distanced from the law by the fact that the town considers him a dummy. Ironically (there's that word again), it is his failure to prosper in the legal world which gives him both his independence in the town and the leisure to follow up his hobby of collecting fingerprint "records."

Prince and Pauper are distinguished only by social position and dress; or whether, to the contrary, he was so disillusioned with American democracy as to accept a deterministic philosophy in which nothing a man does can alter his predestined fate—the absolute antithesis of democratic theory. In a nutshell, it's the age-old question of "nature versus nurture."

In the *Yankee,* great care was taken to mask the author's real views; the framing device, the unreliable narrator, and the "dream versus reality" theme are all employed to keep the reader from nailing down Mark Twain's own feelings. These devices are all absent in *Pudd'nhead,* but they are in part replaced by the deliberate depersonalization of the narrator and by the whole stylized, mechanical, and unreal tone of the novel. Once again, it is hard to pin down exactly what the author himself believes. It is this ambiguity which makes *Pudd'nhead Wilson* (and the *Yankee* too) so difficult to understand. One expects a clear statement, or at least an unambiguous reference to the author's principles; in these books, neither is to be found.

What explanation can we find for this crucial question of interpretation?

It is possible, logically, that Twain himself was not decided between the claims of inherent nature and social nurture as determinants of human conduct, and that, therefore, he gave us both alternatives and left us to weigh them for ourselves.

While I think it likely that Twain did vacillate between the poles of determinism and free will, the idea that he simply made the arguments both ways and left it for the reader to decide seems more than weak to me. I prefer to consider a second possibility, i.e., that the two facets of the author's personality, the Samuel Clemens' side, and the Mark Twain side were at odds on this point.

Clemens, born in poverty and obscurity on the distant and wild frontier, had been transformed into the Victorian American gentleman and would-be millionaire; he was, it appeared, living proof of the proposition that in the freedom of the United States, any man (or at least any white man) could rise to wealth and prominence.

But what if Clemens' rise was partly, if not largely, due to his marriage into a family of wealth and social position? Who knew better than the Mark Twain side of the man that the rise of Samuel L. Clemens was only partly due to his literary skill and was in large measure the result of good luck and a favorable attachment?

What is more, as he was writing *Pudd'nhead*, Mark Twain knew all too well that Clemens was headed for bankruptcy as well as exile. He must have wondered if a malignant destiny was about to condemn him to poverty, despite all his hopes and schemes and labor. He must have known that he was about to repeat his father's experience of bankruptcy in later life, and, worst of all, he had no one to blame but himself. No wonder the note of determinism sounds so loudly in the novel.

If the life of Samuel Clemens stood for the American ideal on the surface, his financial failure as he approached sixty raised the specter of determinism. It may well be that in *Pudd'nhead Wilson,* as in the *Yankee* before it, the two sides of the man gave expression to both concepts.

There is more to say about *Pudd'nhead.* Consider the full title of the novel: *The Tragedy of Pudd'nhead Wilson.* On the surface, nothing could be more inappropriate.

David Wilson is no tragic figure. Not only is he a minor character throughout four-fifths of the novel, he suffers no fall in power or stature, has no tragic flaw which could lead to such a fall, and in fact becomes a hero at the end. The tragic figures in the novel are Roxy, who suffers so much, and in the end, accomplishes nothing; Chambers (the false Tom), who is destroyed by his own flawed character in the classic Greek manner; or perhaps Tom (the real Tom), who finds himself both rich and free at the end of the story, yet completely unable to function outside the society of slaves with whom he has been raised.

Why, then, the title? One explanation is simply that the novel is the companion piece of *The Comedy of Those Extraordinary Twins,* the two stories together forming the literary equivalent of the famous paired masks.

I prefer to look further, however. One way of interpreting the title is to see it in the context of the dominant theme of the book—as an irony. Looking at *Pudd'nhead* this way, we can say that if Mark Twain called the book a tragedy, we should read it as a comedy, just the opposite of what is stated. And indeed, *Pudd'nhead* can be considered a comic novel; not only is there plenty of laughter in it, but, true to the essence of comedy, there is a happy ending in which the villain gets his deserved reward, and the hero, snubbed and ignored through the first eighteen chapters, finally wins his proper recognition and acclaim.

This is a perfectly legitimate reading of the novel, and if I were turning it into a play or an opera, it is the reading I should emphasize; but from the point of view of purely literary interpretation, which can be so much more complicated and complex than the stage allows, I think it is an inadequate one. To read *Pudd'nhead* as a comedy, even as a dark comedy, is to see it as a struggle between "good" as personified by Wilson and "evil" in the form of the false Tom. There is little room in this view for the trials of Roxy—yet no one can read the book without seeing that Roxy, not her son or the lawyer, is the real center of it.

Thus, I go one step further, beyond the ironic explanation, and ask if there is in fact some way that Pudd'nhead Wilson himself can be seen as the victim of tragedy. Not surprisingly, there is.

What is the cause of David Wilson's twenty-three-year-long state of eclipse in the community of Dawson's Landing? His casual remark on first coming to the town, which was misunderstood by the local population and led to his being tagged "a pudd'nhead."

The town declares him to be something he is not; and having once condemned him to the status of "Pudd'nhead," nothing can change his position, even the advocacy of Judge Driscoll, until he solves the murder and forces the people to see him differently. The tragedy of Pudd'nhead Wilson is to be thought of and *called* Pudd'nhead, when he is in fact the smartest man in town.

It does not take much imagination to see, next, that the tragedy of Pudd'nhead is the tragedy of everyone in Dawson's Landing. Roxy, who appears completely Caucasian, is defined as black; her son, the false Tom, is by virtue of his position as the stepson of Judge Driscoll elevated to the highest social status, though in fact he is a gambler, a thief, a murderer, and a complete blackguard. By contrast, the real Tom, raised as Roxy's son Chambers, is no less white than his rival but is by the fiction of color condemned to the life of a slave.

Not only do others force people into unreal roles, but such is the power of social convention that people do the same thing to themselves. The judge, being a Virginia gentleman, is forced to absurdities of behavior in order to keep up "the code" to which he assigns himself.[163]

Trouble results when the community cannot decide which stereotype to apply. The twins are hailed and lionized when they are characterized as nobility, but vilified and castigated when they are presented as foreigners.

The tragedy of Pudd'nhead Wilson is shared by everyone in Dawson's Landing; it is the tragedy of stereotyping, which prevents individuals from seeing themselves as they are or from developing according to their free natures. The tyranny of social casting betrays them all. None are allowed to exist free of

---

[163.] The figure of the freethinking old judge from Virginia is almost certainly based on John Marshall Clemens, the author's own distant and ineffectual father.

tagging and classification; all are forced into defined roles. This relentless labeling is the true tragedy of Pudd'nhead Wilson and all the other characters in the book. For the sake of allowing people to cope with others without thinking by assigning them to specific categories or roles, the society of Dawson's Landing (which is representative of America as a whole) deprives them of the ability to see themselves, as well as others, as individuals.

It is not slavery per se which is the "basic theme" of *Pudd'nhead Wilson,* but the kind of thinking which makes slavery possible—the thinking which accepts the individual only in the context of some larger group or role to which he is assigned. To the extent that we do the same thing today, with our own prejudices and our well-meaning efforts to overcome them by such group-based antidotes as affirmative action or busing schoolchildren to achieve "racial balance," *Pudd'nhead Wilson* speaks as directly to us as it did to Twain's readers of a century ago. In this sense, too, this is a modern, even a contemporary novel.

What is more, the message of the book is driven home by David Wilson's solution to the murder. He has the killer's fingerprints on the knife and evidence of the mysterious girl seen fleeing from the scene, but no female fingerprints he can find match the criminal. Not until he recognizes the false Tom's fingerprints (by accident) does Pudd'nhead recognize his difficulty: "Idiot that I was," he says, "nothing but a girl would do me—a man in girl's clothes never occurred to me."[164] He has failed to solve the mystery, despite having the means at hand, because he has been a victim of the same stereotyping which gave him his nickname. By falling victim to such thinking, he lives up

---

[164.] See Chapter 20.

to his cognomen—this time he really is a pudd'nhead.[165] Can there be any doubt, after this conclusion, that Mark Twain's real object of attack in this novel is our own all-too-universal practice of dealing with people as members of stereotyped groups rather than as unique individuals?

Just as I believe that events in Samuel Clemens' life influenced the introduction of determinism into Mark Twain's *Pudd'nhead Wilson,* so I am convinced that the same factor is responsible for his dissertation on stereotyping in this same book. I have already theorized that Clemens was becoming increasingly dissatisfied with what he was doing with his life and found escape by criticizing his own conduct in the writings of Mark Twain. In everything Twain wrote after *Tom Sawyer,* there is a growing degree of criticism of the behavior of his alter ego, which becomes even more evident and more violently pointed in *A Connecticut Yankee.* In *Pudd'nhead Wilson,* Mark Twain seems to be telling us to disregard social stereotypes; suppose we apply this advice to Samuel L. Clemens?

There was, indeed, a dichotomy between the public Clemens and the private man. He was known to the public primarily as a funny man (partly due to his success in masking the degree of social criticism in his books behind the triple screen of humor, satire, and irony), but he knew himself to be burning with anger at the cruelty, hypocrisy, and dishonesty of the world in which

---

165. Here is yet another irony in a novel of ironies. David Wilson is the smartest, most penetrating intelligence in town, yet he is called "Pudd'nhead." Now, when the situation called for clear-headed reasoning, he fails to consider all the possibilities since he has been blinded by gender. Ironically, he acts just like the pudd'nhead he was called all along. And to the extent that we continue even today to think of people as members of some group rather than as individuals, we are all "pudd'nheads." Once again Mark Twain speaks to us after well over a century.

he lived. To the world, he was a successful author, but he knew in 1893 that he was also a soon-to-be-bankrupt spendthrift who went through his royalties faster than he earned them and who squandered his wife's money as well in his effort to make millions on the Paige machine. To the ordinary American, he was the devoted husband and model family man; but there is reason to believe (and, of course, he knew) that his domestic life was far more complicated and much darker than was known; he even admitted in a letter to Howells that his children were afraid of him, and he was subject to sudden and terrifying rages and to vicious and unfair attacks on others.[166]

In short, the central theme of *Pudd'nhead Wilson*—that what society terms an individual may be nothing like his real self—seems to apply quite directly to Samuel Clemens. He was not in fact what people thought him to be; only the degree to which this is true remains to be clarified. He was living a lie, and he knew it; but his reputation, his fame, and his literary success depended on the truth remaining hidden. Thus, he exorcised his guilt by writing, in the name of Mark Twain, criticism of his own deeds as Samuel Clemens. Exactly what these guilt-producing deeds were, apart from his disastrous investment in the typesetter, I shall discuss in a future chapter.

I suggest, then, that far from being the problematic, disconnected, and somewhat trivial entertainment, which it is frequently considered, *The Tragedy of Pudd'nhead Wilson* is in fact an important and brilliant ironic novel, which fits in logical sequence in the author's canon of work after the *Yankee* and before *The Mysterious Stranger*. Moreover, I see it as being

---

[166.] See Kaplan, p. 362. The letter was written in 1886. Examples of Clemens' rages can be found in his mistaken vendettas against Whitelaw Reid and the *New York Tribune* (Kaplan, pp. 279-281) and his nephew by marriage, the unfortunate Charles Webster (Kaplan, pp. 342-343, 398, 420).

intimately connected with the author's frame of mind at the time it was written—it could not have been created earlier in his career and probably not much later. Finally, it is both thematically and technically the most forward-looking of Mark Twain's novels, in many ways, a book which could have been written today. It should not be ignored.

Late Writings

The *Tragedy of Pudd'nhead Wilson* may be viewed as the last really important novel Mark Twain completed and published in his lifetime. True, it is postdated by *Personal Recollections of Joan of Arc* published by *Harper's* in May 1896, but few Twain readers or critics consider this work a significant addition to the author's canon. After *Joan,* Mark Twain wrote reams of prose—the sheer volume of his output in this period is astounding—but his publications are limited to his last travel book, *Following the Equator,* and a number of shorter works, essays, fragments, and stories. The book generally considered to be his last novel, *The Mysterious Stranger,* was not completed before his death; his first biographer and literary executor, Albert Bigelow Paine compiled it from manuscripts left unfinished and published it in 1916, six years after Clemens' death. Discounting the inferior *Joan* and the uncompleted *Mysterious Stranger,* the author's career as a novelist ends with *Pudd'nhead.*

It seems necessary to discuss *The Mysterious Stranger,* however briefly, for this book states Mark Twain's philosophy at the end of his life. By this time, his financial problems were behind him, but personal disasters had more than taken their place. His beloved daughter Susy contracted meningitis during the summer of 1896, and after a short but painful illness, lost first her reason, next her consciousness, and finally her life. Mark Twain never fully recovered from the shock of this terrible loss; after Susy's death on August 18, 1896, the only major book he was ever able to finish was *Following the Equator* published in 1897.

Just six years after Susy died, Livy Clemens fell seriously ill with heart trouble and goiter, and after an illness of twenty-two months she passed away on June 5, 1904, at the age of fifty-nine. Her death ended a marriage which had endured for more than thirty-four years.

Given these irreplaceable losses, which exacerbated Clemens' already overwhelming feelings of guilt, it is no surprise that his final philosophy, as expressed in the closing paragraphs of the *Stranger*, is nihilistic. "It is true, that which I have revealed to you; there is no God, no universe, no human race, no earthly life, no heaven, no hell. It is all a dream—a grotesque and foolish dream. Nothing exists but you. And you are but a thought—a vagrant thought, a useless thought, a homeless thought, wandering forlorn through the empty eternities!"

In this denial of all reality, Clemens could find some relief from his tremendous load of guilt. If indeed nothing is real, nothing a man does matters: without responsible choices, there can be no guilt. At the end of his life, the aging Clemens used this nihilistic and deterministic philosophy to cope with the private demons which gave him no peace.

I have already pointed out that this conception of life as a dream was in Mark Twain's mind as early as 1873 or 1874, for it appears in *Tom Sawyer*, and that his increasing reliance on deterministic ideas did not develop all of a sudden but grew progressively throughout each of his major works after about 1880. Frank Baldanza, in his study of Mark Twain and his works, argues that indeed the dream philosophy is the "organic outgrowth" of his earliest feelings and experiences.[167] The real question with which we must be concerned is what was behind those tremendous feelings of guilt which increasingly beset Samuel L. Clemens throughout the last half of his life?

[167.] Frank Baldanza, *Mark Twain: An Introduction and Interpretation* (New York: Holt, Rinehart and Winston, Inc., 1961).

Concluding Notes on this Section

The comments which I have made on Mark Twain's major novels are the product of my years of reading and thinking about these books. I had no intention of using the books to prove any particular theory about the life of Samuel Clemens; in fact, I had no such theory.

In the course of my intensive study of Mark Twain's works, however, I found what seem to me to be difficulties which demand explanation, coupled with clues which point to a hypothesis which appears to answer those questions. I believe much of Twain's work can be clarified and explicated in relation to his life as Samuel Clemens; moreover, that Samuel Clemens' life can be clarified and explicated with the aid of hints to be found in Mark Twain's novels.

To put it another way, my thinking about Clemens' derives from my study of Twain, not (as is more conventional) the other way around. In seeking to explain the author's life from the intensive study of his works, I have developed a theory which explains not only the unanswered questions within the novels but also sheds light on the author's thoughts and behavior in his nonliterary life. This theory will be presented in the last section of this book. First, however, let us look at some aspects of Samuel Clemens' life which are as important to my thinking as Mark Twain's writing.

Part III

Encounters of the Second Kind:
Following the Leader

On the Trail of Mark Twain

In the course of my long fascination with Mark Twain, I began to travel to the places where he lived and worked. My purpose was to try to put myself in his place, and to feel as well as see some of the influences which worked on him.

I am a great believer in atmosphere. Visiting an historic site often seems to help me annihilate time and allows me to put myself more readily into the historic event which took place there. In visiting Mark Twain's haunts, I hoped to feel some of the sensations he must have felt, the better to understand the man who first experienced them.

So I began to track Mark Twain around the United States. The trail ran from Missouri to Nevada and California, then back across the continent to Connecticut and New York, ending finally at the Langdon/Clemens gravesite in Elmira. If I could not meet the man, at least I could hope to experience some of the sensations he felt.

To my surprise, however, my odyssey following Twain's spoor produced more than that. It gave me an understanding of some of the forces that shaped the artist and the man, as well as an insight into his personality. Following the Twain trail was a different sort of encounter with the man whose life and work had obsessed me for so long.

The trail begins, of course, in Missouri, so I set out for Hannibal.

Boy's Town

Samuel Langhorne Clemens was not born in Hannibal, the Mississippi River town with which he is most closely associated. His birthplace was the inland hamlet of Florida, Missouri, several miles southwest.

The date was November 30, 1835, and Halley's Comet was making one of its periodic approaches to earth at his birth. Sam was premature, a seven-month baby, and his mother mentioned later, that, when she first saw him she "could see little promise in him." He was a sickly infant who nevertheless managed to survive his childhood, something three of his siblings failed to do.

His father, John Marshall Clemens, came originally from Virginia and had the dignity (if not the financial resources) of an Old Dominion aristocrat. He married Jane Lampton in Kentucky in 1823; she was a witty, lively, and independent woman, little educated but intelligent. Among her comments on her fifth child was: "Sammy is a well of truth, but you can't bring it all up in one bucket."

John Marshall Clemens had come to Florida full of great expectations, but in the wake of the Panic of 1837, he decided to move to a more likely town, Hannibal on the river. The death of a daughter at about this time might also have been a spur to leave. In any event, the family settled in Hannibal in 1839.

Then about twenty years old, Hannibal was a much more substantial community than little Florida. Hannibal counted about one thousand citizens and could boast of some industries: there were a couple of slaughterhouses, a tannery, a hemp factory, and three sawmills. The Mississippi steamboats, which carried the town's commerce, tied up at the wharves lining the waterfront; one block uphill, parallel to the river, ran the principal business street. The town nestled in a little valley between Holliday's Hill on the north and Lovers' Leap, a higher bluff, on the south. Three miles below town was McDowell's Cave, where the boys of Hannibal went exploring. In the middle of the river was wild, uninhabited Glasscock's Island, splitting the Mississippi into two channels. One further significant fact requires mention; the Missouri side of the river was slave territory, while Illinois, across the river, was a free state.

This was the town in which the Clemens family settled. They arrived as substantial citizens—using virtually all his resources, John Clemens had purchased a quarter-block in the center of town, including some rental property and a small hotel on the corner of Main and Hill Streets, where the family lived. He called it "The Virginia" after the home state of his ancestors, but like all of John Marshall Clemens' business ventures, it proved financially disappointing.

At first, the family lived over the hotel, but in 1844, John Marshall Clemens built a house around the corner on Hill Street, the structure frequently thought of these days as the Tom Sawyer house. Across the street lived a girl named Laura Hawkins, the model for Becky Thatcher, Tom's girlfriend in the book, and around the corner behind the house lived Tom Blankenship, the unlettered and unfettered boy who became in literature the immortal Huckleberry Finn.

Sam Clemens lived in Hannibal for about thirteen years in all; he left in 1853, and thereafter returned only for occasional visits. During those thirteen years, he stored up a stock adventures and anecdotes which served him in his books for the rest of his life. One of his biographers, Dixon Wecter, asserts, "No major artist ever made more of his boyhood than did Samuel Clemens."[168]

Both in his books and in private recollections, Clemens frequently thought of his Hannibal years as an idyll. With the river, the hills and the cave to play around, it must have been a pleasant-enough spot. But in truth, Hannibal was less perfect than some of Twain's fiction may indicate. The boyhood of Samuel Clemens may have had plenty of idyllic moments, but there were also a number of ugly, terrifying occurrences. He saw a man shot to death on Main Street, witnessed a moonlight stabbing, encountered a corpse in his father's office (as Justice of the Peace, John Marshall Clemens was in charge of the inquest on the body) and watched the incineration of a drunken tramp who was burned to death when the jail caught fire.

Moreover, Hannibal was a slaveholding town. Even in its relatively mild border-town form, the institution was always cruel and capricious. Sam Clemens could recall the whipping of a girl slave who was punished by order of his own father, the looks on the faces of a group of Negroes waiting on the wharf for the steamboat which was taking them South, and the comment his mother made when he complained that a slave boy would not stop singing at the top of his lungs. She told him that as long as the boy was singing, he was not thinking of his personal tragedy; he had been sold away from his mother and would probably never see her again. Such experiences left a permanent mark on young Sam; he came to despise the institution, which his town and even his own family took for granted. Later in life, he made a personal reparation for slavery by financing a black student through Yale University.

---

[168] Dixon Wecter, *Sam Clemens of Hannibal* (Boston: Houghton-Mifflin, 1952).

With the death of his father, Sam was apprenticed to a printer and was employed in various newspaper offices for most of his teenage years. In 1853, he left Hannibal to see the world. He worked as a printer in New York, Philadelphia, and Cincinnati, but in the sense that his boyhood experiences permeate his best writing, it might be said that he never really left Hannibal.

I came to town about 150 years after Sam Clemens left, only to find that it hasn't let him get away. Entering the town over the Mark Twain Bridge, I immediately passed Mark Twain Avenue—site of the Mark Twain Motor Inn. This is not to be confused with the Mark Twain Motel, which stands on Main Street and houses the Mark Twain Coffee Shop. On the outskirts of town, the Tom and Huck Motel vies for tourist business with the Injun Joe. From any of these hostelries, you can take a Mark Twain taxi to the Mark Twain Dry Cleaners or the Mark Twain Beauty Shop. Everything in Hannibal is shamelessly Mark Twained and Tom Sawyered and Huck Finned and Becky Thatchered. The town's main industries are chemicals, cement, and Clemens, not necessarily in that order. Were he still alive, the old man would doubtless have a delightful time lampooning the way his characters and his name have been exploited in his own home town.

Still, Hannibal is fun to visit. The star attraction, of course, is the Mark Twain Home on Hill Street, built by John Marshall Clemens in 1844. However, the house you see today does not look quite like it appears in many, many photographs taken over the years. This is due to changes made during a reconstruction of the property several years ago. The heavy volume of tourist traffic going through the house destabilized the foundation, and for several years, you could not enter the structure: you could see it only through the windows, while standing on scaffolding erected outside. This was clearly unsatisfactory, so some years ago, the old house was taken apart. Each board was marked, and after the foundation was stabilized, the house was carefully rebuilt. In the course of the work, however, it was learned that the familiar shutters on the front windows had not been there when young Sammy was growing up, so they were not reinstalled. Moreover, it was discovered that the house originally had two more rooms than had been thought. These were added in the restoration so that while the Mark Twain Home is now more true to history than before the reconstruction, it does not look quite the same as it did.

Even with the two additional rooms, one's overwhelming sensation about the house is how small and cramped it seems. One can only imagine what it must have been like when six members of the Clemens family were shoehorned into this little structure during a hot Missouri summer. No wonder Sam spent so much of his time swimming and playing by the river!

The famous fence on the east side of the house, the scene of Tom Sawyer's ingenious plan to get his friends to pay him for the privilege of doing his whitewashing work for him, is not original, but it might just as well be. It still gets whitewashed frequently—I've plied the brush myself once or twice—and it remains one of Hannibal's favorite tourist sites.

Young Sam lived in this house off and on for about ten years, and a number of famous incidents, which he used in his novels, actually occurred here. The downstairs parlor was the scene of Peter the Cat's encounter with Painkiller, as related in *Tom Sawyer*. The side window is the one Peter used to evacuate the room, carrying a couple of flowerpots with him. The window in the boys' bedroom upstairs served as Tom's (and Sam's) midnight escape route. The original fence next to the house inspired the famous whitewashing story, and so on. The Mark Twain Home was given to the City of Hannibal by a local lawyer named George A. Mahan in 1912, with the understanding that it would never be used for profit. Mr. Mahan and his family, who were devoted admirers of Twain, also gave to the city the bronze statue of Tom and Huck which stands at the base of Holliday's Hill (Cardiff Hill in the books).

Adjoining the Clemens' House on the west is a stone structure erected as a museum by the city of Hannibal in 1935. Today it serves as the entry to the house, and as you exit through it you pass through the gift shop. The museum has been relocated around the corner in a larger building on Main Street which offers two floors of exhibit space. Upstairs is a collection of fifteen original paintings by Norman Rockwell illustrating scenes from Mark Twain's books. Here, too, one finds an unusual instrument called an "orchestrelle," a sort of combination organ and player piano which came from Clemens' last home, Stormfield, and was donated to the museum by Clara. According to the *Autobiography,* the author's friend, billiards partner and first literary executor Albert B. Paine played Jean's favorite music on this machine while her coffin was being carried from the house following her sudden death on Christmas Eve, 1909.[169]

About 1846 John Marshall Clemens was forced to give up title to the Hill Street House to satisfy demands of his creditors (the family later regained the home). For a time, the Clemens family lived over the drugstore in the so-called "House of the Pilasters", and it was in this house that Judge Clemens died of pleurisy (possibly pneumonia?) on March 24, 1847. This home, located at the corner of Main and Hill Streets, was prefabricated in Cincinnati in 1836, shipped by steamboat to Missouri and erected in Hannibal. It, too, was given to the city by the Mahan family and is now restored.

The drugstore, which occupies the street level of the "House of the Pilasters," was the scene of an important incident from Sam Clemens' childhood. A countryman named Sam Smarr was shot by a Hannibal storekeeper, whom he had accused of

---

[169]. *The Autobiography of Mark Twain,* edited by Charles Neider (New York: Harper and Brothers, 1961).

dishonesty, and was brought to the pharmacy, where he was laid on the floor. Somebody then placed a heavy Bible on his chest and nine-year-old Sam, who was watching, was long after haunted by the thought that the weight of the book might have caused the man's demise. He remembered the incident vividly, and forty years later, he used it in *Huckleberry Finn.*

Directly across Hill Street from the Clemens' home is the John Marshall Clemens law office. It was in this structure that young Sam stumbled one night over a corpse over which his father was conducting an inquest. Surprisingly, Mark Twain never used this incident in fiction: one would think that such a dramatic confrontation with Death would have found its way into at least one of his novels.

Next to the law office stands the so-called Becky Thatcher House. This was the home of Laura Hawkins, Sam's childhood sweetheart. At the time of writing, it is closed for renovation.

In the block behind the boyhood home, fronting on North Street, is a reconstruction of the Blankenship home—the place where Tom Blankenship, the model for Huckleberry Finn, grew up. This "Huck Finn House" is part of the Mark Twain Home and Museum Complex, although I found it rather uninteresting.

After lunch, I climbed Holliday's Hill. Beyond the Tom and Huck statue, executed by Chicago artist Frederick Hibbard, a path leads up to the top of the hill, where once the Widow Holliday lived in the closest thing Hannibal had to a mansion. She appears in *Tom Sawyer* and *Huck Finn* as the Widow Douglas, although her husband was actually still alive while Sam was growing up.

It is possible to drive up the hill—there's a road which curls up the back side—but Sam and his friends used to walk up, and so did I. This is where the gang used to play Robin Hood, in life as in literature, but my climb did not give me any feel of Sherwood Forest. The city is now too big and too commercialized to give any feeling of the "white town" Mark Twain recalled. I spent a few minutes looking over the river and the modern city, and then I stumbled back down.

There was still one more pilgrimage I had to make before I could feel I knew Hannibal—to the cave. It was privately owned in Sam Clemens' day (by a St. Louis doctor named MacDowell), and it is privately owned today. Two or three miles down the river from town, the cave includes miles of passages cut by a prehistoric underground river. Sam explored it and got lost in it while in the company of a young lady; this incident appears in *Tom Sawyer*. The real Injun Joe, a mild-mannered old fellow, nothing like the bloodthirsty cutthroat in the book, once got lost in the cave and lived on bats until he was rescued. One of the town drunkards wandered around in the darkness for a week until he found a hole and escaped to the riverbank. These events, too, were transformed and used by Twain as elements of *Tom Sawyer*. As the cave figures prominently in Sam Clemens' writing, so it did in his juvenile life.

It's surprisingly drab inside. Dull corridors crisscross every which way, looking even less mysterious in the glare of the electric lights. The passages are bleak and entirely devoid of romance. I can think of no better measure of Mark Twain's skill as a storyteller than his transformation of this pedestrian labyrinth into the mysterious and exciting cavern of *Tom Sawyer*.

Summing up Hannibal as I found it, I asked myself what the town gave to the boy who was to become Mark Twain? True, it supplied him with a rich stock of characters and experiences, which he transformed into great literature. But characters and experiences do not, alone, produce art; the same people and adventures did not inspire Sam's older brother Orion, for example, or anyone else in Hannibal. Samuel Clemens transformed an ordinary river town as he transformed its ordinary cave. As least as much as Hannibal made him, he made Hannibal.

* * * * * * * *

Hannibal sits on the west bank of the Mississippi River about one hundred miles northwest of St. Louis and 280 miles southwest of Chicago. Two main highways converge at the town; US 61, the north-south route which parallels the river from the Twin Cities to New Orleans, skirts the western side of town, while I-72 and U.S. 36 cross the Mississippi north of the town to reach the exit at Mark Twain Avenue. This road skirts the side of Holliday's Hill and becomes Third Street, half a block west of the boyhood home. The old Mark Twain Bridge, which crossed the river directly into Hannibal, has been removed—probably better for the town, but only at the cost of what was once a particularly dramatic approach to the village.

Connoisseurs of Americana will note that our greatest writer and our greatest president came from towns just one hundred miles apart—Twain in Hannibal and Abraham Lincoln in New Salem, Illinois. Lincoln was older by twenty-five years; he was a successful attorney in Springfield, while Sam Clemens was an apprentice printer in Hannibal. The area makes a great travel destination for parents who wish to steep their children in American history and literature—or to enjoy it themselves, for that matter.

On the River

For about four years, from 1857 when he became Horace Bixby's cub until April 1861, when the outbreak of intersectional hostilities shut down steamboat traffic, Samuel Clemens lived and worked on the Mississippi River. For about half of that time, he was a student; then, after obtaining his federal pilot's license in 1859, he was a tolerably successful professional.

Of course, I could not duplicate that experience; but I could visit the river as a tourist on a real steamboat, not all that different from the ones Clemens used to steer. And while sharing Clemens' Mississippi River experiences was not my primary purpose in leading tour groups and lecturing on the *"Delta Queen"* and *"Mississippi Queen,"* those trips did allow me to project myself into the world in which he lived and by which he was influenced.

Not that the river today is the same as it was in Clemens' piloting days. Time and the Army Corps of Engineers have seen to that. The Mississippi has been dredged, channeled, locked, leveed, and bridged. The ornate floating palaces of the past are mostly gone now: today's heavy freight traffic is handled in barges pushed by diesel towboats.

Moreover, even towns and landmarks Clemens knew are gone. Mark Twain himself describes the disappearance of Napoleon, Arkansas in Chapter 32 of *Life on the Mississippi,* and the process has continued through the century since. However much the Corps of Engineers struggles with it, the river is never completely controlled. It is like a circus lion—trained but never tamed. In this, as is many other ways, the Mississippi today is still very like the river Sam Clemens knew.

Even as a mere passenger on the "Mississippi Queen," one thing was brought home to me with stunning clarity—the prodigious learning and remarkable memory demanded of a pilot. Even today, with the aid of radar, radio, powerful search lights, electronic sounding devices, and the like, a pilot must know the whole river in his head. When Clemens worked here, without the advantages of modern technology, the demands were even greater. Not one person in a thousand, perhaps not one in a million, possesses the capacity to steer a boat carrying valuable cargo and priceless lives through a dark, foggy night on the river with a current running and invisible traffic all around, but Sam Clemens did. He writes of the piloting trade in *Life on the Mississippi,* but until one actually goes on the river, one can hardly appreciate what piloting demands today and what it must have demanded in Clemens' time. No one could doubt his genius, having once seen what his piloting career entailed.

One also gets, together with the sense of the difficulty of piloting, a hint of the danger of steamboating and the responsibilities the steersman bore. The average life of a Mississippi River steamer was not more than five or six years—collisions, explosions, and fires did in most boats before they had a chance to become obsolete. To pilot one of the floating palaces demanded that the man at the wheel dismiss from his mind the knowledge that they were also floating coffins. Clemens was able to do this even after the death of his brother Henry, killed when the *"Pennsylvania"* blew up under him totally without warning. A Mississippi pilot had to have not only brains but nerve; Clemens did.

Visiting the Mississippi also brought home another point about Clemens' piloting career. While boatmen do not experience the long weeks of isolation, which are the lot of deepwater sailors, an eight to ten day voyage away from women and families followed by a return trip of the same length must have made a boatman pretty eager for companionship, and in every river port—St. Louis, Memphis, Natchez, New Orleans—there were women ready to fill the need, generally for a price. Mark Twain writes that the river was an education in humanity; he might have specified that the teachers came in both sexes. Having traveled on the Mississippi, I simply could not take seriously the idea of Samuel Clemens as a celibate or a sexual neophyte.

Finally, my own brief riverboating experience quickly taught me to love the river and the boats which ply it, just as Clemens loved it and them. He said later that of all the things he did in his life, piloting career was the job he loved best. Had it not been for the Civil War, he would probably have remained a Mississippi River pilot for the rest of his life, and American literature would have lost one of its greatest figures. In the crazy bookkeeping of history, then, that terrible conflict which cost six hundred thousand lives played a major part in giving the nation one of its greatest treasures—the writer who, more than any other artist, caught the national soul and captured the national spirit.

Carry Me Out to Old Virginny

I n the spring of 1859, after ten years of sporadic and desultory placer gold mining, the greatest bonanza in American history was discovered on the eastern slope of Sun Mountain (also called Mt. Davidson), not far from Carson City, Nevada. Called the Comstock Lode after an early miner, it eventually produced at least $600 million in gold ore and nearly again as much in silver. Comstock mining helped to finance the Union war effort; so important was it to the federal cause that Nevada was admitted to the Union in 1864, despite the fact that it had nowhere near the requisite population. Ore dug from the Comstock paid for the mansions and hotels of San Francisco; the California gold rush of '49 was puny by comparison.

Queen of the Comstock was Virginia City, which started as a tent town near the early placer mines but soon grew into the richest community between Chicago and the Pacific Coast. It got its name from a drunken prospector named Fennimore, who had changed his name to Finney after killing a man in California and then allowed "Finney" to be corrupted into "Virginny." "Virginny" broke a bottle of booze one night and took advantage of the spilled whiskey to baptize the site "Virginia" in his own honor. The name stuck, and as the camp grew, "City" was added.

The Comstock boom brought thousands of fortune seekers to Nevada. Many, of course, became miners, but with the muckers and the stopers came teamsters, cardsharps, merchants, murderers, lawyers, and lawbreakers. Saloons sprang up everywhere, painted women arrived in numbers, and the oldest profession flourished. From California, from the Confederacy, from the Union, ambitious men and women came to Virginia City. They came to get rich, and some of them did. Even for the less fortunate, cash was far more abundant in Nevada than on the hardscrabble farms where many of them grew up. There was money to be made, and not much to spend it on.

Also, there was a thirst for news. Wherever they might come from, Comstockers wanted to know what was happening back in "the States," where the Great War was being fought. There was no telegraph, and it took weeks to get information via San Francisco and the ships from the East. The Pony Express began running in 1860, cutting the wait to days, but news was still at a premium, and a young man named Joe Goodman came to Virginia City to supply it.

He bought a struggling weekly newspaper called the *Territorial Enterprise,* which had recently moved to Virginia City from another mining camp. In a short time, he made it the heart and soul of the Comstock. Possessed of an acerbic wit and a facile pen, Joe Goodman wrote what he thought and backed his words with weapons, if necessary. He fought and won at least one duel against a rival editor, and his credo was that to be a good Virginia City newspaperman, you had to shoot straight—with a pen or a pistol, as the occasion demanded.

Goodman gathered around him a sparkling staff. His right-hand man was Rollin Daggett, a master of invective adjectives. William Wright, who called himself Dan De Quille, specialized in tall stories and pointed satire. Steve Gillis was noted equally for his writing and his fighting; he dispatched copy and dueling opponents with equal facility. Together, they made the *Territorial Enterprise* the liveliest and best-written newspaper in the West.

It was in the spring of 1862 that Editor Goodman began to receive some sketches from a writer in Aurora who called himself simply "Josh." They were humorous, often tinged with satire and cynicism, and Goodman published them readily. One piece in particular, a burlesque of a new and especially pompous judge, caused quite a reaction among *Enterprise* readers, and when "Josh" followed that sketch with another, equally devastating, Joe Goodman decided that this was a writer he wanted for his staff. He sent a letter to "Josh" in Aurora offering him a reporter's position at $25 a week and urged him to come to Virginia City if he were not making more money prospecting. He wasn't—later that year, Dan De Quille left for an extended trip back to "the States," and his replacement on the *Enterprise* was "Josh," fresh up from Aurora. "Josh," of course, was Samuel L. Clemens, who had not yet begun using the pen name Mark Twain. Like Benjamin Franklin a century before, he was making the transition from printing newspapers to writing for them; from artisan to artist.

Technically, "Josh" was supposed to be a reporter, but he soon discovered that Comstockers had little appetite for straight coverage of local events. Besides, Joe Goodman hadn't hired him to write obituaries. What *Enterprise* readers wanted was humor, so humor was what "Josh" produced. He wrote tall stories after the manner of De Quille and burlesques inspired by Artemus Ward. Goodman sent him to cover the sessions of the Territorial Legislature, fully aware that his new reporter knew little or nothing of politics or parliamentary procedure. What the editor expected from his legislative correspondent was colorful writing, and he got it. Clemens' reports from Carson City were read widely and with pleasure. With his growing stature, he decided on a new pen name, and one of his sketches lampooning politicians became the first piece signed Mark Twain.

"Mark Twain" was actually a Mississippi River term, the leadsman's call informing the pilot that the water was two fathoms deep and safe to navigate. Nor was Samuel Clemens the first man to use this haunting river call as a pen name—at least one other old-time river man had signed himself in print that way, although Sam always denied having stolen the name from him.[170] No matter; before he left Virginia City, long before the publication of any of his famous books, Samuel L. Clemens had made Mark Twain his alter ego beyond the possibility of confusion or challenge.

My first trip to Virginia City was made without particular thought of Mark Twain. Victorian mining towns have always attracted me in any case, and Virginia had escaped me until I was past thirty. I found it rather disappointing—approaching from Reno over the Geiger Grade Highway, a contemporary paved road which more or less follows the former stage track, I saw a series of terraces cut into the side of Sun Mountain, with a few church steeples standing sentinel above the commercial buildings. Below the main streets, the houses straggled away into empty lots, and beyond was the awesome, endless emptiness of the desert. Above the town rose the blank gray mountain, peaking in a grim, rocky summit. There were few trees and no streams, few flowers and no songbirds. I had the overriding impression that Virginia City teetered on the extreme outer edge of civilization.

Only when I returned to the Comstock with Twain on my mind did it come alive for me. This time, I followed his route

---

170.   The man was Captain Isaiah Sellers, who signed letters to the New Orleans newspapers "Mark Twain." Clemens may or may not have taken the pen name from him, but it is interesting that the hero of Mark Twain's first novel, *The Gilded Age* (written with Charles Dudley Warner), is "Colonel Sellers."

to Virginia City—along the Carson River to the mouth of Gold
Canyon, then up a steep and twisting road through Silver City
and Gold Hill to the Queen City of the Comstock. Every foot of
this historic trail was once lined with miners' cabins, stamping
mills, and placer works. Enormous piles of tailings bear mute
testimony to years of deep mining. Past the old Gold Hill railway
station, the road climbs even more steeply to the top of the
canyon; there it becomes C Street, the principal thoroughfare
of Virginia City.[171]

The narrow street is lined with two—and three-story buildings,
many with false fronts or pillared galleries. A century ago, these
storefronts served Comstock miners; today, they conduct a
flourishing commerce with traveling tenderfeet. Even more
than Hannibal, Virginia City today lives off the tourist business.

But I ignored the candy stores and the T-shirt shops, for I had
a mission in mind. I had come to Nevada to see Mark Twain's
Virginia City, not the tawdry tourist trap many folks find there.
I parked my car on a strip of flat land along D Street, where the
railroad station used to stand. There, a block away, was St. Mary's
in the Mountains Catholic Church, built originally by Father
Patrick Manogue. He was an ex-miner himself, a veteran of the
California gold rush who had since had a vocation, studied in
Paris, and was ordained just in time to join the rush to Washoe
in 1859. His church is one of relatively few buildings in Virginia
City which dates back to the early period.

[171.] The saddle between Gold Hill and Virginia City was the site of a mock
holdup of Mark Twain, staged by Steve Gillis and some of his other
friends on the occasion of Mark's return to the Comstock to give a
lecture in November 1866. Their object was to keep Mark in town a few
days longer, as well as to have some fun with him; but he did not take the
joke very well and actually left town sooner than he had planned. See
Sanbom, pp. 303-306.

This is due to the Great Fire. Mining towns seem to have been particularly subject to conflagration, probably because they were characteristically flimsy. Virginia City was no exception. On October 26, 1875, a roaring blaze destroyed most of the town. St. Mary's was damaged but rebuilt. A few other buildings—the First Presbyterian Church, the Savage Mansion, the old Gould, and Curry Mining office, later used as the home of John W. Mackay—escaped the fire.[172] They are physical links with the Virginia City of Mark Twain's time. I wondered how many times he had passed the church before which I was now standing.

Even if the majority of the town dates from a later time, there is much more in Virginia City which is unchanged from the early bonanza days. The layout of the town, with its steeply graded cross streets, is exactly as Mark described it over a century ago. He panted his way uphill from D Street to A. I did the same thing, with the same result. The bleak gray mass of Sun Mountain is the same; so is the view of the awesome, seemingly endless sagebrush desert as seen from C Street. If you look behind the tourist traps, there is more than enough of the original Virginia City left to give today's visitor a sense of what Washoe was like when Sam Clemens lived in it, and Mark Twain wrote about it.

There are other reminders, if you know where to look. Maguire's Opera House, where Twain and his cronies watched stunned and delighted as Adah Isaacs Mencken appeared nearly nude in *Mazeppa*, was burned in the Great Fire of '75, but a part of its entryway was made of stone and survived to

---

[172.] Mackay was the greatest of all the Comstock nabobs. From his start as a $4 a day mucker, he eventually became a mine owner and is estimated to have taken a fortune of $100 million from the Comstock—more than any other individual. He later headed the Postal Telegraph Company, and his daughter Ellen married a Russian immigrant songwriter by the name of Isadore Baline. You know him better as Irving Berlin.

be incorporated in a private residence, which still stands on D Street (the current Piper's Opera House is new by Virginia City standards—it wasn't built until 1884). The ruins of the joss house on F Street mark the site of the city's once sizeable Chinatown. I toured the Chollar Mine, a portion of whose main tunnel leading into the mountain is still intact. Once owned by William Sharon, a leading Comstock financier and agent for the Bank of California, the Chollar was once among the region's top producers. Today, its interior contains exhibits of mining equipment and techniques used in the boom days.

That mine visit was instructive. It was a graphic reminder that however romantic Virginia City may seem today, existence in the Comstock was anything but easy. Work was hard and dangerous; life was cheap. At any moment, a miner might be crushed to death by a cave-in or scalded by a sudden flood of underground hot water. Homes and families were far away; even today, Virginia City generates a strong sense of distance from civilization, and in the days before electronic communication and motorized transportation, the sense of isolation must have been overwhelming.

That was why Comstockers needed humor to cope with the conditions under which they lived, and that was why Mark Twain wrote humor. If necessity is the mother of invention, then a writer's market is midwife to his copy, and the demands of Virginia City residents helped create Mark Twain the funny man. Only later, when writing in different circumstances and for an entirely different public, did Samuel Clemens become Mark Twain, the romantic glorifier of boyhood, and still later, Mark Twain, the social critic.

In Virginia City, too, a landmark incident in the growth of Sam Clemens into Mark Twain occurred. Despairing of his work, he came to Joe Goodman one day and said he was going back to Aurora. "I'll never be a writer," he moaned. "You're already one," replied the editor, and his encouragement may have saved Clemens' literary career.[173]

Mark Twain remained in Virginia City less than two years. He was forced to leave in a hurry in May 1864, after challenging another newspaperman to a duel in the romantic tradition of his editor and coworkers. The duel never came off—his opponent backed out at the last minute—but by this time, satisfaction of the field of honor was frowned on by the law of Nevada, and Clemens had made enemies who would have been only too happy to see him jailed. He had the choice of leaving immediately or facing two years in prison, and he chose the 4:00 a.m. stage to San Francisco.

He took with him invaluable newspaper experience, sharpened skills as a writer of humor and satire, and new confidence in his future. He also brought along the best and best-known pen name in America.

I too took something significant from the Comstock—a deeper understanding of how Samuel Clemens grew as an artist. Responding to the stimuli of Virginia City, he attained his first success as a funnyman. By contrast, while he wrote a great deal about Hannibal, he did more to shape it than it did to determine the direction of his career.

Indeed, in the end who can be certain that the hundreds of millions of dollars in gold and silver that the Comstock produced were more important or more long lasting than its literary creation, Mark Twain?

[173.] George Lyman, *The Saga of the Comstock Lode* (New York: Charles Scribner's Sons, 1934), p. 262.

The Cabin on Jackass Hill

Following his hasty departure from Virginia City in May 1864, Sam Clemens made his way to San Francisco. There he took a job as a reporter for a newspaper named the *Morning Call*. He hated the drudgery of newspaper work and spent much of his time getting acquainted with the city's many watering places. In time, he earned the enmity of the powers that be over his intemperate criticism of the San Francisco Police Department. In brief, he made the city too hot to hold him, and in December 1864, Clemens found it prudent to leave town for a while.

His old *Territorial Enterprise* buddy, Steve Gillis (who had accompanied him on that early morning stage out of Virginia City), had a brother Jim, who was prospecting for gold in the Sierras, not far from the town of Angel's Camp. It was to his cabin on Jackass Hill, above the Melones River, that Clemens went.[174]

---

174. Clemens was surprised and pleased to find that Jim Gillis had a fine library in the cabin, including Shakespeare, Dickens, Lord Byron, and plenty of philosophy and other fine literature. See Margaret Sanborn, *Mark Twain: The Bachelor Years* (New York: Doubleday, 1990) p. 257.

The hill had acquired its name from the animals which were stabled there. The pack mules were used to haul supplies to the mines, and on any given night, there might be two hundred of them grazing on the slopes and braying in the dark. The Gillis cabin was at the top of the hill, and its occupants were often lulled to sleep by a chorus of heehaws from below.

For entertainment, the Gillis brothers and their guest would descend the steep hill and head for Angel's Camp, a few miles south. There, Clemens hung out at the bar at the local hotel, known as the Lake, where the proprietor, host, and bartender was a man named Ross (or Ben) Coon. It was from him that Clemens heard the story about a local jumping frog contest won by a stranger who filled the champion frog with buckshot. He found the tale so interesting that he took notes on it, but he did no writing either at Angel's Camp or at the Gillis cabin; his notes went back to San Francisco with him when he returned to the city at the end of February 1865.

Upon his return, he found a letter from Artemus Ward, the well-known humorist whom he had met in Virginia City, among the pile of mail which had accumulated in his absence. Ward had been impressed with Clemens when they met, and now, he invited the former *Enterprise* staffer to contribute a sketch to a book of humor he was compiling. After some delay and further prodding from Ward, Mark Twain wrote down the jumping frog story, changing the names of the leading characters, and sent it off to New York, but the story arrived too late to be included in the book. Ward's publisher, G. W. Carleton, passed it along to the editor of a weekly called the *Saturday Press*. That paper printed it on November 18, 1865; although Twain was not to hear about it for six weeks, it was a huge hit, and he was famous overnight.[175] In the meantime, Twain gave the manuscript of the

---

[175.] See Sanborn, p. 268.

Jumping Frog to his friend Bret Harte, editor of the *Californian*. Harte liked the story and published it on December 16; by Christmas, Mark Twain was an established writer on both coasts of the United States. At the time, he was just over thirty years of age.

So popular was the Jumping Frog story that it was made the title of Mark Twain's first book, a collection of twenty-eight sketches put together by Charles Webb (an old friend from the *Californian*; he was its founder and publisher) and published in March 1867. Incidentally, this first Mark Twain hardcover was printed by the firm of Gray and Green in New York, where Samuel Clemens had worked fourteen years earlier. This delightful quirk of circumstances marked his passage from artisan to artist.

While the cabin on Jackass Hill was not really the place where Mark Twain wrote his first successful story, it was Clemens' base when he first heard the tale, and it was an important landmark in his life before he became a literary success. So while taking my daughter to Sacramento, I made the eighty-mile detour to see the site on my way back to Los Angeles.

Accordingly, I took California 49, the Gold Rush Highway, southward through Drytown, Sutter Creek, Jackson and across the river to Jackass Hill. The turnoff from Route 49 to the Mark Twain Cabin is clearly marked; you go sharply to the east of the highway and right up the steep slope. Private homes line the road all the way to the top, and when you do get to the crest of the hill, the sight is less than inspiring. The ramshackle cabin sits in the middle of a turnaround, protected by an iron fence, and surrounded by contemporary dwellings.

The cabin which stands on Jackass Hill today is not the one in which Mark Twain stayed; that structure burned to the ground about 1890. The collapsing shack we see today was built in 1922 in the hopes of attracting some tourist trade. Its chimney stones may or may not be from the original cabin, depending on whose story you believe. Even the site is not certain, though the Gillis cabin certainly stood on the top of this hill, at most no more than a few yards off.

The condition of the "Mark Twain Cabin" is appalling; it looks as though it might keel over any minute. The floor sags badly, the windowpanes have long since vanished, the boards forming the outside walls are loose and rotting. The shack is at the mercy of the weather; but for the fence and for its isolation, it would be a target for vandals. If this were the original shack, left untouched since Twain's visit in 1865, it could hardly be in worse shape. Besides, the encroachment of contemporary homesteads (not to mention the absence of braying jackasses) makes it impossible to get any feeling for the site as it must have been when Jim Gillis moved his library in.

As for nearby Angel's Camp, where Mark Twain heard the story which was to make him famous—well, it is hardly more inspiring than the cabin, if in better physical condition. The Lake Hotel, where Ross Coon tended bar and told stories, disappeared long ago. The town has grown and retains little (if any) Gold Rush flavor today.

True, it does host the annual Jumping Frog competition each May, a blatant case of capitalizing on the Mark Twain story to bring in the tourist trade. It is too artificial for my taste; too self-consciously cute, like the miniature frogs which you find all over town.

Even the name, Angel's Camp, is a letdown. It has nothing at all to do with messengers from heaven, sent to disclose a gold vein to poverty-stricken but prayerful miners. In fact, Angel's Camp got its name from its founder, a fellow by the name of George Angel, who settled the site back in '49.

Feeling no flavor of the Gold Rush days, when Mark Twain took refuge here from the San Francisco police, I returned to the car and started back to Los Angeles.

From California Bachelor to Connecticut Gentleman: The Metamorphosis of Mark Twain

S amuel Clemens returned to San Francisco on February 26, 1865, an unrewarded California prospector, a bachelor, a poor man, an unknown. Six years to the day afterward he had become a famous writer, a husband and father and a well-to-do Connecticut property owner. Few men lead lives which change so much so quickly. How Clemens performed this spectacular metamorphosis is, I suggest, important to the understanding of his life and later work.

Part of the miracle was due to the combination of undeniable talent and unremitting labor. During his San Francisco period (roughly extending from spring 1865 to December 1866) Mark Twain wrote countless newspaper and magazine articles which appeared in a number of journals throughout the far west. His work appeared in the *Californian*, the *Golden Era*, the *Territorial Enterprise*, the *Alta California* and the *Sacramento Union* to name several. It was the *Union* which sent him to Hawaii (then called the Sandwich Islands) in the spring of '66, and it was while he was serving as a correspondent there that Clemens scored a major news scoop. With the aid of Anson Burlingame, he was able to interview the survivors of the clipper "*Hornet*" who were washed up on shore after forty-three days in an open boat. His story was spread over the front page of the *Union* and earned him further recognition and respect.

His Hawaiian experiences provided Clemens with the material for another new career—that of platform lecturer. He sold out his first house in San Francisco in October 1866 and continued to appear on the lecture platform intermittently for the rest of his life. While he claimed to hate speaking and the travel it demanded, he knew he could always raise substantial sums of quick cash by taking to the lecture circuit, and he did so on several occasions.

Mark Twain's first national recognition as a writer dates from this period as well. His "Jumping Frog" sketch, which appeared in New York in November 1865, made his reputation as a funny man and was later used as the title story in his first hardcover book.

Partially as a result of this work and these varied successes, Clemens got the *Alta* to pay for his voyage on the "*Quaker City*"—the great Pleasure Excursion to the Holy Land and Europe which was to be the single most important undertaking of his life. The trip not only resulted in the publication of *The Innocents Abroad*, an undeniable classic and a runaway best seller, it also resulted in an acquaintance between Clemens and one of his fellow passengers—a young man named Charles Langdon, with whom Clemens became friendly.

The Langdon family was the antithesis of Clemens' own—old, distinguished, and rich. One of Charles' ancestors, John Langdon, had been a signer of the Constitution and governor of New Hampshire. Charles' father, Jervis Langdon, had made a fortune in the coal business and was a leading citizen of Elmira, New York. Charles Langdon himself later went on to a successful career in business, and his son and grandson continued the family tradition, both serving as presidents of major corporations.

Charles had been sent on the *Quaker City* expedition as a sort of last fling before settling down to serious work.[176] He was traveling alone, and Clemens became his closest companion on the ship, despite a fourteen-year difference in their ages.

One day, while the "Quaker City" was resting in the Bay of Smyrna, young Langdon showed his new friend an ivory miniature of his sister, Olivia. Clemens later claimed that he fell in love with her at that moment; in any event, they met in New York City in December 1867. Two years later, after a rocky courtship, they were married at the bride's home in Elmira. Clemens bought a one-third interest in a Buffalo newspaper, and the couple settled into a house purchased for them as a wedding gift by Livy's father. She immediately became pregnant, and on November 7, 1870, delivered Clemens' first child, a son named Langdon.

But life in Buffalo was less than idyllic. The city was intellectually sterile and Mark Twain was no happier as a newspaper editor than he had been as a San Francisco reporter. The death of Jervis Langdon from stomach cancer in August 1870 released the newlyweds from any obligation to remain in the house, which he had bought for them, so Clemens divested himself of his interest in the paper and moved the family to Hartford, Connecticut. This was the home of Mark Twain's publisher, Elisha Bliss; it offered the intellectual climate which Buffalo had lacked, and Clemens had liked the city ever since

---

176. Shipboard romances with members of the lower class were the terror of nineteenth-century nabobs, but Charles was not pursuing a young lady. Also, this was not a mere passenger liner; it was the "*Quaker City*," all of whose company (except Clemens) was properly well-heeled and unquestionably acceptable. So Sam made friends with Charley Langdon, and the rest of his life was altered accordingly.

he had visited it for the first time in January 1868 to negotiate a publishing contract for *The Innocents Abroad*. Hartford was to be the Clemens family's home base for the next twenty years.

Upon arriving in the city, they rented the John Hooker house in which Clemens had stayed during his 1868 visit. They lived in it from October 1871, until their own home was finished in April 1874. Summers were spent at Quarry Farm outside Elmira, the home of Livy's adopted sister, Susan Langdon Crane, and her husband Theodore.

The next year, 1872, was eventful. *Roughing It*, Mark Twain's second travel book, was published in February and received generally good reviews, although it never sold as well as *Innocents*. On March 19, Livy delivered a second child—a girl, christened Olivia Susan Clemens after her mother, grandmother, and aunt, but always known in the family as Susy. Only three months later came a great sorrow: the death of baby Langdon Clemens on June 2. In his *Autobiography*, dictated many years afterward, Samuel Clemens blames himself for his son's death. He tells how he took Langdon for a long drive on a cold day and allowed the child's fur robes to fall off so that the baby was severely chilled, progressively worsened, and finally died.

This account is untrue. Actually Langdon had been a sickly child throughout his nineteen months of life; he never developed the ability to walk or talk, and his skin was an unearthly chalk white. His death was due to diphtheria, not pneumonia, nor was his father responsible for his contracting the disease. However, Samuel Clemens seems to have needed to feel guilty about the death of his son, for which he irrationally blamed himself.[177]

---

[177]. See the *Autobiography*, p. 208. Clemens writes that this passage was his first confession of guilt over Langdon's death. It is curiously unconvincing; it reads as if it were an afterthought. And to top off this strange passage,

He afterward concentrated his affection and attention on his second child, the healthy and entirely normal Susy.

Clemens spent most of 1873 in England, where he was treated as a literary lion. Late in the year, Livy conceived a third baby while Mark Twain published *The Gilded Age,* a satiric novel on which he collaborated with his friend and neighbor, Charles Dudley Warner. The book is most notable for its portrait of the ever-ebullient Colonel Sellers, a character based on James Lampton, a cousin of Clemens' mother.

Livy delivered a second daughter, named Clara, at Elmira on June 8, 1874, and shortly thereafter, the family moved up the hill to Quarry Farm to spend the rest of the summer. There, in the new pilot house study his sister-in-law had built for him, Mark Twain began to write the first of his great novels of the Mississippi Valley—*The Adventures of Tom Sawyer.* This "paean to boyhood" was finished the next summer and finally published in December 1876; it has never been out of print since and probably never will be. A survey conducted not too long ago found *The Adventures of Tom Sawyer* to be the most widely read work of fiction in America today.

While the Clemens family engaged in literary production and biological reproduction in Elmira, architect Edward Tuckerman Potter was overseeing the completion of their new home at 351 Farmington Avenue in Hartford. This house is a classic example of what Henry David Thoreau meant when he wrote that a house should be a portrait of its occupants executed in wood and stone. Restored today as the Mark Twain Memorial, it is the most important monument to the author and his family outside Hannibal, and it was my next stop on the trail of Mark Twain.

Clemens reports the baby's age inaccurately. Langdon died at nineteen months, not twenty-two.

The Curious House that Mark Built

In October 1874, two and a half years after settling in Hartford, the Clemens family moved into their new home at 351 Farmington Avenue. It was and is a remarkable building. Twain himself, in an enchanting piece of doggerel written in 1877, called it "the curious house that Mark built."

It is located in Nook Farm, an area named because there was once a curving stream flowing past the property whose course created a corner or nook. The site was home to such late-Victorian literary figures as Harriet Beecher Stowe and Charles Dudley Warner, but the other houses in Nook Farm were stolid and conventional. Not so the Mark Twain house.

It was planned to reflect the flamboyant man who built it. The style is High Victorian Gothic, with steep roofs, projecting gables, and odd corners and curves. The long veranda (called the Ombra) and the broad rear porch, coupled with the unique way the kitchen projects out front, makes it easy to envision the house as a river steamboat plowing northward toward Farmington Avenue. However, there is no evidence to prove that this was intentional.

Not only the form of the house is unusual. The exterior texture is enlivened by varying the direction, angle and projection of the brick. There are asymmetric gingerbread decorations and non-repeating patterns of brick inlay.

The interior is equally unorthodox. Much of the decor was executed in 1881 by Lewis Comfort Tiffany, who was called in when the house was enlarged after the family's return from two years' residence in Europe. The entrance hall is embellished by geometric designs stenciled against the wood and has a fireplace decorated with wood panels carved in India. Over the mantel is an empty space; this was once filled by a Tiffany stained-glass window. Someday, if it can be located, it may find its way back to its original seat.

The entrance hall also sports a small closet in which Mark Twain kept a telephone. Personally, he hated the instrument and never got much use from it, but as a lover of gadgetry (and a prophet of the new mechanical age), he became one of Hartford's first subscribers.[178]

The drawing room, into which Livy Clemens and the female guests would withdraw after dinner while the men smoked their cigars, had a number of original furnishings and is highlighted by a great mirror, which was moved from the Buffalo house and installed to complement this ornate room. Other pieces owned by the family include the chairs which flank the mirror and the chandelier which is reflected in it.

[178.] One reason for Twain's antipathy to the telephone may have been that he rejected the chance to be an early investor in the device. Too bad—it proved to be a much more useful and profitable invention than the Paige machine into which Samuel Clemens put at least $300,000, only to lose it all.

If the drawing room was Livy's, the dining room was Sam's. It is surpassingly Victorian—and surpassingly ugly, with its gaudy imitation leather wallpaper and grotesque wood furniture. There is a characteristic touch of Twainian humor in the placement of a window directly over the fireplace. It amused Mark to sit at the table and watch the snow fall softly into the fire.

When they were at home, the Clemens family entertained extravagantly. Hartford was conveniently located on the way from New York to Boston, and traveling celebrities were always welcome. It was a rare night when somebody famous or interesting did not show up for dinner at Nook Farm. Among the famous guests at Mark Twain's table were General Sherman, Matthew Arnold, and Henry Stanley (the man who found Dr. Livingston in Africa). In one year, The Clemens family spent the improbable sum of $100,000 on dinner parties alone.[179]

That figure says a great deal about what Nook Farm meant to Sam Clemens. He had been a poor boy in Hannibal and an unsuccessful prospector in California and Nevada. Steamboat piloting earned him a good wage, but it hardly made him wealthy. Thus, with the publication of *The Innocents Abroad, Roughing It,* and *The Gilded Age,* his substantial income from his popular lecture tours (in England as well as America), and with his marriage to a socially prominent heiress, Clemens felt that he had arrived. His nineteen-room mansion, light years from the cramped little wooden house in Hannibal, was his personal symbol of success.[180]

[179.] Although it wasn't presented that way by the guide on the tour, I think this must be in current values. Such a sum in the 1880s would have been more than improbable—it might even have been impossible.

[180.] Justin Kaplan, *Mr. Clemens and Mark Twain* (New York: Simon and Schuster, 1966) pp. 209-211.

Adjoining the dining room is the library, to my mind the warmest and most livable room in the house. Here, the family used to gather after dinner—Sam, Livy, Susy, and later Clara (b. 1875) and Jean (b. 1880). The children would demand that their father tell them a story involving all the bric-a-brac, which stood on the enormous mantelpiece. He would start at one end and work his way across—and woe to him if he left an object or two out.

This mantelpiece was purchased by Clemens at Ayton Castle in Scotland, and it was such a favorite of his that when the house was finally sold in 1903, he had it removed from the room and retained possession. It was returned to the house in 1958 as part of the restoration effort.

Two rooms branch off from the library. One is the conservatory, a glass-enclosed indoor garden overrun with plants.[181] The children used this room to stage family plays, including a memorable adaptation of Twain's story *The Prince and the Pauper*. The other room is the guest bedchamber; the family called it the Mahogany Bedroom, but William Dean Howells, Clemens' friend for forty years and a frequent visitor in the house, dubbed it the "Royal Bedchamber" because it contained an elaborate canopied bed. Adjoining is a bathroom, one of five in the house. This in itself was extremely unusual for 1874, but this room is especially remarkable in that it contained a shower. At a time when indoor plumbing was a rarity, this innovation must have seemed truly radical.

On the second floor is the master bedroom with its incredible hand-carved bedstead brought from Venice. Mark Twain claimed that he and his wife slept with their heads at the

---

[181.] Harriet Beecher Stowe, the Clemens' Nook Farm neighbor, initiated the conservatory fad among her friends and associates. Probably, this room reflects her influence.

bottom of the bed so they could gaze more readily at this riot of carved cherubim. The children played with the removable angels, which decorate the corner posts; it's easy to imagine the three girls storming into their parents' bedroom early on a winter morning and attacking the carvings while Sam and Livy tried to snatch a few minutes more sleep.[182]

Also on this second floor are the guest bedroom frequently occupied by Livy's mother on her visits to Nook Farm; Susy's girlhood room; the room shared by the two younger girls and the schoolroom. This light, airy, roomy space was originally designed as a study for Mark, and it has a broad, comfortable window seat which he had installed for himself. He soon found, however, that the room was too noisy and the window seat too comfortable for serious work. He could get nothing done there, so the room was turned over to the children, and Mark Twain's writing was done in the billiard room on the third floor.

This masculine area at the south end of the house was Samuel Clemens' den, study, and playroom rolled into one. It was his retreat from feminine gentility—he could stay up all night smoking cigars and playing billiards, his favorite recreation. What writing he did in the Nook Farm house was done in this room—most notably the first part of *Life on the Mississippi* and a number of lectures and short speeches. Most of Twain's serious creative work, however, was done during summer vacations at Quarry Farm near Elmira. Mr. Clemens' life as a town squire left him little time for writing in Hartford.

The drawing room may echo Livy, the dining room and the billiard room belong to Mark, but the rest of the home reflects

---

[182.] Years later, Clara recalled that the Clemens girls enjoyed being a little ill because they were allowed to play in the great bed on those occasions when they were sick.

the children. Clara and Jean were born in this house; Susy was two when the family moved in. The girls gave life and warmth to the rambling mansion, and the most prominent of the three was Susy.

She was Mark Twain's favorite daughter, most like him in temperament and wit. Susy was the moving spirit behind the play productions and the story hours. She shared her father's quick temper and his facility with words; when she was only thirteen, she began to write a biography of him, much of which is incorporated into Mark Twain's *Autobiography*.[183] It is a charming document; it's easy to see how this precocious, vivacious child was her father's delight. Moreover, Susy had been the substitute love object when Langdon Clemens, her only brother, died in infancy. No wonder Sam adored her so.

Tragically, she contracted spinal meningitis while visiting Hartford in 1896 and died in the house where she had been raised. Her passing, which took place in the "Royal Bedchamber" downstairs, followed a short, painful illness.

Samuel Clemens never really recovered from the sudden death of his favorite daughter. In effect, the date of her death—August 18, 1896—marked the end of her father's literary career. While he began countless manuscripts in the remaining fourteen years of his life and wrote hundreds of thousands of words, he was able to complete little of what he began and published almost nothing.[184] Of all his major works, only *Following the Equator* (on which he was working on at the time of Susy's death), *The*

---

[183] It has now been published in its entirety for the first time. See Susy Clemens, *Papa: An Intimate Biography of Mark Twain*, edited by Charles Neider (Garden City, NY: Doubleday and Company, 1985).

[184] Bernard DeVoto, "The Symbols of Despair," from *Mark Twain at Work* (Cambridge: Harvard University Press, 1942).

Mysterious Stranger, and the *Autobiography* were not published during her lifetime.

Olivia Clemens was hit equally hard. Never again after Susy's death did she enter the Farmington Avenue house—she could not bear to see it anymore. For the next three years, the family lived abroad in Vienna and London. Although they still owned the Hartford property, they did not live there when they returned to America in 1900. Instead, they rented a home in New York City, where they remained until Livy's failing health brought them back to Europe. They occupied a villa in Florence, Italy, remaining there until Livy died in June 1903. That same year, Samuel Clemens sold the vacant house in Hartford—the family home for twenty years—when he realized that he could never live there again either.

The Farmington Avenue property was purchased by an insurance executive, who occupied it for several years. Later, it was used as a boys' school; finally, in 1929, the Friends of Hartford acquired the house, intending to establish a Mark Twain Memorial. The need to service the mortgage demanded, however, that income be derived from the property. Thus, the library, dining room, and drawing room were leased to the Hartford Public Library for use as a branch office, while the upstairs rooms were converted into apartments. Not until 1955 did the Mark Twain Memorial decide to restore the house to its 1881 appearance, and it took another twenty years of fund-raising, research, and construction before the project was completed. In 1974, on the centennial of its construction, the house that Mark built was at last opened to the public. Three years later, the Mark Twain Memorial received the prestigious David E. Finley Award for significant achievement from the National Trust for Historic Preservation.

Tours of the house include not only the rooms already described but also the interesting Twain Museum in the basement, where the most striking exhibit is the fantastic Paige Automatic Typesetting Machine. Samuel Clemens, the one-time printer's devil, sank a fortune into development of this Rube Goldbergian device. It never worked well enough to market, and in due time, the Mergenthaler Linotype made it obsolete. Sam Clemens went into bankruptcy, and the Paige machine wound up in the Mark Twain Museum.

As a matter of fact, the Paige Automatic Typesetter contributed to Clemens' failure at the age of fifty-eight, but it was hardly the only factor. The Hartford house itself strained his resources. It took six servants to run the place; however successful Mark Twain may have been as an author and lecturer—and he was very successful—still, the house demanded the assured income of a business tycoon. The cost of running it had driven the Clemens family to live in Europe as early as 1891, even before the business slump of 1893. Susy's death ended for good, their plans to return to Farmington Avenue. Samuel Clemens lived too high for even Mark Twain's considerable income.

Here is still another paradox. Mark Twain exposed with devastating clarity the shallow, foolish, and corrupt values of the Gilded Age, but Clemens could not escape from materialism in his private life. Not content with the phenomenal income he earned from his real talent as an author and a lecturer, he was forever trying to strike it rich in some fantastic business venture. Brazilian cocoa, prospecting, publishing, the Paige machine—all failed him, and his overreaching eventually was his ruin. The very house, which was his personal symbol of success, was in fact a symbol of his failure—the failure to overcome dependence on material possessions.

At any rate, the two decades spent at Nook Farm were the artistic and domestic pinnacle of Clemens' life. These were Mark Twain's most productive years as a writer, and his happiest time as a husband and father. Only dark times lay ahead.

*   *   *   *   *   *   *   *

The Mark Twain Memorial and the adjacent Harriet Beecher Stowe House are located on the south side of Farmington Avenue between Forrest and Sisson Streets, not far from the center of Hartford. Take the Asylum Street exit from Interstate 84, and bear left at the intersection where Asylum divides; the left fork is Farmington Avenue. The Memorial is a short cab or bus ride from the Amtrak station and downtown Hartford hotels. Allow at least an hour to see the Twain house and a whole morning or afternoon if you wish to visit the Stowe House as well (admission tickets are sold at the Visitors' Center and a combined ticket is offered).

Quarry Farm and
Woodlawn Cemetery

Hannibal supplied Sam Clemens with much of his raw material; Virginia City shaped him into a successful humorist; San Francisco gave him the foundation for his lecturing career; Hartford was the scene of his greatest social and domestic triumphs, but Elmira was where he did his writing. There he could escape the frenetic pace of life in Connecticut, where he was busy being Mark Twain, celebrity. At Quarry Farm, he could be Sam Clemens, husband and father. Most important, he had time to create. If Hartford was home, Elmira meant even more—for it was there that he had married and had buried his wife, son and two of his daughters before he was laid to rest there himself. I could not have a complete picture of Mark Twain without going to Elmira.

Sam Clemens first came there in 1868, responding to an invitation from Livy's family issued when he first met her in New York the previous December. He found a conventional American small city nestled in the valley of the Chemung River some 250 miles from New York City. Here, Livy's father, Jervis Langdon, settled in 1845. He came from an old New England family; one of his ancestors, John Langdon, was a signer of the Constitution and one of its leading advocates who later served two terms in the United States Senate and five years as governor of New Hampshire. But wealth did not come with John Langdon's pedigree, and Jervis Langdon's branch of the family was not then rich. He made his own fortune in the coal business, and in the years immediately prior to the Civil War, he was one of Elmira's leading citizens. A leading Protestant layman, he was a founder and trustee of Elmira Female Seminary (now Elmira College), an Abolitionist and a doting Victorian father.

To reflect his wealth and position in the town, Jervis Langdon built a mansion for his family on Main Street in the center of Elmira. Nothing remains of it now but a piece of the iron fence which once bounded the property; but judging from its photographs, the house must have been a Gothic horror. Aesthetically, the town lost little when the house was demolished in 1939. But from the historic perspective, Elmira lost a great deal; it was to this house that Sam Clemens came to court Olivia, and it was in its parlor that they were finally married on February 2, 1870. Two of their children were born in the house, and after each death in the family, the coffin lay in state there before burial. Yet despite its historic associations, which made the Langdon house the most important structure in Elmira, it did not survive to the Second World War.[185]

If there remains hardly a trace of the Langdon mansion in town, however, Quarry Farm, the Langdon summer property, still stands hardly touched by time. Lying on East Hill, high above the city, it was purchased by Jervis Langdon and willed to his adopted eldest daughter, Susan Langdon Crane, in 1870.

---

[185]. When the house was demolished, underground tunnels were found beneath it—evidence that it was probably used as a station on the Underground Railroad, the escape route to Canada for runaway slaves from the South. How fascinating it would be to see this house today!

She lived there with her husband Theodore, and for the better part of thirty years, the farm served as the summer paradise for the Clemens and Langdon families. Except when they were in Europe, Sam, Livy, and the children spent nearly every summer here from 1874 to 1903 in company with Charley Langdon's family and the Cranes. Most of Mark Twain's serious writing (after *Roughing It*) was done here.

Theodore Crane suffered a stroke in September 1888 and lingered until the following summer. Sue Crane, left a widow at fifty-four, carried on afterward as hostess at the farm. She never remarried and outlived both her younger sister and her brother-in-law. Upon her death in 1924 (at the enviable age of eighty-nine), Quarry Farm passed to her nephew Jervis (Charles' son), who continued to maintain the property until his own death in 1952. At that time, his son, Jervis Langdon Jr. donated Quarry Farm to Elmira College; today, it houses the Center for Mark Twain Studies. The octagonal study, which Sue Crane had built for Mark Twain, is no longer at the farm; it was moved into the city in 1952, both to increase its accessibility to visitors and to decrease its potential as a target of vandals. Today, it stands on the Elmira College campus in the center of town.

I came to Elmira on a dark, drizzling September afternoon. Postponing a visit to the college, I took map in hand and turned the car toward East Hill. It is a steep climb from the town center to Crane Road, a narrow street turned into a corridor by the trees arching overhead. Samuel Clemens appreciated what that long climb meant to horses, and along the road, he installed four large stone drinking troughs for the relief of thirsty animals. Each trough bore the name of one of the Clemens children. Three of them, now planted with colorful flowers, still line Crane Road (the fourth, bearing Clara's name, has been moved into town and now stands beside the octagon study on the Elmira College campus).

Just below the intersection of Cross Road, I found it—the big white house backed by an even bigger red barn. Before the house stretches an endless expanse of green lawn; beyond it to the west, the property overlooks the valley of Newton Creek and the city of Elmira far below. Quarry Farm is a restful, peaceful spot, equally suited to writing books and raising kids. Vacations there must have been truly summers in paradise.

I parked the car along Crane Road and looked across the low stone wall to the green lawn; and as I watched, I saw that on the other side of that barrier, it was no longer a rainy September day in 1986 but a glorious afternoon in the summer of 1884. The sun was sinking below the treetops in the west, and in its golden glow, I saw the children running and playing on the grass. Susy, twelve, was the leader; Clara, ten, and little Jean, only four, tagged behind with their cousins Julia and Jervis Langdon. On the porch before the house sat Livy Clemens and her sister-in-law, Ida Langdon, chatting and watching the children while Saint Sue served cool drinks. Charles and Theodore would be home soon—the lengthening shadows meant that the time was coming to dress for dinner.

Then from the lawn came a shriek of joy, and the children turned and ran toward the trees overlooking the valley. Looking after them, I saw what they had already seen. A small man was walking slowly toward them, a man with shaggy curls and a prominent moustache. It was Mark Twain, who had been at work all day on his new novel, *The Adventures of Huckleberry Finn*. As he came nearer, the girls ran to him. Susy grabbed at one arm, while Clara took the other and little Jean grabbed his legs. Together, they came up to the house, where Livy waited for them. Mark Twain bent down to pet a couple of his many cats, as the children jumped and jabbered in his ear. Then the whole family disappeared into the big house. Soon there would be dinner, with ice cream for dessert; afterward, games, and before bedtime, stories. Then, at last, as the starry night settled down over Quarry Farm would come quiet, and with it deep sleep. I could see it all so clearly, the way it must have been.

Back in Elmira, I drove up Park Place to the campus. There was the study, standing on a little rise between college buildings. Four wooden steps led up to the door. Inside, a fireplace occupies the opposite wall; the other six sides are of glass. The original furnishings are still there—a round writing table and a few chairs. When it was perched on its hillside, overlooking the town far below, this was a perfect working retreat. The iron fence, which separates the study from the street, came from the Langdon mansion, and it is about all of the old house which survives.

Close by is Watson Hall, containing the Mark Twain Museum. Elmira College has been closely associated with the Langdon family ever since the original Jervis Langdon helped to found it, and its collection contains many exhibits relating to Twain's Elmira connections. The large album of Clemens and Langdon family photographs is particularly interesting.

When I left the museum, I had only one more stop to make on the trail of Mark Twain. I followed him to the Woodlawn Cemetery.

The route to the gravesite is clearly marked. I had no difficulty in finding the Langdon/Clemens family plot. It is not far from the gate, on a hill facing eastward across the valley toward Quarry Farm atop the distant hills. There are two monuments at the site: one, honoring the Langdon family; the second, erected by Clara Clemens Gabrilowitsch, dedicated to her father and her husband. This Mark Twain monument is twelve feet high, twelve feet being two fathoms—"Mark Twain."

The twenty-one graves in the family plot are arranged in rows. To the south side of the central Langdon pillar, the first stone I found belonged to Langdon Clemens, the son of Sam and Livy, who never made it to his second birthday. Next to him lie his grandparents, Livy's father and mother. Lower on the hillside are the graves of Ida Langdon, Charles' spinster daughter, who died in 1964; Theodore Crane, and Susan Langdon Crane, Mark Twain's "Saint Sue."

North of the central monument are three rows of headstones. On the top level, nearest the road, are the graves of Charles Langdon and his wife Ida; their daughter Julia and her husband, Edward Loomis; and those of Jervis Langdon, Sr. and his wife Eleanor. Hers is the newest grave; she died in 1971 at ninety-three.

At the center of the middle row is the grave of Samuel Langhorne Clemens, Mark Twain. Next to him, the ashes of Olivia, brought from Florence, are interred, and beside her is Susy's final resting place. Alone among the markers, hers bears a poem[186]

> Warm summer sun, shine kindly here;
> Warm southern wind, blow softly here;
> Green sod above lie light;
> Good night, dear heart,
> Good night, good night.

Jean Lampton Clemens is buried next to Susy, just below the Mark Twain monument.

On the third row are the graves of Nina Clemens Gabrilowitsch, Clara's daughter; Osip Gabrilowitsch, her first husband, and finally Clara herself. By his request, Gabrilowitsch lies buried at the feet of his father-in-law, Mark Twain. By contrast, Clara's second husband, Jacques Samossoud, is not buried in the family plot—he lies in an unmarked grave elsewhere.

Of course, I never met any of the Langdon/Clemens family; I knew them only from biographies of Mark Twain, secondhand, so to speak. Yet as I walked slowly among their graves, I felt

---

[186.] The verses are attributed to an Australian named Robert Richardson. Supposedly the words had to be changed from "northern" to "southern," owing to the transposition to the Northern Hemisphere.

somehow that this American family, blessed with success and accomplishment, cursed with sorrow and suffering, was my own. Especially, when I read the heartbreaking lines on Susy's headstone, I felt like crying. These were people I felt I really knew.

Woodlawn Cemetery was deserted. The drizzle had changed to a cold, pelting rain. I pulled myself away from the graves and regained the road and the car. As I turned around, I looked back one more time at the grave of Samuel L. Clemens; Mark Twain, I knew, would live forever.

*   *   *   *   *   *   *   *

Elmira is on the Southern Tier Expressway, New York Highway 17, about five hours' driving time from Manhattan. The city actively promotes its Mark Twain connection—the tourist dollars are needed in the local economy these days.

The home at Quarry Farm is not open to the public, but anyone can drive up to it, as I did, and I recommend making the trip. You can see the study on the Elmira College campus from the outside; I understand that the interior can be visited by appointment only. The nearby museum in Watson Hall is quite good, and you should see it before going up to the farm or visiting the graves. The cemetery is open most of the time, and the Langdon/Clemens plot is well marked and easy to find.

Concluding Note on this Section

What to make of my transcontinental odyssey in search of Mark Twain?

Following the trail of Samuel Clemens from Hannibal to Virginia City and California, then east to Hartford and Elmira, illustrated first how remarkable was his sudden metamorphosis from bachelor Western humorist and newspaperman to Eastern father figure and establishment gentleman. From the cabin on Jackass Hill to the Hartford mansion was a journey of three thousand miles across a social gulf infinitely wider, but it took Clemens just nine years to accomplish. One cannot get a sense of just how remarkable his transformation was until one sees these sites juxtaposed dramatically; then one senses that what Clemens did was no less than stunning.

Secondly, this trail sheds light on Clemens' personality. The poverty of his youth in Hannibal explains the extravagance of his adult years in Hartford—he was proving to himself, as well as to the world, that he had overcome his roots. It also explains Clemens' powerful drive toward riches. Whatever else he may have wanted—approval, public adulation, romantic love—he wanted money, lots of money, to erase the stain of a boyhood during which had none.

Third, visits to the Clemens's sites illustrate clearly the fact that what he wrote was keyed to his circumstances. In Nevada, he wrote wild humor because that was what the market called for. In California, he adapted the "Jumping Frog" tale because Artemus Ward asked him for a humorous sketch, having known Clemens from his Virginia City days. But once in Hartford and Elmira, freed by his own success with *The Innocents Abroad* and backed by his wife's money and social position, he became a different writer altogether. He began mining his Hannibal boyhood for material: first (as I think) for his own amusement; later, as the stuff of his greatest book, a novel about good, evil, conscience, and American society known as *The Adventures of Huckleberry Finn*. Still later, he turned his talent to an even more outrageous attack on the world in which he lived in *A Connecticut Yankee in King Arthur's Court*. It is only necessary to pose one question—could this novel have been written by Mark Twain had he remained in the West?—to give the answer. The book could never have been done had Clemens himself not become a Yankee, for it is to a disturbing degree about the man himself.

Finally, seeing the Langdon/Clemens sites in Elmira, Quarry Farm, and Woodlawn Cemetery graphically points out the extent to which Samuel Clemens was attached to the upper-class Victorian world, which Mark Twain was pillorying in his books. The distance between Samuel Clemens and his alter ego is as clearly illustrated here as the difference between Clemens, the bachelor westerner and Clemens, the eastern paterfamilias is in Hartford. Ultimately, my tracking the spoor of Sam Clemens led to questions; how did he accomplish his remarkable metamorphosis, and why did Mark Twain grow so far from his other self?

Part IV

Encounters of the Third Kind:
The Mind of Samuel Clemens

Why?

T hinking about Mark Twain's works and Samuel Clemens' life, one cannot escape the seemingly paradoxical fact that much of Mark's social criticism was leveled at the very Victorian society to which Sam had attached himself and whose values he adopted. One is also struck by the increasing violence, even savagery, of Twain's attacks, and by the growing acceptance of a philosophy of determinism or fatalism which culminates in the posthumous publication of *The Mysterious Stranger* (1916).

At the same time, any student of Clemens' life cannot fail to be struck by his apparent need to assume guilt, even over things for which he was clearly not responsible. Guilt was the leitmotif of Clemens' later years; the *Autobiography* is full of it.

It is easy to see the final philosophy expressed in Twain's writing—that all life is a dream; that man is a mere mechanical creature without significant moral choices, driven by forces beyond his control; that in the end, nothing has meaning—as the product of Clemens' feelings of guilt. If there is no possibility of significant moral choice, then there can be no responsibility for human decisions and actions. The *Stranger* is an anguished denial of responsibility, a shrieking cry, "I, Samuel Clemens, am not responsible and therefore I am not guilty!"

This is perfectly sensible, as far as it goes. But in the larger sense, it begs the vital question—why did Clemens seem to need to take on guilt? Why did he feel the need to exculpate himself by adopting a bleak determinism as his final philosophy of life? Until we can throw light on these questions, we cannot claim to understand fully either Clemens' life or Twain's work, so bound together and simultaneously so far apart.

Guilt

No student of the life of Samuel Clemens can doubt that his dominant emotion was guilt. This was especially true in the last fifteen years of his life. But it is clear that even as a boy, he possessed unusually strong guilt feelings. In the *Autobiography*, he recounts the incident of the drunken tramp who was lodged in the Hannibal jail. Young Sammy Clemens, feeling sorry for him, gave him some matches to light his tobacco, but the tramp accidentally set fire to his bed and was incinerated in his cell before he could be rescued. Clemens recalled that he suffered the torture of guilt for three months afterward, even though he was aware that he was not really responsible for the man's death.[187] There were also numerous other incidents which Sam's hyperactive Presbyterian conscience seized upon, making him notoriously guilt-ridden as a boy.[188]

This tendency to assume responsibility for things not rationally chargeable to his account was a peculiar characteristic of Samuel Clemens' later life; but while his boyhood guilt feelings can be ascribed largely to childish fear of divine retribution, his adult

---

[187.] See the *Autobiography*, pp. 43-44.

[188.] Ibid., p. 45.

need to assume guilt for things he did not do cannot be so easily explained away. Moreover, up until middle age, Clemens was able to cope with whatever guilt he felt. In later years, however, it mastered him to the point of inability to function in the world for at least a couple of years, and to the extent of leading him to the philosophy of fatalism upon which I have already commented. To understand Clemens, and to comprehend Twain, we must first explore the wellsprings of Clemens' guilt.

It will be helpful at this point to cite a study of guilt by psychologist Roy F. Baumeister and colleagues at Case Western Reserve University. This study, published in 1994, explores the nature of guilt and its value to the person feeling it.

"The cultural stereotype," writes Professor Baumeister, "is that guilt is a waste or a worthless emotion, that there is no point in feeling guilty. But guilt seems to have a purpose . . . it seems to benefit relationships. I think the bad reputation [of guilt] comes from the idea that the person feeling guilty doesn't benefit. But in reality, that person does, and so do others. Psychologists have tended to think about guilt in terms of the individual psyche. But the evidence shows that guilt depends on the interpersonal context. Guilt tends to be a two person kind of thing."

The Case Western study indicates that guilt serves three main functions; it helps to maintain relationships, it exerts influence, and it redistributes emotional stress.

"We found that the biggest single cause of guilt people have is not spending enough time with their families. So guilt is a big force making people pay attention to other people." The person feeling guilty tries to make up for it by giving special attention to the other party, and that special attention not only lets the second person know that the guilty one does care but also allows the guilty person to feel better.

Guilt also helps people in close relationships control each others' behavior. The classic formulation is, "If you really loved me, you wouldn't do that!" "The person with less power can get his or her own way by using guilt," says Professor Baumeister. "Guilt is a good strategy for the weaker person in the relationship. Guilt equalizes power."

Finally, guilt can redistribute emotions. If one feels guilty over something done or left undone, and the other person involved knows that, he or she will feel better. "In this way, emotional equity is restored because bad feelings are restored to the person who caused them. Feeling guilty is a way of showing that one cares."

The Case Western researchers also found that guilt arises from the emotions linked to relationships. Basically, they found, there are two sources of guilt. "One is empathy: you feel bad when someone else is hurting. This starts early in life . . . The other cause is anxiety over the loss of a relationship; being rejected or excluded. When you are doing something that may drive someone away, that can produce guilt."[189]

Applying Professor Baumeister's conclusions to the feelings of young Sam Clemens, it seems apparent that his childhood guilt (over the death of the unfortunate tramp, for example) was at least largely of the empathetic type. Whatever relationship guilt he may have felt must have been based on his interaction with his parents.

For love, warmth, and attention, Sam relied mainly on Jane Lampton Clemens, his long-suffering mother, who was also the most potent authority figure in his life.[190] He was forever distressing her, challenging her restrictions, and flaunting his disobedience; but he loved her and he knew that she loved him

---

[189]. The Baumeister study is quoted at length by health writer Shari Roan in the *Los Angeles Times* of Monday, May 2, 1994.

[190]. He recalls in the *Autobiography* that "She had a good deal of trouble with me but I think she enjoyed it (see p. 35)."

as well.[191] In Professor Baumeister's terms, his guilt helped to stabilize their relationship and to redistribute the emotional content of their lives.

With his father, John Marshall Clemens, Sam's relationship was far more distant. The senior Clemens was neither affectionate nor an effective parent, and his business failures and early death (when Sam was eleven) kept him at a distance from his son. After the manner of children, Sam may have felt himself to have been responsible for the failure of his relationship with his father and perhaps even for Judge Clemens' untimely death.[192] It may or may not be significant that Sammy's somnambulism, manifested in early childhood but quiescent since, reappeared immediately after his father's funeral.[193] But if Samuel Clemens felt much conscious guilt over his father's death, he kept it to himself—there is nothing in the *Autobiography* to that effect, nor does there appear to be any other evidence apart from the recurrence of his sleepwalking.

While the boy Sam was tormented by guilt feelings, they seem to have abated during his young manhood. We hear little if anything of such emotions during his years as a journeyman printer and as a cub pilot. Only with the death of his younger brother Henry following the explosion of the steamboat *Pennsylvania* did they return in force.

[191.] The relationship between Tom and Aunt Polly in *Tom Sawyer* appears to be a pretty accurate representation of the relationship between Sam Clemens and his mother.

[192.] While it may be completely irrational, children often blame themselves when a relationship with a parent is unsatisfactory. To the child, a parent is assumed to be perfect; therefore, anything that goes wrong must be the child's own fault.

[193.] See Wecter, p. 118.

Rationally or not, Sam Clemens blamed himself for Henry's death. It was Sam, who got Henry a job on the *Pennsylvania* in the first place; it was Sam's fight with Brown, the pilot, which took him off the boat, leaving Henry on board, and it was Sam who encouraged an inexperienced Memphis doctor to administer morphine to his brother after the accident. The doctor mistakenly gave him an excessive dose and Henry (who might have otherwise recovered, though it is hard to tell) succumbed as a result. A clear-thinking person would have no problem recognizing that on this evidence, Sam's culpability in Henry's death was minimal, if it existed at all; but it brought on an attack of guilt nonetheless.

Following Professor Baumeister's formulation, we may conclude that Sam felt guilt over something he had done in his relationship with his brother; but it is just as likely (if not more so) that his feelings were predicated on his relationship with his mother. Henry had been the "good son" that Sam was not; now "Cain" had killed "Abel" and the good son was dead while the other was left alive. Jane Clemens was suffering, and in his mind, at least, it was Sam who had made her do so. His guilt may well have been that of the survivor, who feels that he was unworthy to have lived while another, better individual died.

But even the death of Henry did not incapacitate Sam Clemens; he went on piloting, got over his guilt feelings, and went out to Nevada, where he seems to have felt no more pangs. He was an unsuccessful miner, then a successful newspaperman, a correspondent, a traveler, a lecturer, and a writer. Not until nearly middle age did Clemens again begin to wrestle with his conscience; and in his later life, he became increasingly unable to cope with his feelings as he had done successfully as a young man. As his guilt grew, his ability to cope with it declined until finally his mental state was reflected in Mark Twain's increasing anger, pessimism, and finally in fatalism.

Why was the younger Clemens able to cope normally with his guilt feelings while the older man was crushed by them? Why did not Mark Twain's writing before 1874 give any hint of the philosophic pessimism which was to dominate his later work?

The usual explanation of the increasing darkness in Mark Twain's books is that it stemmed from Clemens' deepening personal and financial problems. I submit that this theory is inadequate. Were it true, the devastating *Connecticut Yankee* could not have been written in the years 1886-89, when Clemens' financial collapse was still several years in the future, and when his domestic happiness seemed to be at its height.[194] Indeed, while writing the book, Clemens was salivating at the enormous profits he expected from his investment in the Paige typesetting machine. As Justin Kaplan points out, the book and the machine were twinned in the author's consciousness; he was aiming to finish the *Yankee* on the same day Paige completed the typesetter.[195]

Furthermore, if the tone of Mark Twain's writing merely reflected the state of Samuel Clemens' worldly affairs, one would expect the dark clouds to blow away after his rescue from financial distress by Henry Rogers and the final repayment of all his creditors, one hundred cents on the dollar, which was completed by 1898. On the contrary, Twain's later writings

---

[194] I have actually had an academic tell me that the *Yankee* must be an optimistic book, since Clemens' private life had not yet turned sour when it was written. The trouble with such thinking is that it ignores the evidence of the novel itself; the book presents one of the darkest visions in all American literature, and only a willful disregard of its contents could lead to such a ridiculous, inverted conclusion as the one I was given.

[195] See Kaplan, Chapter 14. Its title is "The Yankee and the Machine."

(including the unfinished *Mysterious Stranger*) are even more depressing than his work during the terrible nineties. It is not without significance that one of Mark Twain's most delightful if unsubstantial literary bonbons, *Tom Sawyer Abroad,* was written during the collapse of his finances and published just two days before the Charles Webster Co. declared bankruptcy.[196] There is ample proof, then, that whatever the cause of Mark Twain's fatalism, it was not simply the state of Samuel Clemens' pocketbook. Guilt, not financial disaster, is the apparent cause of Mark Twain's descent into philosophic purgatory. The question remains: what was there in Clemens' life which caused him to feel such an overwhelming burden of grief that even he, who had coped with the deaths of the tramp, his father, and his brother, was unable to deal with it?

In the *Autobiography* and in other late writings and comments, Clemens gives us his own answers. He claimed to have been responsible for the death of his only son, Langdon. "I took him for a long drive . . . it was a raw, cold morning . . . I forgot all about my charge. The furs fell away and exposed his bare legs . . . the child was almost frozen."[197]

This self-accusation does not square with the facts. Langdon Clemens died of diphtheria, not pneumonia, and he died in June—hardly a chilly month in Elmira. At the time of the boy's passing (1872), Clemens expressed no guilt over his death. In fact, he was actually relieved, for the child had never developed normally, and from the date of his birth, he was clearly unlikely to survive. Clemens' attempt to assume guilt for his son's death more than thirty years after the fact was motivated by something

---

[196.] See Kaplan, p. 388. *Tom Sawyer, Detective* also dates from about the same period.

[197.] *Autobiography*, Chapter 37. This account of Langdon's death was dictated at least thirty years after the fact.

other than a mere disclosure of suppressed truth, for the truth was that he was in no way responsible for Langdon's death and showed no guilt feelings at the time.[198]

Clemens also claimed that his "crimes" had made his wife and his daughters "paupers and exiles," and he assumed guilt for doing so. By his "crimes," he was probably referring to his bad business sense, which did indeed result in the squandering of thousands of dollars of his and his wife's money. He made a nearly unbroken series of bad investments, culminating of course in his disastrous backing of the Paige typesetting machine; but while the family did leave America to enjoy the lower cost of living in Europe, and so were in fact self-exiled, they were never paupers or anything close to it. Even at their lowest financial ebb, following the Panic of 1893, the Clemens family lived graciously in European hotels and rented villas. Henry Rogers saw to that Livy kept the valuable copyrights to her husband's books; the family still owned the Hartford mansion, which had considerable value, even during the recession,[199] and Mark Twain's stature was such that almost anything he wrote or any speech he gave was bound to produce

---

[198.] See Kaplan, pp. 168-69 for an account of Langdon's death and Clemens' reaction at the time, which makes an interesting comparison with his statement in the *Autobiography*, written thirty years later.

Kaplan also notes that only once during his forty-year friendship with William Dean Howells did Clemens mention his son, and that was to remark "Yes, I killed him." When that comment was made, however, and in what context, Kaplan does not state. See page 169.

[199.] The house was closed when the family left for the continent in June 1891 and remained untenanted until March 1895, when it was rented to Calvin and Alice Day. They occupied it until the following December, after which John and Ellen O'Neil lived in the house as caretakers.

income.[200] Money may not have been plentiful, but it was never lacking to the point of pauperism.

Moreover, while it might have made some sense for Clemens to berate himself for his mismanagement of the family finances in 1893, it made no sense whatsoever for him to do so after 1898, when all the creditors were repaid in full and he was well-off once again. Yet his self-accusation dates once more from the period after 1900; it cannot be taken at face value any more than can his long-delayed claim to responsibility for the death of his son.

In other words, while guilt was clearly the overriding emotion of Samuel Clemens' last years, the reasons he himself gives for feeling that guilt do not reasonably explain its oppressive bearing on him. We may assume that the guilt he felt was real enough because it paralyzed his thought and action. Therefore, we must look further to find its real causes.

I would suggest that it is possible to find deep, serious causes for the guilt that Clemens experienced if only we use some creative thinking about the events of his life and about Mark Twain's writing. I freely admit that it may be difficult to prove all of my inferences, for the proof may not exist; but I have managed to elaborate a coherent explanation of the sources of Samuel Clemens' guilt feelings, and I believe it is the only theory ever offered, which makes sense of this enigmatic, complex, and difficult personality.

[200.] Proof that this was indeed the case can be found in the success of his 1895-96 round-the-world lecture tour which, together with the book he wrote about it (*Following the Equator*), raised so much money that the creditors of the Webster publishing house, who had accepted an offer of fifty cents on the dollar, were paid off in full.

Sex

My analysis begins with a well-remarked characteristic common to both Samuel Clemens' private life and Mark Twain's published writing—an extraordinary reluctance to discuss or to write about human sexuality or adult love in any but the most romantic and sterilized terms. Mark Twain never created, in any of his novels, a fully drawn, sexually developed female character. He did depict Roxy, the heroine of *Pudd'nhead Wilson,* as a sexual woman—but Roxy, however blonde and brown-eyed she may be, is still nominally black and a slave of whom sexual activity might be expected and in whom it can be discounted. Leslie Fiedler noted this point long ago but did not elaborate on it; it was not his purpose to explore the wellsprings of Twain's reticence.[201] The fact remains, however, that in all of his writing that was intended for publication, Mark Twain never approached anything remotely sexual and avoided writing at length about fully developed adult female characters.

Moreover, Samuel Clemens shows the same reticence toward sex in his personal correspondence to such a degree that some

---

[201.] See *Love and Death in the American Novel* (New York: Stein and Day, 1960).

scholars have thought that he remained a virgin until marriage. Margaret Sanborn has exploded that opinion, but the discovery of one Clemens' letter admitting to sex with servant girls is more in the nature of the exception that proves the rule; so far as I am aware, this is the only confession of sexual activity on Clemens' part, which has yet come to light.[202]

Still, coming from the Missouri frontier, living alone in such cities as New York and Philadelphia, spending several years on the Mississippi as both cub and pilot, living and working as a miner and a reporter in the rip-roaring Comstock and later in California, and liking women as we know he did, it is simply inconceivable that Clemens did not have sexual experience prior to marrying Olivia Langdon. Though neither in his art nor in his letters do we find reference to the girls he met, the romances he had (except for his childhood affection for Laura Hawkins), or the sexual adventures he must have experienced, it is too much to credit that such a full-blooded young man could have lived such a life in such places at such times and yet have remained a celibate.

Besides, we have plenty of other evidence that Samuel Clemens indeed possessed a libido. There exists that scandalous treatise/essay/lecture on the Science of Onanism, which was probably first given as a speech in Paris in 1879 and which only saw print in recent years. In addition, Mark Twain also authored the curiosity known as *1601, or Conversation as it Was in the Time of the Tutors*. Hardly more than an extended dirty joke, this not-very-funny piece dates from the autumn of 1876.

Neither of these trifles was intended for publication and neither makes any pretense to literary distinction. Neither, in

---

[202.] Margaret Sanborn. *Mark Twain: The Bachelor Years* (New York: Doubleday, 1990). See Chapter 15, "Wild Oats", particularly pp. 200-201, quoting Clemens' letter to his sister-in-law Mollie in which he admits to "sleeping with female servants."

fact, is particularly good ribaldry. The significance of these two short exercises is that they demonstrate that Mark Twain was not a plaster saint, as his daughter Clara, his first literary executor and biographer, Albert Bigelow Paine, and even Clemens himself would have us believe. He was human, after all, and not above a bathroom joke or an erotic thought.

So Clemens' extreme reluctance to touch the subject of sex in his own letters, or in any of Mark Twain's creative writing, cannot be contributed to lack of libido. It was a conscious omission on his part. We must ask, then, why he remained throughout his life so completely dedicated to avoiding the subject.

At least some of Mark Twain's reticence about sex can, of course, be put down to his position as an author living in a genteel Victorian society. Twain was writing for a living, and he knew perfectly well that his sales depended on his pleasing the segment of that society which did most of the reading and bought most of the books—that is, upper-class women and their young daughters. What is more, Twain's books were sold largely by subscription, which meant that they were delivered directly to the homes of the purchasers; any comment, any word which offended the sensibilities of these ladies would hurt his sales and his prized reputation as a "proper" author.

These fears can only have been exacerbated by Samuel Clemens' own equivocal position in Victorian society. A wild westerner of questionable antecedents and character, he had fought a long and difficult battle to win the hand of Olivia Langdon and the approval of her parents; he must have had some moments of insecurity despite his success in marrying into such a prototypical patrician family.[203]

[203.] Margaret Sanborn quotes Clemens' own description of the wooing of Olivia Langdon as "the siege of Elmira" and relates that his mother-in-law

Yet I question whether these considerations alone explain Clemens' sexual taciturnity, even if they do Twain's. What Twain wrote for publication was surely influenced by his conception of his readers and their tastes; but what Clemens wrote to his friends was not. One would reasonably expect to find in Clemens' correspondence with the friends of his youth (such as Joe Goodman and the *Enterprise* crew, for one example, or the Gillis boys, for another) some reference to his relationships with women, amateur or professional. On the contrary, to my knowledge, there is practically nothing (save that one letter to his sister-in-law) on paper about the love life of Sam Clemens before he met Olivia Langdon. Even as a very young man, he appears to have been extraordinarily circumspect.[204]

About the time Clemens left Virginia City, one of his rivals spread a story around town to the effect that he was a victim of venereal disease. There was no proof of its veracity then, and it is unlikely that there is any today, but the significance of the incident lies in the fact that it was at least plausible to contemporary Comstockers. In other words, Sam Clemens must have gotten around Virginia City pretty openly but not a whisper of his activities is to be found in *Roughing It* or in his correspondence.

In short, Clemens/Twain appears to have made a conscious decision to avoid any mention of adult sexuality in any context. He avoided the subject to such a degree as to attract my attention to the omission.

---

seems never to have been fully won over until after the marriage. See *The Bachelor Years*, ibid.

[204.] There is plenty of chatter in Clemens' letters about how much he liked girls in general, and there is an account of his juvenile love for Laura Hawkins in particular. But there is nothing at all about his sexual exploits or conquests except that one letter.

I asked myself why an otherwise candid and insightful man would so completely and so unnaturally avoid the subject of sex, not only in print but in correspondence, and I surmised that he did so because he was so uncomfortable with the topic that he wished to sidestep it altogether. The logical follow-up question was, then, why was he so uncomfortable with sexuality; and the conclusion which presented itself was that Clemens may have had some sexual contacts or suppressed desires which he considered so shameful that he did not dare allow even a hint of the general subject to surface. Only a man who thinks he has something to hide shies away from the subject of women so completely.

There is, of course, no evidence at all to support this surmise. In its absence, I have fallen back on creative imagination to discover what there may have been in Clemens' makeup, which he feared so much to disclose.

We may find a clue from Clemens' boyhood in Hannibal. He tells us that one of the important moments of his life occurred one day when he stopped to pick up a piece of paper which was blowing down the street. It chanced to be a page from a book on Joan of Arc, which described her torture while imprisoned by the English.[205] Clemens never got over Joan, and in later life, he wrote *Personal Recollections of Joan of Arc*; he called it his favorite among all his books, although today hardly anybody would claim a place beside *Huckleberry Finn* for this turgid, over-romantic, slow moving, and generally drab work.

---

[205] See Sanborn, ibid., p. 70 for one account of the incident. She says that the first thing Sam did after finding the paper was to ask his bookish brother Henry if Joan was a real person; and he later confirmed Henry's answer by asking his mother. I find this concern interesting in view of my idea about what the story of Joan under torture might have done to young Sammy's hormones. See also Wecter's report of the same incident, p. 211.

Clemens claimed that this early encounter with the Maid of Orleans inspired him with passion and zeal. One wonders if perhaps it did not also stir feelings of sexual excitement in the fourteen-year-old Sam, which he feared to disclose or discuss.

The idea of a woman being physically dominated can have a powerful appeal to some men, and while I claim no knowledge of psychology beyond a layman's superficial ideas, I would imagine that men who were raised in households dominated by females (and who resented it) might be particularly susceptible to this sort of sexual stimulus.

Sam Clemens was indeed raised in this type of environment. His father died when he was just eleven, and for years before that he had hardly been a strong presence in the home. He was distant emotionally from his wife and children alike, and his business failures and ultimate bankruptcy surely did not increase his appeal as a role model or authority figure to a young, active boy. In reality, we know from Sam Clemens himself that his father's failure caused him a great degree of shame and humiliation. Jane Lampton Clemens was clearly the dominant personality in the household, even while her husband was still alive.

What is more, she was not the only female authority figure with whom Sam had to contend. His elder sister Pamela helped to raise him and exerted her dominance over him during his youth. The situation must have been quite like that of the Sawyer family in fiction, with Jane Clemens in the role of Aunt Polly and Pamela as Mary. Significantly, there is no mention of any male authority figure in *Tom Sawyer*—no father, no uncle, no elder brother. Tom Sawyer lives in a completely feminized world. Even his younger half-brother, Sid, is a "good boy," somewhat on the sissy side, and Tom clearly resents him.[206]

---

206. Although, as I have already pointed out (see footnote #19, p. 21), Sid is not really such a good boy at all, and by the end of the novel, we really

Could it not be possible that an active, self-conscious, intelligent boy brought up in such a household might grow to young manhood with deeply buried resentment against the women who ruled his youth, even as he loved and respected them? Is it not feasible that consciously or subconsciously those feelings grew into an adult need to dominate or manipulate members of the female sex or at least to derive secret pleasure from their domination by other men?

Of course, this is dime store psychology, resting on the flimsiest of evidence and the most imaginative of surmises. I cannot prove the truth of it, yet the suggestion that Clemens resented the female authority figures who dominated his youth and privately needed to revenge himself upon them by assuming power over women in his adult life (while all the time keeping his shameful feelings a total secret from others) fits well with what we know of Clemens' later life and helps to explain much about his character, which has heretofore defied rational understanding.

Taking that analysis a step further, is it not likely that a man who fostered such secret feelings toward women, and who was ashamed of them and afraid that they might somehow become common knowledge, would masque his secret sensations and fantasies by acting with extreme courtesy and deference toward women when his dealings with them were subject to scrutiny? Particularly when these women were members of that genteel upper class from which he was most anxious to disguise his shameful secrets?

Here, we have a possible explanation for one of the characteristics of Samuel Clemens' later life—his extreme,

---

wish Tom would give him a good licking for the mean streak which he harbors. Clemens himself said that while Sid was based on his brother Henry, Henry Clemens was a much finer person than Sid Sawyer.

almost embarrassing deference to several upper-class women in his life. One of these was the wife of a Cleveland newspaper executive, Mary Fairbanks, whom he met aboard the "*Quaker City*" and whom he called his social mentor.[207] Although she was not much older than he (thirty-eight to his thirty-one), he soon began calling her "Mother" and submitted his copy to her for approval, as he was later to do with Livy.[208]

Later when Clemens was courting Olivia Langdon, his letters are so obsequious, so full of "I am becoming a good Christian" claptrap as to make one wonder if they could possibly have been written by the same man who had already written *The Innocents Abroad* and who was to produce *Huckleberry Finn* some years later. The Clemens courting letters are so illustrative of what Mark Twain so aptly called "flapdoodle" as to make one want to retch.

But if Clemens could be embarrassingly subservient to ladies of quality, he could also display a surprising degree of authority toward his own daughters. We can infer from his own writings, and from the recollections of Clara Clemens Gabrilowitsch, that he was a holy terror of a Victorian father—a perfect domestic tyrant. His daughters were afraid of him, a fact which he claimed surprised him when he first heard of it.[209] Later, when the family was living in Europe, Clara escaped from the household to study in Germany, but Susy was left a prisoner in the rented villa in Italy. She coexisted with her father by avoiding him—not

---

[207] See Sanborn, pp. 340-343 for an account of Clemens' shipboard relationship with Mrs. Fairbanks.

[208] And, according to Margaret Sanborn, with similar results. He changed what he wanted to change but ignored her comments when he wanted to keep what he had written.

[209] Kaplan quotes an 1886 letter from Clemens to Howells in which Clemens reports being felled by a "thunderstroke"—finding out the day before that all their lives his children had been afraid of him. See p. 362.

coming down to breakfast until he had finished and left.[210] If
Samuel Clemens was not quite the ogre that Elizabeth Barrett
Browning's father was, or Beatrix Potter's, he certainly was not
the jolly, easygoing parent we might have expected the author
of *Tom Sawyer* to be.

In short, Samuel Clemens demonstrated, at different times in
his life, both extreme deference and strong dominance toward
members of the female sex. These inconsistent behaviors may
well be explained if he did have a deeply disguised resentment
toward the feminine authority figures of his youth and a hidden
need to get revenge by dominating women in his adulthood—a
desire which caused him guilt and shame, leading him to
take careful steps so that no one should ever know his inner
thoughts.

For those who might think my theorizing about Samuel
Clemens' sexual proclivities to be unfair to the man, I can cite
some further evidence that he did possess some unusual erotic
leanings. After the death of his wife in 1904, Clemens gathered
around himself a number of nubile young girls he called his
"angelfish."[211] There were twelve of these girls, ranging in age
from ten to sixteen, organized into an "Aquarium Club," with
Clemens as "Curator" or "Admiral." He wrote, "I suppose we are
all collectors . . . Pierpont Morgan collects precious works of art
and pays millions for them . . . as for me, I collect pets: young
girls . . . to whom life is a perfect joy and to whom it has brought
no wounds, no bitterness, and few tears. My collection consists
of gems of the first water."[212]

[210.] See Kaplan, p. 373; also Salsbury, p. 313, quoting a letter from Susy to her
sister Clara.

[211.] See *Mark Twain's Aquarium,* edited by John Cooley (Athens: The
University of Georgia Press, 1991).

[212.] Quoted by Cooley, ibid., p. xvii.

While Professor John Cooley of Western Michigan University, who has collected and studied all the "angelfish" correspondence known to exist, finds no evidence of any "scandal or impropriety," there is at least some reason to suspect that on at least one occasion, the old man indulged in a little indecent exposure with one of his girls. The incident, said to have occurred in Bermuda, was (needless to say) not reported in the press. If it did happen, it can certainly be seen as an old and impotent man's way of asserting power over a young girl, and by extension, over all members of her sex. If it did *not* occur, still Clemens' "collection" of young females, by its very existence, forms an authority situation—the old man an "Admiral," in a position of power and leadership in relation to his "fish." That there were no boys in Clemens' collection seems to me significant in light of my theory about his unspoken feelings about the feminine gender.

What is more, despite Mark Twain's careful avoidance of sexuality, there are some telltale passages in his work which may be perceived as windows on Clemens' sexual fantasies.

In *The Adventures of Tom Sawyer,* we find an incident of gratuitous viciousness. In Chapter 29, Huck overhears Injun Joe describe to his nameless partner his plan for revenging himself on the Widow Douglas; he intends to tie her to the bed, slit her nostrils, and notch her ears "like a sow." Unspoken is the likelihood of sexual abuse to the woman while she is tied to her bed—not, take notice, to a chair.[213]

[213.] Not until after writing this paragraph did I learn that in the original manuscript of *Tom,* Injun Joe actually states that he plans to rape the Widow as his revenge. Robert Keith Miller notes that the passage was changed because Twain was persuaded that rape would be inappropriate in a book, which would be read by children. Mr. Miller wonders, however, why nostril slitting and ear notching were considered any more acceptable—a perfectly reasonable question which must immediately

This passage is so gruesome and so jarring in the context of the novel that it always sent shivers down my spine when I read it as a boy. Indeed, if such behavior were carried out today, it would put Injun Joe in the Charles Manson class. Even his partner expresses horror at the thought, and Joe threatens to kill him if he does not help. It is interesting to note that the intended victim of this unspeakable revenge, the Widow Douglas, is the closest thing St. Petersburg has to the genteel ladies of the Victorian era. As the cream of the town's society, she stands for and is part of the class of women who not only set the standards of conduct for that period but on whom Twain also depended for his sales. He had ample reason to resent them, and in this passage—which is completely unnecessary to the action—he may have been expressing that submerged feeling.

Apropos, there is another very interesting scene in one of Mark Twain's incomplete fragments, the beginning of a novel which was to have been called *Tom and Huck Among the Indians*. This piece was written in Elmira (Quarry Farm) in the summer of 1884, after

---

occur to all of us. Perhaps part of the answer may lie in America's traditional willingness to tolerate violence in preference to sex. I suspect, however, that Twain removed the sexual aspect of his brutal attack partly because it threatened to reveal too clearly his own most secret fantasies. At any rate, I was hardly surprised to hear of Twain's original intent.

The real question is why he wrote the passage into the novel at all, and especially why, once it was criticized, he did not expunge it completely. Presumably, his intent was to make Injun Joe more a fiend than an ordinary villain, and the fact that his frightening plan is thwarted through the intervention of Huck and the Old Welshman made it possible to leave the passage in the book. One wonders, however, what possibly subconscious urges led the author to write it in its original form and put it into the manuscript in the first place.

See Robert Keith Miller, *Mark Twain*, ibid.

the completion but before the publication of *Huckleberry Finn*—in other words, at the very apex of Mark Twain's career and Samuel Clemens' domestic happiness. The manuscript consists of eight and a half chapters, about eighteen thousand words, and it occupied the author for some three months.

Once again we find Huck Finn as narrator, and once again the novel opens with him summarizing the events of the previous novel. Within a few pages, the immortal boys and their friend Jim (now, of course, a free man) decide to run away and live among the red men, just as Huck planned to do at the end of *Huckleberry Finn*.

In the second chapter, Tom, Huck, and Jim meet an emigrant family named Mills—father, mother, three adult sons, a seventeen-year-old daughter named Peggy and her seven-year-old sister. Shortly, the family is attacked by Indians; the four men and the mother are killed and scalped, and the two girls are taken away. Tom, Huck, and Peggy's fiancé Brace Johnson set out to follow their trail.

In Chapter 9, they find a piece of Peggy's dress and four stakes driven into the ground, where she has apparently been spread-eagled with the implication of rape and torture. A few hundred words later, the manuscript simply ends in the middle of a sentence. Twain seems never to have resumed work on it, and it remained incomplete and unpublished until after Clara's death in 1962. Six years later, *Life Magazine* obtained permission to publish *Tom and Huck Among the Indians,* and it appeared in the issue of December 20, 1968.[214]

---

214. *Among the Indians* existed in two forms, a handwritten manuscript at the Detroit Public Library (presumably acquired from or through Clara, who was a Detroit resident for a number of years while her husband was conductor of the Detroit Symphony), and in galley proof among the Mark Twain Papers at the University of California in Berkeley, to which Clara

The story was accompanied by a sidebar written by Professor Walter Blair of the University of Chicago, an eminent Mark Twain authority, in which he speculated on Twain's reasons for breaking off the story where he did. Professor Blair theorized that one reason may have been that Twain was afraid that he was too close to plagiarizing his sources, particularly *Our Wild Indians* by Richard Irving Dodge. Even though Twain rewrote incidents from Dodge's book in Huck's matchless vernacular, Professor Blair feels that he may have been hypersensitive about any suspicion of plagiarism and dropped the work partly for that reason.[215]

Then Professor Blair goes on to add that the second and possibly dominant factor leading to the abandonment of *Among the Indians* was Twain's personal taboo on anything sexual in his books.

Certainly, Twain had such a taboo, as I have remarked; but it appears to me that Professor Blair's analysis does not go far enough on this point. The stakeout scene is not essential to the story and could easily have been written out had Twain wished to save the manuscript. Instead, he threw away three months'

---

willed them at her death. Interestingly enough, the pages mentioning the stakes are inexplicably missing from the Detroit manuscript. Did Twain himself exorcise them? Did Clara? In that event, she may have been attempting to further the image of her father as the wholesome humorist—and as an old woman, may have simply forgotten to edit the galley proofs before she died. Of course, we can never know, now, who was responsible for what.

[215.] The stakeout scene was not original with Twain; Dodge recounts the Indian practice of tying down a white female captive and "abusing her until not infrequently death releases her." One is reminded of the young Sam Clemens reading about the torture of Joan of Arc—did this passage from Dodge affect him similarly?

work. We need to ask as well, if sex was so taboo to him, why did Twain write that scene in the first place?

I can theorize answers to these questions. Perhaps, after living with Tom and Huck for more than ten years, Twain simply grew tired of writing about them. He may have recognized that he had done everything he could with them, save exploiting them to make money (as he later did in *Tom Sawyer Abroad* and *Tom Sawyer Detective* (published in 1894 and 1895, respectively). He may have felt drained after putting all he had as a writer into *Huckleberry Finn,* and he must have realized what is obvious to any reader of *Among the Indians*—that it has Tom and Huck in it but not their magic. Finally, had he wished to save the manuscript leaving the violence in place, he could have done precisely what he did in the case of *Tom Sawyer*—simply desexualize it. He chose not to do so.[216]

I suggest that by the time Twain reached Chapter 9 of *Among the Indians,* he had *already* decided that the manuscript was unprintable. Therefore, to satisfy some private desires, he took the story in an impossible direction and wrote the stakeout scene, expressing on paper, if not in print, his need to dominate women. In other words, I suggest, he did not drop *Among the Indians* because he could not avoid the torture scene; he wrote the torture scene, for his eyes only, because he had already decided to abandon the manuscript. This explanation makes

---

[216.] If indeed Mark Twain gave up on *Among the Indians* out of boredom or from the conviction that he had taken Tom and Huck as far as he could artistically or because he felt burned out writing about them, it may explain his choice of Arthurian England as the setting for his next novel, *The Connecticut Yankee.* Or rather, it may account for the fact that he chose *not* to write again about the Mississippi Valley in 1885, although the idea of doing another book set in England came from his encounter with Malory in that Rochester book shop.

sense of the scene as well as the decision to throw away three months' work.

In any event, the significant fact for our purposes is that the stakeout scene in *Tom and Huck Among the Indians,* perhaps never intended for publication, hints again that its creator harbored a deeply rooted secret resentment of the female sex and a need to express power over women in retaliation for their domination of his childhood.

If, as the evidence I have cited tends to show, Clemens did truly have these feelings, they may account for some of that awesome burden of guilt he was carrying around with him later in life. Surely, however, they do not explain all of it. After all, if my surmise is correct, his feelings of resentment toward women must have emerged, perhaps subconsciously, at about the time of puberty, while the burden of guilt did not weigh heavily on the teenaged Sam Clemens—or on the Mississippi River pilot, the silver miner, the Nevada newspaperman, or the California correspondent either. It was not until Clemens' later life that guilt actually possessed him, an indication that whatever its roots may have been in childhood and youth, other factors have occurred to exacerbate his feelings.

Guilt Revisited

If sexual impulses of which he was ashamed contributed to Samuel Clemens' guilt feelings, but do not account for all of them, we must delve deeper to discover other causes to which those feelings can be attributed. It is also clear that whatever those sources are, they were of a nature that Clemens could not or would not disclose. In other words, they were embarrassing or dangerous to him to such a degree as to compel him to dissemble in order to keep them from being known. Here is the answer to one Clemens puzzle—his seeming hunger to take on guilt not reasonably his. I suggest that he may have adopted these false sources of guilt and placed them before the public in the *Autobiography* so that nobody would search out the true causes, which he wished to keep hidden. Thanks to the Case Western study of guilt, we have a hint as to where those true causes may be found—among Clemens' closest personal relationships with other people. In accord with Professor Baumeister's finding that guilt derives from close ties to others, I have focused on Samuel Clemens' relationships with three key people in his life: his friend, advisor, and financial angel, Henry H. Rogers; his wife, Olivia Langdon Clemens; and his eldest daughter, Susy.

Henry Huddleston Rogers

F ew Americans today have even heard of Henry Huddleston Rogers, but around the turn of the century, his name was synonymous with the worse excesses of rapacious capitalism. With John D. Archbold and William Rockefeller, he was one of the chief operating officers and strategists of the Standard Oil combine, and his business reputation was unsavory. His enemies said that his initials, H. H., stood for "Hell Hound," and Henry Demarest Lloyd considered him one of the archfiends who were turning wealth against commonwealth.[217]

Rogers was a multimillionaire whose commercial interests extended beyond the oil business, and his greatest monument is the railroad he built in the first decade of the twentieth century. Originally known as the Virginian Line, it is unique in that it was engineered virtually without regard for cost and was designed for a single purpose—to carry Pocohontas coal to tidewater for

---

[217.] See Kaplan, pp. 378-382 for a discussion of the Clemens/Rogers association and its implications for Mark Twain's work. As for Clemens' opinion of Rogers' business reputation—Kaplan quotes him as saying, "He's a pirate, all right, but he owns up to it and enjoys being a pirate. That's the reason I like him (p. 380)."

export. It was the most efficient carrier in America and continues in operation today as part of the Norfolk Southern system.

According to Kaplan, Clemens first met Rogers aboard a yacht in about 1891, but their close association began two years later when the financier (who admired Mark Twain's books) arranged to cover a note for Clemens' failing publishing company.[218] By 1894, Rogers had become Clemens' business advisor and backer, and in that role, he arranged to extricate the author from the wreckage of the publishing house and from his commitment to the unsuccessful typesetting machine. When Clemens declared bankruptcy (on Rogers' advice), it was through his influence with the creditors that Livy retained all the Twain copyrights and title to the Hartford house. Henry Rogers, to use Kaplan's phrase, "engineered the financial salvation of the Clemens family."[219]

Rogers made no overt demands on Clemens in exchange for his help, but as Kaplan points out, " . . . it was clear from the start that the price [Clemens] volunteered to pay was public silence."[220] Mark Twain, whose virulent criticisms of moneygrubbing plutocracy go back at least as far as *The Gilded Age,* never criticized the Standard Oil coterie, and Kaplan says that the Rogers' connection was probably responsible for Clemens' bypassing the chance to publish Henry Lloyd's scathing denunciation of that firm—a book which might have saved the floundering Charles Webster company had Clemens accepted it.[221]

In other words, through sponsoring Samuel Clemens and saving him financially, Henry Rogers purchased immunity for

---

[218]. See Kaplan, p. 377.

[219]. Ibid., p. 388.

[220]. Ibid., p. 381.

[221]. Ibid., pp. 381-382.

himself and for Standard Oil from the pen of Mark Twain and the press of Charles Webster. Clemens denied that he had been bought—he was simply being loyal to his friend Rogers, to whom he felt he owed his life and whom he worshipped.[222]

This, I submit, is a distinction without a difference. Clemens took Rogers's advice, accepted his financial backing and support, and in return refrained from writing, saying, or publishing anything which might have affected Rogers or his firm. His denial to the contrary, Samuel Clemens sold out his independent judgment and artistic integrity for a substantial mess of pottage.

He might well have felt guilty over the transaction. True, he saved his family from financial disaster by accepting Rogers' aid, but the cost was part of his soul. Always before, Mark Twain was free to criticize the world of American plutocracy, even while Samuel Clemens was trying to make his way in it; this is precisely what he had done in the *Connecticut Yankee*. After the Rogers transactions, there could have been no more *Connecticut Yankees*, at least as far as Standard Oil was concerned. Clemens' sellout to Henry Rogers might well have been one of the demons which haunted him with guilt in his last years.

222. See Kaplan, p. 381, reporting Clemens' own assertion that he had not been bought and paid for, and treating it with the disdain that it deserves.

Marriage: Livy Clemens

O livia Langdon was not a woman of great wit, and while she was intelligent, she lacked much formal education; fundamentally, she was a Victorian lady raised with conventional sensibilities and tastes. All her life, she was a semi-invalid. At about the age of sixteen, she suffered a fall on some ice and spent the next two years partially paralyzed and unable to even sit up without aid. According to her biographer, Resa Willis, many physicians attended her during her illness, but nothing seemed to help until, in the autumn of 1864, the Langdons consulted a faith healer. As if by magic, Livy rose from her bed and was able to walk a few steps, and within a few months was able to get about unaided.[223]

The exact nature of Livy's illness has never been clear, but it seems to have been related to nervousness and may have been at least partly psychosomatic.[224] In any event, she was never robust

---

[223.] See *Mark and Livy* by Resa Willis (New York: Athenum, 1992) pp. 18-30.

[224.] The healer, James Newton, was paid $1,500, a large sum for the times, but seems to have done hardly more than to throw open the curtains and utter some positive and supportive words. One must wonder, cynically enough, whether after two years in bed Livy simply got tired of being ill

throughout the rest of her life; she eventually developed heart and thyroid diseases which finally killed her at the relatively young age of fifty-nine. However frail she may have been, Livy Clemens nevertheless bore four children and raised three of them; managed a household including, at times, a sizeable service staff; entertained frequently and lavishly: and traveled widely on two continents, not to mention accompanying her husband on a trip around the world. Still, as a somewhat wilting flower without exceptional background or wit, she seems hardly the type of woman Samuel Clemens might have been expected to choose as his life's partner.

Yet the marriage was crucially important to his career. It introduced him to the respectable social circles whose members became his readers; it took him from the Wild, Wild West and put him in contact with the all-powerful Eastern establishment and, in addition to respectability, it brought him instant wealth, for Livy Langdon was an heiress whose net worth amounted to something like a quarter of a million 1870 dollars. Few men's lives have been as dramatically altered by matrimony.

We must ask, then, the unaskable, unanswerable question—did Samuel Clemens choose Olivia Langdon as his wife solely out of love, or because she could bring him so much more?

There can be no doubt that he really did love her, or that they appear to have been a devoted couple through thirty-four years of marriage in good times and bad. Yet when a marriage is so beneficial to one partner—particularly when it is the woman who has the money and position, which the man needs and

---

and used this occasion to stage her recovery. One also suspects her of using her ill health to manipulate her husband and daughters—a not uncommon phenomenon.

wants—one cannot ignore the suspicion that love alone was not the entire motive for the pairing.[225]

This question nagged at Margaret Sanborn, especially because the mushy letters Clemens wrote to Olivia in his courtship of her are so violently out of character with the man who created them. Ms. Sanborn concludes that Clemens " . . . was ably playing a part he felt certain would win the woman that he loved . . . [but] There is no evidence in any of his words or acts then or ever that he regarded this as a practical marriage for him. In fact, [they] counted on living in a boarding house, supported by his income from lecturing and newspaper work.[226]

The trouble with Ms. Sanborn's inference is that it rests on the absence of evidence. She is entirely justified in drawing her conclusions, but negative evidence remains less than totally definitive—for if Clemens *had* been dissembling about his goals in the Siege of Elmira, he would surely have left nothing to show it. We already know that he was capable of keeping secrets—witness his near-total, completely conscious blackout on matters sexual—and he had undoubted talent as an actor (as his success on the lecture circuit clearly demonstrates).

---

[225] The success of a marriage is no proof of its purity of origin. Remember that passage in Chapter 41 of the *Yankee*, where Hank Morgan admits that his marriage to Sandy (which proved to be idyllic) was motivated solely by his concern about her reputation. Could Twain have been hinting here that Clemens' own marriage turned out well, even if it was motivated by the wrong reasons?

[226] See *Mark Twain: The Bachelor Years*, p. 417. But query: would not so astute a man as Samuel Clemens have foreseen that Jervis Langdon would never permit a daughter of his to live in a rooming house, no matter to whom she was married? And in fact, Mr. Langdon bestowed an elegant home on the newlyweds—as I believe Clemens knew he would.

In short, I fear that we cannot reach any definitive conclusions about Clemens' motives, goals, or thoughts simply from the *absence* of evidence. No one could get into Samuel Clemens' mind but Samuel Clemens, even in his lifetime. That remains all the more true today—but I am still trying.

I suggest, then, that Clemens may indeed have had more than pure romantic love in mind when young Charles Langdon showed him the miniature of his sister aboard the "*Quaker City*," and Clemens dedicated himself to the pursuit and capture of Olivia Louise Langdon. Once again, I reiterate the point that he certainly did love her. The question is whether he chose to woo her hand in marriage solely on that account, or because she offered so much more than mere romance.[227]

Proceeding on the assumption that Clemens married for more than love alone, we find that this supposition leads us to some very interesting conclusions. For if he, in essence, took advantage of Livy's social position, family connections, and wealth, he certainly had ample cause to feel guilty about it. Moreover, unlike the possible origins of guilt I have discussed previously, guilt over his marriage would have tended to grow with time and to reach intense proportions during her increasing illness and after her death. Consider Clemens' position in 1905; he was by then probably the best-known and possibly the most generally beloved figure in America, wealthy beyond need of concern and looked up to as an oracle or even a demi-god.

[227.] One must also consider the possibility that while Clemens may have had other things in mind at the time of his marriage to Livy, his love for her grew more profound afterward. This is what happened to Hank Morgan in the *Yankee*, who married Sandy for the wrong reasons, only to discover in her the ideal wife and mother whom he came in time to adore. Was this a picture of Clemens' own marriage? This possibility must not be ignored.

She, on the other hand, was dead. Would Samuel Clemens have attained his eminent position without his wife's emotional and financial support and family position? He needed only to ask himself that question to feel again what he had felt over the death of his brother Henry—the guilt of survival. Those who live through great disasters or shattering crimes, while others close to them die, often feel this kind of guilt. "Why me, Lord?" they ask. "Why did I live when others more deserving of life than I did not?" In our own time, Holocaust survivors have had to deal with this guilt, irrational as it may seem. Soldiers who come home from the wars which killed their buddies confront it frequently. Following the terrible Cocoanut Grove nightclub fire in Boston in 1942, one survivor was so distraught over the death of his wife, for which he blamed himself, that he committed suicide by throwing himself from a hospital window.[228]

Returning to the Case Western Reserve study of guilt cited earlier, we can see that survivorship guilt arises from feelings toward a person or persons with whom the person suffering guilt has been emotionally involved and who did not survive. The apparent randomness or senselessness of one person living while the other dies is the moving cause of the guilt feelings.

In Clemens' case, however, there was even more reason for him to feel guilty toward Livy; for if he in fact did marry her at least partly for her money and position, it was not a random or senseless power that brought out his feelings, but his own

---

[228.] For an account of the fire and its aftermath, including the story of Francis Gotturna, see Paul Benzaquin, *Holocaust* (New York: Henry Holt and Co., 1959) pp. 106-109. Gotturna was unconscious from smoke inhalation and probably could have done nothing to save the life of his wife, but felt so guilty over her loss that all efforts by psychiatrists failed to convince him that he was not responsible. He killed himself about six weeks after surviving the fire.

work in first spotting her, then winning her, and finally using her. What's more, he could never let anyone know what he had done.

"There is no evidence . . . that he regarded this as a practical marriage for him" . . . but what if he did?

Susy

aving proposed a hypothesis in which Clemens secretly married his wife not only for love but also for money and social position, I have accounted for some of the guilt he so clearly felt in the last years of his life; but the burden of that guilt was so crushing that it not only drove Mark Twain into a philosophic pessimism, it drove Samuel Clemens to the verge of insanity. After all, his marriage to Livy, however motivated, was successful, enduring and for all we can learn, happy. Was there yet another source of guilt, beyond his relationship with his wife, which could have borne down so heavily on Samuel Clemens? I suggest that there was.

Langdon Clemens was (according to his father) a premature infant, apparently conceived immediately after his parents' marriage on February 2, 1870 and born in November of that same year. From birth, he had a sickly, chalk-white complexion, and was slow to walk and talk. Both Sam and Livy must have been perfectly aware that the chances of such a sickly infant surviving childhood were small; he was almost a sure bet to contract something virulent. In Langdon's case, that something was diphtheria, which killed him at the age of nineteen months.[229]

Thus, when the couples' second child, a girl, was delivered at the Langdon mansion in Elmira on March 19, 1872, they must have been doubly, triply glad. The child was healthy and normal in every respect. She was named Olivia Susan Clemens, after her grandmother (Olivia Lewis Langdon), her mother (Olivia Louise Langdon Clemens), and her maternal aunt (Susan Langdon Crane). Within the family circle, however, her full name was never used; from babyhood on, she was always known as "Susy."

She was just short of three months old when her unfortunate brother died, and all her parents' love and attention was focused on her. They lavished everything on her, in part because she was a beautiful and intelligent child and partly because her presence helped to overcome the pain caused by the loss of their firstborn.[230] For two years, Susy enjoyed the status of an only child until the birth of her sister Clara on June 8, 1874.

Even after her sister's birth, Susy remained the favorite child in the family, and her status was not changed when Livy gave birth to another baby girl named Jane Lampton Clemens (after her paternal grandmother) but called Jean by the family. The presence of a new baby is sometimes hard on older siblings

---

[229]. Samuel Clemens could recall the deaths of two of his own siblings—Margaret, who died when he was three and a half; and Benjamin, when he was six and a half. He had also had an elder brother, Pleasants, who died as an infant of three months several years before his own birth. Infant and child mortality was more of a norm than an exception in the days before miracle drugs.

[230]. While Sam appears to have felt pain over his son's death for a few days at most, Livy (in whose arms the child expired) was "heartbroken" (See Kaplan, p. 169).

because the infant demands and gets so much attention from the parents, but this does not seem to have happened in the Clemens household.

Susy was always a bright and precocious child, and in her intellect and temperament resembled her father more than did either of the younger girls. While Clara wrote that her father was always impartial toward his three daughters, that statement is simply untrue.[231] Clara and everyone else knew that Susy was first among equals—in fact, Clemens did not bother to hide his special relationship with his eldest surviving child.

In 1885, at the age of thirteen, Susy Clemens began to write a biography of her father.[232] From it, we learn that Clemens'

---

[231]　See *My Father. Mark Twain* by Clara Clemens Gabrilowitsch (New York: Harper & Brothers, 1931), p. 64. She admits that both Sam and Livy loved Susy most, but says that they completely disguised the fact. This is simply hard to credit, given the ample evidence to the contrary. But to have conceded that her father played favorites among his daughters would not have fit the picture Clara was trying to present of her father as the Gentle Humorist and Beloved Old Man of Letters. That she succeeded in her efforts probably helped sell more copies of Mark Twain books, but at a terrible cost; in contrast with European readers, most Americans simply do not take Twain seriously as an adult author.

[232]　Her manuscript has survived and is now in the Samuel Clemens Collection at the Clifton Walker Barrett Library of the University of Virginia, Charlottesville. In 1985 (the 150th anniversary of Clemens' birth and the centenary of Susy's biography), the eminent Twain scholar Charles Neider arranged for its publication as part of his book, *Papa* (Garden City, NY: Doubleday and Co., 1985). While parts of Susy's work had been used by Mark Twain in his own *Autobiography* (accompanied by his comments, written in 1906 and 1907), and other selections had appeared at other times, this was the first publication of the whole manuscript. Neider appended to it some of her letters to her college

affection for his daughter did not go unreciprocated. She wrote of him, "He is an extraordinarily fine looking man . . . the lovliest [*sic*] man I ever saw, or ever hope to see . . ."[233] Plainly she idolized and adored her father and continued to add passages to her little book about him for a year or more. The manuscript became increasingly more a diary than a biography, and the last entry is dated July 4 (1886). It was written at Keokuk, Iowa, where the family had gone to visit Jane Clemens, Sam's mother, who was then an infirm eighty-three. That final entry breaks off suddenly in the middle of a sentence, as if the author had been interrupted in her writing and never returned to it. Susy was then fourteen years and three months of age.

Not only was Susy her father's image in intellect and temperament, she was, if her photographs do not lie, an exceptionally beautiful girl. Even as a teenager, there was something arresting about her. She had deep-set dark eyes, delicate features, and a sensuous mouth. In all her pictures, even as a young girl, those penetrating eyes stand out—intense

---

roommate, Louise Brownell, which were found in the Saunders Papers at the Hamilton College Library, Clinton, NY; and the "delirium notes" Susy wrote in the last few days of her life while suffering from meningitis. Together, these elements combine to make *Papa* much more than a young girl's profile of her father; it is, in effect, a preliminary study of the life of Susy Clemens. Professor Neider's book has been crucial to my own work; had he not published *Papa*, it is more than likely that *Encounters With Mark Twain* would never have been conceived, much less written.

233. See *Papa*, p. 84. These words are from the first paragraph of Susy's biography and were written (according to her father) when she was fourteen and he fifty. This cannot be right, as Susy's fourteenth birthday was on March 19, 1886. Actually, the book (if one can call it that) was begun shortly after Susy's thirteenth birthday. At that time, Samuel Clemens was forty-nine; he turned fifty on November 30, 1885.

and questioning, and strangely compelling. In contrast to her mother, who was quite attractive but nondescript, Susy Clemens must have been impossible to miss in a crowd. Just as her father was a striking man, she was a striking girl, and later, a dazzling young woman. Her sisters Clara and Jean shared some of her features, but their photographs lack her piercing eyes and special aura.

From her letters, it is clear that Susy developed into a lonely, nervous, and passionate young woman. That she had some talent as a writer (although she never managed to master English orthography and her sense of punctuation sometimes failed her) is not surprising, given her father's identity. Indeed, he encouraged her to become a professional writer; instead, she wanted to be an opera singer. She was at least good enough to study with Mme. Marchesi of Paris, one of the greatest vocal teachers of all time,[234] although it seems unlikely that Susy could ever have developed the size and strength to sing the Wagnerian roles to which she seems to have aspired.[235]

As to Susy's personality, her father quotes George Warner (brother of his friend, neighbor, and sometime collaborator, Charles Dudley Warner) as saying, "She is the most interesting person I have ever known, of either sex."[236]

In the fall of 1890, Susy entered Bryn Mawr College outside Philadelphia—the only one of the three Clemens girls who

---

[234] Mathilde Marchesi (1821-1913) was one of the foremost singing teachers of the period. Among her students were Nellie Melba, Emma Nevada, and Emma Eames, to name just three major stars.

[235] Susy was no Amazon, and despite Marchesi's encouragement, it seems ludicrous to imagine her as an Isolde or Brunnhilde. If she had become a successful operatic soprano, one suspects that it would probably have been in the Italian or French repertory rather than the German.

[236] See *Papa*, ibid., p. 67.

ever went to college. The impetus for sending her there came from her mother, who saw to it that she studied for the entrance exams. Bryn Mawr was two hundred miles from Hartford; Livy was making sure that Susy would be out of the house.[237]

It is interesting to note that at college, she went by her given first name, Olivia, which was never used at home. Charles Neider remarks that just as her father had two identities—as Samuel Clemens and as Mark Twain—so now his eldest daughter had two as well. She was Susy at home, and Olivia at school.[238]

Neider quotes one of Susy's classmates as saying (in a letter to Dixon Wecter, written in 1949) " . . . I realized how strong was the tie between her and her father, how much they minded being separated, and also how eager Mrs. Clemens was that she [that is, Susy] should be happy in a new environment, leading an independent life of her own as a college student among girls of her own age, free of the limiting influences of home . . . Mrs. Clemens would come down occasionally for a short stay, I think in order to keep Mr. Clemens from coming, because she told me that he would make anything an excuse, even to bringing down Olivia's [Susy's] laundry."[239]

At Bryn Mawr, Susy (or Olivia) roomed with a slightly older student named Louise Sheffield Brownell, with whom she was to develop an extremely close relationship and while she was homesick and apparently unhappy at the beginning of the

---

[237.] See Kaplan, p. 364. He concludes that Livy wanted Susy and her father to be separated.

[238.] *Papa*, ibid., p. 29.

[239.] The writer of the letter, Mrs. Charles M. Andrews, clearly hints at what she does not actually say—that for a father to be bringing his college-age daughter her laundry over a distance of two hundred miles was certainly unusual behavior. Livy's visits, which were made to forestall Sam's, indicate that she thought so as well.

school year, Susy seems to have adjusted to college life reasonably well.[240]

However successful her freshman year may have been, Susy never finished it. Toward the end of April, 1891, she mysteriously dropped out of Bryn Mawr and returned home to Hartford. Her sudden departure from the college has never been explained. Seeking an answer, Charles Neider visited the school, only to find that all student records for the 1890-1891 academic year have unaccountably disappeared. Even the president's copies are missing.[241] Whatever the reasons for the abrupt termination of Susy Clemens' college career, they are not to be found in suburban Philadelphia.

There may or may not be a connection, but it is a fact that Susy's abrupt departure from Bryn Mawr closely followed a strange incident involving her father. Clemens was invited by the college president, James E. Rhoads, to speak there on March 23, 1891 (four days after Susy's nineteenth birthday). Before his talk, she made him promise not to tell his favorite ghost story, the tale of the Golden Arm.

This is a variation of an age-old folk tale which turns on delivering the punch line—the "snapper," as Clemens called it—with just the right timing to make the audience jump with fright. In this story, the set-up line, repeated several times during the spooky tale, is "Who's got my Golden Arm?" while the snapper is, "You've got it!"

Samuel Clemens had learned the Golden Arm story from the Negroes on his uncle John Quarles's farm in Missouri when he

---

[240.] Much to her father's "private regret," as he admitted to William Dean Howells, "Susy is beginning to love Bryn Mawr." Neider quotes this letter, dated February 10, 1891, in *Papa* (p. 12) and Kaplan also cites it (p. 363).

[241.] See *Papa*, ibid., p. 31.

was just a boy, and it was one of his pet stories. He had mastered the timing and could generally deliver the "snapper" perfectly to get the physical reaction he wanted from the audience. Susy had heard him tell the story many times and, according to Kaplan, was both frightened and discomfited by it.[242]

Sitting in the audience during Clemens' speech, Susy whispered to a friend, "He's going to tell the ghost story! I *know* he's going to tell the ghost story . . . and make them all jump." She was right; despite his promise (which he seems never to have taken seriously), he did tell it, and Susy ran from the room, crying.[243]

Why did Susy react with so much emotion to the telling of this seemingly simple and apparently harmless ghost story, and why was she so upset when her father broke his promise not to tell it?

She told a classmate that she did not want her father to tell the Golden Arm story because it was not right "for the sophisticated group at Bryn Mawr." When he did tell it, delivering the "snapper" with his usual effectiveness, she may have been acutely embarrassed that he acted with such a lack of dignity before her friends.[244]

---

[242] See Kaplan, p. 365, where he indulges in a bit of speculation as to why Susy was so upset by this seemingly innocuous tale.

[243] Ibid. Also see *Papa*, ibid., for Neider's account of the incident.

[244] A young girl may suffer embarrassment over her parents' behavior, which seems to them to be totally innocent. This is understandable (and age-appropriate) in a thirteen-year-old, but at the time of the Golden Arm incident, Susy was not prepubescent or adolescent; she was a fully grown young woman of nineteen. One wonders, then, if mere social immaturity accounted for her overreaction, or whether it grew out of other, more subtle roots.

But if Kaplan can speculate on why Susy was so unsettled by the ghost story, so can I. Is it going too far afield to suggest that her apparent overreaction to the story may have been based on its possessing for her some special emotional impact? Did her father's breaking his promise not to tell the story have particular significance for her? Did this incident perhaps mark a profound moment, even a pivot point, in their relationship? It does seem beyond question that the exceptionally close connection of which Mrs. Andrews wrote cooled greatly after the spring of 1891; also, Susy's mysterious departure from Bryn Mawr occurred no more than five weeks after the Golden Arm incident.

She had little time to spend in Hartford, however. Five weeks after her return from Bryn Mawr, the entire family was en route to Europe. The cost of maintaining an extravagant lifestyle had become too high to handle, so the Hartford house was closed and the Clemens family went to live on the continent, where things were less expensive. Livy and the girls remained in Europe continuously for four full years, mostly in Germany and Italy, while Sam commuted back and forth across the Atlantic trying, to stabilize the family finances. At one point, he was away from his family for seven months.

During this period, the relationship between Susy and her father deteriorated, perhaps almost to the point of estrangement. With his trips to America, the amount of time they spent together was much diminished; and even when Clemens was with the family the old special closeness between his eldest daughter and him seems to have disappeared.

These years were terribly disappointing for Susy. She had little or nothing to do, locked as she was in the gilded prison of upper-class Victorian morality which severely limited the freedom of young, single women. To make matters worse, Clara broke away from the rest of the family to study music in Berlin, while Jean (who was just eleven at the time of the move to Europe) was in school. Susy was left alone with her mother, her books, and her frustrations. She did study voice with Mme. Marchesi in Paris, but on the whole, the four years abroad (Susy's nineteenth to twenty-third years) were not easy ones.

Meanwhile, Henry Rogers had taken over the management of Clemens' business affairs and was planning his financial recovery. Part of his strategy was to send Mark Twain on a round-the-world lecture tour, to be followed by a book on the experience. The trip was planned for 1895-96, and to rest and prepare for it, the family finally returned to the United States in May 1895.

Clemens planned to take Livy and Susy with him on this trip, but Susy declined the opportunity.[245] As a result, it was Clara, next in seniority, who accompanied her parents when they left Elmira on the first leg of the journey on July 14, 1895. Susy came to the railroad station to see them off and stood on the platform, waving as the train pulled away; this was the last time her parents and sister saw her alive.

The lecture tour proved to be a huge success, both artistically and financially, and as a result, Clemens was able to pay off all his creditors 100 cents on the dollar. Meanwhile, Susy continued her vocal studies and tried to build up her strength. She is known to have seen Louise Brownell at least twice during the year her parents were away.[246]

About the beginning of August 1896, Susy was visiting in Hartford and preparing to sail for England to meet Clara and her parents. The family's faithful maid, Kate Leary, who was with her, noticed that Susy began acting restless and ill. A physician was called, but apparently he could find nothing specifically wrong. He concluded that Susy was simply suffering from overwork and

---

[245.] Clemens wrote in his notebook that she disliked long sea voyages. This may or may not have been the reason for her reluctance to go along. See *Papa*, p. 34.

[246.] Ibid.

prescribed relaxation and rest, but Susy did not improve; her aunt, Susan Crane, was summoned from Elmira to be with her.

On August 15, the doctor finally diagnosed Susy's illness as spinal meningitis, a vicious, contagious disease, which before the development of antibiotics was frequently fatal.[247] One of its characteristic manifestations is rapidly rising fever, and by Sunday, August 16, Susy was delirious with temperature. About noon of that day, she became blind, and in the afternoon, she spoke for the last time. She lapsed into a coma, and after two days, she died on Tuesday, August 18, 1896. She was twenty-four years and five months old.[248]

[247.] "Meningitis is an inflammation of the membrane which covers the brain and spinal cord. It may be either bacterial or viral in nature, and it may result from head injuries or infections of the eyes, ears, and nose. It may also result as a complication from pneumonia or syphilis. Transmission occurs by direct contact between people (*Academic American Encyclopedia*. Danbury, Connecticut: Grolier, Inc., 1983)."

So far as I know, there has never been an explanation of how Susy Clemens contracted the disease, or where–in Elmira, or after her return to Hartford.

[248.] In the *Autobiography*, Clemens wrote a description of Susy's death, which took place in the downstairs bedroom at the Hartford house. In it, he mentions those present at her passing—Rev. Joe Twitchell, summoned from an Adirondack vacation; John and Ellen O'Neil, a married couple who were serving as caretakers at the house; Kate Leary, the family maid; her sister Jean; her aunt, Susan Crane; and her uncle, Charles Langdon. Unaccountably, however, Clemens says that Theodore Crane, not Charles Langdon, was at the bedside (see *Papa*, p. 48). He is quite specific in saying that despite Susy's comment, "I am blind, Uncle Charley, and you are blind," she was confused and that it was Uncle Theodore who was present. This is patently impossible; Theodore Crane had died in 1889. In addition, there seems to be no question that Charles Langdon was

Before slipping into her final coma, however, Susy scribbled a series of puzzling notes. Written in her feverish, delirious state, they make no apparent sense, yet seem pregnant with meaning. Charles Neider published them in their entirety in *Papa,* still another of his invaluable services to Mark Twain scholarship. I shall return to these notes later and try to draw some relevance from them.

Samuel Clemens was in England when the news of Susy's illness came. At first, it was reported that her condition was not serious, but the family was upset nevertheless. Livy and Clara began to pack; there was a boat to New York at noon on Saturday (August 15), and they planned to take it if the news turned worse. No further information arrived by cable, and Livy and Clara did board the steamer, Clemens staying at the house they had rented in Guildford. Susy's death occurred while her mother and sister were still en route to America; they reached Elmira in time to attend her burial, which took place on Sunday, August 23. Clemens was informed of Susy's death by cablegram on the eighteenth. The shock was overwhelming, and it is fair to say that he never got over her death.[249]

His writing about Susy, done immediately after her passing, together with a poem he created a year after her death and

---

there—Kate Leary says so (Salsbury, p. 386). It appears to have been Clemens, not Susy, who was confused. Also, one wonders what if anything Susy meant when she said "and you are blind, Uncle Charlie." Did she intend to suggest that Charles Langdon never saw the obvious—the closeness of the Sam and Susy relationship? In her delirious state, she may never have meant anything like this, or even anything at all—but again, one wonders.

[249.] Clemens' discussion of Susy's death in Chapter 66 of the *Autobiography* is some of his most magnificent literary work. It is personal and touching yet remarkably unsentimental and simple. It is a must reading for anyone interested in the life and work of this most fascinating man.

other material pertaining to his feelings about her is also a part of *Papa,* and I shall consider these writings in due time.

Until relatively recently, we have known little more about Susy Clemens than the facts I have already discussed. Our knowledge of her life and character has been greatly augmented, however, by the discovery and partial publication of a series of letters she wrote to Louise Brownell, her Bryn Mawr roommate, after leaving the college.

These letters remained in Louise's possession throughout her life, which was both long and adventurous. After taking an advanced degree and studying in Europe, Louise filled several teaching and administrative positions before marrying, at the age of thirty, Arthur P. Saunders. He became a professor of chemistry at Hamilton College, and the couple had four children. Their marriage lasted fifty-four years until the death of Professor Saunders in 1953. Louise Brownell Saunders lived until 1961, and she willed the letters to Hamilton College as part of the Saunders Papers.

There are thirty-seven letters from Susy (or Olivia, as she was known to Louise) in the Saunders Papers, all but two of them written from various locations in Europe, where the Clemens family was living from June 1891 to May 1895. The bulk of the correspondence was sent between October 1891 and November 1893, with one additional, anguished, pleading letter dated August 1894.

These letters reveal that an extremely close emotional and probably physical relationship existed between Susy Clemens and Louise Brownell. If it was not overtly lesbian (as it may very well have been, judging from Susy's many references to physical contact), it was certainly something far deeper than an ordinary friendship.[250]

[250.] Ms. Michelle Cotton, a history major at Elmira College, wrote a 1982 senior thesis on the Clemens/Brownell letters. She made typescripts of

Once the issue of lesbianism is raised, other evidence supports the possibility. Some of Susy's letters to Clara contain vague, tantalizing references; on February 28, 1893, she wrote from the Villa Vivani in Florence to Berlin, "I am contented here most of the time and satisfied but with me it is different for entre nous I have rather given up expecting much happiness constructed as I am and all."[251] What did she mean by "constructed as I am"? Out of context, this phrase carries no particular connotations, but when Susy's lesbian tendencies are known, it seems full of meaning.

The following November, Susy wrote another letter to her sister, in which she said, "I *wish* you were back here [in Europe—Clara had gone to America shortly before]. I think I depend on you now more than anyone else in the world! Because I love you so much and you are so sweet and then you *understand* and seem to like me as I *am*, without criticising [*sic*]. Oh yes, I have a comfort and rest and pleasure in *you* that I find in no one else [emphasis Susy's]."[252] Again, this comment means nothing if taken out of context, but in the knowledge of Susy's relationship

---

them (a godsend to later researchers, as Susy's handwriting is not always easy to decipher and a number of the letters were written on both sides of thin paper and are today very difficult to make out). She also added an index identifying the individuals discussed in the correspondence, and finally concluded that the relationship between Susy and Louise was probably more than a deep and affectionate friendship—that is, that it was a lesbian love affair. While Ms. Cotton is careful to add that more evidence is necessary before publicly labeling Susy a female homosexual, one cannot read the letters she wrote to Louise without reaching the conclusion that Ms. Cotton's view of their relationship is correct.

251. This letter is quoted by Edith Colgate Salsbury in *Susy and Mark Twain*, p. 323.

252. Quoted by Salsbury, ibid., p. 334.

with Louise Brownell, it seems to indicate that Clara knew of Susy's sexual orientation and accepted her anyway.

There is also further evidence which seems to show that Susy was not Louise Brownell's only female partner. Charles Neider quotes her daughter, Silvia Saunders, to the effect that Louise had a close association with a woman named Jessie Benedict Carter (1872-1917) in Europe, beginning in 1893 (when Susy was writing those impassioned letters to her former roommate) and that "Some of Louise's friends were critical of this relationship." Ms. Saunders did not elaborate further, and Neider wonders whether Susy knew of it and, if so, if she was jealous of it.[253] If indeed this was a romantic lesbian association, it would seem to demonstrate beyond doubt that Louise Brownell was at least bisexual.

As important as Susy's letters are to disclosing her probable sexual orientation, they are at least as important, and perhaps more important, for additional content. For one thing, they make it clear that Susy was holding something back which she was afraid to let Louise know. On June 12, 1893, she wrote from Florence, " . . . the truth is that what I would *tell* you of myself (in person) will not go on paper. It is quite out of the question but it will keep . . . I would rather you knew my sins all of them and my trials too but since they are both strange and vulgar, I am not sure that you wouldn't be shocked by them."[254]

In another letter written three months later, Susy tells Louise, "The point of all this discourse is that I am confirmed in my fear that perhaps it would not be safe for me to tell you as much about myself as I should like to. How do I know you mightn't break off our relations on the spot? . . . I do not say approve only understand forgive and not be weaned. But I don't at all know that you *could* and you might be horrified and repelled and that

---

[253.] Quoted in *Papa*, p. 17.

[254.] Ibid.

would be fatal. As you say to make a friendship satisfactory there must be a complete frank understanding. That is what I should like but there is a *rigorous* something about you that frightens me while I admire it. I believe you are rather *implacable, inflexible, puritanic.* Ah me how I love you and how I would like to meet all the requirements of your most rigorous spiritual self."[255]

Obviously, Susy was terrified that there was something in her background which, if disclosed, might shock Louise so much that she would decide to terminate their relationship. In her desperate state of love, Susy could not tolerate that, so she writes in generalities about her "sins . . . and trials too but they are both strange and vulgar . . ."

What could those dark corners in her past be, that she so feared Louise learning of them? Susy had led a sheltered life; except for her months at Bryn Mawr (where she was actually living with Louise in the dormitory), she had never been away from home . . .

There is a hypothesis which not only explains Susy's "strange and vulgar" sins and makes sense of the Golden Arm incident at Bryn Mawr but also elucidates and illuminates Samuel Clemens' overwhelming guilt feelings in the years following Susy's death in 1896. What if the obvious closeness between father and daughter, which was so apparent at the time that Susy was sent away to college by her mother but cooled afterward, really masked something more profound—a romantic love? It is even possible that this feeling may have been expressed in an incestuous relationship between Samuel Clemens and his favorite daughter.[256]

---

[255]. This letter, dated September 3, 1893, and postmarked Franzenbad, is quoted in *Papa*, pp. 20-22.

[256]. In describing the Sam/Susy relationship on page 6 of *Papa*, Charles Neider says it was "a wonderful relationship, a sort of love affair, between

This is a shocker, as I am perfectly aware. But if such a relationship existed, even if it were not consummated physically, the otherwise mysterious and painful effects on both their lives become clearly explicable. Moreover, there are a great many tidbits of evidence which tend to support the theory. None of them alone seems convincing but worked together into a mosaic they do seem to fit together and to take their places in the picture I am composing.

First, it is essential to discuss incest, to define it and to identify the clues, which often betray its occurrence.

Incest is the last and perhaps greatest sexual taboo in Western society, hardly less powerful today than it was centuries ago. Yet our general conception of incest as something that only happens between Uncle Jed and Miss Rosie in the deepest backwaters of Appalachia is just flat wrong. Incest occurs everywhere—in the cities and suburbs as well as in the hollows—and it is not nearly as unusual as we prefer to think. A recent book, *Incest,* by Anna Kosof, quotes the Kinsey Report of 1953 concluding that 25 percent of American women had been incest victims at some point in their lives.[257]

Moreover, that figure is based on the traditional definition of incest as a sexual physical contact between two blood relatives. Some recent writers argue that this in an inadequate definition because it is too narrow. What if a stepfather fondles a stepchild? They are not blood relatives, so this conduct would not be

---

a father and his daughter." In view of the evidence of Susy's letters which he quotes, and with due respect to Professor Neider's superior knowledge of Samuel Clemens and his family, I wonder if this was merely a figure of speech or whether Neider was hinting at something he was afraid to state more directly.

257. Anna Kosof, *Incest* (New York: Franklin Watts, 1985).

incestuous by the traditional definition, yet the scarring effects on the child are the same.

Taking this into consideration, E. Sue Bloom has suggested that a better definition of incest is the abuse of trust and that neither a blood relationship nor actual touching is essential.[258] This covers the case of the stepfather exposing himself to a stepchild; there is no touching, but the situation is still one of violation of trust in a sexual context and (Ms. Bloom avers) should properly be considered a case of incest. Even according to the traditional definition, she concludes that as of 1990, about a third of American women have had incestuous experiences, while using her more comprehensive definition that figure to rises to between 40 percent and one half!

Incest may appear in many forms, but while brother/sister and mother/son cases do occur, the most common manifestation by far involves an older male and a young female. The man may be father, stepfather, uncle, or family friend; I know personally of one case in which it was the mother's lover. What's more, incest seems not to be bound by social class, economic, religious, or educational distinctions. It appears among all sorts, even among the "best and brightest."[259]

[258.] E. Sue Bloom, *Secret Survivors: Uncovering Incest and its Effects on Women* (New York: Ballantine Books, 1990). Ms. Bloom calls incest the result of a "power trip"; that is, she sees it as the result of a need by the person in the dominant position—generally an older man—to exercise power over the other party. This idea is certainly consistent with my analysis of Samuel Clemens" possible resentment of women and need to dominate or manipulate them in later life.

[259.] Both Bloom and Kosof emphasize this point, dispelling the more comfortable notion that incest only occurs among "*that* kind of people." As a society, we are reluctant to admit the truth—that incest occurs in every social strata.

It is a traumatic experience, so disturbing that an incest victim may block the experience out of her conscious mind. Nevertheless, incest survivors tend to exhibit certain specific behaviors in adult life, and it appears possible to detect from these telltale clues cases of hidden incest, even where the victim has forgotten or repressed the experience.

Bloom has compiled a thirty-five-point checklist of behaviors which may indicate a past incestuous experience, and among these characteristics there are several which were clearly present in Susy Clemens. One is eating disorders, which were a constant problem for her while in Europe, where, according to Neider, she grew thin as a result.[260] Others include a need to be perfect (or perfectly bad); depression; guilt; shame and low self-esteem; the feeling of carrying an awful secret and fear that it will be revealed; withdrawal from or reluctance to trust happiness; sexual dysfunction (although Bloom asserts that homosexual behavior is *not* an aftereffect of incest); feeling crazy or different and creating fantasy worlds or fantasy relationships; swallowing or gagging sensitivity; multiple personality and (most strikingly in Susy's case) a desire to change one's name.[261]

Anna Kosof also offers a list of behaviors common to incest survivors which overlaps but does not duplicate Bloom's. They differ most clearly on the question of lesbianism; Ms. Bloom states that homosexual behavior is not an aftereffect of incest, while Ms.

[260.] See *Papa*, p. 11. Here Neider discusses some of Susy's characteristic behaviors during her four-year exile in Europe. She also suffered from insomnia, nervousness, depression, vague feelings of discontent and unexplained sudden shortness of breath, and experienced manic periods of exultation without apparent cause.

[261.] *Secret Survivors*, ibid. Ms. Bloom emphasizes that her thirty-five-point checklist is not and never can be complete as more data comes to light.

Kosof asserts that it is. She also cites other typical characteristics as follows:

> Feelings of isolation or acute loneliness (a point also emphasized by Bloom);
>
> Difficulty or impossibility of forming normal adult relationships with men after an incest experience in young teen years;
>
> As a rule, the older the victim, the more severe the adult reaction. Some incest survivors develop multiple personalities;
>
> Mothers of incest victims are often passive women and frequently are incapacitated by illness;
>
> Many or most incest victims are distant from their mothers;
>
> Fathers who engage in incest with their daughters often feel themselves inadequate with other adult women.[262]

With the exception of the characteristic of distance from the mother, Susy and her family seem to exhibit each of these behaviors. As her letters to Louise Brownell clearly indicate, she did feel terribly lonely and isolated, and her exile in Europe, away from her closest sister and other relatives as well as from all her college friends could only intensify those feelings. It was like taking a child who was afraid of the dark and turning

---

[262.] See Kosof, *Incest.*

the lights out on her. Her relationship with Louise Brownell is characteristic of incest survivors according to at least one source; she clearly had low self-esteem; she exhibited fear of a terrible secret in her past which she was afraid Louise might learn; she did seem to withdraw from and distrust happiness. She did seem to demonstrate obsessive-compulsive tendencies, and she was apparently manic-depressive. She was unable to form normal relationships with men her own age. If she did not develop a true multiple personality, she certainly started down that road by creating a second identity for herself at Bryn Mawr, where she actually did change her name. Her mother was indeed a passive woman at least partially incapacitated by illness. Her father, as I view him, probably resented the authority of women in childhood and had a secret need to dominate and manipulate members of the female sex in later life. He may very well have felt inadequate with other women, and it is not impossible that this may have been one of his reasons for choosing a weak and semi-invalid woman as his mate. To fit one or two characteristics of incest survivors would not be significant, but Susy seems to have shared many if not most of them, insofar as I have been able to find out.[263]

Other points are raised by Carol Poston and Karen Lison in their book, *Reclaiming our Lives.*[264] They found that adult incest survivors frequently set impossible goals for themselves and are perfectionists to an excruciating degree. They also emphasize the frequency of eating disorders among incest survivors, and they point out that using illness as a tool to manipulate others

---

[263.] On Bloom's checklist are such other items as wearing a lot of clothing, or baggy clothes, suffering from gynecological disorders and phobias, which Susy may or may not have shared, but which are beyond my power to discover.

[264.] Carol Poston and Karen Lison, *Reclaiming Our Lives* (Boston: Little, Brown and Co., 1989).

is also a common characteristic of people who have been incest victims. We already know that Susy Clemens did suffer from eating problems, did appear to be a perfectionist, and did set for herself a wildly improbable if not impossible goal—to be a Wagnerian soprano, a career for which her physical makeup was not suited. She did not, so far as I can determine, use illness as a manipulative tool—but her mother did throughout her entire life. One wonders if Livy Clemens herself may have had some incest experience, although there seems to be no other reason to raise this supposition. In any event, Susy had watched her mother in action for many years, and perhaps this experience led her to eschew the practice of using illness to manipulate others. The point is made one way or another—Susy Clemens shared many of the characteristics common to incest survivors and did so to a marked degree.

Having defined incest, and having noted that Susy Clemens exhibited many of the indicative behaviors found in incest survivors, we may now examine other bits of evidence which seem to support the hypothesis that something more than a normal father-daughter relationship existed between Samuel L. Clemens and his eldest daughter.

If I am correct about Clemens' need to dominate and manipulate women, and if my suggestion that his marriage was motivated by factors other than mere love, it is certainly not going too far to suppose that conditions favorable to an incestuous relationship existed in the Clemens house. On the one hand, there was Livy—virginal, semi-invalid, and intellectually and temperamentally less than a match for her husband. On the other hand, there was Susy—precocious, passionate, and physically attractive, her father's favorite from birth, and the one of his children who most closely resembled him in talent and temperament.

We also know from his "Aquarium Club" that Clemens enjoyed the company of young, unspoiled girls. It has long been supposed that in collecting his "pets," Clemens was trying to recapture the magic lost when Susy died; but in reality, they had not been close for five years before her passing. What he was really trying to recapture was the Susy of the late eighties, not the adult daughter of the nineties. This seems to me to be a significant point.

It is essential to recall that Susy was not just the only one of the Clemens daughters who went to college, but that, she was sent away from home by her mother, who clearly wanted her out of the house and far enough away to keep her apart from her father.

The "Golden Arm" incident, which upset Susy so much, may also make more sense if we review it in the context of the incest hypothesis.

If there had been a romantic relationship between Sam and Susy, it was almost certainly over by March 1891. By that time, having been more or less forcibly separated from her father by her residence at Bryn Mawr, Susy had already begun her relationship with Louise Brownell. Did his breaking of his promise not to tell the story constitute for her a final betrayal of her trust?

As to the story itself, was it possible that the Golden Arm in the ghost story could have been associated in Susy's mind with her father's "Golden Arm"—the arm which wrote *Tom Sawyer* and *Huck Finn* and which presumably had aroused her sexually? Did his delivery of the snapper—"You've got it!"—symbolically mean to her that *she* no longer possessed it, and that it was slipping away from her into the common possession of her classmates? From the other side, did Clemens tell the story (despite his promise not to do so) because he sensed that Susy was no longer his special daughter but a grown woman, who was inevitably slipping away from him? Was this his way of breaking off their intimacy? Whether or not these speculations have substance, it is clear that by the time the family left for Europe, a matter of weeks after the

Golden Arm incident at Bryn Mawr, the exceptional closeness upon which Mrs. Andrews commented had been replaced by a decided coolness between them. In short, did the Golden Arm incident symbolically mark the end of a relationship which by that time was probably already dead? If so, Susy's extreme upset over the telling of an innocuous ghost story suddenly makes sense.

Likewise, Susy's choosing to be known at Bryn Mawr as Olivia takes on new significance in light of the incest hypothesis. Olivia was not only her own given first name and that of her grandmother—it was also her mother's name, or, to put it another way, the name of the woman to whom her father was married. Was Susy's choice of this name consciously or unconsciously indicative of a desire to usurp her mother's position? Was it a way of safely announcing her special relationship with her father? Certainly, these are plausible possibilities.

Bryn Mawr was something of a villain to Clemens. I have already quoted his letter to Howells, expressing his regret that by February 1891, Susy was beginning to love the college.[265] In addition, there is a cryptic remark in Mark Twain's notebook: "Bryn Mawr began it. It was there that her health was undermined."[266] Up to now, that comment has defied explanation. As Neider puts it, how was her health undermined? What health did he mean; physical? Mental? Emotional?

Let us now reexamine that conundrum in the light of the incest hypothesis, coupled with what we know of Susy's relationship with Louise Brownell. Suppose that Clemens saw his place in Susy's life disappearing, and suppose that somehow he knew or

---

[265.] See p. 176.

[266.] *Mark Twain's Notebook,* edited by Albert Bigelow Paine (New York: Harper and Brothers, 1935).

suspected that it had been taken by a woman.[267] Would that not account for his frustrated and distressed remark? "Bryn Mawr began it" would then refer to the progressive dissolution of their special relationship, and "her health was undermined" would mean, in coded terminology, her clearly lesbian tendencies.

If, as I have suggested, a special relationship existed between Sam and Susy, even if it was not physical, we may have a hint as to its beginning date.

Susy's biography ends, as I have said, in mid-sentence. On July 4, 1886, she wrote, "We have arrived in Keokuk after a very pleasant . . ." She broke off suddenly at that point and never again continued. The reason has never been satisfactorily explained.[268]

I suggest that as Susy sat in her grandmother's house writing her entry for July 4, she was interrupted in her work by the opening of a door and the entrance of another person. There was conversation; Susy left her desk, and then something happened

---

[267]. Is it credible that Susy might have informed her father that she was breaking off their relationship and that she preferred women her own age? If she did, he would have been hurt but could hardly have expressed himself on paper except in the most guarded terms; hence his cryptic comment about her health.

[268]. Clemens' own explanation, found in his notes to Susy's biography, seems to me both vague and inadequate. He writes, "Interruptions came, her days became increasingly busy with studies and work, and she never resumed the biography, although from time to time she gathered materials for it [see *Papa*, p. 229]." He makes no comment on the nature of the "interruptions," which must have been very important to make Susy suddenly stop working on a project which had occupied her for more than a year. It is only fair to note, however, that her interest seems to have been flagging anyway, for the number of entries greatly diminishes after April 1886. There seems to be just one in June.

that so radically altered her relationship with her subject that she never returned to her biography. That something could have been the beginning of their romantic relationship, or at least their mutual recognition that something out of the ordinary already existed between them. The onset of an incestuous relationship would be just the sort of dramatic trauma which would cause Susy to drop her writing project for good, leaving that puzzling half-sentence to tease Clemens students a century afterward.

If I am correct in my view of Samuel Clemens' feelings toward women, and in the suggestion of a romantic relationship between him and his eldest daughter; and if that relationship began in his mother's house, the implications would be doubly and triply interesting. I claim no knowledge of psychiatry, but if a man is motivated by resentment of his female-dominated youth and begins an incestuous relationship with his daughter in his mother's home—the scene of his youthful humiliation—it does not seem unreasonable to suppose that in the act of sexually possessing his daughter he might symbolically be conquering and dominating the two women against whom his resentment was really (and secretly) directed; his sister and his mother herself. What a terrible revenge to exact for the tyranny of a female-dominated youth!

Nor are these the only reasons for supposing an affair between Sam and Susy. If we refer to her delirium notes, as published in *Papa*, we find that she mentions Maria Malibran several times, most prominently as an "equal and superior" to whom she (Susy) bows and obeys.[269] Malibran is treated almost as a female deity

---

[269.] To appreciate my argument here, it is absolutely essential that the reader make himself familiar with Susy's delirium notes. They are quoted in full in *Papa*, pp. 44-47. Disjointed and at times seemingly incomprehensible, the notes (which were written while Susy was burning up with fever and

(in fact, Susy anticipates modern feminists in her delirium notes by referring to the Lord in the feminine gender).[270]

Malibran's prominence in the delirium notes demands that we discuss her life story, which is extraordinary. Like Susy Clemens, she was the daughter of a great artist—the Spanish tenor, composer, conductor, and teacher, Manuel Garcia, widely regarded as the leading singer and vocal instructor of his time.[271] He was also, like Samuel Clemens, a dominating and domineering father. His younger daughter, Pauline Viardot-Garcia, followed in his footsteps as a vocal teacher as well as a stage performer.

His eldest daughter, Maria, was born in 1808. He was determined that she should be a great soprano, and he literally beat her into a vocal career. She became a legend while still in her teens; even today, she is often considered the greatest female opera singer of all time, partly because of her phenomenal range (from deep contralto to high soprano) and partly because of her charismatic personality. To get away from her father, she married, at eighteen, an older man named Eugene Malibran. Not long after the wedding, she deserted her husband and lived openly with the Belgian violinist Charles de Beriot, whom she afterward married. Six months later, while pregnant, she was

---

no longer rational) may express the concerns of her subconscious mind and should not be ignored. Whether it is valid to draw conclusions about Susy's life from these notes is a question each individual must decide for himself. Clearly, I think it is both possible and legitimate to do so.

270. "There is no appeal from my command and [statutes?] of the inexorable Lord. She is not unjust (p. 45)."

271. He taught many great singers of the nineteenth century but probably his most famous pupil was Jenny Lind, the "Swedish Nightingale." She was brought to America by P. T. Barnum and became an astonishing success even among people who would never have dreamed of going to the opera; she was the greatest "crossover" artist of the time.

thrown from a horse and died of her injuries on September 23, 1836, when she was only twenty-eight years old.[272]

Susy was certainly familiar with Malibran's career, and in fact may have known details about her not generally appreciated. This was because Susy's teacher Mme. Marchesi was herself a pupil of Manuel Garcia, Jr.—Malibran's brother.

There are a number of parallels between Susy's life and that of Maria Malibran, who was obviously a role model and almost a goddess to her. Neider enumerates them on page 50 of *Papa*; both were eldest daughters of exceptional and overbearing fathers; both were passionate and temperamental; Malibran was a great singer, and Susy aspired to be one—and both died tragically, terribly young. There is another possible similarity, however, which Neider does not discuss.

I asked the president of the local Maria Malibran society (yes, she has a fan club in Los Angeles even today, a century and a half after her death) whether there was any indication of an incestuous relationship between Maria and her father, the senior Garcia; the answer was that it was certainly possible. If there was such a relationship, Susy might well have known about it through Marchesi and have carried her identification with Malibran further than is generally thought. This would explain the appearance of the great soprano in the notes Susy wrote while in a delirious state shortly before her own untimely death. It is a small point, certainly, but it makes sense, and it fits neatly into the jigsaw puzzle I am putting together.

The delirium notes also contain other tantalizing references. She writes, "Yes my black Princess. You and Miss Two will meet on equal terms and on [dissimilar?] ground in future. You are

---

[272.] For data on the lives of Marchesi, Garcia, Viardot, and Malibran, I have referred to *Prima Donnas and Other Wild Beasts* by Alan Wagner (New York: Collier Books, 1963). One of the most delightful books I know.

her superior in strength and power and intellectual courage. She is yours in purity and character and peace . . ." One can only speculate as to whether Susy was expressing something of her own two personalities; Miss Two, "Olivia," and the black Princess (Susy Clemens). If it is valid to draw such inferences from the delirium notes, they would seem to support the premise that Susy unconsciously conceived of two warring personalities within her. The black Princess (the Susy Clemens part of her) enjoys strength and intellectual superiority but is somehow morally tainted (by incest?) while Miss Two (her Olivia alter ego) is superior in "purity, character, and peace" but inferior in the other areas. Along the same lines, the delirium notes are full of light and dark imagery; and while the references are confused, there seems to be some reason to associate the black Princess with darkness and Miss Two with light. I should be glad to hear from someone experienced in psychiatry on the possible implications of these delirium notes.[273]

In the light of other facts concerning the Clemens/Langdon family, I also wonder to what degree a tendency toward mental illness can be inherited.[274] Remember that Livy spent two years

---

[273.] It is also interesting to note Susy's many references to Mrs. Charles Dudley Warner, a woman who was the mother of Susy's girlhood friend and who seems in the note to be associated with the Olivia (or pure but weak) side of Susy's personality. Neider wonders whether Mrs. Warner may act as a stand-in for Susy's own mother in the notes. I also muse on the possibility that Susy may have felt a lesbian attraction for this older woman, which, of course, she could never express directly. Finally, for what it is worth, Mrs. Warner's given name was Susan.

[274.] There is no doubt that at least some mental disorders are influenced, if not entirely caused, by genetic factors.

"Schizophrenia tends to run in families. The incidence . . . is about 12 percent in the children of one schizophrenic parent; about 45 percent

in bed after the teenaged fall on the ice; that Clara later suffered a nervous breakdown and spent some time in a sanitarium; that Clemens himself seems to have struggled (successfully in the end) with the increasing divergence of his own and his Mark Twain personalities, and that in the next generation, Nina Clemens Gabrilowitsch, Clara's daughter and Clemens' only grandchild, eventually committed suicide. The whole family was edgy and high-strung, leading me to wonder whether the tendencies which seem to be present in Susy just before her death could have had a genetic basis.

There are other facts, in themselves seemingly meaningless, which when viewed in the light of the incest hypothesis tend to support it.

A year after Susy's death, in August 1897, Twain wrote a poem in her memory.[275] In it, he follows Poe's lead in metaphorically

---

in the children of two; about 10 percent in brothers or sisters of a schizophrenic; and about 50 percent in identical twins of schizophrenics. Adoption studies show that these family concordance rates . . . are largely accounted for by heredity rather than environment . . . Nevertheless, schizophrenia cannot be entirely genetic because the concordance rates for identical twins is not 100 percent (*Academic American Encyclopedia*, Vol. 17, p. 124).

It would be presumptuous and wrong to attempt to diagnose the Clemens family with any particular mental disease, at a distance of over a century. Still, it seems likely that the family did have some problems, for Sam, Livy, Clara, Susy, and perhaps Jean as well all exhibited symptoms of distress.

[275.] It was published in *Harper's Magazine* for November 1897, and Neider quotes it in full in that invaluable little book, *Papa* (pp. 59-62). He notes that it does not merit reprinting as a work of poetry, per se—"Clemens was no poet," as he accurately observes—but as a testimonial to the author's attachment to Susy.

describing Susy as a temple, as Poe described Roderick Usher as a house. The lines read, in part:

> Strangers from the outer world
> Passing, noted it with tired eyes,
> And seeing, saw it not:
> A glimpse of its fair form—an unanswering momentary
> thrill—
> And they passed on, careless and unaware.
> They could not know the cunning of its make;
> They could not know the secret shut up in its heart;
> Only the dwellers of the hamlet knew . . .

What, one must ask, was so secret about Susy's nature? It was not as if her remarkable qualities were unknown to anyone close to the family, or indeed to anyone who met her. What secret then was "shut up in her heart"? What was the "cunning" of her? Out of context, the poem seems innocuous; in the light of the incest hypothesis, it seems remarkably suggestive.

The circumstances leading to the composition of this poem are also interesting. It is marked "Lake Lucerne, August 18, 1897," the first anniversary of Susy's death. One would have expected the parents of a beloved daughter to spend that day together in mutual consolation, but they did not. Samuel Clemens went off by himself to commune with his muse under the trees, while Livy took a steamer up Lake Lucerne and spent the day at an inn alone.[276] While this is certainly a small point, it seems so out of keeping with what one would expect a pair of devoted parents to do on such a harrowing occasion that it makes me wonder

---

[276.] Kaplan gives this account of their day (p. 400) but draws no conclusion from their behavior. I find it so incongruous as to almost demand some explanation.

why they acted this way. A special relationship between Sam and Susy would explain, perhaps, why he wanted to be alone with his thoughts on the anniversary of her death, and why he wrote that peculiar poem on that particular day.

Nor is the mysterious analogy linking Susy's hidden nature to the seen but unremarked temple Clemens' only cryptic reference to her in print. There are at least two remarkable passages in Twain's published works, which seem unfathomable if taken alone but which appear to make complete sense when examined in the context of the incest hypothesis.

The first of these occurs at the end of the notes he wrote to accompany Susy's biography. Part of her work, accompanied by his comments, is included in the *Autobiography* (Chapter 41). The rest, however, was omitted and appears in *Papa*, the first complete edition of Susy's biography to reach the public. Clemens' comments were dictated, according to Neider, in 1901 and 1906.[277] I quote his concluding passage as Neider gives it:

"When I look at the arrested sentence that ends the little book, it seems as if the hand that traced it cannot be far—is gone for a moment only, and will come again and finish it. But that is a dream . . . a feeling, a longing, not a mental product: the same that lured Aaron Burr, old, gray, forlorn, forsaken, to the pier day after day, week after week, there to stand in the gloom and the chill of the dawn gazing seaward through veiling mists and sleet and snow for the ship which he knew was gone down—the ship that bore all his treasure, his daughter."[278]

To understand the implications of this seemingly innocuous but puzzling passage it is necessary to know something of Burr's story. He was the most enigmatic and controversial figure in the

---

[277]. See *Papa*, p. 6.

[278]. Ibid., p. 229.

history of in American politics, and to this day, not all of his actions can be satisfactorily explained.

Burr was a power in New York politics, where he was a rival of Thomas Jefferson for leadership of the Republicans and of Alexander Hamilton for power in the state. In 1800, he was Jefferson's running mate, destined for the vice presidency except that through some misunderstanding Burr and Jefferson wound up tied in the electoral college. The decision thus devolved on the House of Representatives, voting by delegation; the swing vote was New York's. The Federalists in that delegation held the controlling votes, and thus were in the unusual position of deciding which of their two sworn enemies, Jefferson or Burr, was to be the president of the United States. Alexander Hamilton, though he despised and feared Jefferson's policies, hated Burr even more and worked to swing the New York Federalists behind Jefferson. He was duly elected, with Burr becoming the vice president.

Four years later, Burr was dumped from the Republican ticket in favor of George Clinton, who became Jefferson's second vice president. Jefferson had mistrusted Burr from the beginning, and his mistrust turned to outright hatred.

Exiled from Washington, Burr returned to New York and ran for governor in 1804. Again Hamilton went to every possible length to beat him, and Burr lost the election. He subsequently challenged Hamilton to a duel, and early on the morning of July 11, 1804, the two met on the field of honor at Weehawken, New Jersey. In the duel, Hamilton was fatally wounded.

Burr went on to conspire with James Wilkinson in a plot whose object is unclear even today. Jefferson alleged that it was a treasonous attempt to detach the West from the United States and ally it with Spain, and he ordered Burr's arrest and trial. The conspiracy, whatever it was, collapsed, but Burr was acquitted despite everything Jefferson could do to obtain a conviction. Burr went to Europe for a few years but returned to the United

States in 1812 and continued to live in this country until he died in 1836 at the age of eighty.

What immediately strikes the reader on reading of Burr's career is that he managed to earn the fierce hatred and enmity of both Jefferson and Hamilton. In fact, almost the only thing these two completely antithetical Founding Fathers agreed on was their utter contempt for Burr, even though he was Jefferson's political ally and Hamilton's fellow New Yorker. One must ask why both these men, who were at opposite ends of the political spectrum and who hated each other, were united in despising Burr.

Part of the reason may have been mere political rivalry, particularly in Hamilton's case; but the enmity goes beyond that. It was not only political—it was personal (as Hamilton's letters and public comments clearly demonstrate).

This extreme animosity toward Burr by both Jefferson and Hamilton rested in part on Burr's close relationship to his adult daughter, Theodosia. Like Susy Clemens, she was a brilliant woman; unlike Susy, she was exceptionally well educated. Her relationship with her father was widely noted; she wrote, herself, "I would rather not live than not be the daughter of such a man." She did eventually marry a prominent planter and politician from South Carolina named Joseph Alston, and by him, had a son. In 1812, Theodosia and her little boy took a ship for New York to see Burr, but the vessel was lost at sea and no trace of it was ever found.

It was whispered at the time that Burr and Theodosia were something more than merely father and daughter—in fact, that they were incestuous lovers. It was this feeling about Burr, which made him such a pariah among people like Hamilton, who hated him not only for his ambition and his politics but for what they considered his moral degeneracy.

It is barely possible that Clemens was unaware of Burr's reputation, but knowing how well-read he was in history, one has trouble believing that he could have mentioned Burr and his daughter, obviously knowing of their closeness, without having also heard the suspicions about it. Why, then, did he deliberately identify himself with Burr in those notes intended for the *Autobiography*? Did he refrain from including them in it because he realized that perceptive readers might realize their implications? Why, then, did he write them at all? Was this another example of a Clemens tendency we have seen before—to disclose in writing, in guarded terms, something he would never have revealed directly? Clemens could not possibly have written these lines without knowing that he was deliberately calling attention to his own relationship with Susy, likening it to Burr's possibly incestuous pairing with Theodosia, yet he wrote them. Was this his response to the terrific pressure of keeping the secret—to put it down on paper, in cryptic terms and without intending it to be published in his lifetime, just to ease the oppressive weight on his mind? He appears to have done the same thing with that famous passage in *Tom Sawyer,* and with the suppressed torture scene in *Tom and Huck Among the Indians,* which I believe were safety valves for his feelings about dominating women.

With this tendency in mind, we must now return to *A Connecticut Yankee in King Arthur's Court.* I have already pointed out that this is Mark Twain's most problematic, most tortured book; but it includes still another mysterious element, which I have not yet discussed.

Hank Morgan, the Connecticut Yankee of the title, is forty years old at the time of his excursion into the sixth century.[279] At home in Connecticut, however, he tells us that his own true love is the fifteen-year-old telephone operator, Puss Flanagan; the joy of his life is to pick up the instrument and say, "Hello, Central!" He is so involved with her that when he is in Camelot, tossing and turning in the night, he utters those words in his sleep so

---

[279.] He tells us in Chapter 40 that King Arthur is about his own age—forty.

frequently, and with such evident feeling, that Sandy imagines them to be the name of "some lost darling of mine" and bestows it upon their baby daughter.[280]

We also find out a bit more about Puss Flanagan in the novel, although the evidence is contradictory. When Hank first refers to her, he mentions that they are "as good as engaged," and that she comes from the same place he does—East Hartford.[281] But in Chapter 39, as Hank Morgan prepares to battle the knights, he thinks of "the dear image of a certain hello-girl of *West* Hartford, and I wished that she could see me now."[282]

What do I make of these seemingly trivial points? In view of the incest theory, a good deal. We know that Twain was at work on the *Yankee* as early as January 1886, when the first chapters were written—six months before the trip to Keokuk, which marked the end of Susy's biography. He worked on the manuscript through 1887 and 1888 in his usual stop-and-go fashion, rushing it to completion by May 1889, with the intention of completing the book at the same time Paige finished the typesetting machine. Susy Clemens turned fifteen on March 19, 1887, during the composition of the manuscript and nine months after the Keokuk visit. Did her father deliberately write Hank Morgan's romance with the fifteen-year-old Puss Flanagan into the novel to commemorate their own secret relationship? Can anyone give me any other reasonable explanation of why this episode is in the book?

What is more, the inconsistency of Puss Flanagan's residence also appears to have meaning. East Hartford, which is Hank Morgan's own home, was the site of the big arms factory—the industrial, blue-collar area which one would expect to be the

---

[280.] Chapter 41.

[281.] Chapter 11.

[282.] Emphasis mine.

home of plant foremen and telephone girls; but West Hartford, which the Yankee mentions as Puss' home later in the book, was where the Clemens family, the Warners, the Hookers, the Beechers, the Gillettes, and the Stowes all lived. It was an upper-class area not likely to spawn fifteen-year-old "hello girls"; but it was home to Susy Clemens.

Another peculiarity of the Puss Flanagan story is that when we first hear of her as Hank's love in Chapter 11, her age is not given. Not until Chapter 15 (!) do we learn that she was fifteen, the same age as Susy had attained in 1887. The possible import of this fact is obvious—when he wrote the earlier chapters, before the Keokuk trip, Mark Twain did not think of Puss as being fifteen. Later, when he continued (or rewrote) the manuscript, he gave her Susy's age and Susy's home address—after their romantic involvement had begun. One wonders what Susy said when she learned that her father had written their relationship into his novel.

What lends such importance to these passages is that they appear to be completely gratuitous and meaningless when read without reference to the incest hypothesis. Unless we are prepared to believe that Mark Twain, a great literary artist, deliberately wrote the Hank Morgan—Puss Flanagan romance into the story, made her Susy's age, and moved her from East Hartford in Chapter 11 to West Hartford in Chapter 39 with no reason, we are obliged to make some sense of this sequence. I can offer no other theory which so completely clarifies this material, nor am I aware that any alternative explanation has ever been proposed.

In this connection, the complicated, obfuscating triple-framing device, which surrounds the *Connecticut Yankee,* becomes even more significant. As I have already pointed out, one of its effects is to make it impossible for the reader to assign responsibility for anything that happens in the book; we can never know whether it is Hank Morgan, Mark Twain, or Samuel

Clemens, who speaks at any particular moment. Thus, the frame hides Mark Twain's attacks on his own alter ego—for his folly in allowing himself to be gulled by Paige, for his stupidity in vainly chasing quick riches, for his spendthrift habits, and for his indefensible love for his juvenile daughter. No wonder Twain regarded the *Yankee* as a book that could only be finished "with a pen warmed up in hell."[283] No wonder Hank Morgan ends in insanity and death.

Nor was "Puss Flanagan" to be Susy's last incarnation in a Mark Twain novel. Beginning in 1893, he undertook the composition of *Personal Reminiscences of Joan of Arc*, which he claimed was written not with a view toward publication but "out of love."[284] His description of the Maid of Orleans was not based on the historical Joan, who was tall, ungainly, and not particularly attractive. Instead, he based her on Susy.[285]

---

[283] CF that famous letter to Howells dated September 22, 1889, quoted by Kaplan (p. 354) and previously referred to in a footnote in this manuscript. The incest hypothesis with its accompanying conclusion that Mark Twain was really attacking Samuel Clemens lends new and deeper significance to this remark. Incidentally, it astounds me that as perceptive a reader as Howells, who recognized that the *Yankee* was a satire, could still as late as 1908 call the book ". . . the most delightful, truest, most humane, sweetest fantasy that ever was (Howell's remark is quoted by Kaplan, p. 346)." Did he read the last five chapters at all?

[284] See Kaplan, p. 371, quoting Twain to this effect. We may ask, love for whom?

[285] See Kaplan, p. 397. Nor is Joan the only character Twain created whose physical portrait is based on Susy, although she is the most famous. It does not seem to have been much noticed by critics, but Mary Jane Wilks in *Huckleberry Finn* clearly reflects the real-life Susy Clemens. Huck describes her as a redhead, naturally nice to other people, but with a flaming temper which shows itself when she learns of the deception the

This is a most interesting point when one recalls that wind-blown piece of paper he picked up from a Hannibal street. It was certainly his first introduction to the story of Joan; and if my theory is correct, it may also have been the stimulus which made his libido alert to the degradation of women. One expression of that degradation could well have been incest; did Samuel Clemens act out with his own daughter the terrible, powerful drive which he had kept hidden inside him from puberty? Was the romantic and possibly physical conquest of Susy, a psychological act of revenge against the dominant women of his youth? Was his identification of Susy with Joan of Arc

---

king and the duke have played on her and her family. She has plenty of what Huck calls "sand" in her character—that is, she has guts and is not afraid to stand up to others. Susy Clemens was also red-headed and hot-tempered, naturally kind and good-hearted and equally capable of love and rage.

One passage in the novel describes how Mary Jane's nostrils flare open when she is angry (Chapter 28). Judging from photographs of Susy, that is a characteristic Twain probably borrowed from his eldest daughter. He was an acute and sensitive observer, and he could hardly have overlooked the fact that Susy's nostrils were a key component in her facial makeup, as her photographs attest. Physically at least, and probably in character as well, Mary Jane Wilks is closely modeled on the young Susy Clemens.

Incidentally, there are three Wilks sisters, just as there were three Clemens girls; but only the eldest (Mary Jane/Susy) is drawn in detail. Huck does have difficulties with Joanna (the "harelip," as Huck writes it!), who is smart enough to catch him every time he slips. Her sharp questions may have been inspired by the discussions the girls had with their father in the Hartford house, where they would demand that he tell them stories and then jump on any mistake or omission he might make.

therefore more than mere casual modeling? These are fearsome and perhaps fantastic ideas which cannot be substantiated, yet they seem to offer a cogent explanation for the guilt of Samuel Clemens and a clarification of much that is mystifying in the work of Mark Twain.

There are still other points which seem to me to support the incest hypothesis, though they appear to have no significance when viewed out of that context.

After Susy's death, Clemens searched desperately for some sign that he had been in her thoughts, and that she loved him. It was his hope of finding some message from her that led him to have all of her papers, including the delirium notes, preserved. He wrote to his wife, asking her if Susy had left "any little message" for him.[286] He seems to have been desperate for some proof that before she died, Susy had left some indication that she loved him.

One's immediate reaction is likely to be, "How pitiful! How touching!" On second thought, however, one realizes that this is a very unusual reaction for a father to have. Why should Clemens have needed such reassurance of Susy's love unless he had some strong reason to *doubt* that he had it? If, God forbid, one of my adult daughters should suddenly pass away, I would feel pain and grief, but it would never occur me to seek posthumous written proof that she loved me.

I submit that Clemens' need for reassurance was based on the fact that it was not ordinary parental love with which he was concerned. He wanted to know if Susy still loved him in the romantic, not the filial sense.

In this context, there was ample reason for him to doubt. Since she had left home for Bryn Mawr, the closeness between them had visibly lessened. Her letters to Louise Brownell tell

---

[286.] See Kaplan, p. 373.

us what Clemens must have felt intuitively—that he was no longer the most important person in her emotional life. While the family was living in Florence, there was tension between Sam and Susy—so much tension that she dreaded going down to breakfast with him.[287] When she was offered the chance to accompany her parents on the round-the-world lecture tour of 1895, she declined the opportunity, and Clara went instead.[288]

At the date of her death, then, Clemens had not seen Susy for a year, and before that, she had rejected the chance to travel with her parents. He knew she was striving for an independent life, and he knew or suspected that he was no longer the central love object in it. No wonder he worried whether she still held any romantic love for him! If familial love was all that had been at stake, he would have had no need for concern but a romantic relationship left him wondering. Thus, the incest hypothesis helps to explain Clemens' surprising need for reassurance about Susy's love, clarifying another of the otherwise mysterious circumstances in the life of this complicated and secretive man.

Another indication of the truth of the incest hypothesis may be found in the guilt felt by Susy herself. On the occasion of her eighteenth birthday (March 19, 1890), she wrote a curious letter to her aunt, Susan Crane. It is full of vague references to "eliminating the soul" and attaining self-mastery and self-possession. Edith Colgate Salsbury quotes it at length in *Susy*

[287.] See Kaplan, p. 373; also Salsbury, p. 313.

[288.] Clemens wrote later that Susy did not go because she hated long sea voyages. This may be true, but it seems likely that she had other reasons for remaining in America. One was the presence of Louise Brownell in the United States; another was Susy's desire to make a career for herself as an opera singer; and to create an independent life of her own. It may also have been that after four years in Europe, Susy simply did not want to go globetrotting again.

and Mark Twain. Susy wrote, "I should like to realize that it is not only my duty but my privilege to suffer all and do all that I can for others in this world. But, Oh! One's horrible earthly weaknesses! There's the trouble. It is so hard to control them. While one can have a good sized piece of sky in one's sight, though, one must possess some consciousness of Eternity—even if it be an unconscious consciousness.

"Tomorrow I am eighteen. Eighteen! I dread to have to say I am so old! And nothing done and such unsettled notions of things . . . I am ashamed I am not a more reliable, serene character, one to be depended upon. I know so well what a girl of eighteen should be."[289]

It is not necessary to make sense of everything Susy writes in this strange letter to see that she feels that she has been an inadequate person, falling short of "what a girl of eighteen should be." She also clearly felt the victim of her "horrible earthly weaknesses," which she found it difficult to control. One can only surmise exactly what she meant, but she explicitly felt guilty about what she had done or failed to do.

The incest hypothesis offers a framework within which the vague feelings Susy expresses here become intelligible. If there was a relationship between her and her father, the responsibility for it was not all on one side. Susy had a passionate nature, as her letters to Louise Brownell later clearly demonstrate, and she says herself that she had difficulty controlling her "horrible earthly weaknesses." She certainly loved her father very much, and it is possible that she had an Electra complex—even if there was never a physical relationship between them. If there actually was, it almost certainly resulted from a mutual passion too strong

---

[289]. Edith Colgate Salsbury, *Susy and Mark Twain* (New York: Harper and Row, 1965) pp. 276-276.

to be restrained. If this was the context, then Susy's remarks to her aunt, otherwise obscure, are immediately explained.

In any event, she seems to have paid as high a price in guilt as he did. Her life was warped, not only by the guilty secret she was keeping but also by the emotional instability and unhappiness which followed. Between the last entry in her biography, which was full of sunshine and uncomplicated joy, and her eighteenth birthday, when she produced this problematic and self-critical letter, something powerful and damaging affected Susy's self-esteem. The incest hypothesis provides a possible explanation, where no other has been proposed.

Further support for the incest hypothesis can be derived from another of Samuel Clemens' proclivities—his tendency to confuse his wife with his eldest daughter. Helen Keller recounts a striking occurrence of this phenomenon in *Mainstream.*[290]

Ms. Keller and Mr. Clemens were old acquaintances, having met for the first time in 1894 when she was only fourteen. They shared the patronage and support of Henry H. Rogers, who not only extricated Clemens from his bankruptcy but also paid for Ms. Keller's education.[291] On the occasion of a later encounter

---

[290.] Helen Keller, *Mainstream. My Later Life* (Garden City: Doubleday, 1929) pp. 50-51.

[291.] See Kaplan, p. 380. It is ironic that his sponsorship of Helen Keller, perhaps the most unselfish thing Henry Rogers ever did, should remain almost totally unknown today. Annie Sullivan may have been (as the play called her) "The Miracle Worker"; but the miracle would never have been worked had it not been for the old pirate Henry Huddleston Rogers, who paid for it.

Incidentally, when Helen Keller visited Clemens at Stormfield in 1908, shortly after he took up residence there, he said to her, "I don't know much about women. It would be impossible for a person to know less about women than I do." Having been raised by a mother and a

in 1905, Clemens told Helen of his loneliness since Livy's death
the previous year, and how his thoughts kept running back to
his wife and his daughter. He then quoted to her the lines of the
poem he said were engraved on Livy's headstone—and spoke
the lines of the Richardson poem which is chiseled on Susy's![292]
Whether Clemens' error was a conscious attempt to mislead,
a self-delusion, or merely an unconscious mistake, the point is
made—he did, intentionally or otherwise, confuse his wife with
his eldest daughter. This, I submit, can be taken as a subtle clue
that there was more of a romantic than a merely paternal cast to
his relationship with Susy.

Along the same lines, Clemens wrote (in the *Autobiography*)
"Tomorrow is the 5th of June, a day which marks the disaster of
my life—the death of my wife."[293]

While the loss of Livy after thirty-four years of marriage was
certainly painful for him, one simply cannot accept at face value
his assertion that it was "the disaster" of his life. At the time of
her death, Livy Clemens had been suffering for two years from
heart and thyroid disease. She was fifty-nine years old and had
had a full and for the most part reasonably happy life. Clemens
himself was by this time nearing seventy, and most of his creative
career was behind him. He knew his wife was dying, and her

---

sister, married for thirty-four years and the father of three daughters,
Clemens of all men should have known something about the female sex.
If he didn't, what man ever could? One can only wonder what he meant
when he made this statement.

[292] See p. 243 of this manuscript for the text of the poem. Livy's stone has
no verse at all—in fact, none of the Langdon or Clemens' graves do, with
the sole exception of Susy's. Since Livy had died only the year before, it
is difficult to believe that Clemens could have forgotten this fact so easily.
Factors other than mere time were probably at work.

[293] See the *Autobiography*, Chapter 67 (dictated about 1906).

condition was such that her passing could only be a relief from suffering. Both of them had plenty of time to anticipate her death.

No, it was not Livy's demise which was the disaster of Clemens' life but Susy's. She fell victim to a sudden and agonizing disease which killed her unexpectedly at the tragically young age of twenty-four. Her death effectively put an end to Mark Twain's serious literary career and to Samuel Clemens' domestic happiness as well. In short, once again what he said of Livy was actually more true of Susy; once again, we can infer from this a more than paternal relationship between her and her father.

There is still another Clemens trait on which the incest hypothesis may throw some light—his notorious tendency to turn on people who drew too close to him. Perhaps the most notable incident of this unpleasant Clemens' characteristic was his treatment of Charles Webster, his unfortunate nephew-in-law.[294] Clemens first put the young man in charge of the publishing venture; later he blamed Webster for all the evils of his life. Nor could Webster defend himself—he died in 1891, at only forty years of age.

Bret Harte, once a close friend who bought Mark Twain's "Jumping Frog" story for the *Golden Era,* also became the object of Clemens' scorn.[295] To a lesser degree, he did the same to Dan De Quille, a former *Territorial Enterprise* staffer who, with

---

[294.] Webster married Annie Moffett, daughter of Clemens' sister Pamela; he was trained as a civil engineer, and the family connection seems to have been his only qualification for the executive position which Clemens bestowed upon him.

[295.] On the occasion of Harte's death (in London in 1902), Clemens wrote of him, "Bret Harte was one of the pleasantest men I have ever known. He was also one of the unpleasantest . . . He hadn't a sincere fiber in him. I think he was incapable of emotion, for I think his heart was merely

Clemens' encouragement and support, wrote a history of the Comstock, only to see his old friend become cold and distant. Later in life, Clemens also turned on his secretary, Isabel Lyon, whom he accused of stealing Mark Twain monies. In fact, I can think of only two outsiders who were able to maintain long-term intimate friendships with Samuel Clemens—William Dean Howells and Pastor Joe Twitchell.

Could it be that Clemens withdrew from close associations with outsiders out of fear that somehow his guilty secrets would be discovered? That the fear may be irrational does not mean that Clemens might not have felt it. In any event, this theory does offer at least a plausible explanation for one of Clemens' most unpleasant personal characteristics.

In reviewing the evidence I have amassed in support of the incest hypothesis, I find that there are no less than twenty-one points—twenty-one pieces of the puzzle—which when fitted together form an interlocking and mutually supportable whole. These twenty-one points may be summarized as follows:

1. Susy's character, temperament, and special good looks.
2. The extraordinary closeness known to exist between Susy and Sam.
3. Livy's transparent effort to get Susy out of the house by sending her two hundred miles away to college.

---

a pump and had no other function. (Quoted in Metzler, *Mark Twain Himself*, p. 117)."

For what it may be worth, my friend Anna Howland, who is an acute student of both Twain and Harte, suggests that Clemens in his attacks on his former friend was actually criticizing his own characteristics, and that part of his enmity grew out of his jealousy of Harte—a man who left his wife and daughters, while Clemens remained with his family.

4. The Golden Arm incident, closely followed by Susy's unexplained departure from Bryn Mawr.
5. Susy's relationship with Louise Brownell.
6. Her refusal to accompany her parents on the world tour.
7. The delirium notes, disclosing Susy's own divided and tormented personality.
8. Susy's congruity with present-day profiles of incest survivors.
9. Susy's hints at something secret and terrible in her past.
10. Clemens' character and personality, coupled with Livy's relative infirmity and passivity.
11. Clemens' remarks about the effects of Bryn Mawr on Susy's health.
12. The sudden breaking of Susy's biography of her father.
13. Clemens' poem.
14. Clemens' behavior on the anniversary of Susy's death.
15. Clemens' comparison of himself to Aaron Burr.
16. The relationship between Hank Morgan and Puss Flanagan in A *Connecticut Yankee in King Arthur's Court*.
17. Clemens' use of Susy as his model for Joan of Arc, and also for Mary Jane Wilks.
18. Clemens' anxiety about whether he still commanded Susy's love at the time of her death.
19. Susy's own feelings of guilt and inadequacy.
20. Clemens' confusing Livy and Susy.
21. Clemens' withdrawal from outsiders, possibly because he feared disclosure of his hidden secrets.

No one fact by itself demonstrates the existence of an exceptional, romantic relationship between Samuel and Susy

Clemens; there is no smoking gun. But the total picture, once all the puzzle pieces are locked in place, strongly suggests the existence of such an affair. The cumulative force of the evidence, when all the pieces are taken together, is impossible to ignore. In addition, the incest hypothesis clarifies much that is otherwise inexplicable, and makes sense of points which otherwise seem meaningless, to such a degree that it simply cannot be dismissed without serious consideration.

Let me emphasize that in keeping with the modern definition of incest, I do not believe it is necessary to demonstrate that a physical, sexual relationship existed between Sam and Susy, though it is possible that it did. What is important is that a relationship existed in which there was a violation of trust in a sexual context; on the evidence, it is not hard to believe that such a thing did occur, though it cannot be positively proved.

Since Albert Bigelow Paine and Clara Clemens Gabrilowitsch thoroughly edited Samuel Clemens' letters and papers after his death, for the purpose of presenting to the public a sanitized, "wholesome" author whose sales would not be jeopardized by unbefitting revelations, there is probably no way to prove or disprove by direct evidence the incest hypothesis. If there ever was a paper trail (and there may well never have been one), Paine and/or Clara would surely have destroyed it.[296] Researchers seeking to substantiate or refute the incest hypothesis will probably have to find their evidence in materials which were not subject to Clara Clemens Gabrilowitsch's control; it is very unlikely that such materials ever existed and even less probable

---

[296.] In her efforts to present a sanitized portrait of her father which would protect both the family name and the income from royalties, Clara suppressed for many years some of Mark Twain's writings on religion, politics, etc. She would certainly not have let a word escape about such far more incendiary topics as incest or lesbianism.

that they could have survived for a century undetected and unrecognized. My opinion is that the incest hypothesis will stand or fall on the bits and pieces of evidence which I have presented, for this is likely to be all the relevant material now in existence. Either the reader will be convinced, or he will not; but once raised and cogently supported, the idea is so consistent with what we know of both Sam's and Susy's lives, and explains so much, that it is simply impossible to dismiss it out of hand.

One of the things it explains is Mark Twain's turn to the philosophy of pessimism and moral vacuum in *A Connecticut Yankee*. Until now, it has been difficult for critics to accept the awful despair in this book, which ends with scenes of mass destruction and insanity because it was written while Samuel Clemens was still financially solvent and domestically happy. In 1889, he was not only still living in the Hartford dream house but was looking forward with enthusiasm to the limitless reaches he envisioned from the Paige typesetting machine. There was at that time no apparent reason for Mark Twain to adopt the philosophy of moral vacuum, pessimism, and determinism, which is found in the *Yankee*.

The key word here is "apparent." Given the incest hypothesis, Twain's philosophic despair suddenly falls into place. The strain of conducting an illicit, secret love relationship with Susy caused enormous new guilt for Clemens, just as his marriage appears to have done twenty years before; and Clemens dealt with the new guilt in the *Yankee* just as he had dealt with the earlier feelings in previous works of Mark Twain.

Clemens' conscience may have harassed him over his marriage—and Mark Twain responded by killing his conscience in "Carnival of Crime" and devaluing it in *Huckleberry Finn*. In his possible affair with Susy, Clemens may have committed what society thought of as an absolute moral wrong—and in Mark Twain's next novel, he concluded that there is no morality in the world and that good and evil are matters of chance; that is, that moral choice does not exist. Clemens worked out ways to cope with his personal guilt through the writings of Mark Twain.

Moreover, the incest hypothesis offers the *only* cogent explanation I have seen of the dark strain in the *Yankee*. No other source of guilt had arisen at this time in Clemens' life; no other crisis of conscience had to be coped with in 1889. Here is a solution to a major Mark Twain mystery—what happened between the publication of *Huckleberry Finn* and the *Connecticut Yankee* which made the later book turn so violently pessimistic, determinist, and bitterly critical of its "hero," Hank Morgan himself?

I submit that it was the development of a love relationship between Sam and Susy Clemens, whether or not it was physically consummated, which brought Mark Twain to write his acerbic confessional satire, *A Connecticut Yankee in King Arthur's Court,* in which we find the first full statement of the dark philosophy most closely associated with the author's later life.

The Totality of Guilt

However important the incest hypothesis is to my conception of the character and mental makeup of Samuel Clemens/ Mark Twain, I must emphasize that it forms only a part of my analysis of the sources of that overwhelming, paralyzing guilt which afflicted Clemens in the last years of his life. Clear wellsprings of that guilt were (I have theorized) Clemens' secret feelings of resentment toward and the need to dominate and manipulate women; his pangs about his marriage, which, while it was a love match, was also a key to the door of his success; and his sellout to Henry Rogers, in which he traded material security for the artistic freedom to criticize and condemn the American plutocracy, at least insofar as Rogers and the Standard Oil Company were concerned. With the combined burden of all these doings bearing down on him, it is no wonder Clemens nearly went to pieces after Susy's sudden death, and a few years later, Livy's passing left him vulnerable to the awful contrast between what the world thought of him and what he knew himself to be.

By 1904, the year of his wife's death, Mark Twain had become something more than America's best-known writer. He was in all probability the most famous man in the world, known from Southampton to Sydney, from Perth to Pretoria, through his books and his world tour. He had become something of a national icon as well as a prophet, raging against lynching, Mary Baker Eddy and the king of Belgium. Beginning on the occasion of his testimony before a joint committee of Congress in December 1906, he adopted his trademark white suit, which made him stand out even more clearly from the crowd.

Yet while Mark Twain would stroll down Fifth Avenue, drinking in the adulation of the multitudes (of which he could never get enough), Samuel Clemens knew all too well that if his true thoughts and his full conduct had been known, he would have been the target of scorn and derision instead. He was leading a double life. The front he presented to the world was a false one, and he knew it; the dishonesty of his life could only increase that already staggering burden of guilt.

I believe that Samuel Clemens was a weak man, unable to resist the temptations of wealth, social position, and romantic excitement that periodically offered themselves to him.

At the same time, however, another part of him abhorred the things he was doing and made him pay in guilt for the gratifications he obtained. He was, I think, a deeply troubled man who won great success and popular adulation partly through his own great talent but also partly through sham and deceit. He repeatedly gave in to his desires and generally got what he wanted—but he hated himself for doing so.

How could such a man live with himself? Clemens found a way, through the personality of Mark Twain. In the books he wrote as his alter ego, he vented his self-hatred by attacking the world of Samuel Clemens, the actions of Samuel Clemens and at last, the personality of Samuel Clemens.

Mr. Clemens and Mark Twain

When Jason Kaplan published his landmark biography of the author in 1966, he chose the title *Mr. Clemens and Mark Twain,* implying that the two identities were not the same. I believe he was entirely right in this perception, but I should go even further than he did in emphasizing the degree to which the two sides of this complex man grew apart from and hostile toward one another. Sam and Mark may not have been alternative personalities in the same body, like Dr. Jekyll and Mr. Hyde; but if the printer, steamboat man, miner, lecturer, publisher, inventor, and failed investor, *and* the author, satirist, ironist, humorist, and social critic were not two separate people, they were well on the way to becoming so. In recognition of the extent to which Samuel Clemens and Mark Twain became not only divergent but actually hostile identities lies, I think, the key to understanding the man's life and the author's works.

I doubt that Clemens had any inkling of what was in the future when he first signed one of his dispatches to the *Territorial Enterprise* with the name, Mark Twain. It began as just a pen name, more euphonious than Thomas Jefferson Snodgrass or W. Epaminondas Blab; more dignified than just plain Josh. Those two short syllables have a haunting quality. They reverberate naturally; once heard, they are unforgettable. No author ever chose a better pen name.

But in Mark Twain's first two long books, *The Innocents Abroad* and *Roughing It,* the pen name became something more—a character who appears in the books signed with his name.[297] Mark Twain in these travel books is a distinct personality, based on but not completely identifiable with Samuel Clemens.[298] He is credulous, naïve; one of the "Innocents" of the first book, a tenderfoot in the second. One might compare this character with Jim Smiley in the "Jumping Frog" story or with many similar unsophisticated figures of fun in the tradition of American humor. Mark Twain the character is often the butt of the joke.

However, Mark Twain the author grew far beyond the literary character bearing the same name. The decisive turning point was *The Adventures of Tom Sawyer,* in which for the first time, Mark Twain the author began to attack the world and the character of Samuel Clemens. Many of the attacks misfire, and much of the ammunition is shot off, as it seems, randomly and without careful aim; but in reading and re-reading *Tom Sawyer,* it becomes blindingly clear that a reversal has taken place. Mark Twain the character has disappeared, and Mark Twain the author has turned Samuel Clemens (in his juvenile persona as Tom Sawyer) and his society into the object of attack. Moreover, in the course of writing this book, Mark Twain appears to have first discovered

---

297. This so-called "double device," where the name of the central character is also used as that of the author, was picked up many years later by Frederic Dannay and Manfred B. Lee when they created "Ellery Queen." Whether they got the inspiration from Twain, I cannot say.

298. This is also true of the Cub Pilot in *Life on the Mississippi,* who does not actually bear the name Mark Twain, but who might just as well do so since he is just the *Innocents* and *Roughing It* personality transferred to the river.

and then circumvented the limitations of the Tom character; he created Huckleberry Finn, who becomes the central figure in the later, greater book.

What happened between *Roughing It* and *Tom Sawyer*, which so dramatically changed the relationship between Samuel Clemens and Mark Twain? I suggest that the key event was Clemens' success in the Siege of Elmira, when he breached the walls, stormed the citadel, and married Olivia Langdon.[299] At a stroke, he had it all—position, respectability, and the money which liberated him from the necessity of writing for a quick payoff. At the same time, the conscience in him knew that he (as I believe) chose his wife because she brought him not only love but also those other tangible and valuable assets.[300] He began using her the moment the ink was dry on the marriage contract, and he continued to manipulate and to use her for the rest of their life together. He paid the price for his conduct in private guilt, while hiding his feelings behind the cloak of love and of devotion to his wife.[301]

I believe that there is great significance in the fact that Mark Twain emerged as a novelist within a couple of years of his marriage. *Tom Sawyer*, the first of his Mississippi Valley books and the first novel in which the themes of his adult literary career are introduced, had its genesis in the Boy's Manuscript of 1870—written during the first year of the Clemens' married

---

299. *Roughing It* was actually written after the wedding, but, of course, it is based on Clemens' Nevada experiences while he was still single.

300. Clemens knew what he wanted—Livy Langdon's hand in marriage—and he pulled out all the stops to get it. Remember those sickening, phony love letters, and Margaret Sanborn's observation that he played the parts he knew he had to play to win her over (see p. 309).

301. This was not difficult for him to do because he really did love Livy; but, as I have suggested, love was not the only motive for his marriage.

life—and was finished by 1875. Among other themes, it introduces the author's probing of the meaning and significance of conscience. Mark Twain was to wrestle with this question in each of his novels thereafter.

I cannot but think that his preoccupation with this subject is intimately connected with the single most important event in Clemens' life—his wedding. What other experience did he have which could have raised in him such concern for conscience, and eventually such an attitude toward it? In these first years after his marriage, we find Samuel Clemens coping with feelings of guilt through the critical writing of Mark Twain—the first time he had employed his alter ego as in this capacity but certainly not the last. In short, Clemens' pangs of guilt seem to have led him to find a new role for Mark Twain. Having begun as a mere nom de plume, Mark grew into a figure of fun; now he became Clemens' literary conscience, attacking in his works the things which Clemens was doing in his life but felt guilty about.

Thus, Mark Twain came to blast the headlong pursuit of wealth, the constant craving after glory and adulation, the heedlessness of others' feelings, the selfish manipulation of other people for private ends, the cost of thoughtlessness, and so on. And the more guilt Clemens felt about his conduct, the more pointed and more violent grew Mark Twain's attacks.

This process culminated in that horrifying, powerful, bleak, destructive, dark, flawed masterpiece, *A Connecticut Yankee*. It is not only a great satire on Victorian America, it is a personal attack on Hank Morgan, the Yankee himself.

But Hank Morgan not only represents the Victorian America of which he is the avatar; he is, as Justin Kaplan has recognized, in large measure Samuel Clemens himself.[302] And it is Hank

---

[302.] See Kaplan, p. 349.

Morgan, who is the target of Mark Twain's most ferocious, most bitter attacks.

There is an explanation readily at hand. By the time Mark Twain finished the *Yankee*, Samuel Clemens had not only spent thousands of his own and his wife's dollars on the Paige machine in the hope of getting untold riches from the invention but he had also (as I have suggested) violated the ultimate sexual and social taboo by falling in love with his own daughter. His self-hatred must, by this time, have become almost overwhelming. He coped by escaping into his Mark Twain identity and writing a novel in which he expressed the contempt and disgust he felt not only for the world to which he pandered but also for himself.

It has been said (although I cannot recall by whom) that each novelist creates his characters out of pieces of himself—that each literary personality represents one isolated piece of the creator's integrated psyche. In the case of Mark Twain, one can clearly identify Tom Sawyer and Hank Morgan with Samuel Clemens the would-be plutocrat, a figure closely identified with a corrupt society whose values he seeks to emulate. On the other hand, there is Huckleberry Finn, the social outcast who somehow recognizes that "sivilization" is impossible to live with and who has the nerve to escape it. Like Huck, Mark Twain stood outside society and freed himself from it; Samuel Clemens, like Tom, never tried to do so, but on the contrary, he accepted the standards of his surroundings and only tried to exemplify them more completely. He wore the mask of respectability at all times, and stood with the community, not outside it or against it. From this disintegration of the man into two increasingly antagonistic personalities came the sanity of Samuel Clemens and the literary art of Mark Twain.

In view of this explanation of the relationship between the life of Samuel Clemens and the work of his alter ego, some of these recurring themes, which characterize Mark Twain's writing from

Tom Sawyer onward, take on new significance. Conscience, of course, is one; I have already touched on how Clemens' struggle with his own superego is reflected in Twain's work. Another is the question of the relationship between nobility, character, and conduct; as Clemens sought guides to "good" behavior, so Twain reflects the question of what constitutes noble conduct and from what source it derives. Related to this question is the question fundamental to democracy: Is education really everything? Do clothes really make the man, or are some individuals born to the purple while others are destined never to arise above the level of human muck? Twain's answer to this query appears to change in the course of his work, as Clemens' guilt led him increasingly toward the philosophy of determinism, which was his final refuge from responsibility for his actions. After the probing which occupies *Tom Sawyer, Huckleberry Finn,* and the *Connecticut Yankee* Mark Twain finds a heart of darkness at the center of the universe—that no guide to good or bad behavior is adequate, and that man may do good while attempting what he thinks is evil (as in *Huck*), or work evil while trying to do good (as in the *Yankee*). He discovers that the universe lacks a moral center; the inevitable next step ("What is Man?" and *The Mysterious Stranger*) is that life is meaningless and moral choice nonexistent.[303] In

---

[303]   In reaching this conclusion, which I believe is the undeniable message of the *Connecticut Yankee,* Mark Twain anticipates contemporary writers in declaring, in essence, that God is dead. For the period in which he was writing, this was an extremely radical thought. But even as Mark Twain foresaw the carnage of World War I in the last chapters of the *Connecticut Yankee,* so he also anticipated the postwar disillusionment which has left such a mark on twentieth-century literature.

   In thinking of Twain as a modern writer, I was struck by the similarities between his career and that of the contemporary humorist, writer, and filmmaker Woody Allen (Alan Koenigsburg). Granted the difference that

this philosophy, Clemens found relief at last from the internal demons which tormented him.

Allen has worked primarily in a medium which did not exist in Twain's time, there are surprising parallels between them. Mark Twain started his writing career with humor sketches; Woody Allen began as a teenaged joke writer. Twain moved into performing as a platform lecturer; Allen became a stand-up and then film comedian. Twain turned toward serious themes—social criticism, conscience, moral responsibility; Allen, as a director, has gone in the same track. Indeed, in their maturity, each of these original American geniuses has produced a major work which is difficult to explain, yet totally absorbing and absolutely personal. Mark Twain wrote *A Connecticut Yankee*; Woody Allen made *Crimes and Misdemeanors*. And now, to these creative parallels, we may add this personal one—in 1992, Woody Allen admitted having an affair with his young stepdaughter. Compare this with the incest hypothesis involving Sam and Susy Clemens.

The Great Twain Theory: Final Summation

After thirty years of reading and thinking about Samuel Clemens and Mark Twain, I am convinced that these two personalities represented opposite sides of the man who was both. Mark Twain's novels make it apparent that the two sides of the man were not only divergent but increasingly hostile, yet they were forever bound together in the same physical being, not unlike those remarkable twins, Luigi and Angelo Capello.[304] This disintegration of personality was born of Clemens' self-hatred and of the guilt he felt. In accord with the Case Western study, I believe that guilt arose out of Clemens' relationships with other people—his mother, his wife, his patron and business savior, Henry H. Rogers, and his eldest daughter, Susy.

I believe that Clemens resented the domination of his youth by the female authority figures of his mother and his elder sister. While he loved his mother, his chafing at her authority over

---

[304.] In my opinion, Twain's fascination with Siamese twins and other paired but opposite characters (prince and pauper, Tom and Huck) may derive in part from his own dual identity.

him led him to grow up with deep-seated, hidden needs to take revenge by dominating and manipulating women. His feelings in this direction were stirred by his encounter with the story of Joan of Arc under torture, and he undoubtedly felt some guilt over them.

One way in which Clemens' need to dominate members of the female sex was satisfied was in his choice of the semi-invalid Livy Langdon as his wife. He could and did manipulate her for the duration of their marriage. In addition, Clemens probably had other reasons, besides love, for marrying Livy. She brought him instant social position and she was an heiress, much of whose money he eventually ran through. Even though there seems to be no doubt that Sam Clemens did love Livy, his additional motives in choosing her—of all the women he might have selected as his wife—gave him abundant cause for guilt feelings about his marriage.

Clemens had equal cause to feel guilty about his relationship with Henry H. Rogers. By accepting the patronage and support of the "old pirate," Clemens forfeited his artistic freedom insofar as Rogers and the Standard Oil Company were concerned. Not only did Mark Twain never attack that firm or its owners and managers in print but Clemens also rejected the chance to publish Henry Demarest Lloyd's *Wealth Against Commonwealth* out of deference to Rogers, even though it might have been a valuable property for his shaky publishing house.

Finally, and most guilt-provoking of all, there was Clemens' relationship with Susy. It was certainly far more intense than ordinary father/daughter associations and *may* have gone so far as consummated physical incest. In any event, it was a powerful, secret, and emotionally searing relationship which left both father and daughter scarred for life.

These real sources of Samuel Clemens' guilt were impossible for him to disclose. As a result, in the *Autobiography*, he "admitted" responsibility for things for which he was not truly to blame—his son's death and the "exile and pauperism" of his family. Discovery of the deeper source of Clemens' self-hatred explains for the first time his apparent need to assume guilt for things he did not do.

With the deaths of Susy and Livy, with Clemens' emergence from bankruptcy (engineered by Rogers) and Mark Twain's ascension to new heights of adulation and fiscal success, Clemens' guilt reached new levels. While Mark Twain was being lauded around the world as a sage and almost as an icon, Samuel Clemens knew only too well that his life was a fraud and a deceit. It is no surprise, then, that he dictated much of his notoriously unreliable and perhaps even willfully dishonest *Autobiography* in the years following Livy's death.

Actually, the closest Clemens came to a true statement of his life and his feelings about it had been written years before. *A Connecticut Yankee in King Arthur's Court* contains Mark Twain's violent attacks not only on the world of Samuel Clemens but also on Clemens himself in his guise as Hank Morgan. The ultimate irony of Clemens' life is that his self-criticism and confession, made in this novel, is almost completely overlooked. In fact, Mark Twain's status in the pantheon of American writers is equally ironic—today, many of his countrymen dismiss him as a writer of children's stories.

I believe, and I hope to have demonstrated, that on the contrary, Mark Twain was a far more serious and far greater writer than most of his contemporary readers are aware. He was a superior literary craftsman and almost beyond challenge as this nation's finest satirist, ironist, and humorist. No American writer has surpassed his talent for vernacular speech or for using dialogue to create unforgettable characters. No American writer of his century treated such deep and powerful thematic material with such consistent, probing analysis. Mark Twain's real concerns are the questions of how the individual relates to society, how good and evil occur, and how human thought may relate to human behavior. That his ultimate conclusion was both depressing and frightening—that there is no moral center in the universe, that moral choice is impossible, and that good and evil are beyond human control—only makes him the greater thinker who saw beyond the smugness and self-satisfaction of his era. Mark Twain foresaw, in the final pages of the *Yankee,* the carnage of modern warfare, which is the product of the marriage of moral vacuum and technological proficiency. If he did not envision the Hitler Holocaust as well, he certainly did recognize the conditions which made it possible. No nineteenth-century writer compares with Twain's deadly analysis of the coming future. He is incomparably the most "modern" of Victorian novelists.

This is the case not only philosophically but technically as well. Twain gets little credit as a literary innovator, but his experiments with language, point of view, and the device of the "Greek chorus" in *Pudd'nhead Wilson* distinguish him as a writer far ahead of his time. By any measure, be it of his thought or his literary skill, Mark Twain deserves far more recognition as a great writer than he generally receives.

Perhaps one can best describe this fascinating man in terms of the immortal characters he created. His Samuel Clemens side was Tom Sawyer and Hank Morgan—perfect reflections of an imperfect world. Clemens accepted the prevailing goals and standards of post-Civil War America and sought to exemplify them. He wanted money and glory, and he sought them through business and marriage into the upper middle class.

But he was also Huckleberry Finn and Jim, characters who stand apart from the corrupt society around them. Huck observes the foolishness, cruelty, and cupidity of "sivilization" and opts to escape it. Jim, consigned by skin color to the status of an automaton, exemplifies the deepest capacity of humanity for love and warmth. The writer who created them, Mark Twain, was the most incisive and most devastating social critic American literature has produced, and the paramount target of his greatest scorn was Samuel Clemens, his own other self.

Out of Clemens' guilt over his way of life grew Mark Twain's literary accomplishments. Clemens did not change his behavior—he was too weak for that—but he eased his guilt by attacking in print not only the society to whose standards he subscribed but also his own flawed personality and indefensible conduct. No wonder that the more I came to know Samuel Clemens, the less I liked him; while the more I understood Mark Twain, the greater grew my admiration for him. The necessity of understanding both these divergent and hostile personalities and their relationship to each other is what made it so difficult—and so rewarding—to study the man who was both Tom Sawyer and Huckleberry Finn, both Samuel Clemens and Mark Twain.

Part V

A Mark Twain Chronology

1823 (May 6)	John Marshall Clemens m. Jane Lampton at Columbia, Kentucky.
1825 (July 17)	Orion Clemens b.
1827 (September 13)	Pamela Clemens b.
1828-29 (?)	Pleasants Hannibal Clemens b. (d. three months later)
1830 (May)	Margaret Clemens b. (d. August 19, 1839 at Florida, Missouri)
1832 (June)	Benjamin Clemens b. (d. Hannibal, Missouri, May 12, 1842)
1835 (November 30)	Samuel L. Clemens b.
1838 (June 13)	Henry Clemens b. (killed in a steamboat explosion near Memphis May 1858)
1839 (November 13)	John Marshall Clemens sold out all of his holdings in Florida, Missouri, and moved to Hannibal, thirty miles away. Took up residence at Virginia House; the home at 206 Hill Street was probably built about 1844.
1842 (May 12)	Death of Benjamin Clemens after a short illness.
1847 (Mar 24)	John Marshall Clemens died, probably of pneumonia, after a two-week illness. Contrary to his own recollection, Sam (then eleven and a half) was not sent to work immediately but stayed on in school for at least one more year.
1848(?)	(Probably, according to Dixon Wecter, at the end of May or in early June) Sam Clemens apprenticed to printer Joseph Ament at age thirteen.
1850 or 1851	Orion returned to Hannibal and bought a newspaper after the owner went to California; Sam worked for him as a printer's devil.

1850	Within two years of his apprenticeship, SLC found a page from a book about Joan of Arc in prison (Wecter, p. 211).
1851 (January)	SLC left Ament on the promise of $3.50 a week from Orion but was (to his own recollection) never paid a cent.
1851 (September)	Orion consolidated his *Western Union* with the older *Hannibal Journal*.
1851 (September 20)	Pamela Clemens m. Will Moffett in Green County, Kentucky. She was then twenty-four and close to becoming an old maid. They settled in St. Louis, Missouri.
1852 (Jan 29)	Fire damaged Orion's printing shop.
1852-53	SLC printed various humorous sketches in the *Journal*.
1853 (May 27?)	SLC left Hannibal, proposing to go to St. Louis but with the actual intent to see the East. Visited his sister Pamela in St. Louis and worked as a printer for the *Evening News* there (June-August) to earn money for a New York trip.
1853 (August 24)	Arrived for his first visit to New York City.
1853 (Summer)	SLC worked in New York as a journeyman printer; one of his employers was the firm of Gray and Green. According to his own account, he spent many of his evenings reading and studying.
1853 (Fall)	Moved to Philadelphia, where he spent the winter.
1854 (Fall)	After a year in the East, SLC returned to St. Louis, where he worked for a newspaper as a printer. He roomed with a man named Frank Burrough, who introduced him to the works of Scott, Thackeray, and Dickens.

1855	SLC went to Keokuk, Iowa, where Orion had bought a newspaper. Sam worked for his brother for a year and a half. The youngest Clemens brother, Henry, was also in Keokuk part of this time.
1856 (Fall)	SLC left Keokuk with the object of going to South America. However, he got no further than Cincinnati, where he spent the winter of 1856-57 working again at the printing trade.
1857 (April)	Took passage on the steamboat "Paul Jones" for New Orleans, still intending to reach Brazil. Instead, met pilot Horace Bixby, and with money borrowed from his brother-in-law William Moffett, became Bixby's cub and undertook to learn the Mississippi River.
1858 (May)	SLC and his brother Henry were working on the steamboat "Pennsylvania" (John Kleinfelter, Master). An ill-tempered pilot attacked Henry, and Sam got into a fight with him over it. As a result, Sam went ashore to wait for another berth, while the "Pennsylvania" steamed north. Near Memphis, she blew up with the loss of 150 lives, one of them Henry's. SLC later blamed himself for Henry's death.
1859 (Apr 9)	After two years as a cub, Samuel Clemens was licensed as a Mississippi River pilot. He worked at this trade for the next two years.

1860 (December 20)	South Carolina seceded from the Union. In the following 60 days Mississippi, Florida, Alabama, Georgia, Louisiana, and Texas also declared themselves out of the Union; the seven states formed the Confederacy at Montgomery, Alabama in February 1861.
1861 (April 12)	South Carolina attacked the Union garrison at Fort Sumter; Lincoln called for volunteers to enforce federal authority in the South. Virginia seceded April 17; Arkansas, Tennessee, and North Carolina in May. With the outbreak of fighting, river commerce was shut down.
1861 (Spring)	SLC returned to Missouri. Joined "Marion Rangers," a Confederate auxiliary, and was elected a second lieutenant. Served two or three weeks, and then, in his own words, "Quit."
1861 (July)	Left for Nevada by stagecoach with his older brother Orion.
1861 (August 14)	Arrived at Carson City. Sam served as Orion's secretary until the following January.
1862 (January-February?)	Left Orion and went silver prospecting at Aurora, where he lived with Cal Higbie and Robert Howland and worked a claim at Esmeraida Hills.
1862 (Spring)	Began sending letter to the *Territorial Enterprise*, signing himself "Josh."
1862 (Summer)	Received offer of staff position on the *Enterprise*. After a delay of some weeks, decided to accept. Left Aurora on foot and tramped to Virginia City.
1862 (August)	Arrived in Virginia City and went to work for Joe Goodman on the *Enterprise* at $25 per week.

1863 (January)	Sent by Goodman to cover the Territorial Legislature at Carson City. On February 2, signed one of his reports with the name "Mark Twain," his first use of it in print.
1863 (December)	Met Artemus Ward, who was touring the West. Ward spent 12 days in Virginia and was impressed with Twain's humorous writing.
1864 (May)	The Sanitary Commission flour sack reached Virginia City. SLC got into trouble over "miscegenation society" remark and was challenged to a duel.
1864 (May 29)	Rather than fight or be arrested, SLC and his friend Steve Gillis left Virginia City by stage for San Francisco.
1864 (Summer)	Took a reporter's job on the *Morning Call* newspaper; also wrote pieces for the *Golden Era*. Later moved to the competing *Californian* newspaper, which paid better. Criticized the SF police for their handling of anti-Chinese mobs and made himself unpopular.
1864 (December)	To allow things to cool down, left SF for Angel's Camp, where he lived with the Gillis brothers in Jim Gillis's cabin atop Jackass Hill.
1865 (January-February)	While hanging out at the bar of the Angel's Camp Hotel, heard Ben (or Ross) Coon tell a story about a frog-jumping contest. SLC took notes on the story and brought them with him when he returned to San Francisco.

1865 (February 26)	Returned to San Francisco. Received a letter from Artemus Ward, inviting him to submit a humor piece to a new collection. SLC wrote out the "Jumping Frog" story, but it arrived too late for inclusion in Ward's book.
1865 (March-December)	Lived and worked in San Francisco, writing for various newspapers, including *The Californian. Golden Era* and *Territorial Enterprise*.
1865 (October 8)	While strolling down Third Street one Sunday noon, SLC experienced a sizable earthquake. He wrote extensively about the experience.
1866 (March)	Sent to Hawaii (then known as the Sandwich Islands) as correspondent for the *Sacramento Union*. Twain's travel letters from the Islands began appearing in April and were very popular.
1866 (June 21)	Though suffering from boils, Twain scored a journalistic coup when, with the help of Anson Burlingame, US minister to China who was on his way across the Pacific, he interviewed fifteen survivors from the burned clipper ship "Hornet," who had washed up on shore after forty-three days in an open boat. Twain stayed up all night to write his story and just did get it aboard a California-bound ship the next morning.
1866 (July 19)	The *Sacramento Union* printed Twain's "Hornet" story on the front page. That same day, SLC left Hawaii for California.
1866 (August 13)	Returned to San Francisco.

1866 (October 2)	Using his Hawaii material, Mark Twain embarked on another new career: he delivered his first platform lecture to a sold-out house in SF. He continued to lecture intermittently for the rest of his life with great success, although he hated the platform circuit and resorted to it mainly as a source of quick cash when needed.
1866 (December 15)	Left San Francisco aboard the steamer "America" on the first leg of a proposed world tour, sponsored by the *Alta California* newspaper. He planned to cross the Isthmus, then take another steamer to New York, and to visit Missouri and home before leaving.
1867 (January 12)	Arrived in New York after a terror-filled trip from Nicaragua on the cholera-stricken ship "San Francisco." Took rooms on East 16th Street. Saw and was enthralled by "The Black Crook" at Niblo's Garden but was completely unimpressed by Barnum's Museum. Wrote letters for the *Alta*.
1867 (February 1)	Saw advertisement for the Great Pleasure Excursion to Europe and the Holy Land and got the *Alta* to send him in lieu of going around the world. The paper paid his passage ($1,250) and promised him $20 for each letter.
1867 (March 2)	Left New York for Missouri and his first trip home in six years.

1867 (May 1)	Charles Henry Webb, whom Twain had known in San Francisco, put twenty-seven of Twain's California humor sketches into a book, headed by and titled *The Celebrated Jumping Frog.* This was MT's first appearance between hard covers. Coincidentally, the printer was the firm of Gray and Green, which had employed SLC as a journeyman in 1853.
1867 (May 6)	Delivered first New York lecture.
1867 (June 8)	Sailed aboard side-wheel steamer "Quaker City" with sixty-six other passengers for the five-month cruise across the Atlantic. Twain wrote fifty-three letters for the *Alta,* plus another nine to New York papers—about three letters per week for the duration of the trip. Aboard were Mrs. Mary Mason Fairbanks, Dan Slote, and John "Jack" Van Nostrand with whom, among others, MT became friends.
1867 (July)	Visited Paris; got a kick from the cancan.
1867 (August 26)	In port at Yalta; met Czar Alexander II.
1867 (September)	In the Bay of Smyrna. Charles Langdon showed SLC a miniature portrait of his sister Olivia. Clemens claimed to have fallen in love on the spot.
1867 (November 19)	"Quaker City" returned to New York. The next day, Clemens wrote a piece on the trip for the *New York Herald.*
1867 (November 21)	Negotiated contract with the American Book Company (E. Bliss) for a book about the "Quaker City" trip. Showing unwonted business acumen, SLC rejected a flat $10,000 fee in favor of a five-percent royalty. The book appeared in 1869 as *The Innocents Abroad.*

1867 (November)	Served briefly as private secretary to Senator William Stewart of Nevada. They did not get along, and SLC soon was on his own again.
1867 (December 27)	First met Olivia Langdon at the St. Nicholas Hotel in New York. SLC spent thirteen hours on New Year's Day with the Langdon family.
1868 (January 2-3?)	First date with Livy. They went to hear Charles Dickens lecture; neither was much impressed.
1868 (January 21)	Signed contract with Bliss for *The Innocents Abroad*. First visit to Hartford, Connecticut.
1868	With William Swinton, formed a newspaper syndicate and served as Washington correspondent for a dozen small-time newspapers. Twain was no more impressed with Congress than he had been with the Nevada Legislature in 1863. Some of his observations were used in *The Gilded Age*. To earn additional money, Twain lectured extensively in 1868-69, while simultaneously writing *The Innocents Abroad*.
1868 (March)	Trip to California to negotiate with the *Alta* for the rights to use his "Quaker City" letters in *Innocents*.
1868 (August)	Visited Livy at the Langdon family home in Elmira. After two weeks, SLC proposed to Livy but was turned down. Nonetheless, he kept up the pursuit.
1868 (November)	Livy confessed to SLC that she was in love with him.
1869 (February 4)	Formal engagement of Olivia L. Langdon to Samuel L. Clemens announced.

1869 (July 20)	*The Innocents Abroad* was published by the American Book Company of Hartford, Connecticut (Elisha Bliss). The book was an instant success.
1869 (August)	With the aid of a $12,500 loan from Jervis Langdon (Olivia's father), Clemens purchased a one-third interest in the *Buffalo Express* newspaper and became editor.
1869 (November 10)	Met William Dean Howells for the first time at the offices of Ticknor and Fields in Boston. Their friendship continued for the next forty years, until SLC's death in 1910. First Boston lecture delivered.
1870 (February 2)	Wedding of Samuel L. Clemens to Olivia L. Langdon celebrated at the Langdon family mansion in Elmira, New York. The pastors were Thomas Beecher (brother of Henry Ward Beecher) and Joseph Twitchell. After the ceremony, the entire wedding party went on to Buffalo, where Jervis Langdon presented his daughter and new son-in-law with a surprise nuptial gift—a furnished house on fashionable Delaware Avenue.
1870 (August 6)	Jervis Langdon died of stomach cancer at age sixty-one. The stress of his death helped to bring on the premature birth of SLC and Livy's first child two months later. Livy Clemens became an heiress.
1870 (September)	Twain began writing *Roughing It*.
1870 (November 7)	Langdon Clemens b. two months prematurely (like his father before him).

1871 (April)	SLC, unhappy with the drudgery of newspapering and wishing to be closer to his publisher, Bliss, sold his share in the *Express* at a loss. Aided by Livy's inheritance, the family left Buffalo and spent the summer at Quarry Farm, while planning a move to Hartford in the fall.
1871 (Summer)	Twain worked on *Roughing It*. Livy became pregnant for the second time.
1871 (October)	SLC rented the John Hooker house in Hartford (where he had stayed on his first visit) until they could build a home of their own. For the next twenty years, the Clemens family lived most of the time in Hartford, with summers at Quarry Farm, Elmira.
1871-72	Lecture tour to raise cash and pay off debts.
1872 (February)	*Roughing It* published. Sales did not meet SLC's expectations, despite a favorable review from William Dean Howells in the *Atlantic*.
1872 (March 19)	Daughter Olivia Susan Clemens, "Susy," born in Elmira at the Langdon home.
1872 (June 2)	Langdon Clemens died of diphtheria, aged nineteen months. He had never progressed normally and still could not walk at the time of his death.
1872 (August 21)	SLC sailed for England, his first visit there. Livy and Susy remained in America.
1872 (November)	SLC returned to America full of Anglophilia after a successful trip during which he was lionized everywhere in Britain. Bought the land at 351 Farmington Avenue and began planning his house. Wrote the earliest version of *Tom Sawyer*—as a play.

1873 (January-April)	SLC and Charles Dudley Warner collaborated on *The Gilded Age.*
1873 (May 7)	Mark Twain's self-pasting scrapbook, the most financially successful of his inventions, patented.
1873 (May)	SLC returned to England, this time with Livy. Even more well-received than the previous autumn. Took Livy and Susy home in October, then immediately returned to England alone for a three-month lecture tour.
1873 (September)	Banking house of Jay Cooke & Co. collapsed. Clemens lost some money; Livy's income was reduced when the Langdon family coal interests suffered losses.
1873 (December)	*The Gilded Age* published by Bliss in the United States and by Routledges in England. It sold thirty-five thousand copies in its first two years, then faded out.
1874 (January)	Clemens returned to America. Livy pregnant for the third time in their four years of marriage.
1874 (April)	Clemens family moved into the new home in Hartford, which was to be their home for the next seventeen years. It cost $70,000 to build, exclusive of the land and furnishings.
1874 (June 8)	Clara Clemens b. at the Langdon house in Elmira.
1874 (Summer)	SLC developed a play version of *The Gilded Age*; wrote "A True Story" for the *Atlantic* (it appeared in the November issue); and began *Tom Sawyer* (he completed about four hundred MS pages by September 4, then laid the book aside until the next summer).

1874 (September 16)	The stage version of *The Gilded Age* opened in New York, with John T. Raymond in the role of Colonel Sellers. It was a hit and ran for two years, producing royalties for Clemens of as much as $900 per week, making it by far SLC's greatest success as a playwright.
1875 (January)	"Old Times on the Mississippi" began running in the *Atlantic*. It appeared in seven episodes between January and June. Much of the writing was done in the billiards room on the third floor of the Hartford house; this was the most important creative work done by Mark Twain in the city.
1875 (June)	The family returned to Quarry Farm for the summer. Twain picked up the manuscript of *Tom Sawyer*, where he had left off the previous autumn and completed the book by the first week in July. He copied the manuscript on a typewriter (patented by Christopher Latham Sholes in 1868 and put on the commercial market by Remington no earlier than 1873), making *Tom* perhaps the first novel to appear as a typescript.
1875	Assisted Dan De Quille (William Wright) in the writing of his history of the Comstock, *The Big Bonanza*, and contributed an introduction.
1876 (January)	Wrote "Carnival of Crime in Connecticut" and delivered it as a speech to the Monday Evening Club (January 24).
1876 (June)	"Carnival" appeared in the *Atlantic*. On returning to Quarry Farm, SLC wrote "1601."

1876 (August)	First disclosure that Twain was at work on *Huck Finn*. He wrote to Howells (August 9) and mentioned that he had written four hundred MS pages but liked the book only "tolerably well." At the end of the summer, he set the MS aside for three years.
1876 (October)	Collaborated with Bret Harte on a play, "Ah Sin." The object was to make big money from the stage, which Harte in particular needed.
1876 (Dec)	"Ah Sin" finished. *Tom Sawyer* finally published, over a year after it was finished and too late for the Christmas trade. Angry with Bliss, SLC began to think about a new publisher.
1877 (May 7)	"Ah Sin" opened in Washington; it was not a success.
1877 (May)	Trip to Bermuda with Joe Twitchell.
1877 (July)	Nationwide railroad strike, accompanied by rioting and violence which ended only when federal troops were called out. Like many Americans. SLC was frightened and dismayed.
1877 (Summer)	"Ah Sin" opened in New York and managed to run five weeks before closing with a loss to the producers. Twain threw most of the blame on Harte but did recognize that it had been a bad play and that he was partly responsible.
1877 (Summer)	Still bewitched by the quick, big profits to be made from the theater, Twain worked on another play, "Simon Wheeler, Detective." It was never produced; two years later, in rereading it, he saw why—it was "dreadfully witless and flat."

1877 (November 23)	First notes for *The Prince and the Pauper* written.
1877 (December 17)	Whittier Birthday dinner. Twain's attempt at humor was ill-received, and he feared he had offended Longfellow, Holmes, and Emerson. In later years, he tended to magnify the size of the social disaster far beyond its real scope.
1878 (April 11)	SLC and family sailed for Europe on an extended tour, which would last seventeen months. Summer in Germany.
1878 (August)	With passage and expenses paid by Clemens, Twitchell arrived from America. Walking tour of Germany and Switzerland, collecting material for *A Tramp Abroad*. Twitchell stayed six weeks before returning to America.
1878-79	Resided in Munich for the winter.
1879 (February)	Moved on to Paris for the spring.
1879 (February)	Speech to the Stomach Club on "The Science of Onanism" (not publicly printed until 1952).
1879 (July-August)	Family spent the summer in England, sailing for New York late in August.
1879 (September 3)	SLC and family arrived in the United States after sixteen months away.
1879 (November)	Livy became pregnant for the fourth time. Mark Twain at work on *A Tramp Abroad*.
1880 (January 7)	The completed manuscript of *Tramp* was delivered to Bliss.
1880 (March)	*A Tramp Abroad* published. It sold sixty-thousand copies in the first year—Mark Twain's biggest hit since *The Innocents Abroad*.

1880 (July 26)	Jane Lampton Clemens, "Jean," b., last child of Sam and Livy Clemens.
1880 (September 28)	Elisha Bliss, Mark Twain's regular publisher, died of heart disease.
1880 (October 19)	Kate Leary entered the household as Livy's maid. She remained with the family for thirty years to the day (October 19, 1910).
1881 (April)	Clemens appointed his nephew by marriage, Charles Webster, as his business manager. Then twenty-eight, Webster was married to Pamela Clemens Moffett's daughter Annie; the family connection seems to have been his only qualification for the position.
1881	A new kitchen wing was added to the Hartford house, and interior decoration by Tiffany & Associates executed. The expansion and renovation cost $30,000.
1881 (December)	*The Prince and the Pauper* published by James Osgood of Boston. Actually, SLC was the true publisher himself, in that he paid all the costs; Osgood acted as sales agent, earning a royalty for his efforts (Kaplan).
1882 (April-May)	Trip down the Mississippi from St. Louis to New Orleans, then back to St. Paul in the company of Osgood and a stenographer named Roswell Phelps. In New Orleans, met Joel Chandler Harris (author of "Uncle Remus") and George Washington Cable. Spent three days in Hannibal on the way back north; traveled upriver on the steamboat "City of Baton Rouge," whose master was his old piloting teacher, Horace Bixby.

1882 (Summer)	Worked simultaneously on *Life on the Mississippi* and *Huckleberry Finn.*
1883 (July)	*Life on the Mississippi* published over Osgood's imprint; as with *Prince*, Clemens was actually the sole financier of the project. Sales were disappointing, and Clemens blamed Osgood.
1883 (Summer)	Worked on *Huckleberry Finn,* completing the manuscript, then revising and rewriting through the fall and on into the following spring. With the MS finished, he wrote in September to his British publisher, Andrew Chatto, that it was "a rattling good book."
	Charles Webster & Co. publishing firm founded.
1884 (November 5)	Twain, in need of cash, begins joint lecture tour with Cable (ran through winter '85).
1884 (December)	*Huckleberry Finn* published in England.
1885 (February)	*Huckleberry Finn* published in the United States, after a delay caused by a mischievous engraver who altered one of the illustrations, making it patently obscene. Sold fifty thousand copies in its first three months.
1885 (February 28)	Lecture tour ended in Washington. Former President US Grant signed a contract with Webster & Co. for publication of his memoirs.
1885 (July 23)	Death of Grant.
1885 (Fall)	Webster & Co. published Grant's memoirs. Over two hundred thousand sets were sold, producing royalties of half a million dollars for the Grant family and a $200,000 profit for the publishing house.

1885 (December)	"History of a Campaign that Failed" appeared in *Century* magazine.
1886 (January)	First chapters of *A Connecticut Yankee in King Arthur's Court* written.
1886 (February 6)	Clemens buys half interest in the Paige Machine. The book and the machine were linked in his mind, and he was determined that both should be finished simultaneously.
1886 (July)	Trip to Keokuk to see Jane Clemens, then eighty-three. Last entry in Susy's biography/diary (July 4).
1887 (June)	Twain receives honorary MA from Yale.
1887	The machine was swallowing $3,000 per month; Clemens was drawing money from the publishing house to subsidize the cost. By December, he had already sunk $50,000 into the machine.
1887 (Cont)	Webster & Co. published Father Bernard O'Reilly's *Life of Pope Leo XIII*. Clemens' expectations of a bonanza of "at least one hundred thousand copies" fell flat. Henry Ward Beecher, whose autobiography the firm was to have published, died in February, leaving an unfinished manuscript and a loss to the publishing house.
1888	Webster, in poor health, resigned from the publishing company. Theodore Crane suffered a stroke in September and was nursed by the Clemens family in Hartford. Mark Twain at work on *Yankee*; the Paige Machine seemed near success.
1889 (January 5)	Paige demonstrated the machine for Clemens, with apparent success—then disassembled it again to refine it further.

1889 (May)	Twain completed manuscript for *Yankee*.
1889 (July 3)	Theodore Crane died at Quarry Farm.
1889 (December)	*Yankee* published by Webster & Co.
	Full ownership of the Paige Machine assumed by Clemens.
1890	The machine was now costing Clemens $4,000 per month. In the summer following the death of Theodore Crane, the family went not to Quarry Farm, but to the Onteora Club at Tannersville, New York, for the summer.
1890 (October)	Susy entered Bryn Mawr College near Philadelphia as a freshman student. Her roommate was Louise Brownell. Clemens made frequent trips to Philadelphia to see her; Livy made some to forestall his going even more often.
1890 (October)	Jane Lampton Clemens died, age eighty-seven. She was buried in Hannibal.
1890 (November)	Olivia Lewis Langdon (Livy's mother) died, age eighty. She was buried in Elmira.
1891 (March 23)	Clemens lectured at Bryn Mawr, telling a ghost story. Susy cried.
1891 (March)	*The American Claimant* finished.
1891 (April)	Susy left Bryn Mawr and returned to Hartford; her departure from the college was never explained. Correspondence between Susy and Louise Brownell begins.
	Charles Webster dies, age forty.
1891 (June 6)	Family leaves Hartford for Europe, closing the house (which had become too expensive for them to maintain). Winter 1891-92 in Berlin.

1892 (June)	Clemens made a business trip to America for a month, alone.
1892 (September)	Lived in Florence. Twain wrote *Puddn'head Wilson* and worked on *Joan of Arc*. Without telling Susy, he based his Joan on her.
1892	Jean, age twelve, began to show alarming personality changes (diagnosed as epileptic four years later).
1893 (September)	Met Henry H. Rogers in New York.
1893 (December)	*Pudd'nhead Wilson* serialized in *Century*, running through five issues (to April '94).
1894 (March 3)	Visited Nicola Tesla in his laboratory.
1894 (April 16)	*Tom Sawyer Abroad* published by Webster & Co.
1894 (April 18)	Clemens declared bankruptcy on the advice of Henry Rogers.
1894 (Spring)	Twain finished *Joan of Arc* in Paris.
1894 (Summer)	Spent summer in America, trying to raise money to stave off financial disaster. Panic of 1893 had cut off Livy's income from her inheritance.
1894 (October)	The Paige Machine received a trial by the *Chicago Herald* newspaper. It broke down by December, and Rogers advised that it be written off as impractical.
1895 (January)	Finished *Tom Sawyer, Detective* and *Joan of Arc*.
1895 (March)	Met Helen Keller, then fourteen. Encouraged Rogers to support her—he did.
1895 (May)	Family returned to America after four years abroad. Twain rested and prepared for a round-the-world lecture tour to pay off his $100,000 in debts.

1895 (July 14)	SLC, Livy and Clara left Elmira for Cleveland on the first leg of the lecture tour. Susy, who chose not to go, saw them off at the station. It was the last time they saw her alive.
1896 (May)	*Joan of Arc* published by Harpers.
1896 (July 15)	Lecture tour concluded in Cape Town. The family sailed for England, where they rented a house in Guildford and waited for Susy, Jean, and Kate Leary to arrive.
1896 (August 18)	Susy died at twenty-four of meningitis, in the guest room on the first floor of the family home in Hartford.
1896 (Fall)	Living in London, at twenty-three Tedworth Square, Twain began *Following the Equator*.
1897	Wrote *What is Man?* (Not published until 1905.)
1897 (May)	Completed *Equator*.
1897 (November)	*Following the Equator* published by American Book Co., now run by Elisha Bliss' son, Frank. Twain was back where he had started with subscription publishing. Sold thirty thousand copies immediately.
1897 (December 11)	Orion Clemens died in Keokuk, Iowa, aged seventy-two.
1898 (January)	Money from the lecture tour and sales of *Equator* was sufficient to pay off all creditors 100 percent and still leave $13,000 for the family. Within a year they were well-off again, with investment revenues and cash in the bank. Family lived in Vienna 1898-99. Twain wrote *Concerning the Jews*.

1899	Frank Bliss published twenty-two-volume set of *The Writings of Mark Twain*.
1900 (October 15)	After nearly ten years spent living in Europe, Sam and Livy returned to America and took a furnished house at 14 West 10th Street in New York City. Clara prepared for her debut as a singer.
1901 (February)	Published "To the Person Sitting in Darkness."
1901 (June)	Honorary Litt.D from Yale.
1901 (Summer)	Family spent the summer in Elmira and at Saranac Lake, New York.
1901 (Fall)	Rented house in Riverdale, where the family lived until June '03.
1902 (April)	Clara moved to Paris to be with Osip Gabrilowitsch.
1902 (May)	Trip to Missouri. Visited Hannibal for the last time in May, spending five days there. Visited family graves at Mt. Olivet Cemetery. Distributed high school diplomas; had dinner with Laura Hawkins Frazer and Helen Garth.
1902 (June 4)	Received Litt.D from the University of Missouri.
1902 (Summer)	Sam and Livy summered at York Harbor, Maine.
1902 (August)	Livy became ill with heart trouble and goiter. Clara returned from France. Livy never fully recovered.
1902 (October)	Family returned to Riverdale for the winter, traveling by special train. During the fall and winter Livy was isolated in her room, and Clemens was forbidden to see her. They communicated mostly by notes.

1902 (December)	Income over $100,000; Clemens was rich again.
1903	Hartford house, unlived in since Susy's death, was finally sold to the president of an insurance company.
1903 (Summer)	Last family visit to Quarry Farm. Twain worked in his "pilot house" study for the last time.
1903 (October)	Clemens signed a contract with Harper's making that firm his sole publisher (deal negotiated by Rogers). The contract guaranteed him an income of $25,000 yearly for five years. The family then left for Florence, Italy on the advice of Livy's doctors. They stayed at the Villa di Quatro outside Florence throughout the winter, but Livy's health steadily declined.
1904 (January)	Began dictation on his *Autobiography* to Isabel Lyon, his private secretary.
1904 (June 5)	(Sunday evening) Livy died at age fifty-nine. Following her passing, Clara had a nervous breakdown, and Jean suffered a seizure.
1904 (Fall)	SLC returned to New York. He rented a house at 21 Fifth Avenue, where he lived for the next four years. Clara entered a sanitarium and was sequestered there for a year; Jean and Kate Leary remained with him (The house, on the SE corner of Fifth Avenue and Ninth Street, was torn down in 1954.)
1904 (January)	Orion's wife, Mollie, died.
1904 (December)	Pamela Moffett died.
1905 (November 30)	Clemens' seventieth birthday.

1905 (December 5)	Seventieth Birthday Dinner at Delmonico's, staged by George Harvey, Editor of *Harper's Weekly.*
1906 (January 7)	Albert Bigelow Paine called at the Fifth Avenue house and proposed to become Clemens' official biographer. They began at once, with Clemens dictating over five hundred thousand words in the next thirty months.
1906 (Summer)	Summer at Dublin, New Hampshire; Dictated *Autobiography.*
1906 (September 22)	Clara's singing debut in Norfolk, Virginia.
1906 (December 7)	SLC testified before Joint Committee of Congress on copyright law; revealed his white suit, his characteristic outfit in his later years.
1908 (June 18)	Moved into his last home, "Stormfield," near Redding, Connecticut. Designed by Howells' son John and named by Clara because it was partly paid for by royalties from "Captain Stormfield."
1907 (June 26)	Honorary degree from Oxford. On this, his last visit to England, Twain met George Bernard Shaw at St. Pancras Station. He also met Barrie and Beerbohm. His "Aquarium Club" angelfish replaced his own daughters; Clara was now thirty-three and Jean quarreled with him; they did not get along well.
1908 (August)	Samuel Moffett, Pamela's grandson and SLC's great-nephew, drowned.
1909 (May)	Sudden death of Henry H. Rogers, SLC's patron and financial advisor/savior.

1909 (October 6)	Clara married Osip Gabrilowitsch at Stormfield. Joseph Twitchell performed the ceremony, as he had for SLC and Livy thirty-nine years earlier. The couple left immediately for Europe, leaving Jean to live with (and serve as secretary to) her father.
1909 (November)	Visited Bermuda for a month, returning to Stormfield in December.
1909 (December 24)	Clemens' final tragedy: Jean died, having suffered an epileptic seizure while in the bath. Twain's tribute to her, written on Christmas Day, was his last writing.
1910 (January 5)	Last meeting with Howells.
1910 (January 6)	Left for Bermuda to spend the rest of the winter. Clemens was suffering from angina pectoris and gradually growing weaker.
1910 (April 12)	Feeling himself failing, sailed for New York and home.
1910 (April 14)	Arrived at Stormfield.
1910 (April 21)	(6:22 p.m.) Died at Stormfield, aged seventy-four years, four months. Buried in Elmira, Woodlawn Cemetery.
1910 (August 18)	Nina Clemens Gabrilowitsch, SLC's only grandchild, born. She was born on the fourteenth anniversary of Susy's death.
1923 (July 25)	Stormfield burned to the ground; a replica was rebuilt on the site and still stands.
1936 (September 14)	Osip Gabrilowitsch died, age fifty-eight.
1944 (May 11)	Clara married Jacques Samossoud. She was just short of age seventy.

1962 (November 19)	Clara died, age eighty-eight.
1966 (January 16)	Nina committed suicide in Los Angeles. She was fifty-six years of age.
1966 (June 13)	Samossoud died. His ashes are buried at Woodlawn but in a separate plot.

Bibliography

Adams, Charles Francis, Jr. and Henry	*Chapters of Erie* (New York: Henry Holt, 1886.)
Allen, Jerry	*The Adventures of Mark Twain* (Boston: Little, Brown & Co., 1953.)
Andrews, Kenneth	*Nook Farm: Mark Twain's Hartford Circle* (Cambridge: Harvard University Press, 1950.)
Baldanza, Frank	*Mark Twain: An Introduction and Interpretation* (New York: Holt, Rinehart & Winston, 1961.)
Bellamy, Gladys, C.	*Mark Twain as a Literary Artist* (Norman, OK: University of Oklahoma Press, 1950.)
Benzaquin, Paul	*Holocaust.* (New York: Henry Holt & Co., 1959.)
Blair, Walter (Ed.)	*Mark Twain's Hannibal, Huck and Tom* (Berkeley and Los Angeles: University of California Press, 1969.)
Bloom, E. Sue	*Secret Survivors: Uncovering Incest.* (New York: Ballantine Books, 1990.)
Bloom, Harold (Ed.)	*Modern Critical Views: Mark Twain* (New York, New Haven, Philadelphia: Chelsea House, 1986.)
Blufarb, Sam	*The Escape Motif in the American Novel* (Columbus, OH: Ohio State University Press 1972.)

Brashear, Minnie, M.

Mark Twain. Son of Missouri (Chapel Hill: University of North Carolina Press, 1934.)

Canby, Henry, Seidel

Turn West, Turn East (Boston: Houghton-Mifflin, 1951)

Clemens, Susy

Papa: An Intimate Biography of Mark Twain introduction Charles Neider (Ed.)

(Garden City, NY: Doubleday and Company, Inc., 1985.)

Cooley, John (Ed.)

Mark Twain's Aquarium: The Samuel Clemens Angelfish Correspondence 1905-1910 (Athens: The University of Georgia Press, 1991.)

DeVoto, Bernard

Mark Twain at Work (Cambridge: Harvard University Press, 1942.)

Fatout, Paul

Mark Twain in Virginia City (Bloomington, IN: Indiana University Press, 1964.)

Fiedler, Leslie

Love and Death in the American Novel (Revised Edn.) (New York: Stein and Day, 1966.)

Gabrilowitsch, Clara, C.

My Father, Mark Twain (New York: Harpers, 1931.)

Harnsberger, Caroline, T.

Mark Twain's Clara (Evanston, IN: The Press of Ward Schori, 1982.)

Haycroft, Howard

Murder For Pleasure (New York: D. Appleton-Century, 1941.)

Hemingway, Ernest

Green Hills of Africa (New York: Scribner's, 1935.)

Hill, Hamlin

Mark Twain: God's Fool (New York: Harper and Row, 1973.)

Howells, William, D.

My Mark Twain: Reminiscences and Criticisms (Baton Rouge: Louisiana State University Press, 1967.)

(New York: Harper & Bros., 1910.)

Kaplan, Justin   *Mr. Clemens and Mark Twain* (New York: Simon & Schuster, 1966.)

Keller, Helen   *Mainstream: My Later Life.* (Garden City, NY: Doubleday, 1929.)

Kosof, A.   *Incest.* (New York: Franklin Watts, 1985.)

Lyman, George   *The Saga of Comstock Lode* (New York: Scribner's, 1934.)

Metzler, Wilton   *Mark Twain Himself. A Pictorial Biography* (New York: Bonanza Books, 1960.)

Miers, Earl, S.   *Mark Twain on the Mississippi* (New York: Collier Books, 1957.)

Miller, Robert, K.   *Mark Twain* (New York: Frederick Ungar Publishing Co., 1983.)

Neider, Charles (Ed.)   *The Autobiography of Mark Twain* (New York: Harper & Bros., 1959.)

Neider, Charles (Ed.)   *Papa* (Garden City, NY: Doubleday, 1985.)

Paine, Albert B. (Ed.)   *Mark Twain's Notebook* (New York, London: Harper & Bros., 1935.)

Poston, Carol and   *Reclaiming Our Lives* (Boston: Little, Brown & Lison Karen   Co., 1989.)

Pratt, Fletcher   *Ordeal By Fire: A Short History of the Civil War.* (New York: Perenial Library, 1966.)

Salsbury, Edith, C.   *Susy and Mark Twain* (New York: Harper & Row, 1965.)

Sanborn, Margaret   *Mark Twain: The Bachelor Years* (New York: Doubleday, 1990.)

Seelye, John   *Mark Twain in the Movies: A Meditation with Pictures* (New York: Viking Press, 1977.)

Seuss, Dr.   *Fox in Sox.* (New York: Beginner Books, 1963.)
(Theo. S. Geisel)

Smith, Henry, N. (Ed.)   *Mark Twain: A Collection of Critical Essays*
                           (Englewood Cliffs, NJ: Prentice-Hall, 1963.)

Smith, Henry, N.   *Mark Twain of the Enterprise* (Berkeley and Los
(Ed.)   Angeles: University of California Press, 1957.)

Smith, Henry,   *The Mark Twain-Howells Letters,* Vol. 2 (Cambridge,
N. and Gibson,   Mass: Harvard University Press, 1960.)
William, M. (Eds.)

Taper, Bernard (Ed.)   *Mark Twain's San Francisco* (New York:
                           McGraw-Hill, 1963.)

Wagner, Allan   *Prima Donnas and Other Wild Beasts* (New York:
                           Collier Books, 1963.)

Wallace, Irving and   *The Two* (New York: Simon & Schuster, 1978.)
Amy

Wecter, Dixon   *Sam Clemens of Hannibal* (Boston: Houghton
                           Mifflin Co., 1952.)

                           Mark Twain in Hartford (Hartford: Mark Twain
                           Memorial, 1958.)

Willis, Resa   *Mark and Livy.* (New York: Atheneum, 1992.)

Works by Mark Twain:

The Jumping Frog and other stories. (1867)
The Innocents Abroad (1869)
Roughing It (1872)
The Gilded Age (with Charles Dudley Warner) (1873)
The Adventures of Tom Sawyer (1876)
A Tramp Abroad (1880)

The Prince and the Pauper (1881)

Life on the Mississippi (1883)

The Adventures of Huckleberry Finn (1885)

A Connecticut Yankee in King Arthur's Court (1889)

The Tragedy of Pudd'nhead Wilson (1893) (as a magazine serial)

Tom Sawyer Abroad (1894)

Personal Reminiscences of Joan of Arc (1896)

Following the Equator (1897)

Albert, B. Paine (Ed.), *The Mysterious Stranger* (posthumously) (1916)

Charles Neider (Ed.), *The Autobiography of Mark Twain* (First Edition) (1924)

Periodicals

LIFE Magazine December 20, 1968, "Tom and Huck Among the Indians."

Los Angeles Times May 2, 1994, "Quoting Prof, Roy F. Baumeister about his study of guilt."

Other

Cotton, Michelle. Elmira College Senior Thesis on the Susy Clemens—Louise Brownell Letters, 1982.

Academic American Encyclopedia (Danbury, Connected: Grolier, Inc., 1983) Volume "M": data on meningitis.

Index

The letter n *after the page number refers to footnotes. The number following it refers to the footnote number.*

S

Sacramento Union, 6, 259, 392

Salsbury, Edith Colgate, 361
  Susy and Mark Twain, 361

Samossoud, Jacques, 278, 411

satire, 22

Saunders, Arthur P., 333

Sawyer, Sid, 36

Sawyer, Tom, 36–40, 41n20, 42,
  44, 46–47

Scott, Walter, 76n54, 102–3

Scott, Walter (steam boat),
  96n66, 99–104, 106, 127

Sellers, Isaiah, 250

Seymour, Jane, 69

Sharon, William, 253

Sign of Four, The (Doyle), 202

sivilization, 43, 90, 92, 97, 111,
  122, 136, 148, 178, 183, 377,
  383

social criticism, 52–55, 64, 85–86,
  127, 192–93, 285

Stevenson, Robert Louis, vi, 51

Stormfield, 12–13, 240, 363,
  410–11

St. Petersburg, 34–36, 44–46, 48,
  52–53

Study in Scarlet, A (Doyle), 202

Sullivan, Annie, 363

Susy and Mark Twain (Salsbury),
  361

switching identities, 71, 73, 132

T

Temple, Alfred, 37–38

Territorial Enterprise, 248–49, 256

Thatcher, Becky, 28, 30, 33–34,
  37, 211, 236

"Those Extraordinary Twins"
  (Twain), 200

Tiffany, Lewis Comfort, 265

Tom Sawyer Abroad (Twain), 198–
  99, 293, 309, 406

Tragedy of Pudd'nhead Wilson, The
  (Twain), 199, 202
  interpretations of, 217, 219,
    221, 223
  irony in, 215, 217
  other elements of, 206–7, 209,
    211, 214–15
  plot of, 203–4, 206

Tramp Abroad, A (Twain), 8, 68,
  74–75, 401

Tudor, Mary, 69–70

Twain, Mark, vi, 5, 53, 54n32, 77,
  249
  Adventures of Huckleberry Finn,
    The, v, 58, 63, 82–84, 182,
    187
  Adventures of Tom Sawyer, The,
    24–25, 75, 84, 134, 263, 374
  Ah Sin, 67–68, 400
  "Carnival of Crime in
    Connecticut," 399
  Connecticut Yankee in King

Edwards Brothers Malloy
Thorofare, NJ USA
May 1, 2012